PAYBACK

BRIAN GALLAGHER

POOLBEG

Published 2003
Poolbeg Press Ltd.
123 Grange Hill, Baldoyle,
Dublin 13, Ireland

Email: poolbeg@poolbeg.com

1 3 5 7 9 10 8 6 4 2

A catalogue record for this book is available from the British Library.

ISBN 1-84223-110-3

Typeset by Patricia Hope in Palatino 10/13.5
Printed and bound in Spain by
Litografia Rosés S.A., Barcelona

www.poolbeg.com

ABOUT THE AUTHOR

Brian Gallagher was born in Dublin. He is a full-time writer whose plays and short stories have been produced in Ireland, Britain and Canada.

He has written extensively for radio and television, and is one of the script team on RTE's successful drama series *Fair City*.

He collaborated with the composer Shaun Purcell on the musical *Larkin*, for which he wrote the book and lyrics.

His novels *Invincible* and *Flight* won widespread praise, and he is currently writing a new novel, *Pursuit*.

Outside of writing, his interests include travel, tennis, music, and inland waterways. He lives with his family in Dublin.

Also by Brian Gallagher

Invincible
Flight

ACKNOWLEDGEMENTS

Once again I'd like to thank Chief Inspector Kenneth Eccles for his patience in answering my many questions on police procedure. As ever, any deviations from the norm stem from artistic licence on my part.

My sincere thanks also go to my editor Gaye Shortland, to Paula, Sarah and Brona in Poolbeg, to Ber Faughnan and Kevin MacCourt who kindly read the manuscript and then allowed me to pick their brains, and to all of the following who cheerfully answered my seemingly endless queries: Sian Quill, Clare Dowling, Vincent Smith, Pat Moylan, John Rooney, Darina O'Flanagan, Clare Garrihy, Patricia McCormack and David O'Sullivan.

Finally, but most importantly, my thanks go to my family, Miriam, Orla and Peter, the best supporters anyone could have.

This book is dedicated to Orla: avid reader, eagle-eyed critic, loyal fan – and daughter in a million.

Prologue

Gellert Hill, Budapest

January 2000

Abdullah Majid had finally tracked down his quarry. The search had been painstaking, but now the moment of reckoning was at hand; tonight he would kill his enemy.

It was a dark, moonless night, ideal for his purpose. Flurries of snow swirled in the wind that gusted up from the river, and the wooded slopes of Gellert Hill were deserted. Majid looked down the hill to where the broad expanse of the Danube flowed swiftly beneath the twinkling lights of the Szabadsag Bridge. Beyond that again he could see the floodlit buildings that stood like majestic sentinels on the Pest side of the river.

The lightly falling snow lent a fairytale air to what was already a striking view, but Majid hardly noticed. Tonight wasn't about scenery, it was about vengeance. For five years in an Israeli jail, and for almost two further years since his release he had imagined the moment when he would catch up with Moshe Avram. He had fantasised about it, played it out in innumerable ways in his head, and now, finally, it was about to happen.

Majid quietly stamped his feet against the cold, then scanned again all the approaches to the summit of Gellert Hill. He had read in his guidebook how Bishop Gellert, the Venetian martyr, had been thrown by pagans from this very hilltop, trapped in a barrel spiked with nails. It was exactly the kind of death Majid would have liked to inflict on Moshe Avram when he met him tonight.

Back in 1992 Avram, an Israeli agent, had led a Mossad team that raided the camp where Majid had been training in guerrilla warfare. The training camp, located in the Sudan, had been run by Mujahadeen, veterans of the war in Afghanistan. Everyone in the camp had considered the Sudan too hostile an environment and too far from Israel for a ground operation to be launched by Mossad. They had been wrong, and an audacious and well-executed Israeli raid had destroyed the camp, killing and wounding many of its occupants.

Majid and several others had been captured and driven by lorry to a remote spot on the Sudanese Red Sea coast, from where a Greek-registered, but Israeli-run freighter had transported the prisoners to the Israeli port of Eilat.

Moshe Avram had interrogated Majid relentlessly during the two days of the voyage, and Majid still felt sick with shame and anger each time he recalled it. With Majid's hands and feet securely bound, Avram's henchmen had held him over a tub of seawater into which the Mossad officer had pressed his victim's face whenever he was displeased by his answers. During the interrogation it had reached the stage where Avram had only smirkingly to make a pressing motion with his thumb for Majid to feel his stomach tightening with fear. He had held out for as long as he could, but eventually the Israeli had broken him.

He had hated Avram for the brutality of the torture, but he had hated him even more for the self-loathing induced by being made to talk about the camp's command structure, staff and objectives. He had tried to blur the truth as much as possible and had mixed half-truths and evasions into the information they had extracted, but his pride had been badly damaged by the loss of dignity caused by being broken.

Now, seven years later and half a continent away, it was time to settle the account. On learning that Avram was in Budapest, Majid had suppressed his excitement and concentrated instead on devising an approach that he felt would hook the Israeli. It had to be something enticing enough to make a professional like Avram agree to a solo meeting at an isolated venue. After much thought, Majid had opted for Hamas as his bait. He knew that the Israeli had a particular hatred for the Lebanese terror group, and so he had sent a note to Moshe Avram at the Israeli Embassy saying he had valuable information on Hamas. No point in pretending to be an Israeli sympathiser; a cynic like Avram would be more convinced by a commercial motive. He had offered therefore to sell first-class intelligence on Hamas, insisting first on a meeting alone with Avram to discuss money and communication methods. Two in the morning at the Liberation Monument on Gellert Hill had been Majid's chosen rendezvous, and he had come an hour and a half early to scout the area and be in position long before the Israeli arrived. On a snowy winter night the area had been deserted, with just the occasional car travelling up the hill and on towards the Citadel, a former military base now converted into a restaurant.

Majid had looked through his night-sight glasses every few minutes, scanning all approaches to the Liberation Monument. He had stood in a cluster of trees from where he could see the monument itself, the road to the Citadel above that, and the paths leading to the river below. Dressed in black and with his face encased in a woollen balaclava, he knew that he would be virtually invisible in the absence of moonlight.

As time had passed the cars threading their way up the hill had dwindled in frequency and, hearing one approaching now, Majid realised that it was the first vehicle that had passed in some time. He glanced at the luminous hands of his watch: one thirty, half an hour to go. *Unless they come early*, he thought.

The Liberation Monument, commemorating the Red Army's liberation of Budapest from the Nazis, consisted of a tall column on top of which stood a woman holding aloft what looked like a palm leaf. The significance of the imagery wasn't clear to Majid, but it was a good rendezvous point – near the city centre, yet off the main roads and surrounded by wooded parklands. On his arrival he had used a sophisticated infrared scanner to check the area carefully, but no body-heat images had shown up from any of the surrounding thickets, and he was reassured that an Israeli trap was not set in place.

That had been an hour ago and despite the cold he had waited patiently.

The car he had just heard had passed now, but in the distance he thought it sounded as if it had come to a halt. Instinctively his hand closed around the silenced Beretta in his pocket. Probably only a taxi going to the Citadel. *Or Moshe Avram arriving early and approaching surreptitiously.* Still holding the gun, he lifted the night-sight glasses that hung around his neck and looked up towards the road. Nothing whatsoever was stirring there. And yet . . .

He had underestimated the Israeli once before and Avram had taken him by surprise. Tonight he had to be the one springing the trap. He lowered the glasses and took off his gloves, wanting to be ready for action. He slipped the pistol into his jacket pocket, then took out the infrared scanner. Taking care to shield it from anyone on the road above, he switched on the screen. He pointed the scanner in the direction of the Citadel and immediately picked up an image. His heart began to pound, but he forced himself to breathe deeply. From the infrared image, it was clear that someone was walking down the road from the Citadel.

Majid strained his ears, but with the wind he could hear no footsteps. Standing stock-still, he watched the image on the screen approaching, then slowing. He looked away from the screen and up towards the road. Using the night-glasses again he stared hard, but he could see nothing in the swirling snow. He lowered the glasses, then from the corner of his eye he caught a movement and, looking back at the screen, saw that the target was moving again. This time the image was moving away, and he realised that the person was beginning to descend the road leading down the hill.

Majid breathed more easily. Probably just a late-night stroller who had slowed for a view over the city. He checked the infrared image again, but the person was still descending. One part of Majid was almost disappointed that it wasn't Avram arriving early to try to out-manoeuvre him. It would have been satisfying to surprise the Israeli as he tried to spring his own trap.

He glanced again at the screen and his pulses quickened. The person was no longer going down the hill. Instead the image was moving sideways. Whoever it was had left the road and gone into the parkland. Majid felt the familiar thrill that always hit him when going into action, but he refused to give full rein to it. Whoever had left the road might have nothing to do with the rendezvous. It could be someone who had simply gone into the bushes to urinate. Except that the image was still moving. Slowly but surely the person was travelling in an arc that would eventually take him onto the main path below the Liberation Monument.

Majid looked away from the screen and down the wooded slopes, trying to gauge the area that the person would have reached. He used the night-glasses, scanning what he thought was the appropriate area, but failed to pick up any movement. Lowering the glasses, he shifted the scanner and gazed at the screen. What he saw caused him to swallow hard. A second image was now approaching from the direction of the Citadel. It could simply be a coincidence, but Majid didn't believe in coincidence, certainly not on operations like this.

A stab of fear tightened his stomach as it occurred to him that perhaps he had gone from being the hunter to being the hunted. No, he thought, they couldn't know who he was or what he had in mind. If the two images were of Avram and an accomplice, the chances were that they were staking out the area and providing a hidden back-up for Avram when he made the rendezvous. They couldn't know that he knew there were two of them; he still had the upper hand. Plus he knew where they were, but they didn't know his location. *Unless they too had IR heat sensors . . .*

No, he decided, there was no reason for Avram to assume that his contact would remain hidden in the woods. Even if they didn't know his whereabouts however, he knew that the situation was going to be tricky. To do what he wanted with Avram he would have to kill the back-up, but without alerting the Israeli. Difficult, but not impossible. The problem was that he didn't know which of the two images was Avram. Probably the second one, he reasoned – that way Avram could appear to arrive normally along the path leading from the roadside, while his accomplice was in place to cover him from below the monument.

He would deal with the one in the bushes first. He switched off the IR scanner, then moved carefully along the snow-covered ground in the direction in which the first person had been heading. After a moment he reached a clearing where several paths met, then he stepped back into the cover of the trees and raised his night-glasses. By his reckoning the first person had been heading this way and would be exposed when crossing the clearing. He looked through the glasses and waited. Sure enough, after a moment he heard a slight rustle, then saw a figure moving stealthily through the trees.

The figure reached the clearing, looked about, then stepped back towards the bushes. As Majid had expected, it wasn't Avram. He hadn't seen the man's face properly, but Avram was over six feet tall, and this man was small and stocky. Majid kept the glasses trained on the figure as he moved into the shrubbery. It looked like he was taking up a position. The next moment all Majid's suspicions were confirmed. The man turned his head and, through the night-glasses, Majid saw that he was wearing a miniature microphone and earphones set.

It was good news and bad news. Good in that there could be no further doubt about what he was up to. Bad in that Majid couldn't kill him without alerting Avram. The dynamics of the situation had changed – he was outnumbered now, and the prudent course might be to retreat. Majid considered his options, recalling the rules that his trainers in the Sudan had stressed. Always consider the odds, always weigh up the possible gain and loss, never act just for the sake of acting. All things considered, the wise move now would be to withdraw. But Majid hadn't come all this way to be wise. His business with Avram was personal, a blood feud, and he wanted it settled, tonight.

Besides, he thought, maybe the radio mikes weren't an insuperable problem. In his note, he had insisted that Avram come alone, that if there was anything untoward the meeting would be aborted. Which meant that Avram couldn't approach the monument wearing earphones and a mike. And if Majid used the silenced Beretta on the stocky man *after* Avram had removed his earphones, he could still take the Israeli by surprise. But it wasn't a sound plan, he knew. There were too many imponderables, the chief one being: when would Avram take off the earphones?

Majid realised that he would have to use the scanner to determine Avram's location and trust that on arriving near the monument the Mossad man would have slipped off the communications gear. Majid moved slowly backwards into the shrubbery, knowing that he couldn't switch on the scanner here, with its light being visible to the watcher in the bushes. He worked his way in a circle, taking care not to snap any twigs, until he was about fifteen yards behind the stocky man.

Majid switched on the scanner and pointed it towards the monument. The image showed the second person moving slowly in that direction. Majid reckoned that he would have just left the road. If Avram were taking off the earphones, he would surely be doing it now. Majid slipped the scanner into his jacket pocket and withdrew the Beretta. Using his left hand, he held the night-glasses firmly to his eyes, then with his right hand he wedged the gun against the branch of a tree to steady his aim. He knew that the silencer would lessen his accuracy, but on the positive side he was an excellent marksman and the Israeli in the bushes was unmoving.

He held his breath, pressing the gun hard against the tree to minimise shaking, then squeezed the trigger twice. The noise of the wind dampened the thump of the silencer, and he saw his target slump to the ground. He fired two more shots into the body, then made for the nearby path, transferring the gun to his left hand and holding it just inside his pocket. He would have preferred to make absolutely sure that the first Israeli was dead, but he couldn't risk taking that much time. In case Avram was still wearing a mike, Majid knew that he had to get to him before he called in again with his colleague.

He moved swiftly towards the base of the Liberation Monument. Then suddenly he saw Avram. There was no mistaking the bulk of the tall Israeli standing in the snow-covered clearing. Majid felt his mouth go dry now that the moment had finally arrived, but his adrenaline kept him moving forward.

Hearing the approaching footsteps, Avram turned, and Majid saw his face in the faint light spilling down from the streetlamp on the road above. There was no sign of any microphone or earphone, and Majid felt a surge of exhilaration. "Mr Avram, I presume," he said, holding out his right hand to shake as he drew near. He had worked out in advance exactly how he would play this.

Speak in English – Arabic would make Avram instinctively suspicious. Hold out the right hand to shake hands – most people by reflex hold out their right hand in return. That way

Avram would have to use what would normally be his gun-hand.

It worked perfectly. Avram held out his hand, and in one continuous movement Majid shook hands, pulled the gun from his left pocket and pushed it against Avram's temple. "One move and I'll blow your brains out!" This time he spoke Arabic, in which he knew Avram was fluent, and he saw the flicker of fear cross the Israeli's face. "Understand?" he said, pressing the gun harder into the other man's temple.

"Yes."

The Mossad agent's voice was steady, and Majid noted that he had seemed to regain his composure pretty quickly. *He'd soon change that.* Keeping the gun pressed to Avram's head, Majid moved behind him, then shifted the barrel to press into the back of the Israeli's head.

"Put your legs wide apart," he ordered.

Avram complied, then Majid took a step back, the gun still trained on the other man's head.

"Now slowly, very slowly, raise your hands onto your head."

Again the Israeli complied.

"Start moving forward. Keep your legs apart!" Majid enjoyed seeing the Israeli moving forward awkwardly at his command. He followed closely behind, his aim never wavering, then told Avram to halt. They were now out of view from the road above. "Keep your hands on your head, then turn around slowly," he ordered. Standing just far enough back to be out of lunging range, Majid reached up with his free hand and

11

removed the balaclava. "Face look familiar?" he asked.

"I can't see you properly," answered Avram.

Majid was almost going to move closer for the pleasure of seeing the Israeli's fear on recognising his face, but he stopped himself. This bastard was both cunning and dangerous – drawing near would be a mistake. "Sudan ring a bell?" he said instead. "Little sailing trip up the Red Sea? Torturing a helpless man?"

Avram made no response, and Majid felt his anger rising. "Turn around," he snapped. "Turn around!"

The Mossad agent turned his back as ordered, and Majid quickly swung the Beretta, smacking the Israeli hard on the back of his neck. Avram stumbled and cried out in pain, but didn't fall to the ground.

"That's just for starters, you Zionist pig! Oh, and in case you're wondering – your friend in the bushes won't be helping. Ask me why. Ask me why, pig!"

"Why?"

"Because I blew his brains out!"

The Mossad agent said nothing, but Majid knew he must be feeling sickened. Frightened too, with no-one now to rescue him. "You thought you were so smart, didn't you?" he goaded. Avram didn't answer, and Majid felt his anger rising again. "I'm talking to you, pig!"

"I'm not talking to you, scum!"

Majid felt a surge of rage at the Israeli's defiance and he swivelled the gun in one flowing movement and fired a shot. Avram screamed in agony, then stumbled to the ground, clutching his shattered kneecap. Keeping the gun trained on his captive, Majid kicked him hard in the ribs and was rewarded with another cry of pain.

"Don't show disrespect again, pig. Understood? I said *understood*?"

"Yes . . ." Avram whispered, still holding his knee.

Majid looked at the Israeli contemptuously. "Not so good at taking it, are you? Really good at giving it out, when your victims are helpless – not so tough on the receiving end. Are you, pig?"

The Israeli stared up at him, but didn't answer. At first Majid thought the man was distracted by pain, then he realised that Avram was defying him. If he had any fleeting regard for the other man's bravery, it was swiftly overtaken by rage. Even when wounded and taken prisoner, the Israeli arrogance that Majid hated so much was in evidence.

"Answer when I speak to you, pig!" he said, but still the Mossad man held his gaze and made no reply. Majid aimed the gun at Avram, his finger tight on the trigger, but still the Israeli refused to answer. Majid shot twice, the bullets aimed for the other kneecap, and Avram screamed.

Majid relished the sight of the prostrate and blood-soaked Israeli, but even as he did another part of his mind was operating objectively. *Time to finish it.* The scream and Avram's earlier cry might have been heard. He drew closer. He went behind the Israeli and buried his knee in his back, then jerked the man's head backwards with his left hand. "You've tortured your last Arab, pig. Time to die . . ." Majid slipped the gun into his pocket with his right hand and pulled out an ornate dagger. He quickly wedged the dagger-case between his knee and Avram's back and unsheathed the weapon with one hand, allowing Avram to see its finely honed blade. The Israeli's head was pulled taut to expose his neck, and Majid saw the flash of fear in his eyes.

Enough, he thought; then in one swift movement he slit the Israeli's throat. Avram struggled and cried out as the blood spurted from his severed carotid artery, then eventually his struggles ceased and he went limp, and Majid allowed him to fall onto the crimson-stained snow.

Majid stared in triumph for a moment at his enemy's body before wiping the blood off his weapon in the snow and sheathing the knife. Exhilarated at paying off the first part of his debt so spectacularly, he took one last look at the body, then set off down the hill.

1

London

September 2000

Penny Harte walked along Victoria Embankment, following the route to her destination on autopilot. The summer sunshine sparkled on the waters of the Thames, but Penny barely noticed as she mentally prepared for her appointment. She was dressed in a smartly cut, lightweight business suit and white silk blouse, but she had slipped the jacket off because of the strong sunshine. The admiring stares she drew from several of the men she passed on the Embankment were lost on her today. She was thirty years old, slim again after the birth last year of her first child, and with her black hair, sallow skin and dark eyes she was used to admiring glances. Sometimes it was an irritant, sometimes flattering; this morning it barely registered with her.

She passed under the railway bridge leading to Charing Cross station, savouring the cool breeze that came from the river, but only half-noticing the traffic that plied the waterway. She continued along by the Thames until she came to Westminster Bridge, then paused for a moment. Better put on her jacket, she thought. It was essential to get into the right frame of mind, important that she project the right businesslike image. At the same time, she couldn't pretend that this was a normal business meeting.

So what was the correct demeanour for meeting your former lover, whom you hadn't seen for seven years? It depended, she knew, on a great many things. How you had parted, why you had parted, which of you had made the break, which of you had requested to meet again. As it happened, the summons to appear at his office had come out of the blue, and if Penny's superiors knew that she had once had a relationship with Colin Mathieson, no-one had mentioned it. Since the summons, she had played the moment of their coming meeting over in her mind from many different angles. Should she be cool? Friendly? Businesslike? Should she make no reference to their past relationship, or would it be better to allude lightly to it? A sort of 'I'm-happily-married-now, that-was-the-distant-past, no-hard-feelings' approach?

She hadn't been able to make up her mind, and as she made her way down Millbank now and arrived at her destination she knew that she would have to play it by ear. The building she entered had a foyer, and she crossed as confidently as she could to the reception desk. A burly young man with a shaven head looked up on her arrival. "May I help you?" he asked, and Penny was slightly surprised by his middle-class accent.

"I have an appointment to see Colin Mathieson," she said.

16

"Ah," the young man answered, quickly opening an appointments book. "And you are?

"Detective Inspector Penny Harte."

"If I might just see your identification, please?"

Penny showed him her badge, and the young man smiled. "Thank you, Inspector Harte. Mr Mathieson is expecting you."

The office was spacious, clearly the domain of a senior figure, with large windows through which the morning sunlight shone brightly. Penny took in the details automatically, but her attention was on Mathieson as he rose smilingly from behind his desk and crossed the room to greet her.

The years have been kind to him, thought Penny. He had been in his late forties when they split up, but he still had a lean, athletic build, the likes of which few men in their fifties could boast. She had been twenty-three when they met, working on her first major case back in her native Yorkshire. Mathieson had been quite a senior MI5 operative, and when the case ended Penny had been flattered that he asked her to dinner. He was handsome, witty and urbane, and in spite of the age-difference they had become lovers. Before he had returned to London he asked Penny to join him on holiday, and they had spent an idyllic two weeks in Sardinia. On their return to the UK however, it became clear that Mathieson's first passion would always be his career and that his plans didn't include a long-term relationship with someone twenty-five years his junior. What had been a pleasant interlude to Mathieson had been more significant to Penny, however, and it had taken her some time to get over the affair. And now, seven years later, she had been summoned to his office without explanation.

"Penny, you're looking wonderful," Mathieson said, shaking hands and kissing her lightly on the cheek.

"You're looking well yourself, Colin."

"Please, take a seat. Tea, coffee?"

"No, I'm fine, thanks," she answered, sitting in one of several leather armchairs.

Mathieson sat opposite and looked at her smilingly. "It's good to see you again."

"It's . . . *surprising* to see you again," she answered.

If Mathieson sensed a hint of a barb, he gave no indication of it. "Yes, I dare say you're wondering why we asked to see you."

"It had crossed my mind . . ."

"We thought you might be just the person for a certain job."

"We?"

Mathieson shrugged in acquiescence and then smiled. "All right – guilty of a royal we. *I* thought it, OK?

"In what capacity?"

"My capacity as a Deputy Director."

So he had been promoted, thought Penny. "Actually, I meant in what capacity you sought *me*."

"Ah," he said. "Misunderstood."

The story of our lives, thought Penny. "Congratulations, by the way, on the promotion."

"Thank you. Likewise on your own in rank."

Penny nodded in acknowledgement.

"Sergeant at twenty-five," he continued, "special Police College at Bramshill, an Inspector at twenty-seven – it's rather impressive."

It was also rather evident that he had read her file. Then he nodded, and she sensed that the pleasantries were at an end.

"So, the reason that you're here . . ."

"Yes?"

"I've requested that you be seconded for three weeks."

"To whom?"

"To liaise with us."

"To liaise with the Security Service?"

"Yes."

"Surely Special Branch are the police officers who do that?"

"In the normal course of events. We have a situation however that isn't quite normal . . ."

Penny looked at him, curious despite her reservations about being embroiled again with Mathieson, albeit professionally.

"Why me?" she asked.

"Two reasons. One, you're a lateral thinker. First class at it."

"Am I?"

"No false modesty, Penny. You know you are."

"I dare say there are plenty of lateral thinkers in the force."

"Frankly, I doubt it. Whereas your work when we were together on the Walker/Adams case was excellent."

"You said there were two reasons?"

"Quite. The other also relates back to the case."

"Yes?"

"We want someone with an intimate knowledge of Harrogate."

"I'm actually from Leeds."

"Same neck of the woods. Plus you were all over Harrogate when we were hunting Mary Adams."

It was true. It had been her first case with CID and she had immersed herself enthusiastically in working with the Security Service, which had been on the trail of Dave Walker and his wife Mary Adams.

"I transferred from Bramshill straight to the Met," said Penny. "I haven't been based in Yorkshire since '95."

"I'm aware of all that."

"Then why not use someone currently based in Harrogate?"

"We will, of course, use the local force. But we'd like you there in addition. A three-week secondment's been cleared with your superiors. Assuming you're prepared to help."

Penny looked away, her mind racing. Despite the polite phrasing, she knew Mathieson wasn't simply making a request. Had he been, she would have said no. Aisling, her baby girl, was only eighteen months old and although Shane, her husband, could look after her perfectly well, Penny hated the idea of being separated from her child for three weeks. The reality however was that her secondment had already been cleared by MI5 – she still thought of them as MI5, despite the name-change to the Security Service – which meant her superiors would expect her to co-operate. And although Mathieson had given no details of the operation, obviously it had to be something of importance. She couldn't just walk away – there was no point going to the elite police academy to fast-track your career if you were going to undo that by balking at a special assignment.

Mathieson had her and he knew it. But was seeking her out purely business on his part? Could he possibly also be hoping to rekindle an old relationship? Or seeking to enliven a stay in Harrogate with the chance of a fling with an old flame? He was still a good-looking, attractive man, but Penny wasn't interested; her life had moved on. She would make that clear if need be, she decided. Meanwhile she consciously forced herself back into police-officer mode.

"OK," she said.

"You'll go?"

"Yes. What's the operation?"

Mathieson looked at her evenly. "We think it began last February. Now – it's shaping up as a security nightmare . . ."

Puerto Banus, Southern Spain

February 2000

Abdullah Majid stood in the bow of the yacht as it cruised majestically into the harbour. The setting sun stroked the sky with purple, casting a soft light on the rows of sleek, multi-million-pound craft moored at the marina. A playground for the rich and idle, Majid thought. You could almost smell the money in the air. Despite the preponderance of luxury yachts, the admiring glances of those strolling along the quayside was evident as they took in the size and elegance of the *Tigris*, the craft on which he was the sole passenger.

Majid had left Taormina in Sicily two and a half days previously, the dramatic bulk of Mount Etna silhouetted against a clear blue winter sky as they left the harbour behind. Between the spectacular views and the sumptuous luxury of his quarters on the *Tigris*, it had made for an impressive start to his voyage. All part of the softening-up process, of course – Majid had realised that at once – but impressive nonetheless. When the millionaire shipping magnate Omar Rahmani had requested a meeting, Majid had been intrigued. Although Iraqi like Majid, Rahmani lived mostly outside the country. He still maintained a palatial home in Basra, the city of his birth, but these days he spent more time in his villas in Sicily and southern Spain.

Rahmani had been unwilling to indicate what he wanted to discuss with Majid, but he had stressed that a meeting could be mutually beneficial. Would Majid honour him by being his guest on the *Tigris*, which would transport him to Rahmani's current location in Spain?

Majid had been fascinated and, despite himself, a little flattered. Omar Rahmani was one of the most wealthy and powerful men in Iraq. It was said he had left school at eight, a penniless urchin who sold dates and trinkets to the British soldiers occupying Iraq after the Second World War. He had gone from that to pimping for sailors and tourists, before graduating to gunrunning and smuggling, at which he had made his fortune. A millionaire before he was thirty, he had been careful to support Saddam Hussein's Bathist Party, without ever becoming involved directly in politics himself. Then, in the seventies, he had boosted his fortune even more by illegally shipping goods to Rhodesia in defiance of UN sanctions. He was now in his early sixties and had a large fleet of tankers and merchant ships, and trade contacts all over Europe and the Middle East.

So what could he possibly want from me? Majid wondered for the hundredth time as the *Tigris* smoothly came to anchor. He would find out soon enough, he thought, as a metallic silver Mercedes came to a halt on the jetty, even as the crew made the vessel fast to the quayside capstan.

"Sir."

He looked around to see the captain of the *Tigris*, immaculately dressed in naval uniform. "Captain."

"I hope your voyage with us was pleasant."

"Very much so. Your hospitality was superb."

"Thank you." The captain indicated a gangplank which was being secured and at the base of which stood the chauffeur from the Mercedes. "Mr Rahmani awaits you."

"I'll just organise my luggage."

"We'll send that on, sir. Mr Rahmani would like to see you right away."

Majid hesitated, suppressing a flicker of irritation, then he decided that if this was some kind of power game he would allow Rahmani this opening move. If he were to challenge the older man, he would do so on something more significant.

"Fine," answered Majid with a smile. "And thank you again, Captain, for a most enjoyable voyage." Without waiting for a reply, he made for the gangplank and quickly descended.

The chauffeur drew forward, then bowed. "Good evening, sir. I'm instructed to escort you to Mr Rahmani's residence."

"Good."

The man opened the rear door of the Mercedes and Majid entered, the faint aroma of leather upholstery touching his nostrils like an expensive perfume. Again the smell of money, thought Majid, as the car pulled away smoothly, leaving the harbour behind as the driver made for the main coastal road.

They cruised for several minutes, heading west towards Marbella, then the driver turned left, following a narrow road that wound upwards. The car came to a halt at a set of gates, and Majid saw the words *Casa Verde*, then the gates soundlessly swung open and the car proceeded up a driveway flanked with cypress trees. Eventually they reached the villa, an imposing building behind which Majid could see a large swimming-pool and beautifully manicured lawns. The chauffeur opened the car door for Majid and escorted him towards the villa's main entrance. Inside, he led him across a panelled hallway, then stopped and knocked respectfully on a heavy teak door.

"Enter," cried a voice for within, and the chauffeur ushered Majid into Rahmani's study.

"Your visitor, sir."

Rahmani dismissed the chauffeur with an imperious wave of the hand before advancing smilingly towards Majid. The shipping magnate was overweight, with heavy jowls and a lumbering gait, but his thick grey hair was expertly coiffured and Majid reckoned that his tailored suit would have cost a small fortune. They shook hands and Rahmani kissed Majid on the cheek.

"So good of you to come."

"My pleasure."

"A comfortable trip, I hope?"

What else would it be on a luxury yacht? thought Majid. "Most comfortable, thank you."

Rahmani indicated to Majid to sit on an ornately

decorated sofa, then lowered his bulk into a nearby armchair. "You'll have coffee, mint tea?"

"Nothing for me, thank you. I had refreshments on board ship."

Majid knew most visitors would be expected to allow Rahmani to play the role of traditional Arab host, but he wanted to tilt the older man just a little off balance, to let him know that he was not in any sense a supplicant.

"As you wish," answered Rahmani with no indication of offence taken.

Majid decided that he would push matters a little more by dispensing with protracted pleasantries – he had after all spent nearly three days getting here by sea so that Rahmani could impress him with the lavishness of his hospitality. "You're an important man, Mr Rahmani," he said, "so I won't waste your time. Perhaps you would tell me how we can assist each other?"

This time Rahmani slightly raised an eyebrow as though to indicate that he wasn't used to being rushed. "Indeed," he said, looking levelly at Majid.

"Well?"

"I've taken the liberty of checking your background."

"I wouldn't expect to be alone with you if you hadn't," said Majid with a small smile.

Rahmani didn't smile back, but looked at Majid thoughtfully. "I've taken another liberty. I've opened a bank account in Zurich for you."

This time it was Majid's turn to raise an eyebrow.

"I've arranged with my banker that it's accessible by either of us. Two and a half million pounds sterling has been lodged in it."

Majid tried to show no surprise, but he had to concede that if Rahmani's tactic was to seize his attention, it had certainly succeeded.

"Should you agree to my proposition, that money will be available to you at once. Should you succeed in the task I have in mind, a further two and a half million sterling will be lodged."

"Five million pounds – clearly a task of some difficulty," said Majid wryly.

"Great difficulty. Great danger too – we may as well be honest from the start. But difficulty and danger are no strangers to you, I think."

"Perhaps . . ."

"Anyone who survives five years in an Israeli jail and repays them with the panache you showed last month – such a man is a force to be reckoned with."

Majid was taken aback. "I'm not sure what you're referring to –"

"Budapest. Highly impressive . . ."

Majid looked at the older man, surprised by the range of his knowledge. The number of people who knew of his operation against Moshe Avram was small; obviously, Rahmani had excellent sources. "You're remarkably well informed."

"I make it my business to be."

"So what precisely are you proposing?"

"A similar act of vengeance. But on a much more impressive scale."

"Against whom?"

"Our mutual enemies."

"And who would they be?"

27

"The Americans and the Europeans who attacked Iraq during the Gulf War. The butchers who mowed down helpless Iraqi soldiers, who bombed innocent civilians."

Majid said nothing but waited for Rahmani to continue.

"I know you lost your mother and sisters when they bombed Baghdad," said Rahmani. "And both your brothers were killed in action during the butchery on the road to Basra."

Majid felt a sudden anger at having old wounds calculatedly opened to force his hand on whatever scheme Rahmani was hatching. "You know a great deal about me, Mr Rahmani – maybe too much."

"Do not be angry with me, my young friend. Channel it where it belongs."

Majid breathed deeply, annoyed at himself for not controlling his emotions. "And your role in all of this?"

"I, too, lost family," said Rahmani simply.

"Really?"

"My first wife and two grandchildren were killed by missiles. So-called 'smart bombs' that killed women and children."

"I'm sorry."

"Let us together make those sorry who should be sorry," said Rahmani.

Majid considered the other man's reply, then looked at him. "Before we go any further there's something I must ask you."

"Please."

"The Gulf War ended nine years ago – why are you only acting now?"

"It's said that vengeance is a dish best eaten cold."

"But nine years . . .?"

"Circumstances have provided an opportunity just now."

"Yes?"

"Firstly there's yourself, a fellow Iraqi with the motivation, the daring, and the ability to take the fight to the enemy."

"And secondly?"

"The perfect chance to hit our enemies in a spectacular fashion."

"And what is this chance?"

"Before we discuss that, I must point out something to you."

"Let me guess. If you reveal your plan, and I choose not to become involved, I'm a liability."

"Were you ever to discuss it with a third party – yes."

Although the older man spoke evenly, Majid knew that someone of Rahmani's power could afford to make a lethal threat with courteous phraseology. "I've survived as long as I have by knowing when to keep my mouth shut," said Majid. "If I don't accept your offer, this conversation will never have taken place."

"Your grasp of the situation does you proud," said Rahmani, then he smiled. "Of course if you agree to my offer, this conversation is equally non-existent."

"Of course."

"Very well. The opportunity I mentioned occurs next September."

Majid was taken aback. "That's seven months away."

"I imagine you'd need plenty of time to prepare for what I have in mind."

"Which is?"

"The death of every Foreign Minister in the European Union."

Majid made an effort not to show surprise, and waited for Rahmani to elaborate.

"It's been announced that they're holding a conference from September the twenty-fourth to the twenty-sixth. And here's the best part: the conference will be addressed by the American Secretary of State."

Despite his efforts to show no emotion, Majid felt his excitement mount. "That would be quite a prize."

"The perfect retribution for what was done to us, our families, and Iraq."

Majid said nothing, his mind racing.

"The money I mentioned, that would be for you personally. I would fund all expenses, though of course I must never be traceable in any way to this operation."

"Where is the conference to take place?"

"England. The International Conference Centre in Harrogate, Yorkshire."

"I see . . . Do you have a plan on how to kill them?"

"No, that would be entirely up to you. May I take it that you're interested?"

Majid thought for a moment, then looked Rahmani in the eye. "Yes. It will take a great deal of planning. But come September, justice will be done . . ."

London

September 2000

Penny looked at Mathieson, unable to mask her eagerness to hear about the security nightmare to which he had referred.

"Before I go into detail," he said, "I do have to mention the Official Secrets Act . . ."

"'Idle talk costs lives'"?"

"Something like that," answered Mathieson with an apologetic smile. "Look, I know you'll be discreet. It's just something I have to refer to when anyone's seconded to us."

"Fine. Well, now that it's been referred to –"

"You want the gory details. Problem is, it *could* be gory if things go badly."

"So, what is this security nightmare?"

"A terrorist attack on the EU Foreign Ministers' conference next month."

"I see."

"For good measure the conference will be addressed by the American Secretary of State."

Penny raised an eyebrow. "Plum targets."

"I'm afraid so. And they'll all be together in the Conference Centre in Harrogate."

"What makes you think an attack is planned?"

"We've received intelligence pointing to just such a plan."

"Forgive me if I'm stating the obvious," said Penny, "but isn't this . . .well, isn't it always the case?"

"How do you mean?"

"Any major political conference must be potentially a terrorist target. I mean, we had two G7 summits in London in recent years. Can't the same precautions be taken for this as for the G7s?"

"They will be," said Mathieson. "This is different though."

"In what way?"

"At a G7 summit, or anything similar, the threat is theoretical. We still bend over backwards to guard against it – but it's non-specific."

"And this threat is specific?"

"Yes."

"So who's making it?"

"We don't have a name," replied Mathieson, "but it emanates from Iraq."

"Iraq?"

"You sound surprised."

"Well, I am a bit," said Penny. "I thought they were pushing hard to have the UN embargoes lifted."

"They are. But this threat is not state-sponsored."

"Who *is* sponsoring it then?"

"Again we don't have a name. What we do know is

that there's a wealthy backer in place, and there's a plan in place."

"Can't the Iraqi government be pressurised to try and stop the operation?" asked Penny.

"Not very effectively – if we've no name to give them. From Saddam's point of view it's all rather appealing actually."

"Yeah?"

"He can hardly be blamed if some fanatic makes a solo run that has absolutely no official backing. At the same time if the operation succeeds, Saddam privately laughs his head off."

"Right," said Penny reflectively. "So this information that we have – where does it come from?"

"We got it from the Israelis."

"Where did they get it?"

"From a visit to Sidon."

"Sidon – in the Lebanon?"

Mathieson nodded. "They launched a raid there last February. Mossad were after a terrorist leader called Duraid Kizili – along the way they flushed out someone else . . ."

Sidon, Lebanon

February 2000

Majid smiled his most charming smile as he crossed the bedroom with the drinks. He had picked up the woman in a local hotel, a voluptuous Turkish dancer who, with a little persuasion, had accompanied him to the villa. She smiled back at him now as he gave her the glass, her jet-black hair ruffled by the evening breeze that wafted in from the balcony. Majid touched his glass against hers, then reached out his left hand and ran it slowly down her cheek. She closed her eyes as though savouring his touch, and Majid put down the glass and drew her to him. Her skin was flawless and smelt faintly of musky perfume and when she opened her eyes and looked at him boldly he leaned down to kiss her. That was when he heard the first scream. The woman's eyes widened in shock, and they both turned towards the door.

The sound had come from downstairs, but before they had time to consider it further there was a volley of shots followed by another scream. Majid was already moving as footsteps pounded up the stairs. Ignoring the cries of the woman, he made towards the balcony. He heard a nearby bedroom door being kicked open and the sound of shouted orders from the landing. His already pounding pulses raced even faster on recognising the language. *Hebrew. Another fucking Mossad operation!*

All of Majid's instincts told him to flee. But if his instinct was to run, his training had drilled into him the importance of not panicking. A second or two weighing up the options could be the difference between life and death. His money, his passport, and more importantly his gun were in a travel-bag in the wardrobe to his right – he swung back, made for the wardrobe and grabbed the bag. He heard another bedroom door from across the corridor being smashed open, followed by more screams. *Your door will be next. What are you going to do?* It was the kind of scenario they had made him address during his training in the camp in the Sudan. That was over seven years ago now, yet he was still able to detach himself enough to make split-second decisions under pressure. *The Israelis had to be slowed down.*

He sacrificed a precious second or two in pulling the gun out and swivelling to face the bedroom door. Without pausing, he fired three quick rounds at the door. With luck he might have hit someone, but at the very least it would make the attackers hesitate before entering the room.

The Turkish woman had started to scream, but Majid ignored her and sprinted towards the balcony. A swift glance showed no-one visible in the garden below, and Majid was over the balustrade in one flowing movement.

35

He lowered himself by his arms to minimise the drop, then heard the door to the bedroom being smashed in. Immediately he let go, falling down into the garden. He heard the Turkish woman screaming hysterically as he rolled to his feet. Suddenly the earth beside him seemed to erupt, and he knew it had been raked with machine-gun fire. The Mossad agents were using silenced Uzis, he realised, as he threw himself frantically for the cover of a low garden wall.

He couldn't let himself be taken prisoner a second time by the Israelis. Then again maybe they weren't taking prisoners – maybe this was a search and destroy mission. He crawled along the base of the wall, and chips of masonry flew past his head as another burst was fired down at him from the balcony. He reached a point where he was out of the line of fire and quickly scrambled to his feet and zigzagged towards the rear wall of the grounds. More shots thudded into the ground to his left, and for a second he was tempted to turn and fire back, but instead he kept moving. He had seen the muzzle-flashes of the Israeli on the balcony; to fire back would have meant muzzle-flashes from his own gun. There were probably at least half a dozen Israelis on the raid – all it would take was another member of the Mossad team to spot his muzzle-flashes and he would be dead.

Majid ran with the Beretta in his hand, leaving behind the screams and shooting. Would the Israelis come after him or would they concentrate on those within the house? Hard to know, but he had to assume they would pursue him. He knew enough of Mossad

operations to realise that they would probably have the
rear of the villa covered, and so instead of making for
the rear entrance he held his course for the boundary
wall that separated the safe house from the estate next
door. *Safe house, that was some joke. But whoever had betrayed
them to the Israelis would pay for this!* First though he had to
get away, and for all he knew the agent who had shot at
him from the balcony might have dropped down into
the garden to sprint after him.

All of a sudden, he reached the boundary wall and,
without slowing, he jumped upwards. He used his
right foot to continue his momentum and, catching the
top of the wall with his left hand, he hauled himself
upwards, still clutching the Beretta in his right hand. If
the Mossad unit was close behind he was a sitting duck,
he knew, and as he hauled himself astride the wall he
half-expected a bullet to slam into his back. No shots
were fired at him, however, and he quickly dropped
down on the other side of the wall.

It was darker here, away from the lights of the villa,
and he was setting off again when he heard approaching
voices from the far side of the wall. He quickened his
pace, spurred by the knowledge that the Israelis were
after him. He raced in what he thought would be the
direction of the house into whose grounds he had
escaped. If he reached the house, there would be a way
to the road, possibly a car he could take. It was a bigger
estate than he had imagined however, and with his
lungs on fire from running he found his way blocked by
another boundary wall. He realised that he must have
skirted the house. This wall was higher than the one he

had climbed and was topped with razor wire. Catching his breath, he tried to think clearly. He heard the sound of traffic and figured that there must be a public road on the other side.

He set off again, following the wall in the direction that lead away from the safe house and after several moments he came to a side entrance. Without pausing, he grabbed the handle of the wooden door and pushed it. It barely budged. Majid swore under his breath. He tried it again, but the door was locked. Just then he heard a twig cracking some distance away and he knew the Mossad agents were closing in. He wiped the sweat from his hands, raised the Beretta and aimed it at the door. He fired three times, splintering the lock, then kicked at the door. Shards of wood flew in all directions, but the remains of the door swung open and Majid ran through the gap. As he expected, he was out on a public road and was the focus of attention for pedestrians and drivers as he ran forward, gun in hand. He didn't waste precious seconds checking if the Israelis were pursuing him, but instead made for a nearby young man who had stopped his motorcycle to see what was happening.

"Off! Now!" screamed Majid, pointing the Beretta.

The terrified youth dropped the motorbike, its engine still ticking over. Majid grabbed the handlebars, swung it upright and mounted it. As he did so, two men in commando uniforms and with blackened faces came through the shattered gate. Majid fired two shots, and the Mossad agents dived for cover while the local inhabitants screamed and scattered for safety. Majid shoved the gun into his waistband, revved the motorbike's engine, then threw it into gear and careered away down the road. He zigzagged at speed in case the Israelis managed to get off any shots, then he reached a corner and took it sharply, heading in the direction of town and away from the safe house.

For a minute or two he drove at high speed, feeling it was important to put some distance between himself and the Israelis even at the risk of drawing attention to himself – then as he began to approach the centre of town he slowed to a normal speed. There was a good deal of evening traffic, and he pulled his jacket forward to cover the Beretta in his waistband. After a while he relaxed a little. He was an Arab in an Arab city – the Israelis were the interlopers here and probably would want to withdraw pretty quickly, now that the raid had drawn attention.

He slowed down, pulled in to the side of the road, and reflected for a moment. It had been a close call. Someone would pay for this, he vowed. First things first though. For now, he needed to go to ground. It wouldn't be a problem. He had his passport, his credit cards, and plenty of money. He would find somewhere to hole up, and later exact a price for tonight's events. He switched off the engine and pulled the motorbike up onto its stand. He slipped a handkerchief from his pocket and surreptitiously wiped the handles of the bike to remove any prints, then strolled casually away, glad to disappear into the back streets of the city.

London

September 2000

Penny looked at Mathieson, her curiosity aroused by his tale of the Israeli incursion. "So, was this Kizili character picked up when they raided the villa?"

"No. Seems he had a hidden passage in his bedroom. Used it as an escape hatch."

"Very James Bond," said Penny with a wry smile.

Mathieson didn't smile back. "These people live on the edge. It's not a game to them – or to us."

"Right," said Penny a little apologetically. "And the guy we're interested in?"

"Got away in the confusion. Though Mossad weren't actually after him – his presence was simply a bonus."

"How so, if he got away?"

"Because we know he was there," answered Mathieson, "and we know now what he was doing in Lebanon."

"Which was?"

"Recruiting and organising."

"For an operation in Harrogate?"

Mathieson nodded his head. "I'm afraid so."

"How do we know this, if they both got away?"

"The Israelis picked up Duraid Kizili last week. Spotted him attending a funeral in the West Bank."

"I see . . ."

"Stroke of fortune," said Mathieson. "Damn lucky for us though that they did."

"And was Kizili working with this guy on the operation?"

"No, that's the thing. Although he's a terrorist of some standing, Kizili has nothing to do with Harrogate – he was simply providing a safe house."

"Not very successfully."

"No. Though as I said, the Israeli raid wasn't connected to our business – they were working to their own agenda."

"How do we know about Harrogate if Kizili wasn't involved?"

Mathieson allowed himself a small grin. "It seems Kizili's duties as a host didn't extend to privacy. He'd bugged the bedroom our man was in."

"Why would he do that? Aren't they all more or less on the same side?"

"You must be joking!"

"Well, I know there are lots of factions. But I assume they're all anti-Israeli, anti-Western . . ."

"It's the Middle East, Penny. Everyone has his own agenda. Information is power. So, if you have a guest staying in your safe house, as distinct from in a hotel . . ."

"It's because he has something to hide."

"Precisely. And if you know what it is, that gives

41

you an edge. If he doesn't *know* that you know, you have even more of an edge."

Penny nodded. "Has Kizili revealed a name for this guy?"

"The visitor called himself Ali, but all visitors using the safe house had pseudonyms."

"Hadn't Kizili ever met him before?"

"He swears he hadn't – nor did he actually meet him this time."

"Even though the man stayed in his villa?" queried Penny.

"Yes. Apparently there's a network out there where people ring people, proper names aren't exchanged, people stay for a night or two, questions aren't asked."

"Right," said Penny thoughtfully. "This tape that was made – can we hear it?"

Mathieson shook his head. "'Fraid not. The raid took place over six months ago – Kizili had wiped the tape."

"That's really a pity."

"It is, but there you have it."

"For all we know, this Kizili could be making the whole thing up."

" I wish he were."

"How are you so sure he's not?" Penny persisted.

Mathieson hesitated, then appeared to reach a decision. "There's a senior chap in Mossad called Samuel Lubetkin. Our interests have sometimes coincided and . . . let's say he owed me for a past favour. So when he rang me personally about this, it had to be taken seriously."

"Fair enough. How did the Israelis get Kizili to reveal it in the first place?"

"You don't want to know," answered Mathieson, and Penny felt a stab of distaste, knowing she was entering a murky world where unspeakable acts were rationalised by the end justifying the means. "Take it from me, they'll have extracted all the information Kizili had and it will have been accurate."

"And what exactly did this Ali character disclose about the mission?"

"Kizili said he spoke to someone in his room. It seems he has ample funding from an Iraqi supporter."

"But definitely not the Iraqi government? Even in a covert form?"

"No. It was apparent the operation – and that word was actually used – it was apparent it was to be privately sponsored. The second person there used the phrase 'your countryman' when referring to the sponsor, so we reckon our suspect is Iraqi."

"And Harrogate? Was it actually mentioned by name?"

"Yes. Plus the dates of September the twenty-fourth to September the twenty-sixth – which coincides exactly. He also spoke about taking a circuitous route to the UK. I'm afraid it all adds up."

"So what do we do?"

"All the counter-terrorist stuff we always do – and then some."

"And my role?"

"A) You know the area, and B) you're coming to this fresh. I want you to join our team, liaise with the local police – your old boss Jack Thompson will be involved at the Yorkshire end – and look at this from every angle. Be unorthodox, think laterally."

"Right . . ."

"Try to look at this with a terrorist's eyes. What would you do if you were him? How would you circumvent the measures he must know will be in place? How would you organise back-up, money, transport, weapons, communications gear? What would you do to make your actions unpredictable? Immerse yourself in it – and see what you can come up with."

"I'll try," said Penny.

"Try hard," said Mathieson, looking at her evenly, "try very hard. Because if this guy has his way, there'll be slaughter in Harrogate."

Eastern Mediterranean

August 2000

Abdullah Majid had known there was a problem the moment Rahmani rang him. Firstly, by virtue of the older man making contact at all, then by the tone of his voice. The shipping magnate had requested an immediate meeting, to which Majid had no option but to agree. With a little over three weeks to go to the operation, Majid could hardly believe that Rahmani would entertain second thoughts, yet there was no mistaking the tension in the older man's voice during their brief telephone conversation.

Majid had driven to Tripoli, where Rahmani's yacht was berthed. As with their first meeting in the villa in Spain, no public contact took place and only a handful of Rahmani's staff were aware that their master was meeting Majid, whose name was never used.

Both men were now seated in the luxuriously appointed boardroom of the *Tigris*, but Majid had no time to savour the opulent surroundings. "Obviously there's a problem," he said, wanting to get to the heart of the matter.

"I'm afraid so."

"Well?"

"There's been a security breach. It relates back to Sidon."

Even now, six months after the raid on the villa, Majid felt his hackles rise. He had never been able to discover how they had been betrayed to the Israelis. Duraid Kizili had gone to ground and so Majid had never been able to establish that the raid was to apprehend Kizili and had nothing to do with his own presence. "A breach regarding our project?" he asked.

"Yes."

"How so?"

"The Israelis picked up Kizili several days ago – he'd gone to the West Bank to attend a funeral."

"Stupid of him to take the risk," said Majid, "but he knows nothing of our operation."

"That's where you're wrong. He'd bugged your room in Sidon."

Majid felt his stomach tighten and he swallowed hard. "Bastard!"

"You should have been more careful," said Rahmani.

"I was told it was a safe house!"

"You still should have been more careful. I emphasised from the start that I must never be traced to this."

"I never mentioned your name to anyone!"

"You indicated that you had backing."

"I never said who from. They'll never know it was you – how could they possibly?"

Rahmani thought for a moment, then to Majid's relief he seemed to accept this. "But the dates of the Conference were mentioned," said Rahmani. "The Israelis have already put two and two together."

"Damn!" Majid tried to gather his thoughts. Then he looked at Rahmani. "How do you know all this?"

"I have a source."

"Inside Israeli intelligence?"

"Obviously."

"How reliable a source?"

"Extremely reliable. I pay top dollar."

Majid reflected a moment, trying to keep his anger in check. "So," he said, "Kizili betrayed me . . ."

Rahmani looked at the younger man coldly. "Indeed. Though some would blame you for not exercising more caution."

Majid accepted the rebuke, knowing he deserved it and hating himself for having let his guard down in the safe house. "It will never happen again," he said softly.

"Another lapse would be fatal," said Rahmani, looking him in the eye.

Majid knew he was being threatened and ordinarily would have become angry, but he knew better than to cross Rahmani in these circumstances. Instead, he nodded briefly. "Point taken."

Rahmani allowed a moment to elapse, emphasising the point, then he continued. "We have important decisions to make."

"You're not thinking of aborting the mission?"

"Aren't you?"

"They don't know who I am," answered Majid,

"they don't know who's backing me, they don't know how I'll strike –"

"They know when you plan to strike, they know where – the odds have shortened."

"Not that much. Kizili and I didn't meet face to face when I stayed in the villa, so he won't be able to do an Identikit for them. And there would always have been high security . . ."

"Now it will be stepped up and they'll be awaiting you."

"Let them. I'm prepared to take that risk."

"I'm not certain I am," replied Rahmani.

"It will be my neck on the block."

"It will be my neck too if they catch you and link you to me."

"That won't happen."

"How can you be sure?"

"I'll succeed or I'll die," said Majid simply. "I won't be captured again."

"You might not have a choice. Supposing you were shot in the leg and couldn't run?"

"They'll get no information from me, I swear it."

"Brave words, my friend, but anyone can be broken, given time."

"No. I have a capsule. I swear to you on the grave of my father, I'll die rather than talk."

Rahmani looked at him quizzically and Majid sensed that the older man was wavering. In his heart of hearts the shipping magnate wanted the mission to go ahead, Majid reckoned, and he sensed that Rahmani had been swayed by the oath to die rather than betray him. He had been tempted to argue that the mission had already started, with an accomplice in place, but he suspected that Rahmani wouldn't care about wasted money and effort. No, better to say nothing further for now and let Rahmani reach a decision of his own accord.

After a moment the older man nodded. "Very well. Sometimes the bold gesture is required."

"We continue then?"

"Yes. To come this close, yet not avenge my family . . ."

"I understand."

Rahmani looked Majid in the eye. "You're a courageous man. However this turns out, I want you to know I respect you."

"Thank you."

"You really think you can still do it?"

"I will still do it," said Majid with conviction. "They will pay in blood, I promise you . . ."

2

Monday September 11th 2000

Laura Kennedy sang along enthusiastically as 'Hit Me With Your Rhythm Stick' played on the car radio. She enjoyed the zaniness of the lyrics and the pulsating melody, despite the frustration of Dublin's slowly moving traffic. She saw an irritated-looking, middle-aged man in the next car looking at her askance and she smiled at her own behaviour. She had always liked the Ian Dury song, a number one hit at the time of her ninth birthday in 1979.

No congested traffic at eleven in the morning back then, she thought. On the other hand, jobs hadn't been plentiful, as they were now. She recalled the previous evening and her father voicing the frustration of Dublin's motorists when he had said: "Roll on the recession!" It had been said half-jokingly, yet Laura knew that many drivers in her native city were nostalgic for the less congested roads that existed before Ireland's economic boom of the late nineties. It was a selfish thought, she knew, and she herself was one of the people whose lifestyle had been enhanced by the so-called Celtic Tiger economy. Pity the roads hadn't kept pace with the economy, she thought for perhaps the hundredth time, then the instrumental riff that ended 'Hit Me With Your Rhythm Stick' caught her attention and her mood lightened again.

No point moaning about the traffic – better to make the best of it. She switched on the mobile phone mounted below her dashboard, deciding the sluggish traffic would enable her to get some calls made. She hesitated a moment, then dialled the number for Eamon McEvoy, the Deputy Editor of *The Sunday Clarion*. It was a call she had been putting off, but it had to be made. Although she had started her career as a trainee journalist on the *Clarion*, she had resigned after several years to go freelance, in order to have more freedom to pursue the stories that interested her. McEvoy still liked Laura to keep him posted though, especially when, as now, he had commissioned her to do an exclusive story. She heard the phone ringing twice, then it was abruptly answered.

"McEvoy."

"I know who you are and I know what you did," said Laura in a high-pitched American accent. *Might as well get him in good humour*. She was rewarded by the sound of a chuckle.

"Laura?"

"That's what they calls me, Master."

"Very droll. I was expecting to hear from you before now."

"Didn't want to bother you unless I'd something to report."

51

"Slow progress then?"

"Tricky area, Mac. You can't just ring the Continuity IRA and say you want to do a feature."

"Presumably you've made some headway?"

"Absolutely. I've an important meeting lined up for today." *Well, she was meeting a guy in a pub.*

"Have they agreed to co-operate on an article?"

"Not yet, but –"

"Look, I know you're keen on this one," interjected McEvoy, "but you could wait and wait and still wind up with nothing."

"I really think it's worth it, Mac. I mean these guys are loose canons – they could wreck the Peace Process. A glimpse into their thinking could be very telling."

"If they're willing to open up. You've already spent a fair bit of time without much return."

"But it could all pay off. It's a good scoop if I get them to talk."

"If . . ."

"Come on, Mac, give me a break. I've paid my dues."

"Meaning?"

"I've done the cub-reporter stuff. I've covered the hurling-club fashion shows, I've covered the amateur drama festivals."

"And been paid for it."

"Could *anything* pay for sitting through yet another amateur production of *Riders to the Sea*?"

"Pity about you!"

Notwithstanding his words, Laura heard what she thought of as a smile in McEvoy's voice and she decided to go for broke while she had him in good humour. "Come on, Mac, cut me some slack on this one."

"I don't know why I should."

"I've orphaned children to support."

"You're too much of a yuppie to have children."

"I've a silver-haired mother wandering through the snow in search of food."

"Yeah? Left her large, detached house in Glasnevin, did she?"

Laura laughed. "You've got a good memory."

"The hide and the memory of an elephant. All right," continued McEvoy resignedly, "stay on the story. But I'd like some progress sooner rather than later."

"Thanks, Mac."

"Don't thank me, come up with a good piece."

"Will do. Talk to you soon."

"Yeah. Regards to the orphans."

Laura smiled again. "Yeah, see ye, Mac."

She switched off the phone just as the traffic around her began to speed up. Good omen, she thought, then she accelerated, eager to get to her meeting and to make progress on her story.

It was the kind of pub Laura hated. The television blared in the background and, despite the broad expanse of the bar, the air was already smoky and stale-smelling at midday. She hadn't wanted to argue however when it was suggested for her rendezvous, and now she dismissed the tackiness of her surroundings and concentrated on the two men sitting opposite her. They each had a pint of beer on the table and they seemed relaxed, but these men were dangerous.

She had expected a one-to-one meeting, but had known better than to comment when Fergus Boyle had shown up accompanied by another man whom he had introduced as Gerry O'Donnell. Both men appeared to be in their mid to late thirties, but there the resemblance ended. Boyle, who was obviously the more senior of the two, was smoother and more authoritative – vainer too, thought Laura, taking in his layered hair, cowboy boots and tight jeans. O'Donnell was dressed more shabbily in tracksuit bottoms and a Glasgow Celtic football jersey, and where Boyle was lean and muscular, O'Donnell was heavily built but overweight.

Boyle leaned forward now, piercing Laura with a gaze from grey eyes that seemed both knowing and calculating. Killer's eyes, she couldn't help thinking, but she held his gaze nonetheless, sensing that he was the type who would respect strength and exploit weakness.

"So, Laura, tell me why we should help you.'

"You shouldn't help me," she replied, and she knew immediately it was the right kind of answer, that she definitely had his interest now.

"Then why are we here?" asked Boyle.

"Because we may be able to help each other. It only works if it's a two-way thing."

"So tell me how this two-way thing would work."

"We have a newspaper that wants to tell interesting stories. You, I presume, have a philosophy you want to get across to the public."

"Go on."

"So I interview you. Explore your motivations, your methods, your objectives – try to let our readers see what makes the Continuity IRA tick."

"We don't feel we have to justify ourselves. Our cause is a noble one."

"That attitude would be part of the story then."

For the first time O'Donnell leaned forward, his bulk an unspoken threat as he looked Laura in the eye. *"That attitude?"*

"That attitude, that approach, that philosophy – call it what you will."

"Supposing we call it resistance to a foreign oppressor?" said O'Donnell.

It had the ring of a phrase he had learned off, but Laura simply shrugged in response. "If we do the article, you'll have the chance to make that case."

"Let's just be clear about something," said Boyle. "If we agree to an interview, it won't be to justify ourselves to you or your readers. It'll be to counterbalance the unrelenting stream of British propaganda."

"Fair enough," answered Laura, "but I have to be straight with you. I'm not offering you a propaganda piece. It will be an in-depth article, covering the pros and the cons. I promise I'll report your views, fairly and accurately. No more, no less."

Boyle's cold grey eyes gave no indication of how he felt, and it occurred to Laura that it wouldn't be fruitful to appear to be backing him into a corner. *Time to change direction.* She had noticed that O'Donnell's pint glass was already almost empty and so she stood and pointed at it. "Why don't I get us a refill and you can talk it over between you? Same again?"

"Yeah," said O'Donnell without hesitation, then Boyle nodded assent also. "And a small one to go with the pint," added O'Donnell.

"Right. Won't be long," said Laura. As she made for the bar she saw from the corner of her eye O'Donnell closing his fist and clenching his elbow in a sexual gesture, then she heard laughter from both men. She felt a surge of distaste. It would be easy to imagine these men laughing with equally casual disdain after planting a car bomb, she thought. Then she rebuked herself. She mustn't give way to personal dislike; she had to be professional and non-judgemental. Being a reporter meant dealings with criminals, terrorists, all sorts of unsavoury people – being polite to them didn't mean you accepted their values, it just went with the job. Besides, a lot rode on her landing this feature. She had worked her way up the ladder from the least glamorous newspaper jobs to getting interesting features fairly regularly, but she knew that a good scoop here would boost her standing considerably. She simply had to mask her feelings and persuade Boyle to do the interview.

The barman took her order, and as she waited for the drinks she calculated that she was in with a good chance of getting what she wanted. The meeting had been set up by a republican sympathiser who owed Laura a favour, but presumably the Continuity IRA had an agenda of its own if it was even considering co-operating on an article. The trick was not to put any kind of obstacle – personal or otherwise – in the way. And while the crude sexual gesture had been offensive, it wasn't altogether surprising. With thick, wavy brown hair, a slim figure, and clear blue eyes Laura was used to the full gamut of male responses, from good-humoured flirtation through to O'Donnell's puerile machismo. She would pretend she hadn't seen the gesture and concentrate instead on getting Boyle's agreement.

She looked at him now as she waited for the drinks and she was struck by the man's innate self-confidence. When setting up the meeting he had given her his real name without a moment's hesitation. Admittedly the conversation was strictly off the record and he would be referred to simply as a source if the article went ahead, but nonetheless Laura was surprised by his lack of furtiveness. Or maybe the arrogance involved was a form of psychological warfare. *I know I can give you my name because if you break any confidence you know what will happen to you.* And she was under no illusions about his propensity for violence. She had made enquiries, and it emerged that Boyle was a figure of some renown in the Republican movement. He was said to be both fearless and cruel, and stories were told of him throwing petrol bombs as an eight-year-old during the turbulent summer of 1969 when a loyalist mob had tried to drive his family from their home. Two years later he had attacked a British officer with a kitchen knife when the army had burst into their house to intern his father. It was hardly surprising that he had ended up in the Continuity IRA with other dissident republicans who refused to accept the IRA cease-fire or the terms of the Good Friday Agreement.

The barman handed Laura her change. She pocketed the money and placed her drinks on a tray, then glanced over at O'Donnell. He hadn't featured in her enquiries, and she would have put him down as a minder-cum-sidekick for Boyle, but for the fact that Boyle was the kind of man who seemed well capable of minding himself. Probably Boyle's gofer, she decided, the kind of dim-witted guy you got in terrorist movements everywhere who sensed that the only way he would ever have any standing in his community was as a member of an illegal organisation. Little wonder that the cease-fire would hold little appeal for him or for Boyle – the transition from power-wielding buccaneer to mundane citizen had been traumatic for lots of revolutionaries.

Laura returned to the table and placed the drinks down before the two men.

"Good enough," said O'Donnell, downing the small whisky before Laura had regained her seat.

"Well?" she asked.

Boyle ignored the pint she had placed in front of him and looked at her unblinkingly. "I'll do the interview, " he said, "but . . ." He raised his index finger warningly.

"But what?"

"I want final approval before it gets published."

"I'll certainly consult you fully –"

"No. I said final approval."

"Mr Boyle, I'm a professional journalist," said Laura, keeping her voice reasonable.

"So?"

"No reputable journalist will let the subject write the article. I'll consult you, I'll show it to you before publication, no problem. But the final say on the contents of the article lies with me and my editor – that's the way it works."

"So you expect me to trust you? Or even worse, you and your editor?"

"I give you my word that any article we do won't be distorted. I'll record whatever's said accurately, and the article will be fair and balanced."

There was a pause, and Laura held her breath, knowing that to say any more would be overselling herself.

"Balanced, fair and accurate?"

He was going to go for it – she could feel it.

"Yes," she answered.

Boyle pointed at her and when he spoke his voice was soft but threatening. "It better be. It better be . . ."

Laura felt a shiver of fear, but tried not to show it. "OK," she said.

"All right, let's start then," said Boyle.

"Right now?"

"Right here, right now."

It was strange being back, Penny thought, as she made her way through the centre of Leeds. She had decided to walk from the train station to her rendezvous with Detective Chief Superintendent Jack Thompson, her old boss, and she wondered how they would get on, five years after they had last worked together. Back then she had been his protégé and their rapport had been excellent, but since that time she had risen to the rank of Detective Inspector, while Thompson had received what would probably be his last promotion before retirement, in being made a Chief Superintendent. Although a senior rank, it was less senior than his ability warranted, and Penny knew that it was due in part to the fact that Thompson had always been something of a maverick, never keen to engage in the manoeuvring associated with office politics. He had always been a hell of a detective though, and she was glad that they would be working together in Harrogate. She just wasn't sure if they could slot back comfortably into their old relationship after all this time. They had kept in loose contact after she had moved south, but the last time Penny had seen her former boss had been the previous year when his wife, Alice, had died of cancer. Penny had travelled up for the funeral and had heard subsequently that Thompson had coped with his loss by immersing himself in his work. She hoped he was keeping well and that they would still get on. Then she told herself to stop fretting; she would have all her questions answered soon enough.

She made her way up Briggate, past the beautifully restored Victoria Arcade, every corner and minor landmark seeming to hold memories for her – either of childhood or her days as a rookie constable here in Leeds. She reached the junction with The Headrow and turned right, opposite the Odeon cinema where she had gone years previously on her first date. She smiled to herself, remembering the innocence of finding it thrilling to hold hands with a boy from school as she sat in the darkened cinema. She had loved the film – *Witness*, starring Harrison Ford as a streetwise detective – and she had blurted out to her date that she too was planning to be a detective one day. And now, fifteen years later, she *was* a detective. Except that unlike Harrison Ford, with his adventures in the picturesque countryside of the Amish, she was going to workaday Harrogate. And far from engaging in fictitious thrills and spills, she was trying to apprehend a real-life killer who was bent on causing death and destruction.

She carried on down Eastgate, her mood a bit more sombre now, then she came to the police station and entered. She showed her ID to the desk officer and said she was expected by Superintendent Thompson.

"Top floor, Inspector," the man said. "Left when you come out of the lift, then down to the end of the corridor."

"Thank you," said Penny, resisting the temptation to tell him that she had been in that office countless times during the three years she had worked with Thompson. Still, she was gone over five years now – she could hardly expect new staff to know that she had once worked here. She took the lift to the top floor, made her way to Thompson's office, knocked twice, and stepped in.

Thompson smiled broadly on seeing her and rose from behind his desk. He was tall and heavily built, with lightly oiled grey hair, and he still looked fairly fit, Penny noted, although he was now sixty-one years old. She wasn't sure exactly what effect she had feared his recent grief might have had on him, but outwardly he seemed largely unchanged.

"Great to see you again, Penny," he said, coming from behind the desk to greet her.

"You too, Chief," she answered, "you too."

They hugged each other, then Thompson stood back and looked at her. "You're looking well. Motherhood must suit you – that and soft southern living."

"Yeah, can't beat the old three-in-the-morning feeds to keep you looking good."

Thompson laughed. "You're surely not at that stage still?"

"Not really, but it was the best answer I could come up with."

Thompson smiled. "How old is Aisling now?"

"Eighteen months."

"A handful, I'd say?"

"Two hands full – and then some," answered Penny.

"I know. My son, Peter, has a baby ten months old."

"Congratulations. Boy or a girl?"

"Girl. They called her Alice . . ."

"Oh. . . right. I – I was so sorry, Chief . . ."

"I know."

"How have you been managing?"

"Not too badly. Working hard, playing a bit of golf, playing a bit of bowls . . ."

"Yeah?"

"Going to the odd football match, baby-sitting my grandkids. Coping."

"Good." Penny wondered if she should say more, but she knew that Thompson wasn't a man who was comfortable talking about his feelings and she felt that perhaps enough had been said.

Then Thompson himself changed the subject. "So, a Detective Inspector at thirty. Not bad, not bad at all."

"Thank you."

"Enjoying it?"

"Yes," answered Penny, then she smiled ruefully. "Well, most of the time anyway."

"Tell me about it," said Thompson with a grin. "Here, have a seat. Would you like tea or a coffee?"

"No thanks," answered Penny as she sat. "I had something on the train."

"Fair enough." Thompson regained his swivel-chair, then leaned forward. "Well, to business."

"Right."

"I'll bet you weren't expecting to land back up here?"

"No," said Penny. "You know who had me seconded to this?"

Thompson nodded. "Our mutual friend, Colin Mathieson."

"I hadn't seen him since . . . well, since we'd split up, years ago."

"Must have been a bit of a surprise."

"It was. And not entirely pleasant, but it wasn't the kind of assignment I could turn down."

"No," said Thompson, "I can see that. And while we're in nostalgia mode, there'll be another old face present when we get to Harrogate."

"Oh?"

"Len Carrow."

"You're not serious?"

"Afraid so. He's handling the Special Branch end of things."

Penny sighed. Carrow had been the Special Branch officer in charge of liaising with Thompson back on her first major case, and she and Carrow had disliked each other from the moment they met.

"Just like old times, eh?" said Thompson.

"Unbelievable."

"Not really. Like you, he has a Yorkshire background and a detailed knowledge of Harrogate. It was always a runner that he'd be in on this show."

"Right."

"And I'll save you asking."

"What?" said Penny.

"The answer is yes, he's still as much a pain in the arse as he ever was. Worse actually."

"Thanks, Chief," said Penny with a laugh, and she knew in that moment that her fears had been unfounded and that there would be no problems working again with Thompson. "That's just what I needed to hear."

"Just thought I'd get it out of the way," he said with a grin. "Anyway, the four of us are scheduled to meet in Harrogate tomorrow morning at eleven."

"That should be interesting."

"Yes. After our deliberations the full team will be briefed. I assume you've given the case some thought already?"

"You could say that," answered Penny.

"Why don't you fill me in on your ideas on the way up there?"

"OK. When were you thinking of going?"

"As soon as you like. Did you want to contact your folks before leaving Leeds?"

"No, I'll ring Mum from the hotel tonight – maybe see them later in the week, work permitting."

"Right, well, we're all booked into the Moat House Hotel."

"Can't get closer to the Conference Centre than that."

"That's why it was chosen," said Thompson. "So, will we head up there now?"

"One slight snag. I left my luggage in the train station – didn't know if you'd be free to leave now or whether I'd have to take the train."

"No problem, we'll pick it up en route."

"Great," said Penny. "Now that I'm near, I'm kind of eager to get into action."

"Well, Harrogate's where the action's going to be – one way or another."

"Right then, let's get to Harrogate . . ."

Laura had known they would reach the omelette argument somewhere in the interview, and sure enough, Fergus Boyle was getting there now.

"In any war there'll be civilian casualties. It's unfortunate, but –"

"You can't make an omelette without breaking eggs?"

The pub was filling up with the onset of the lunch-time trade and the air was even smokier now, but Laura hardly noticed as Boyle looked searchingly at her, recognising the challenge in her tone.

"Don't get sarcastic with me," he said.

"I'm simply repeating a line that gets trotted out as justification," Laura answered.

"The Continuity IRA doesn't trot out justifications!" snapped O'Donnell. "Doesn't have to – not to you or to anyone!"

"I think maybe you do," said Laura.

"Do you now?" said Boyle.

His voice was quieter than O'Donnell's but somehow more menacing for that. They had crossed swords in milder fashion several times during the interview, but this was different. Civilian suffering was a key issue, and she couldn't let herself be bullied out of asking the hard questions.

"I think you need to explain how you justify putting innocent civilians at risk when your war, as you see it, is with the British authorities."

"We don't set out to injure civilians."

"They just get killed and maimed when you plant a bomb."

"We don't have to listen to this crap!" said O'Donnell.

"What good is an interview that's afraid to tackle the issues?"

"What good's a fucking interview at all?!" replied O'Donnell.

Laura paused, suspecting that O'Donnell's aggression was partly fuelled by the amount of alcohol he had managed to consume during the hour they had spent in the pub. The decision to grant the interview wouldn't have been his however, and so she turned instead to Boyle, forcing her voice to sound reasonable.

"Look, this is the very kernel of public concern. Even people who might be sympathetic to an armed struggle are sickened when innocent bypassers are killed and maimed. There's no getting away from it as an issue."

"I'm not trying to get away from it," said Boyle. "The Continuity IRA is at war with the British. In any war innocent people die; it's regrettable, but that's the reality."

"But aren't you consciously fighting in such a way that ordinary people are certain to be casualties."

"Every side in every war does that," countered Boyle.

"How are the British authorities doing that?"

"They massacred thirteen unarmed civilians in Derry on Bloody Sunday."

"Which was completely wrong, but –"

"Which was completely in character."

"No –"

"Yes! Don't give me any holier-than-thou stuff on the Brits. When it comes to killing civilians they leave us in the ha'penny place. Machine-gunning people in Amritsar, fire-bombing people in Dresden, smart bombs that slaughtered civilians in Baghdad – the list is endless."

Although Boyle spoke with animation, Laura sensed that this was an argument he had prepared in advance, and she decided to probe him a little more. "You believe they were wrong to do those things?"

"Yes, I do."

"Then why do your people adopt the same approach, albeit on a smaller scale?"

"We do what has to be done . . ."

"So two wrongs make a right?"

Boyle stared hard at her again, and Laura had to suppress a shiver.

"Don't put words into my mouth," he said.

"But isn't that what it amounts to?" she persisted.

"We're fighting a war. There's no clean way to do it."

"A lot of people would argue there's a cleaner way to do battle than planting car-bombs."

"You don't know what you're fucking talking about!" said O'Donnell.

"Really? Well, I *do* know what our readers will ask," countered Laura. "And they'll ask how car-bombs can ever be justified, how they further your cause."

"They further the cause by bringing the fight to the enemy," said Boyle. "They hit him in his homeland, where it hurts. They make him see that there'll always be a price for their occupying our country."

"And that justifies their use? Despite civilian casualties?"

"What would you have us do?" asked Boyle. "Take on the British army out in the open? All their weapons, all their technology, all their manpower? You want us to fight them on their terms?"

"I don't want you to fight them at all."

"Your precious readers then?"

"I'd say most of our readers don't want you to fight them either. The vast majority here voted for peace – which brings me to my next point."

"I can hardly fucking wait," said O'Donnell.

"Leave it, Gerry," said Boyle, then he turned back to Laura. "What's your next point?"

"Democracy. The will of the Irish people. They had their say and they voted for peace under the Good Friday

Agreement. So how can you justify a continued armed struggle?"

"Very simply. The original will of the Irish People was for a fully independent Ireland – that's how the first Dáil was set up – to govern the whole country."

"You're talking about back in 1918?"

"Yes. Sinn Fein won the election by a landslide. But the people were sold out. The legitimacy of subsequent governments was flawed – *fatally flawed* – by recognising partition of our country. They lost the mandate to govern when they conceded the six counties of Ulster to the British."

Laura paused, considering her next move. She knew that the Continuity IRA had its origins in a Sinn Fein split in 1986 when a group of veteran republicans left the party because it had dropped the traditional republican policy of not taking seats in the Dáil. She knew too that activists like Boyle justified their activities by claiming to be the inheritors of the mantle of the original IRA. Time to push Boyle a bit further, she decided, and steeling herself, she looked him in the eye.

"So because of an election eighty-two years ago, you feel entitled to ignore all subsequent elections – would that be right?" she asked.

"Elections held by quisling governments are flawed."

"So what are you saying – that you know best what the Irish people need?"

"I'm saying the Irish have an inalienable right to independence, irrespective of elections or treaties."

"Is it not incredibly high-handed to set yourself up as the ones who'll decide on the rights of the Irish people?"

"Isn't that what Pearse and Connolly did when they launched the 1916 Rising?" answered Boyle, and Laura knew that these were arguments in which Boyle was long practised.

"And do you think patriots like Pearse and Connolly would approve of car bombs?" she asked. "Blowing up discos and hotels?"

"I think Pearse and Connolly regarded damage to private property as secondary to their goal – which is the same as my goal – an independent, united Ireland."

Laura was about to respond when the mobile on their table rang and O'Donnell reached forward to answer it. On arrival, he had thrown it down on the table in the ostentatious manner that Laura associated with people trying to impress. It was what she thought of as the 'I'm so important I must always be contactable' syndrome; and it seemed particularly apt for O'Donnell who clearly wasn't as significant a player as he would like to be.

"Hello . . . yes, just one second, he's here," said O'Donnell. He held the mobile out to Boyle.

"Excuse me," said Boyle to Laura, then he reached out and accepted the phone.

Laura was surprised that he didn't leave their company to take the call, then she surmised that perhaps it was an innocuous call that he knew he would be receiving about this time. Whoever the caller, she decided to listen carefully while appearing to go through her notes.

"Hello," said Boyle. "Good man . . . it's ready now? Great . . . two-bedroomed, is it?

Perfect . . . yeah, two of us . . . maybe about two weeks . . . no, I don't know the area that well . . . listen, I'm with someone just now, can I ring you back in a few minutes and we'll go through the directions? OK, give us the number."

Boyle clicked his fingers, and O'Donnell produced a biro for him from the pocket of his jeans. "OK, shoot," said Boylan.

O'Donnell smiled on hearing the phrase and pointed his finger at Laura as though it were a gun. Laura held his gaze long enough to let him know that she found it neither funny nor intimidating, then went back to her notes, pen in hand, as Boyle jotted down the number on a beer mat. She realised that Boyle and O'Donnell were being accommodated somewhere by the caller and she glanced across the table at the number that Boyle had written down. It was upside down from where she sat, but as Boyle finished the call she worked out what the seven-digit number was and, without quite knowing why she did it, jotted it down among her notes.

Boyle switched off the mobile and handed it back to O'Donnell, and Laura was conscious of his eyes upon her. Could he have noticed her reading the number, she thought, her heart suddenly pounding?

"So . . ." he said, looking her in the eye.

Laura tried not to flinch from his gaze, and resisted the temptation to cover up the sheet of paper on which she had written the number.

"You've got quite a bit of information, haven't you?" he said.

Could he be referring to the phone number? Laura's pulses were racing madly. "Yes," she answered neutrally.

"And I've had enough of this. You should have more than enough to write the article."

Laura had to make a conscious effort not to show her relief. "Yes, I think most points have been covered."

"Fair and balanced, that's what you promised, isn't it?"

"Yes."

"Make sure you keep that promise," said Boyle with a smile that didn't extend to his eyes.

"Can I contact you, when I have it written?" asked Laura.

This time it was O'Donnell's turn to smile. "We'll contact you, love."

They rose to go, and Boyle turned to Laura. "We'll ring you," he said, looking her in the eye. "We know where to get you . . ."

Laura made herself look back at Boyle as though the phrase was entirely innocuous, then he nodded and the two men left. She sat down and breathed out a sigh of relief. She had got her article. Mac would be pleased, and she herself should have been delighted. Instead, the meeting had left a bad aftertaste. She sat unmoving in the smoky pub, glad to have gotten her scoop, yet unable to shake off a sense of unease.

3

Tuesday September 12th 2000

Abdullah Majid waited patiently for his victim. The hot Lebanese sun beat down relentlessly, the mid-morning heat shimmering up off the earth, but Majid sat, patient and unmoving, in the shade of a cedar tree. He had learned the need for patience during his years as a prisoner in Israel, and before that during his time in the training camp in the Sudan.

You must learn the skill of waiting, his instructor had insisted. *You must wait in difficult conditions, uncomplaining even to yourself – patient, yet never letting your concentration lapse.*

It had been good training and he had often had to use it in the intervening years, to the extent that now it was a matter of honour with him not to acknowledge boredom or discomfort, but to see and feel only what he allowed himself to see and feel.

Despite the shade provided by the cedar tree a bead of sweat ran down into his eyes and he wiped it away, then raised his binoculars again. He was careful not to let the sun reflect off the lenses as he gingerly parted the foliage that concealed him to get a better view of the house that he was staking out. It was about one hundred and fifty metres away at the bottom of a hill and he could see a black Toyota Land Cruiser and a blue Renault Laguna parked in the shade of a row of mature trees, but there was no sign of any activity around the house.

The building was a large suburban villa on the outskirts of Beirut, similar to the one from which Majid had had to flee the previous February, and the similarity seemed apt to him, bearing in mind the respective owners. He had sworn that he would be avenged for the betrayal that had almost cost him his life at the hands of the Israeli commandos, but Kizili, the villa's owner, had gone to ground so thoroughly that Majid had been unable to locate him. In the normal course of events he would have bided his time and waited until Kizili re-emerged, but two things had changed his plans.

Firstly, he had received the news that Kizili had foolishly attended the funeral in the West Bank, after which he was abducted by Israeli Intelligence. And secondly, Majid was due to leave the day after tomorrow for his mission in Harrogate. With Kizili in Israeli custody there was little likelihood of being able to get at him for the foreseeable future, yet Majid felt that the near miss at Sidon couldn't go unanswered. And so he had travelled to Beirut to send a message to Kizili, via his brother, a wealthy shipping agent who lived in the villa at the base of the hill.

Majid had studied the man's movements, and each morning the shipping agent drove from his suburban home to the company's offices. He didn't keep completely predictable hours, but Majid was prepared to wait until he emerged, knowing that he would eventually make the trip to town. His principal worry was that the man might change his routine today and, instead of leaving alone, might decide to give a lift to his wife or his children.

Still, no use expending energy worrying about matters beyond his control; the odds still favoured another solo trip to the office. Majid lowered the binoculars and wiped the sweat from his eyes, then caught a movement from the front of the house. He saw a figure stepping out the hall door and quickly raised the binoculars again. It was his target. Majid felt his heart begin to beat a little faster. He kept the binoculars trained on the front entrance, hoping that no-one else would emerge. To his relief, the door stayed closed and Kizili's brother walked alone towards the cars.

The man carried a heavy briefcase and before he reached the vehicles he had already mopped his brow. Even in a finely cut, lightweight suit, the fact that he was seriously overweight, combined with his having just left the air-conditioned villa, was causing him to sweat. Majid felt his own perspiration increasing as his target drew level with the Renault Laguna. Majid's plan depended on his taking the Land Cruiser as he normally did, but there was always the risk that today he might take his wife's car.

Majid held his breath, then breathed out in relief as

the shipping agent walked past the Renault and on to the Land Cruiser. He watched the man open the door and throw his briefcase onto the passenger seat, then slide awkwardly behind the wheel. He started the engine immediately, eager presumably to get the air-conditioning working, then turned left on emerging from the shade of the trees and accelerated down the drive.

Majid kept the binoculars trained on the vehicle, then when it was about halfway to the entrance he pressed the electronic triggering device and detonated the bomb. The Land Cruiser exploded in a blinding ball of flame, the shattered remnants of the car falling back to earth amidst a black plume of smoke. Already Majid was moving down the hillside in the opposite direction. He moved briskly along a predetermined route and within a minute he had reached the byroad on which he had parked his car.

He got into the vehicle, put it into gear and drove away at a moderate speed, drawing no attention to himself. After a few moments he reached the main road leading back to town. He turned onto the road, joining a long stream of cars.

As he cruised along, he dialled the florists whose number he had memorised earlier. He gave the address of the house which he had earlier kept under observation and requested that the pre-paid bouquet of flowers be delivered there in the afternoon.

"Any message, sir?" asked the florist.

"Yes."

"Go ahead, sir."

"A closed mouth catches no flies."

"I'm sorry…"

"A closed mouth catches no flies!" repeated Majid more forcefully.

"Very good, sir."

"Thank you," said Majid, then he switched off the mobile. The message would get through to Kizili, he knew. It wouldn't necessarily be linked to Majid however – there were probably lots of people who had suffered because of Kizili's loose tongue. Still, the point had been made. The account had been settled for Sidon, and now Majid could again devote all his energy to his mission in England. Pleased with his morning's work, he drove contentedly down the highway.

Penny felt a sense of déjà vu as she sat at the conference-room table in Harrogate police station. Just like old times, Thompson had said ironically yesterday, and in fact today's meeting did bring her back eight years to the summer of 1992 and her first major case. The respective MI5, police and Special Branch senior officers had been Colin Mathieson, Jack Thompson and Len Carrow, and looking across the table at Carrow now, Penny felt the same dislike that she had experienced the first time they had met. Carrow had been arrogant and sexist in his dealings with her and there was little in his manner this morning to suggest that he had altered his mindset in the intervening years. He was a heavy-set man of about sixty, his ginger-coloured hair a little greyer and more receding than when Penny had seen him last. He still favoured tailored tweed suits and expensive brogues, she noted, and his artificially modified Yorkshire accent confirmed again for Penny her image of him as a working-class social climber anxious to camouflage his roots and adopt a country-squire image.

He leaned forward now and looked Penny challengingly in the eye. "Seeing as you're here, Inspector, for your renown in lateral thinking, maybe you'd share your thoughts on the case?"

Penny decided to ignore the sarcasm, reasoning that the best way to deal with Carrow's disapproval of her was to act as though it wasn't an issue. She saw Thompson and Mathieson looking at her expectantly and despite the misgivings she had felt about working again with Mathieson, she suddenly found herself wanting to justify his choosing of her. Well, here goes, she thought; then she began to speak, consciously keeping her voice low-key but assured.

"The thing that strikes me most forcibly about this case is the amount of preparation our would-be assassin needs to engage in. He'd have to be aware that we'll have stringent security measures in place. Yet clearly he intends to circumvent them. That takes a hell of a lot of planning and organising. He's going to need transport, he's going to have to get weapons into the country and then here to Harrogate, he's going to need money, communications systems, accommodation. All of these potentially leave a trail. Our job, as I see it, is to seek out that trail proactively. It'll be a race against time. We need to get to him before he gets into position – whatever or wherever that may be."

"That's all very well in the abstract," said Carrow, "but how does it translate into action?"

"Well, I know that we're flooding Harrogate with police officers between now and the conference," said Penny.

"Overtime budget gone through the roof," added Thompson with a wry smile.

"Obviously a lot of their efforts will be along the usual lines," Penny continued. "Combing the Conference Centre for suspicious devices, sealing off approaches, checking ID's – all the normal, but vitally important stuff."

"Presumably you have some other tasks in mind for them?" said Mathieson.

"I think we need to channel as much manpower as possible into locating our suspect before the conference ever starts," said Penny.

"How exactly?" asked Carrow.

"Well, when Mr Mathieson here assigned me to this case he suggested that I try to look at it through a terrorist's eyes. When I did that, I decided the key action for an assassination bid to have any chance is reconnaissance. Our man has to know in detail the layout of the Conference Centre. He has to know access routes, possible escape routes, where our checkpoints are likely to be. In other words he has to get to know Harrogate intimately."

"Your point being?" prompted Carrow.

"My point, sir, being that to do all that – and to organise accommodation, transport and all the rest – our target needs to spend a fair bit of time in Harrogate."

"The conference doesn't start until Monday week – that still gives him almost two weeks," said Mathieson.

"More if he's already here," suggested Thompson.

"Walking around the streets, checking out the Conference Centre, looking into car hire, organising a place to stay – that all involves risk, a chance of being noticed," said Penny.

"You still haven't said how you propose to find him when he goes about any of these things," said Carrow.

"We won't find him going about any of those things," answered Penny. "At least I don't think so."

"Why not?" asked Mathieson.

"They're too risky, and he'll know that."

"A minute ago you had reconnaissance as being vital – which is it?" asked Carrow.

"It's vital, but he won't have to do it if my theory is right."

"So what's your theory?" asked Mathieson.

"He won't have to do it because he's *already* done it," answered Penny.

The intelligence officer looked at her with interest. "When?"

"Months ago. Probably shortly after the conference was announced. Much easier back then to hang around hotels, check things out in ways that would arouse grave suspicions now."

"Fair point," said Mathieson.

"When exactly was the conference announced?" asked Thompson.

Carrow flipped over a sheet of paper on the table in front of him. "February the twelfth last."

"Ample time for our man to come here, suss things out, make his arrangements and only come back to carry them out much nearer to the time," suggested Penny.

80

"It *does* make sense," said Thompson, and Penny was pleased to see Mathieson nod his head in agreement.

"How does it bring us any closer to catching our suspect though?" asked Carrow.

"If he's been here he'll have left some kind of trail."

Carrow looked at her, unconvinced. "The trail – if there is one – could be six months old."

"Granted," said Penny, "but if we look hard enough we could still uncover something. This conference is top priority, so we can get the manpower we need. If we do that and check the records of all hotels, guesthouses, airlines, car hire companies –"

"Hang on a minute," said Carrow, "have you any idea how many people visit Harrogate each year?"

"No, sir, but –"

"I have," said Carrow forcefully. He flicked through his paperwork and quickly produced a one-page document. "I got this from the Conference Centre. It's visitor statistics. Want to know how many delegates attended conferences and exhibitions in 1998/99?"

"Why don't you just tell us?" said Thompson.

"Two hundred and nine thousand three hundred and eleven. Want to know how many attended trade fairs that year? *One hundred and forty-seven thousand eight hundred and fifty*. Even if we knew what we were looking for we couldn't *begin* to follow up that number of enquiries."

"It's a lot of people, sir, but we can cut it down. Those figures were for an entire year. If we were to limit our enquiries to – say a window of three months after the announcement of the conference – we'd cut the figure by seventy-five per cent."

"Great," said Carrow sarcastically, "so we're down to – what, ninety thousand?"

"Quite a bit less if we remove all women visitors," suggested Mathieson. "Less again if we remove all men over the age of thirty-five."

"We're not certain of his age," objected Carrow.

"Kizili's description to the Israelis was probably late twenties, early thirties," said Mathieson.

"*Probably*," replied Carrow, "but he didn't meet our man. That's a second-hand description Kizili got from a maid in the villa."

"The description still narrows things a bit," said Thompson.

"Yeah, dark hair, brown eyes and sallow skin – that really narrows things down!" said Carrow sarcastically.

Mathieson looked at the Special Branch man. "Come on, Len. You know as well as I do that in situations like these you can't cover everything, so you work the percentages. Thirty-five years old is a reasonable cut-off point."

Penny said nothing, happy to let her boss make some of the running, but Carrow wasn't having it and he turned and looked at her directly.

"So tell me, Inspector," he said, "assuming we factor out women, and men over thirty-five, and anyone who's fair-skinned, or blind, or paralysed, and we get the figure down to – oh, let's say fifteen to twenty thousand suspects – how do we find our man amongst those?"

"I think we try to narrow it further, sir."

"Clearly you've given some thought as to how we might do that," said Mathieson, his tone encouraging, in what Penny suspected was a deliberate counterbalance to Carrow's abrasiveness.

"I tried to put myself in the shoes of an assassin coming here to reconnoitre, perhaps last March or April," she answered, "First question was, do I travel alone or with accomplices?"

"Alone I would have thought," said Thompson. "Keeps it simple."

"That's what I thought too," agreed Penny. "Plus, before getting the lie of the land, he may not have decided on how he'll make his assassination attempt. Therefore he may not have decided how many accomplices he'll use, or if he'll use any at all."

"Go on, " said Mathieson.

"I think if I were coming to a place like Harrogate I'd pose as a businessman – one more man in a suit among thousands attending conferences and exhibitions. That means staying in a fairly good hotel."

"Not necessarily," countered Carrow. "He could have stayed in a guesthouse."

"Possibly," conceded Penny, "but a hotel is more impersonal, so you're less likely to be remembered there. It also fits in more convincingly with the businessman image."

"Which he may or may not have adopted," said Carrow.

"Granted again, sir, but for better or worse my scenario was a solo businessman staying in a good hotel. That means they'd have taken details of his credit card on arrival. My other assumption is that if he's Iraqi he's likely to travel on some kind of a Middle-Eastern passport rather than a false – or indeed legitimate – European one."

"Why so?" asked Thompson.

"Easy for him to get one, no complications if an immigration official somewhere speaks to him in Arabic. Also there's the racial issue."

"Which is what?" demanded Carrow.

"Lots of Europeans still think of Europe as basically Caucasian. If he looks or sounds Arabic but travels on a British passport, a Dutch passport, whatever – it stands out a little more than an Arab travelling on a passport from an Arab country."

"Even though there are huge numbers of Arabs with French passports, loads of Indians and Pakistanis with British passports?" said Carrow.

"I appreciate the value of your playing devil's advocate, Len," said Mathieson, "but I think Inspector Harte's point is valid nonetheless."

Penny smiled to herself, knowing that in his own elliptical way Mathieson had suggested that Carrow should back off a little.

"It's really a pity the Israelis haven't been able to supply you with a photograph, Colin," said Thompson.

"I know. I asked them to go through their files, dig out photos of terrorists they have listed or any prisoners they've held who have Iraqi backgrounds, but it's a needle in a haystack. Prisoners and terrorists – of whom there have been thousand upon thousand – they lie about their names, their backgrounds, everything. Nevertheless I've leaned on Samuel Lubetkin to send photos of any likely Iraqi who fits the age profile."

"And what was the response?" asked Thompson.

"He'll do what he can, but with all the unrest out there the Israelis have their hands pretty full."

"To get back to our imaginary assassin in the hotel," said Carrow, looking once more at Penny. "How do we find him?"

"I know it's a big task," she answered, "but suppose we were to list every hotel guest who meets the character profile I've given. Then we cross-check him against car rental, airline tickets, ferry tickets. See what the cross-check shows, see can we narrow the net. If a person who showed up on some of those lists were to book into Harrogate again around now, it would certainly give us someone to talk to."

Carrow stared at her. "What you suggest isn't a big task – it's mammoth."

"Nevertheless, we have to start somewhere," said Thompson.

"Are you prepared to commit your constables to what might be a total wild-goose chase?" asked Carrow.

"A certain number of them, yes," answered Thompson.

"Very well, gentlemen," said Mathieson, "perhaps we'll leave it at that for now. I know time is of the essence and that you both have staff to be briefed, so I won't take up any more of your time. I think DI Harte has given us all food for thought and we'll decide how to proceed when we've had time to weigh up what she's suggested."

"Fine," said Thompson.

"Right," said Carrow more curtly, rising as he spoke. "And you won't forget our date for tonight?"

Mathieson smiled and caught Penny's eye before glancing back to Thompson and Carrow.

Penny felt a little uneasy, even though the use of the word 'date' had been playful. She knew Mathieson was referring to a suggested brainstorming session over drinks in the hotel later that evening, and part of her feared that Mathieson might be hoping Thompson and Carrow would be too busy to attend, leaving him alone with her in a semi-social setting. She knew she was possibly being a little paranoid, yet she was relieved when Thompson said he would definitely make it.

"Len?" asked Mathieson.

"Yes. Eight thirty, I'll see you then."

"Fine," said Mathieson.

Pity, thought Penny, one session with Chief Superintendent Carrow in a day was enough – but she nodded farewell with the others as the Special Branch Officer left.

"Right," said Mathieson, "I'm off too. I'll leave you with Superintendent Thompson, Penny, and see you this evening."

"OK."

Thompson waited till Mathieson had gone, then he turned to Penny and smiled. "What did I tell you? Just like old times!"

"Absolutely."

"Don't let Carrow get to you. He's probably just peeved because most of what you said was smart and well thought out."

"Thanks, Chief."

"So . . . ready to find this fugitive of yours?"

"Ready to try," answered Penny.

"Right," said Thompson, "let's go to work."

Laura drove into the parking bay in front of her apartment block in Clontarf, but remained sitting in her car. Warm September sunshine dappled through the gold-tipped leaves of the sycamore trees that separated the bays in the parking lot, but Laura was oblivious to her surroundings as news came in on the radio of a car bombing in Beirut. She listened with unease, the subject of car-bombing being fresh in her memory after yesterday's interview with Boyle and O'Donnell. Car-bombing had always seemed to her to be a particularly cowardly course of action, the type of tactic where the end could never justify the means. The newsreader went on to say that the victim, a married man with three children, had been killed instantly, and Laura felt a sharp stab of disgust. Yet here she was, interviewing and giving a platform to terrorists herself.

She reached out and turned off the radio, then sat looking blankly out the window. She told herself that as a journalist it was her job to deal with people like Boyle and O'Donnell, that however she might be disgusted personally by terrorism she was still obliged to protect her sources. Just as Catholic confession was predicated on the absolute discretion of the priest, so too did freedom of the press demand occasional supping with the devil. It was the dirty part of her trade, a grey area of compromise and favours traded. She rationalised that when the press was curtailed things were always far worse, that tyranny thrived in societies that didn't have the counterbalancing effects of investigative journalism, but despite the logic of her arguments she still felt dissatisfied.

The more she reflected on it, the more she felt tainted by her dealings with Boyle and O'Donnell. She had already begun writing the article based on their conversation, but despite her determination to remain detached and professional she had found herself returning to how she had felt while in their company. *Uncomfortable*, she thought. *Wary. Defensive*. The reality, she knew, was that they enjoyed making people uncomfortable; they got a kick out of being feared and having others defer to them. Yet she could hardly drop the article at this stage. Apart from incurring the anger of the Continuity IRA there was the matter of her editor, Eamon McEvoy. She had pressed him to allow her to stay on the story, and he had been pleased last night when she told him about the interview. No, she thought, she was committed now. She would have to finish the article and continue her dealings with Boyle and O'Donnell. If she took the phone in her study off the hook and applied herself now, she could have it finished by tonight. She breathed out, tried to dismiss the Beirut story from her mind, then got out of the car and made for her apartment.

Majid rose eagerly and made for the departure gate on hearing his flight being called in Damascus airport. The start of any mission was always exciting, but this was an operation that could make history. It was a thrilling thought, and Majid found himself smiling at the pretty airline worker who took his boarding pass. He was still on a high after the strike against Kizili's brother, and it boosted his morale to set out on what he knew would be a challenging mission with such a satisfying success under his belt.

He had driven across the Lebanese border to take a flight from the Syrian capital to Paris, and from France he planned to make his way to Harrogate via Brussels and Dublin. It was a deliberately circuitous route, but he reckoned it would enable him to enter the UK with the least likelihood of interception, while allowing him to collect vital equipment in Ireland.

He boarded the plane, returning the practised greetings of the cabin crew. He took a newspaper from his travel bag before stowing it overhead, then occupied a window seat, fastened his seatbelt and began to peruse the newspaper. The paper would preclude the need for conversation with fellow passengers while awaiting take-off, and once airborne he would simulate sleep until his arrival at Paris.

He settled back behind the newspaper, but he was too wound up to concentrate on any of the articles. It reminded him of his first trip away from home, when as an eighteen-year old he had left Baghdad to do his military service. Although only twelve years previously, it now seemed like another age, but he recalled the same sense of setting out on an adventure, the same inability to concentrate on any kind of reading matter.

Back then he had regarded himself as lucky, and his timing as a conscript had indeed been fortunate in that he was spared involvement in the murderous war between

Iran and Iraq that had just ended. He was fortunate again that his army service had finished before the summer of 1990, during which Iraq had invaded Kuwait. He had been less fortunate however in having completed less than one year of his studies as a medical student when the Allies had attacked Iraq. Less fortunate too when his mother and sisters had been bombed in Baghdad and his brothers killed on the road to Basra. The Iraqi medical system that he had planned to join had gone from being the most advanced in the Arab world to being catapulted back to primitivism as a consequence of the war. Majid had seen surgeons having to perform caesarean sections by lamplight, had seen diabetics undergoing amputations for want of insulin, had seen post-operative pain management that consisted of nothing more than aspirin.

He had been outraged that despite the fact that UN sanctions precluded health commodities, all such items were in disastrously short supply due to the trade embargo that lessened government revenue with which to buy them. Allied to his grief at the annihilation of his family, he had felt a burning rage, and he had turned his back on medicine and vowed instead to take the fight to the enemy. And now he was going to have the most glorious opportunity to do so.

He settled back in his seat as the plane taxied out onto the runway, then watched the lights of Damascus spread out below him as the 747 took to the air. He continued to gaze out the window, watching the twinkling lights of towns and villages, then suddenly the lights ended and he knew they were over the Mediterranean and heading west towards his target.

He closed his eyes and let his mind drift, going over again all that would have to be done if he were to succeed in his mission. A vital element, he knew, would be the performance of his two accomplices in Harrogate. The first one he had sought was Jemail Zubi, a Lebanese in his early thirties whom he had met during his imprisonment in Israel. Recruiting Jemail was what had brought Majid to Sidon the previous February, and the tough *Hezbollah* fighter had agreed to join Majid in his operation, albeit after some haggling over fees. Majid knew that the haggling had nothing to do with his commitment however. Jemail was zealously anti-Israeli, and by extension anti-Western. It was simply part of the man's make-up not to accept the first fee offered, and Majid had anticipated a certain amount of bartering before Jemail finally shook hands and solemnly agreed to be part of the mission. Tamaz Akmedov, the other accomplice, had been a more difficult piece of recruiting.

Majid remembered with amusement the look of surprise on Omar Rahmani's face when they had discussed the matter in the shipping magnate's Spanish villa the previous March.

"You want me to find you a waiter?" Rahmani had asked.

"As soon as possible. You handle a lot of imports into Germany, yes?"

"Yes . . ."

"And you'd have a lot of trading contacts in Turkey?"

"I have trading contacts in many places. What is your point?"

"There are three million Turks living in Germany. Quite a number of them must be waiters. For my

BRIAN GALLAGHER

operation to work I need an experienced waiter who speaks good English, who'll keep his mouth shut, and who's prepared to work abroad for the next six months and then vanish."

Rahmani looked at Majid searchingly. "You intend to plant a sleeper in the Conference Centre?"

"It's a part of my plan. Better though, I think, if you don't know any more operational details."

Rahmani held the younger man's eye, then nodded. "Very well. So this waiter – he must be Turkish, but living in Germany?"

"For preference. Germany and Britain are both EU countries so there's free movement between them. Also Turkey is deemed more pro-Western than most Islamic countries – there'll be less suspicion of a Turkish national than someone from an Arab country."

"Assuming we find someone who fits the bill, how can you be sure he'd get a job in the Conference Centre?"

"I've checked it out on the Internet," answered Majid. "It's a big place with a large staff. There's sure to be a turnover. If our man is an experienced waiter with good references – which we'll make sure he has – then he's very likely to be taken on."

"Supposing he's not? Suppose we find someone who's perfect, and he goes to Harrogate, and at that point there's no staff turnover?"

"If need be, we make sure there *is* a turnover."

"Are you suggesting what I think you are?" said Rahmani.

"No, there mustn't be anything to arouse suspicion. Instead, we'd head-hunt a waiter or two with offers that couldn't be resisted. You have enormous power and resources. Without it ever being linked to you, strings can be pulled, restaurant owners bribed or leaned on. You know how such things work."

Rahmani looked thoughtful, and Majid spoke reassuringly. "Look, it probably won't ever come to that. But we need to move on this."

"On the basis that they won't be suspicious in hiring staff six months before the conference takes place?"

"Exactly."

Rahmani still looked doubtful. "To get someone who's prepared to do this may not be easy. If you kill the Foreign Ministers, they'll move heaven and earth to find out who did it."

"Our man can go to ground. Deeply. Then later he can be provided with a new identity."

"You really think it will be possible to recruit someone who'll do all that?"

"For a million dollars, yes. That sort of money means he could start a new life, never be a waiter again as long as he lives."

"A million dollars?" said Rahmani.

"Small change to you, a fortune to someone on a waiter's wages."

"Indeed . . ."

Majid looked at the older man challengingly. "I hope you're not going to quibble, Mr Rahmani. You said you'd meet all operational expenses. We've got to make this attractive enough for someone to take the initial risks, then change identity and start a new life."

Rahmani raised his hands in a placatory gesture. "I

take your point. There'll be no difficulty with finances. Finding the right person . . . that may be another matter."

"It's essential that this be done."

"I understand. But it will have to be done in such a way that there is absolutely no trail linking me to the enquiries that unearth our waiter. That will take very careful handling."

"I've complete confidence in your ability to have your wishes implemented," said Majid.

"How flattering."

Majid ignored the sarcasm. "Also the person we choose must have a background that would withstand a security check."

"Really? Anything else?"

"No. Once you've identified some candidates, I'll take care of everything else."

"Take care, as in?"

"I'll choose which to approach. I'll be the one to make contact – you won't have to get involved in any way."

Rahmani nodded. "An experienced Turkish waiter, with good English, who'd withstand a security check yet be prepared to be an accomplice to spectacular killing – and then vanish? Getting such a person is not going to be easy."

"For a million dollars, we'll find the right person. Believe me . . ."

And he had been right, reflected Majid now, as the 747 cruised through the evening sky towards Paris. Rahmani's powerful organisation had compiled a list of candidates and after careful consideration of the dossiers provided for each waiter, Majid had selected Tamaz Akmedov as his first choice. He was a fifty-year-old man who had been born into poverty in the town of Urfa, in the south-eastern region of Turkey. Leaving home at seventeen, he had gone to work in a hotel in Tripoli, where he had married a teenage Jordanian chambermaid. The marriage had broken down after several years, and as his wife had an extended family in the Tripoli area, and Tamaz worked long and irregular hours, it had been decided that she would raise their baby daughter after they split up. Tamaz had then worked in Cyprus, where he had learned to speak good English, all the while sending home money for the maintenance of his child. From Cyprus he had moved on to Germany, working in Berlin, Hamburg, Cologne, and finally Munich. His trips back to Tripoli had stopped after his daughter, then ten years old, had died with her mother in a car crash, and he now lived alone in an apartment on the outskirts of Munich.

Perfect, Majid had decided. One of life's losers, someone who had always been dealt a poor hand, someone who might well jump at a chance to change his fortune. The man's dossier said that he was servile in demeanour, which again appealed to Majid. It meant he would be easy to manage, yet after thirty years of servility and hard knocks he might well be uncaring of what would befall a group of privileged Foreign Ministers. Not that Majid intended to give him any more details regarding the operation than were strictly necessary.

As it turned out there had been little problem in

persuading Tamaz Akmedov to leave Germany and to perform the role prescribed for him. To Majid's surprise, he hadn't balked to any great degree at the notion of having to go to ground or of living thereafter with a new identity. And if he had any moral qualms about violent action against Western politicians he hadn't let them hold him back. Presumably the million dollars was sufficiently dazzling to overcome any reservations, as Majid had hoped.

In keeping with the stipulations given to Rahmani, the man spoke good English, was an experienced waiter and had a pleasant if timid manner. It hadn't even been necessary to create a vacancy for him by head-hunting other waiters. The Conference Centre had, in fact, been glad to recruit a well-turned-out and experienced waiter who wasn't insisting on top-of-the-scale payments.

Within a week of arriving in England Tamaz had got the job, and within another two weeks had located a two-bedroomed terraced house for rental in Starbeck, a working-class neighbourhood of Harrogate. Tamaz had signed a lease for a year's rental, and he and Jemail Zubi were now installed there and awaiting Majid's arrival.

Most of the pieces were in place, Majid thought – it just remained to carry out his own preparations. He leaned back further in his seat as the 747 carried him towards his destination, his mind racing in anticipation of all that lay ahead.

The hotel meeting room reflected exactly the mixture of

informality and efficiency that Penny had expected Mathieson to adopt. A waitress was serving drinks to everyone present, but on the table lay writing pads and pencils, neatly laid out for the four participants.

Penny noted that Thompson and Carrow had both opted for beer and Mathieson for a gin and tonic, and she smiled to herself at the predictability of their choices as she sipped her own glass of white wine.

Mathieson tipped the waitress, then as soon as the woman had left he turned to the others. "Thank you for coming to our brainstorming session. You know the drill: any idea, no matter how outrageous, is noted – no analysis or criticism until later."

"We've been through it before," said Carrow.

"Quite," answered Mathieson. "Well, I'm sure you've all had your thinking caps on. I'll act as facilitator and recorder of suggestions." He looked around. "So, any ideas on how our man might launch an attack on the VIPs at the conference?"

There was a moment's hesitation, then Thompson spoke. "Well, just to get the ball rolling, how about something really obvious, like a mortar or rocket attack?"

"Duly noted," said Mathieson, scribbling on his pad.

"Helicopter assault?" suggested Penny.

"Poison introduced into the food or drinks," said Carrow.

"A tunnel under the Conference Centre, packed with explosives and detonated at the appropriate time," said Thompson.

"Nice one," said Mathieson, jotting down the idea.

"Poison gas introduced into the air-conditioning system," suggested Penny.

"OK."

"Straightforward frontal assault," said Carrow. "I know it's extremely unlikely, but they might expect us to virtually dismiss it for that reason."

"It's all right, Len, you don't have to qualify the suggestions," said Mathieson. "Anything else?"

"A waiter or Conference Centre employee who'd act as a suicide bomber," said Penny.

"Good, good."

"High-altitude aerial assault, using a guided missile," suggested Thompson.

"OK."

"Sniper attack by a marksman as the VIPs arrive at or leave the Conference Centre," said Carrow.

"Or as they arrive at or leave Harrogate itself," added Penny.

"An explosive device that's already in place that will be set off at the right time."

"Fine," said Mathieson, then he looked around on hearing no further suggestions. "Anything else? No?"

The others nodded.

"All right," said Mathieson, sipping his gin and tonic, "a few interesting ones there. Let's take each and look at counter-steps."

"The aerial assault's easily blocked," said Carrow. "We'll have the RAF on alert. That'll take care of the helicopter assault also."

"Less so perhaps," said Penny. "A high-altitude jet assault would show on radar. But if someone had a chopper hidden in a nearby area they might fly in under radar."

"Fair point. We'll check every commercial helicopter rental," said Thompson, "then during the conference enforce a no-fly zone in the vicinity."

Mathieson looked at his list. "OK, countermeasures for sniper attack?"

"We've already identified lines of sight onto the entrance to the Conference Centre," answered Carrow. "Any building offering such a shot to a sniper will be checked by our people."

"How often?" asked Mathieson.

"Every day. Plus we'll have plainclothes officers in the vicinity of all such buildings whenever the conference is in session or the delegates are expected to enter or leave the hotel."

"Though of course we'll encourage delegates to use the enclosed bridgeway from the hotel to the Conference Centre," added Thompson.

"Right," said Mathieson, jotting down a note. "Rocket or mortar attack?"

"Similar to the sniper approach," answered Carrow, "without the line of sight consideration of course. We'll flood the area within the range of such weapons with plainclothes and uniformed officers, particularly when the delegates are in session or arriving or departing."

"Any further steps needed?" asked Mathieson.

"Not if everyone is alert to the dangers. My Special Branch officers are trained for this, the uniformed constabulary less so."

"Don't worry about the constabulary," said

Thompson. "I'll make certain they're all up to speed."

"Really?" said Carrow, a note of challenge in his voice as he turned to look at Thompson. "What should they be looking for in the case of mortar or rocket attacks?"

"Vehicles that can't be readily seen into," answered Thompson without hesitation. "Specifically trucks or vans whose rear doors could be opened quickly to fire off mortar rounds. Yes?"

"Yes," conceded Carrow, and Penny had to suppress a smile, knowing that Thompson would have enjoyed scoring a point off Carrow.

"A tunnel under the Conference Centre packed with explosives," said Mathieson quickly, in what Penny recognised was a desire to pre-empt conflict between the other two men.

"We need a thorough examination of the architect's plans for the building," suggested Penny. "Any underground passageways or ducting to be checked by sniffer dogs on a regular basis."

"Sounds good," said Mathieson. "Have we got the architect's plans?"

"Yes," replied Thompson. "We'll get someone with architectural knowledge to identify the kind of areas Penny's mentioned."

Mathieson nodded. "I think that also covers the notion of an explosive device already in place. All right, an attack as delegates arrive at or leave Harrogate itself?"

"Heavily armed escorts, fast-moving motorcades, armour-plated cars. Can't see it as an attractive option for a terrorist," said Carrow. "Too difficult, targets too mobile."

"Could they do something to hinder that mobility – create a stationary target?" asked Penny.

Carrow fixed his gaze upon her. "How, exactly?"

"Phoney roadworks, a temporary stop sign, then the road workers produce a bazooka or whatever?"

"There'll be no roadworks allowed in Harrogate from the time the delegates are due until they depart," explained Thompson.

"What about between Harrogate and the airport?" asked Mathieson.

"The same," replied Thompson. "Anyone trying to stop the motorcades will be regarded as hostile and treated accordingly."

"Good." Mathieson glanced down at his list, then turned back to the others. "Frontal assault, then?"

"Roadblocks manned by armed police officers to prevent easy access to the area of the Conference Centre," answered Thompson. "Army back-up as required."

"Consisting of?"

"Marksmen on rooftops, Special Forces units in and around the site itself."

Mathieson nodded in satisfaction. "OK. That leaves us your idea, Len, of poison in the food or drink, which I think we'll link with Penny's poison in the air-conditioning."

"I think maybe we could also lump in my suicide bomber," suggested Penny. "In order to work, all three methods require access. And the only way that kind of access can be gained is through collusion from within."

"Granted. So, how do we prevent that?" queried Mathieson.

"Strict enforcement of access procedures to all sensitive areas to begin with," said Thompson. "Badges with photographic ID for all staff."

"And security checks on all staff in the Conference Centre and hotel," said Carrow. "Likewise for any contract caterers, barmen, waiters."

"There are no contract caterers for the conference," responded Thompson. "It's all done in-house."

"You're certain about that?"

Thompson looked Carrow in the eye. "I wouldn't be saying it if I weren't certain."

Again Penny had to suppress a smile as Mathieson intervened before the latent hostility between Carrow and her old boss could flare up.

"I'd like some of the initial screening to be done by Special Branch," said Mathieson.

"Or to put it another way," said Carrow, "we do the donkey work before your people step in and take over?"

Mathieson smiled wryly. "I'm sure your combativeness is an asset in Special Branch work, Len. This mission, though, calls for a multi-discipline approach. Let's all work together and save the battle for our real enemies, all right?"

Although delivered with a lightness of touch, there was no denying the element of rebuke in Mathieson's comment, and Penny wondered if Carrow would lock horns with Mathieson, who was the senior man present. She knew only too well that behind his almost languid courtesy Mathieson could be single-mindedly ruthless when the occasion demanded. Although he had rarely talked about it when they were a couple, she knew he had been decorated for bravery as a young army officer serving in Aden and Oman. He wouldn't have reached his present rank in MI5 without the steely resolve that was masked by his cultured manner. Part of her wanted to see Carrow getting his comeuppance by defying Mathieson, but the Special Branch man had the necessary cunning to know when to back down, as he did now.

He shrugged, as though the matter wasn't worth arguing about. "Security Service or Special Branch – the important thing is that we check out the staff."

"Quite," said Mathieson.

"Between permanent staff and part-timers we're talking about almost two hundred employees in the Conference Centre and a hundred and twenty-five in the hotel," said Thompson. "To do security checks on all of them will take a hell of a lot of effort."

"There's no choice, though, is there?" said Mathieson. "We'll need the names and personal details of every employee."

"I've been on to their personnel section already," answered Carrow.

"Good."

"Guy in charge started moaning about data protection and privacy, but I soon marked his cards for him."

"Not too vigorously, I hope," said Mathieson. "We'll want as much co-operation as possible."

"Don't worry, he'll co-operate," said Carrow. "I'm

meeting him first thing in the morning to start on his staff files."

"OK." Mathieson looked at the others. "Anyone got any other thoughts?"

"There is one thing," said Thompson, "though maybe this isn't the place . . ."

"Anything that might have a bearing, Jack."

"It's the Americans. I know their Secretary of State would be a plum target, but their security people are . . . let's say they're a bit over the top."

Mathieson smiled and shook his head. "The American Secret Service – they're a law unto themselves."

"That's just it," said Thompson. "Every country sending a Foreign Minister here has security considerations, but the Yanks act like the whole thing is their show. It's like the UK is a satellite of the US and they don't feel constrained by our laws."

"It's a tricky one, Jack – they're our allies. If they had their way they'd actually be at meetings like this one." Mathieson raised his hands before the others could protest. "I know, we're on British soil, so the security will be co-ordinated by us. On the other hand, being our close allies, I'm under political pressure to keep them happy."

"So when they stick their noses in or ride roughshod over our rules, do I tell them to bugger off, or say 'Hands-across-the-water, all-chums-together – work away'?"

Penny saw Mathieson smiling fleetingly, and this time she didn't bother to hide her own grin. She had forgotten how much she used to enjoy her old boss when he was blunt with his superiors.

"Somewhere in between the two extremes, perhaps?" suggested Mathieson. "When they try your patience, bear in mind that the Americans have paid a fair bit when it comes to terrorism and assassinations. And when all is said and done, we're usually on the same side."

"I'll try to remember it next time I'm questioned by some prat with a crew cut and chewing-gum," answered Thompson, a hint of a smile playing around his lips.

"Thank you. Well, I think we've covered quite a bit tonight and I'm grateful for your efforts," said Mathieson. "If there's nothing else . . .?" He looked around the table, but nobody had anything further to add. "I think another drink might be in order, then. And enjoy it, folks. Because from now until the conference is safely over we're going to be rather busy . . ."

4

Laura looked across the sitting-room card-table at her
mother, knowing what was coming next. Laura's father
and her sister Roisin were picking up their cards, but
her mother was more interested in the direction the
conversation had taken than in the family game of
Newmarket. "Why don't I say it for you, Mam – then we
can get it out of the way?"

"What are you talking about, Laura?"

"Marriage and childbirth – lack of same. This is
where you say that when you were thirty you'd already
had Alan and Roisin, and were expecting me."

"Well, it's true, I was."

"And they were just preparing to land on the moon,
the Beatles hadn't released 'Abbey Road', Ireland had
never won the Eurovision . . ."

"What's any of that got to do with it?"

"It was a different world then, Mam."

Laura's father tapped the table in the manner of one

106

about to enter a room. "Excuse me? Are we playing cards or studying sociology?"

"The cards are only a smokescreen, Dad," said Roisin. "We're really here to sympathise with Laura for being a spinster."

"You're hilarious," said Laura.

"All I did was ask how things are with Declan," protested Laura's mother.

"And we all know what that means!" said Roisin.

As her father and her sister laughed, Laura found herself smiling too. Although she had left home as soon as she finished college, she still enjoyed family gatherings, and on Wednesday nights there was a loose arrangement whereby anyone who was free dropped in to the family home in Glasnevin. Tonight her brother Alan was on duty at the hospital where he worked as a paediatrician, and Roisin's little girl had gone swimming with her father, so that it was just Laura, Roisin and their parents. Alan and Roisin were both married with young children, and the desire of Laura's mother for her to follow suit had become something of a running gag.

It was a year and a half now since Laura and her boyfriend Declan had taken the apartment in Clontarf and, despite the vigour with which she fended off her mother on the topic, Laura had found herself thinking recently that perhaps it would be nice to formalise things. As a sought-after film sound-engineer, Declan travelled abroad a lot, but despite the opportunities for dalliance that went with his job, Laura had few doubts about his commitment. Although he had never pushed the matter, she knew he would be quite happy to get married. Perhaps when he returned from Prague, where he was on location for the next three weeks, she would raise the subject with him.

"So are you going to pick up your hand, Maeve, or go on haranguing your daughter?" said Laura's father.

"I wasn't haranguing, merely showing an interest."

"Right. Well, can we all show an interest in our hands now?"

"Hark the Cincinnati Kid," said Roisin.

Laura smiled, knowing that even in a family game her father found it hard to rein in his card-playing enthusiasm. At sixty-two years of age he had sold the family's lucrative locksmith franchise the previous January, and since retiring he had become a stalwart member of the local bridge club. Like herself, he was tall and slim – his nickname of Chubby referred to his former business rather than his build – and Laura knew that people said she was the one who had inherited his energy.

"Right, whose lead is it?" asked her mother.

"Yours, Mam," answered Roisin.

"Oh . . ."

"Planet Earth, to Maeve! Come in, Maeve!" said Laura's father.

Just then a mobile phone began to ring. "Oops," said Laura, "mine, I'm afraid."

"Those blessed things are a curse," said her mother.

"I know," replied Laura apologetically. "I'm sorry, but it could be Declan." She rose and crossed to where the mobile was ringing in her handbag.

"Take the call!" said her father. "Encourage him.

When your mother was thirty she'd already had Alan and Roisin and was expecting you!"

Laura laughed, then switched on the phone. "Hello?"

"Is this the lovely Laura Kennedy?"

Having half-expected it to be Declan, Laura was thrown for a moment, but now she recognised the northern tone. *Fergus Boyle.* Laura turned back to her family, the frivolity of the previous moments suddenly banished. "Excuse me for a minute." She moved out into the hall, closing the door behind her. "Mr Boyle," she said.

"Miss Kennedy. I hope I'm not disturbing anything?"

Again the tone was mocking – suggestive almost.

"No, that's all right."

"So, have you been a busy beaver?" asked Boyle.

"I've worked on the article, if that's what you mean."

"Is it finished?"

"More or less. I'm just polishing it."

"Good, I want to see it. Can you e-mail it tonight?"

Let him wait, thought Laura, *he's much too accustomed to having things his own way.* "No, not tonight. I'll send it to you tomorrow if you give me the address."

There was a slight pause as though Boyle was deciding whether or not this was acceptable, then he gave her the e-mail address.

"What time tomorrow?" he asked.

"Maybe late afternoon."

"Don't you work in the mornings?"

"Yes, and when I've finished going over the article with my editor tomorrow morning, I should be able to send it to you in the afternoon."

Again there was a pause and Laura knew that she had irritated him. In one way it felt petty, and yet she couldn't help but feel she had won a small victory by not yielding to a timetable of his choosing.

"See that you do," said Boyle. "Just see that you do."

The line went dead and Laura stood there a moment, then switched off her mobile. This guy could be a problem, she thought, especially if he objected to the thrust of the article. Which he might well do. Despite her attempts to be even-handed and to present arguments that she found repugnant, the article was far from being a propaganda piece for the dissident republicans that Boyle represented. Well, so be it. She would deal with Boyle when she had to. She slipped the phone into her pocket, tried to put the implications of the call from her mind, and went to rejoin her family.

Abdullah Majid adopted the bored nonchalance of the international business traveller as he made for passport control at Dublin airport. He had travelled on an evening flight from Brussels, and most of the passengers appeared to be business people returning from the European Union's centre of administration. Majid was travelling on a Belgian EU passport – a forgery of impeccable quality – knowing it gave him the right as an EU citizen to move freely between member states. He had chosen the flight deliberately, reasoning that a late flight carrying mostly business people and EU bureaucrats might receive a more cursory scrutiny than a normal daytime one.

The body of passengers moved towards the passport-control booths and Majid made sure to position himself neither at the front nor the rear of the group. There were two officers on duty, dressed in civilian clothes, but to Majid's trained eye they were still clearly policemen. For the most part they were exchanging a word or two with passengers and then ushering them through without examining passports. Occasionally however they would stop passengers, check their passport photos and question them in more detail. In most cases, Majid noted, this happened to those who were not white-skinned. Clearly there was a watch being kept for illegal immigrants. Majid's own complexion wasn't all that dark, but compared to the fair-skinned Irish travellers all around him he knew he must look foreign.

What of it, he told himself. His cover was plausible: he was a foreign businessman coming to do some work in Ireland. Which wasn't entirely untrue, he thought wryly, as the line moved forward towards the passport booths. The policemen on duty were engaging in easy conversation and greetings with the arriving passengers, but Majid wasn't fooled. He knew the officers would be listening carefully as their apparently casual greetings were returned. He knew too that they would be much more likely to spot-check the passports of passengers who didn't sound Irish. Although he felt confident that his forged passport would hold up to scrutiny, Majid made it a point never to bring himself to official attention any more that was strictly necessary. He reached the head of one of the two queues and casually held up his passport. He neither caught the official's eye nor conspicuously avoided it.

111

"Good evening," said the passport officer smilingly, and Majid had to look at him.

"Good evening," he answered.

"Can I see the passport, please?" the man asked.

Accent or complexion, Majid wondered as he opened the passport and handed it over.

The policeman looked at the photograph, then looked at Majid. The chances of his picture being on file in Ireland because of his conviction in Israel in 1992 were remote, Majid told himself, and he made himself smile pleasantly as the policeman nodded.

"I think that's yourself all right," the official said with a grin. "And the purpose of your visit?"

"Business trip."

"And what business would that be, Mr Lefevre?"

"Computer software."

"Fine." The man handed out the passport. "Have a nice trip."

"Thank you." Majid took back the passport, then started along the passageway leading towards the baggage carousels. After walking for a few moments he reached the carousel for the luggage from Brussels and waited for his suitcase to appear.

He thought of the exchange with the passport officer, irked in retrospect at being stopped on racial grounds, however discreetly it may have been handled. He had frequently found on his travels that even when officials were pleasant, as had been the case here, there was an innate air of superiority about them. It could be a subtle message – though frequently it was blunt – saying they were the ones in charge, and you'd better toe the line. He knew that with his middle-class background he would have been better educated than the vast majority of such people, but he had been taught never to let either irritation or superiority show. During his training back in the Sudan, it had been drilled into him that in most situations it was more clever *not* to appear clever. Better to resist making too much of an impression, better not to draw attention to yourself. If you wanted to fade into the background you never scored points with officialdom, you didn't tip hotel staff too little or too much, you blended in whenever possible and resisted the temptation to feed your ego by appearing smart and thus standing out.

Majid's reverie was broken by the baggage carousel kicking into life, and within a few minutes he had collected his suitcase and was making for the blue EU channel at customs.

With the exception of his false passports and other papers stowed in a perfectly concealed hidden compartment, the contents of his suitcase were entirely innocuous. Unless the suitcase was actually taken apart, Majid knew that nothing untoward was going to be found were he stopped at customs. Nevertheless he felt his heart beginning to beat a little faster as he approached the blue channel. Once again he contrived to be in the centre of a group as he walked through, and he avoided eye contact with the customs official. This time he passed by unchallenged and emerged into the arrivals hall. He made for the sign indicating the taxi rank and was pleased to see the small queue there being swiftly reduced by a line of advancing taxis. Within a couple of moments he reached the head of the queue and a taxi-driver approached and took his suitcase. "Where to?"

"Gresham Hotel," answered Majid.

"Right you be. Hop in."

Majid climbed into the back of the cab, took some paperwork out of his travelling bag, and immersed himself in it at once, as he habitually did when in the field. No point getting into conversation with loquacious taxi-drivers and perhaps lodging in someone's memory.

The taxi-driver took the hint and drove towards the city with the car radio on for company. Majid kept the paperwork propped up on his knee for appearance's sake, but let his gaze drift out the window as they drove through the suburbs towards the city centre hotel. Although he should be in no danger here, as nobody knew he was arriving in Ireland tonight or where he was staying, he still felt a little vulnerable to be travelling without any weapon. Moving through airports ruled out a gun, of course, but tomorrow he would need to organise a weapon. Nothing elaborate, he thought – a sharp knife could be made to appear fairly innocuous while still being deadly in experienced hands.

The suburbs now gave way to the city, and Majid looked out the window with interest as the taxi negotiated brightly lit streets that mixed Georgian architecture with the occasional modern eyesore of glass and concrete. They reached the top of a really broad thoroughfare whose central section stretched away in a line of trees and statues, and the taximan looked over his shoulder.

"O'Connell Street. The Gresham's over there."

Majid gathered his papers as the taxi drove down the city's main street, then they pulled in to the front of the hotel and Majid collected his suitcase and tipped the taximan the ten per cent that the Irish guidebooks recommended. The taximan nodded his thanks and pulled away, and Majid allowed the hotel porter to carry his suitcase in to reception.

The hotel was old but well appointed, with a marble-floored foyer and an elegant lounge and bar stretching away behind it. Comfortable without being ostentatious, Majid thought, just the kind of place in which the fictitious Mr Lefevre would stay. He moved to the check-in desk where his registration was handled with courteous efficiency and within five minutes of stepping from his taxi he found himself in a tastefully decorated bedroom at the rear of the hotel. Majid left unpacking his case for later and instead unzipped his travelling bag and removed his mobile phone. It was only half past nine, not too late to make his call, he reckoned. He took a slip of paper from his jacket, noted the telephone number on it, then dialled on the mobile. The phone was answered on the second ring. *Maybe they're as eager as I am,* thought Majid.

"Hello?"

The man's voice sounded harsh, his accent grating to Majid's ear.

"I'm calling about Hamlet," said Majid, using the agreed code.

"All's well in the State of Denmark," answered the man.

"Excellent. Meeting on Friday then?"

"Yes. We'll call you and confirm the exact time."

"Fine."

The line went dead. No wasted words or loose talk there, thought Majid with approval. He switched off the phone and sat down on the bed, pleased at the confirmation that all was in hand. It seemed that Rahmani's Libyan contacts had been as good as their word, which meant that the final pieces of the jigsaw were falling into place. He felt a surge of excitement and allowed himself to savour it. After months of planning, it was now about to happen. Finally, the mission was operational.

5

Thursday September 14th 2000

"What's the point having a husband who designs software if I can't get his advice?" asked Penny.

"Advice is no problem – it's *free* advice I shy away from."

Penny grinned, happy to be chatting again with her husband Shane, even if it was only by telephone. She had stayed in her hotel room, having arranged for him to call at breakfast time. Since she had gone to Harrogate they had been in telephone contact each day, with the exception of the previous day when Shane had to fly to Warsaw in pursuit of a software sale to a Polish bank. Knowing that their schedules might not correspond as a consequence, Penny had suggested an early call this morning instead.

She had noticed that Shane had sounded more affectionate than usual when they spoke on Tuesday night and it had occurred to her that perhaps he felt a little uneasy at the idea of her spending three weeks in close proximity to her ex-lover. Nothing explicit had been said by either of them, but it had struck her that Shane might be in need of a little reassurance. Somehow the notion made him seem all the more endearing and she was glad to hear him in such good spirits this morning. She realised however that many men would find a potential rival like Colin Mathieson somewhat unnerving. Although in his mid-fifties now and thus twenty years older than Shane, he was still a very attractive man, and Penny knew that lots of women would find the combination of his urbane charm and classic good looks difficult to resist.

Despite the slightly uncomfortable history between them, Penny herself had warmed to him a little since arriving in Harrogate. The previous night they had found themselves alone after yet another security conference, and for the first time he had dropped his professional air and asked her if she was happy. The question had taken Penny by surprise, yet she had sensed that Mathieson wasn't hoping for a negative reply, the better to promote his own prospects of having an affair with her. She had hesitated to answer, part of her feeling that Mathieson had no right to ask; then she had decided against taking umbrage and replied truthfully that since marrying Shane and having Aisling she had never been so happy.

Mathieson had said he was glad for her, and to Penny's relief he sounded sincere. He had added that she deserved to be happy, then smiled warmly. The smile had awakened memories, and in providing a glimpse backwards in time it reminded her of why she had once been so strongly drawn to Mathieson. But that was then and this was now, and she had no intention of letting Mathieson come between herself and Shane.

She had met Shane Nelligan at a dreadful party in a house in Reading and had immediately been attracted to him. He had been born in England of Irish immigrant parents who made their fortune in Britain. Shane had inherited his mother's sense of humour – a mixture of sarcasm and a sense of the ridiculous that was distinctly Irish – and his sense of fun had been apparent from the start. That first night in Reading he had made Penny laugh by proposing a mass suicide by the unfortunate party guests in the nearby Thames, and she had sensed soon afterwards that a future with this man would be an attractive possibility.

And now, four years later, he could still make her laugh, as he just had in his retelling of Aisling's exploits with her grandparents. Many of Shane's extended family, including his parents, lived in the Windsor area where Penny and Shane had their home, and the Nelligan grandparents had happily taken Aisling while he was in Warsaw overnight.

Having missed her daughter all week, Penny had listened absorbedly to his tales, before finally switching to the technical query for which Shane was playfully demanding payment.

"Come on, Nelligan, free advice has to be one of the perks in marrying a computer geek!"

"Are my ears deceiving me or could I possibly have heard the word *geek*?"

Penny laughed. "All right – technological wizard."

"That's more like it."

"Oh, and talking of technology, I saw a quote yesterday that I wrote down for you."

119

"Why do I just know this will be offensive?"

"Hang on, I have it here," said Penny, reaching for her notepad. "Who said 'Technological progress is like an axe in the hands of a pathological criminal'?"

"The Chief Constable?"

"Try again."

"Mother Teresa."

"Shane –"

"The person who designed Gatwick airport."

"Give in?" asked Penny.

"All right, who said it?"

"Albert Einstein."

"You're kidding?"

"Scout's honour."

"Albert Einstein?"

"Yeah."

"Sure what did he know?!"

Penny laughed. "Anyway, to get back to the computer advice . . ."

"Shane speaking, how may I help you?"

"Seriously, Shane, I don't know how feasible what I'm suggesting is. I don't want to look foolish by approaching our IT people half-cocked."

"Give us the gist of it."

"Supposing we wanted to find someone who'd visited the UK. Harrogate in particular. Could a computer programme be written that would check all hotel registrations, airline passenger lists, car-hire applications, ferry passenger lists and so on – to see if he showed up on several of them?"

"Have you got this person's name?"

"No."

"Right . . . well, you've got a couple of problems here. First off, the hotels and airlines and so on probably aren't all using the same type of systems. Some would be on ORACLE, some on SYBASE."

"So, what are you saying? Different systems aren't compatible?"

"They wouldn't be immediately interchangeable. But ways could be found around that. Your big problem is not having something specific that can be searched for."

"Well, we do have some profile of our man," answered Penny.

"How defined is it?"

"Iraqi male, aged twenty-five to thirty-five, likely to be travelling on a passport from an Arab country. Black hair and sallow complexion – but that will hardly be recorded anywhere."

"It's not much. The problem here, love, is numbers. The numbers flying and staying in hotels and so on – we're talking millions. What you'd normally do is a sort and merge on the various databases. By narrowing the search the computers have to make, you get an extract from the data field. Then you can start scanning for matching correlations."

"Right," said Penny.

"Age, sex and nationality are a start, but that's still really broad. The numbers are so vast you need to refine the sort and merge with specific data. The more names the computers can eliminate the better your hope for some kind of meaningful matching correlations."

"We're working on that," said Penny.

"Work on it hard. It's like the Internet – the more you can refine your search the more likely you are to find what you seek."

"But broadly speaking, it is possible to do the kind of thing I'm suggesting using computers?"

"Broadly speaking, it's possible. Practically speaking, you need more data."

"OK. And thanks, Shane."

"No sweat, the bill is in the post."

"Settle for payment in kind?"

"The minute you get home!"

Penny smiled. "It's a deal. Listen, I'd better get to work . . ."

"Constabulary duties to be done . . . "

"Afraid so. I'll call you later tonight, all right?"

"Great. Talk to you then."

"And, Shane?"

"Yeah?"

"Love you."

"You too. Bye."

"Bye."

Penny hung up, then crossed the room, picking up her jacket on the way to the door.

She made her way to the hotel carpark, her mind still going over the conversation with Shane, but no matter how she looked at it, unless Mathieson's Israeli contact came up with something, she could think of no way to put a name or a face on their target.

She drove through the centre of Harrogate, the early morning air still balmy in the September sunlight. She turned left on passing the train station and drove past the Odeon cinema, idly noting that the film *The Patriot* was still playing here. Was her antagonist a patriot, she wondered? Or simply a deranged fanatic? Or maybe someone more mercenary, somebody planning an act of terrorism for the money? Or perhaps even a combination of all three?

She was still pondering the matter when she pulled to a halt in front of the large redbrick building that was Harrogate's police headquarters. She parked the car, then went inside, returning the greetings of various officers as she made for the rooms that were allocated to the conference security operation. She entered the main office to find Mathieson there alone and going through paperwork that was spread out on the desk before him.

"Morning, Penny," he said.

"Morning."

"You sound a trifle down."

"I was just talking to Shane about the computer search."

"Ah. . ."

"Really brought home to me how little we have on our suspect."

"Quite."

"Mind you, I still believe we should plough our way through the records of every hotel in Harrogate. Airline and car-hire lists too, however laborious it may be."

"I'm inclined to agree."

"It's donkey work, and it'll take manpower, and probably enrage Chief Superintendent Carrow and Special Branch –"

"Don't worry about Special Branch," said Mathieson. "I'll handle them."

"Good. Like I say, it's donkey work that's still worth doing, but . . ."

"But what?"

Penny grimaced. "It's not inspirational. I can't help feeling we need a flash of inspiration on this one."

"That or the opposition to make a mistake."

"Right."

"This is the awkward stage, Penny. Have to keep plugging away and hoping for the best." Mathieson shrugged. "It could be that this threat will come to nothing. If our man doesn't show up, or is deterred by our efforts, then we've won. If on the other hand we uncover something, at that stage we'll act decisively."

"It's if we uncover nothing, and something still happens, that I have nightmares about," said Penny.

Mathieson looked at her. "Me too," he said frankly. "Me too . . ."

Laura Kennedy entered the newsroom of the *Clarion* with a spring in her step. Eamon McEvoy had rung her to say that he liked the Continuity IRA article and that, subject to some careful editing, the paper was going to run it. She crossed the busy newsroom now to meet him, cordially exchanging greetings with several journalists, and it struck her how much she missed the camaraderie of being a staff member on a major newspaper. She had never had serious regrets about going freelance, loving the flexibility and the opportunity to pursue stories that interested her, but there was a price to pay in terms of relative isolation. She normally only had cause to come in to the *Clarion* about once a month and she missed the gallery of colourful characters with whom she once worked on a daily basis.

"Laura! Summoned to the Principal's Office?" cried Jimmy Sullivan, one of the sub-editors.

"Something like that."

"Tell me it's not a spanking?"

"Even if it is, Jimmy, I'll try not to enjoy it!"

Jimmy grinned and Laura passed by his desk, on which he had a sign stating: *The mission of the modern newspaper is to comfort the afflicted and afflict the comfortable*!

"Hey, Laura," cried Dave Murray from behind the can-strewn desk at which he wrote the social diary. "I have one for you. Why should a journalist have a pimp for a brother?"

"I don't know, Dave," she answered with a straight face. "Why should a journalist have a pimp for a brother?"

"So he'll have someone to look up to!"

Laura laughed, then continued across the open-plan office. She reached the door of Mac's office, knocked twice, and entered. Mac was on the phone, but he nodded in greeting and indicated for her to sit. She took a chair on the opposite side of his desk as he mouthed the words "Accounts Department" and threw his eyes to heaven while continuing to listen to the person on the other end of the phone.

She smiled sympathetically and raised a hand to indicate that she was in no hurry. She glanced around the room, wondering yet again how Mac could run a newsroom with such efficiency from an office that looked so disorganised. The bookshelves overflowed with reference books, magazines, and typewritten manuscripts, files were stacked on the floor, and Mac's desk was an ocean of scribbled handwritten notes. The room was bare of adornment save for one framed photograph of Mac, his wife and their four children, and a blown-up newspaper headline in bold type that ran the length of the wall behind the desk, proclaiming Richard Daley's infamous quote: *A newspaper is the lowest thing there is!*

After a moment the Deputy Editor managed to end the call and swivelled round in his chair to face Laura.

"Nice work, Kid."

"Thank you."

Mac was only in his mid-fifties, but anyone who was less than about forty-five and with whom he was on good terms was "Kid" to the Deputy Editor. "I went through the article with our solicitor," he said.

"Well?"

"We made a couple of adjustments, but they're small. Nice piece of work – you tackled the heavy issues but without leaving us open to lawsuits."

"I tried to tread carefully."

"I could see that. And you managed to do it without ever sounding timid, which is great . . ."

Laura looked at him carefully. "Why do I sense there's a *but* looming on the horizon?

Mac smiled briefly, then shrugged. "*But* with a small "b", maybe."

"So what's the problem?"

"With the article itself, nothing. It's incisive, it's detailed, it's even-handed, and it gets us into the mindset of these people."

"But there is a problem?"

"Might be. With this guy you dealt with," answered Mac.

"Fergus Boyle?"

"Yeah. You haven't done him or his people any favours."

"I never said I would."

"I know that, Laura, but you know how things are in the real world. Even when you warn a subject that a profile isn't a PR exercise, they'll often take umbrage if there isn't a bit of rose-tinting."

"You're not suggesting I soften the piece?" asked Laura. She looked anxiously at Mac, hoping this wasn't what he wanted. Apart from the professional problem such a request would present, she didn't want her opinion of Mac to be diminished. She had always respected him as a tough-minded but fair editor who didn't buckle under pressure. It would be disillusioning to discover otherwise now.

"No softening whatsoever," he answered. "You won't have any problem with the *Clarion* – you may have with Mr Boyle."

"You said yourself that the article is even-handed. If Boyle didn't believe me when I said it wouldn't be a propaganda piece – well, that's his problem."

"I'm just saying be prepared for him flaring up when he reads it."

"Tell me one thing, Mac. If he rings here and objects, will the article be spiked?"

"Absolutely not."

"Rewritten?"

"Absolutely not."

Laura nodded, reassured by her boss's unequivocal response. "Thanks, Mac."

"However . . ." Mac leaned forward and looked Laura in the eye, "and there *is* a 'however', Kid."

"What is it?"

"The fact that this guy's not your normal subject. If he doesn't like what he sees it may not be just an angry phone call, or a solicitor's letter."

"You think he'd threaten me?"

"It's possible."

Laura looked thoughtfully out the window, considering her options.

"Look, we may be jumping the gun here," said Mac. "None of this may happen. But in a worse-case scenario . . ."

"What?"

"If you want – and I'm only putting this forward as a possibility – we could publish the piece without your by-line."

"No way. This is my story, my name has to be on it."

"Just, if he became threatening, you could tell him it was the paper's decision to go ahead – it was no longer your article. You'd still be paid, of course, and the people who matter would know that it was your scoop, but if you need to placate him I'm offering to let the *Clarion* take the heat."

"I appreciate the concern, Mac, but I'm not hiding behind you, or the paper, or anyone else."

"Well . . . if you're sure?"

"I'm sure. Absolutely sure."

"OK. When are you supposed to be sending it to him?"

"Probably later on today. Whenever we agree the final version."

"All right then," said Mac, reaching unerringly for the article amongst the many mounds of paper on his desk. "Let's get to it . . ."

Majid pushed the room-service tray aside but retained the wooden-handled steak knife that had come with the dinner. He wiped the knife clean with a tissue, handling the sharp blade with care. He had deliberately ordered a three-course meal, reasoning that when he left the tray in the corridor outside his hotel room it would be filled with the used crockery and cutlery from the various courses. That way the absence of a steak knife would be much less obvious than if he had tried to purloin one from the hotel restaurant, where the courses would be served one at a time.

He had originally considered buying a more lethal commando-type knife from one of the army surplus stores he had seen in Dublin during his exploration of the city during the day. He had decided against it however, reasoning that it would entail bringing himself to the attention of a shop assistant, however fleetingly. No point having someone wondering unnecessarily why a foreign visitor wanted such a weapon. It was unlikely that he would need to use it while in Ireland, he knew, but he felt vulnerable at being unarmed while on a mission. Besides, on Friday he would be meeting the people that Rahmani's Libyan contacts had set up. Those on the Irish end had already been paid half the fee for the equipment they were providing, but with Majid due to pay the balance with a bank draft there was always the possibility of an attempted double-cross, and Majid felt he couldn't attend an illicit rendezvous without a weapon of some kind.

Although a silenced Beretta would have been his first choice, the people in Ireland from whom he could have obtained one were the very people he was going to meet. Still, the value of a sharp knife tended to be underestimated. For those with the stomach to do it, the quick slitting of a throat could be both silent and lethal.

Satisfied with his choice, he wrapped a thick paper napkin around the steak knife as a scabbard, then slipped it into the pocket of his jeans. Although it had been a balmy September day, the evening had now grown cool so he pulled on a casual jacket, then made for the door of his room. He walked down the corridor towards the lifts, aware that his jeans and sneakers were a little at odds with the smarter dress code adopted by most of the guests. No matter, he thought, he would be out of the hotel within a minute and it was more important to look the part when he got to his destination.

Earlier in the day he had pored over a local newspaper, the *Evening Herald*, going through the small ads until he found a column of motor cycles for sale. By buying a second-hand motorbike for cash he would acquire the transport he needed, yet avoid the need for car hire with its attendant paperwork and identity requirements. He had rung several of the numbers listed and had arranged to visit a house in Kilmainham, where a Honda CB 250 was for sale.

Majid reached the ground floor of the hotel and crossed the lobby quickly, then he descended the steps outside the Gresham and crossed to the O'Connell Street taxi rank.

"Where to, boss?" asked the taxi-driver

"St Patrick's Terrace, Kilmainham."

"No problem."

Majid got into the back of the taxi, taking the *Evening Herald* from his jacket and immediately immersing himself in it.

"Cold aul evenin', what? After such a nice day," said the driver, notwithstanding the presence of the newspaper.

"Yes," answered Majid curtly, then immediately returned to the paper.

The driver shrugged philosophically, as though he had done his part in the civility stakes, and Majid was relieved when he made no further attempts at conversation. Occasionally turning the pages of the tabloid newspaper to give the illusion of reading, Majid in reality was looking admiringly out the car window as the taxi made its way past the imposing floodlit edifices of Trinity College and the Bank of Ireland in College Green. The taxi continued up Dame Street past

City Hall and a large Gothic church that Majid knew from his guidebook must be Christchurch Cathedral. They carried on past the Guinness plant, once the largest brewery in the world, and Majid noted wryly that for the price of a taxi-fare he was getting quite a good tour while en route to Kilmainham.

Several minutes later the taxi swung off the main road and pulled to a halt in a narrow cul-de-sac.

"St Patrick's Terrace," said the taxi-driver, but without the warmth with which he had originally greeted his passenger. "What number?"

"This will do fine," said Majid. He quickly calculated a tip of ten per cent, then paid the driver and got out of the car. As the taxi-driver did a three-point turn, Majid walked to the end of the terrace, as per instructions, and cut down an alleyway that led to an adjoining street. He checked the number of the corner house, the first in a row of squat cottages. It was number twelve, his destination. The cottages had tiny front gardens, and Majid opened the gate and approached the front door of number twelve, noting the weed-strewn mess that constituted the garden.

He rang the doorbell and a moment later an overweight man in jeans and a lumberjack shirt opened the door. The man was in his early thirties, with long thinning hair, and he smiled when he saw Majid. "Fair play to ye, pal! You showed up like you said."

"You have the motorbike?"

"Round the side entrance. Mind the bin there."

Majid followed the man round the litter-strewn front garden and in through a side door. Behind the door was a side passage containing the Honda. The man's appearance and the state of the garden hadn't been confidence-inspiring, but the motorbike looked clean and well-maintained.

"There ye are. Sings like a bird."

"Sorry?" said Majid.

"The engine. Sings like a bird."

"Ah."

The man pulled the motorbike from its stand and kick-started it. Immediately the engine sprang to life. "Listen to that. Tickin' over lovely. Service her meself."

"It sounds good," admitted Majid.

"Goin' perfectly. You can have a test drive if we agree on the aul spondulicks." He switched off the engine.

"The what?"

"The spondulicks – the money. God, you're not here long, are ye?"

"Eh, no . . ."

"Thought so. What do you work at – or are you a refugee?"

"I work . . . as a waiter . . ."

"Ah, the aul tax-free tips, what?"

Majid felt like strangling the man, but the persona of a foreign waiter wanting to get a bargain dictated that he remain patient.

"Where are ye from anyway?"

Majid hadn't been expecting such a quizzing and he lied off the top of his head. "Holland."

"Holland?!"

The man looked at him with real interest, and Majid

immediately regretted his answer, despite having no idea what the other man was thinking.

"Ye bastard ye! Ye done us in Euro 88!"

"Sorry?"

"Wim fuckin' Kieft! Put us out of the European Cup!" The man grinned and looked at Majid.

"Ah . . . soccer . . ."

"What else!"

Majid took in the man's physique. He was at least ten kilos overweight, but Majid knew he would be the type who would scream abuse at players from the sideline.

"Then ye did us again in Orlando. Jonk gets another jammy goal – and we're out of the bleedin' World Cup!"

"Yes," said Majid, trying for an apologetic smile and wishing he hadn't chosen Holland for his false nationality.

"To say nothin' of the qualifier in '95."

"Right . . ."

"Great piss-up in Orlando all the same. The Irish and the Dutch livened that kip up, what?!"

"Yes. About the bike?"

"Ah sure, I have to give you a good deal now, don't I? Getting the aul wheels meself."

Majid presumed this was slang for a car, and he saw an opportunity. "Are you selling a helmet also?"

"Absolutely. Lovely job too. Tinted visor and all."

Perfect, thought Majid. Wearing that he wouldn't look like a foreigner – instead he would be just one more faceless man on a motorbike. And this gibbering fool would have provided him with transport and a mask, untraceable as a cash deal.

"OK," said Majid. "Let's talk about money . . ."

Penny stopped in her tracks and pointed. "Possible weak spot, Chief."

Thompson followed her gaze to where a service entrance ran downhill from Kings Road, the thoroughfare flanking the Conference Centre buildings. "All the entrances will be cordoned off," he answered.

"I know. But most of our attention will be on the entrances being used by the delegates."

"We'll still man all service entrances with armed officers," said Thompson.

"I'm just thinking out loud," said Penny, "but I can't help feeling that this one's a bit of an Achilles heel, even with the metal bars."

"How so?" asked Thompson.

"It leads down into the heart of the centre. If somebody once gained access that way, they could make towards any of the five conference halls. It's also immediately accessible from the public road here, so a vehicle could approach at speed to break through a cordon if the security bars were lifted."

"Point taken."

"And even if the bars are in place they could use a heavy vehicle – we need to be able to stop anything short of a tank."

Thompson scribbled onto the clipboard he was carrying. "Duly noted," he said.

They continued their survey, walking along Kings Road, then turning down towards the carpark that served the Moat House Hotel. It was seven thirty in the

evening and there were lots of cars in the surface carpark.
Penny looked at them, then turned to Thompson.

"Are you thinking what I'm thinking, Chief?"

"Car-bombs?"

"Exactly. Between this carpark and the one serving
the Conference Centre it's a hell of a lot of vehicles.
Checking the boot and the underside of each for
explosives before they park would cause chaos."

"There'll be opposition to closing the carparks,
mind. We're ruffling a lot of local feathers as it is."

"I don't see what choice we have, Chief."

"We have no choice," said Thompson. "I'd already
decided to close the Moat House carpark and to keep
the Conference Centre one solely for accredited and
security-cleared people."

"Right."

"From the day before the delegates arrive we'll have
to close both carparks to the general public."

"That'll make us popular," said Penny with a grin.

"Can't be helped – have to err on the side of caution."

"Talking of which, I had an idea."

"Yeah?"

"It's a bit of a belt and braces job, admittedly –"

"Belt and braces is fine. Let's have it," said Thompson.

"Well, I know we'll be issuing passes to allow people
other than hotel and Conference Centre staff to pass
through the security cordons –"

"Fire Brigades, ambulances, and so on?"

"Precisely. Why not also give them a code-word to
be used in addition to their ID if they need to gain
access?"

136

"Just in case our villain somehow got ID?"

"Yes. It would give us one more strand of protection. And we could change the code-word daily while the dignitaries are here."

"Good thinking, Penny."

"Thanks, Chief."

"I'll organise it with the appropriate people. Shouldn't be too difficult to set up."

"Easier than welding manholes," said Penny with a grin, and Thompson smiled wryly.

"Too bloody true."

Earlier that morning Colin Mathieson had had a run-in with the head of the advance party from the American Secret Service, who had wanted manhole covers in Kings Road welded shut in advance of the arrival of the US Secretary of State. Even allowing for the Americans' rigorous attitude to security the demand had been regarded as somewhat over the top, and retellings of the clash had quickly spread amongst those working on the operation.

"If he thinks that's bad, wait till next week," said Thompson.

"How do you mean?"

"He'll have the cloak-and-dagger lot from every EU country throwing in their tuppence worth."

"From what I gather from Colin, most of them will only have limited forces here."

"How limited is limited?" asked Thompson.

"Three or four officers for each Foreign Minister. The Germans and the French are the most pushy about it apparently – they'll have somewhat bigger groups."

"That's all we need," said Thompson with a grin. "The Intelligence equivalent of the Eurovision bloody Song Contest."

"I'd say that part's the least of Colin's worries right now," said Penny.

"Oh?"

"I think he's finding Mr Carrow rather heavy going."

"Him and the rest of the human race."

"Security checks on the hotel and conference-centre staff take a lot of co-ordinating," said Penny. "Seems Special Branch aren't enamoured with Colin calling the shots, however diplomatically done."

"More like Len Carrow is the one who's not enamoured – he always wants to be the one in the limelight. So, how are the security checks coming along anyway?"

"I think Colin is going to brief you this afternoon. So far they've got one barman whose father, long since deceased due to a heart attack, was in the IRA about thirty years ago. We have two waitresses who are anti-nuclear protesters –"

"CND?"

"Yes."

"My own niece is in CND," said Thompson.

"Still *potentially* subversive – in the eyes of Special Branch."

"Anyone else?"

"One kitchen porter, aged sixty, who was a member of the Communist party of Great Britain for about a year."

"What year?"

"1961."

Thompson smiled briefly. "That's it?"

"So far," answered Penny. "Still a lot of staff to check out."

"Is priority being given to those hired in recent times?"

"I'd imagine so. I left Colin's office to meet you without going into that sort of detail."

"Not to worry – we'll hear from him if there's anything to hear."

"No doubt."

"Well," said Thompson, "best get on with our survey."

Penny turned to move off, but Thompson paused.

"And Penny?"

"Chief?"

"Keep your eyes peeled. And keep on thinking belt and braces all the way. I've a bit of a funny feeling on this one . . ."

6

Majid accelerated out of the bend, tilting the Honda CB 250 as he followed the curve of the road. It was years since he had ridden a motorbike and it brought back memories of going to college in Baghdad on the gleaming Triumph that had been the pride and joy of his youth. Ahead of him now stretched the Cooley Peninsula, and to his right the waters of Dundalk Bay sparkled in the morning sunshine. The Irish countryside had as many shades of green as the guidebooks had said, but Majid wasn't in the right frame of mind to savour his surroundings.

It was always this way when he was on a mission – his senses heightened, adrenaline flowing through his veins. Normally he wouldn't have attended an important rendezvous like this morning's alone, but on balance he had decided against bringing Jemail Zubi to Ireland. Simpler to let Jemail make his own way to Harrogate while he took care of arrangements at this end. The fact that he was to pay today for the equipment he was collecting had Majid on edge, but the people he was buying from had insisted on the final half of their fee being paid on delivery of the goods. The one element of the rendezvous that Majid could control was timing, and so he had driven up early from Dublin in order to be in position long before the appointed meeting time.

He slowed the Honda down on seeing a signpost ahead. According to his calculations, it should be the turn for the village of Carlingford. Sure enough, the sign indicated Carlingford to the left and Majid knew his rendezvous point was drawing near as he picked up speed again and continued on the road to Greenore.

After a few moments he saw a small turn ahead on his right and he brought the Honda down through the gears on seeing his landmark, a pub called the Cooley Inn. Majid turned off the main round and followed a quiet byroad that passed the pub and a small cemetery, then began to curve back in the direction of the main road. A bank of trees on his left shielded him from being seen from the main road and he followed the instructions he had been given and pulled in to a large patch of waste ground on the right of the road. On the far side of the waste ground was a barn-like building that was padlocked, and nearby were a wrecked car and a rusting transport container. There was no sign of anybody and when Majid switched off the engine all he could hear was birdsong and the sound of the occasional car coming or going towards the port of Greenore.

It was a good location for what had to be done, he thought, near the road, yet out of sight of passing traffic. He dismounted and pulled the bike up onto its stand, but kept his helmet on. The likelihood of encountering passers-by in a spot so off the beaten track was slim, but from now until the deal was brokered ultra-caution would be his guiding principle.

He looked around, his practised eye seeking possible hiding places and access routes, then he took the Honda down off its stand, wheeled it to a corner of the wasteland and hid it behind some bushes. He unclipped the sealed envelope containing the bank draft from the motorbike's pannier, then carefully concealed it about twenty metres away in a separate corner of the site. Finally he choose a spot from where he could see any approach to the wasteland, hid himself from view and settled down to wait.

"She's some bitch! I knew from the minute we met her that she'd be a pain," said O'Donnell.

"She's a journalist," answered Boyle. "They're all pains."

"Surely she can't just print the article if we don't agree?"

"Keep your eyes on the road, Gerry," instructed Boyle, and O'Donnell switched his attention back to the R173. It was a secondary road that was taking them eastwards and they were sitting in the cab of a large lorry being driven by O'Donnell.

"She can't just print it without our say-so, can she?" persisted O'Donnell.

"Of course she can," snapped Boyle. "Unless she states something libellous – and she's too cute to do that

– it's hard to stop her. And even if we were libelled, we'd have to identify ourselves if we wanted to go to law."

"Who said anything about the law?" asked O'Donnell. "We could lean on her ourselves. She'd soon change her tune then."

"That could backfire badly. Much better if we could get her to expand those parts of the article that lay out our philosophy."

"Our *philosophy*? Jaysus, there's posh!"

Boyle looked at the other man with irritation. "Have you got anything between your ears at all?!"

"Sorry, Fergus. Only kiddin'."

"What was the purpose of meeting her in the first place?"

O'Donnell considered briefly. "Eh . . . to counter British propaganda."

"So it's hardly good PR for the organisation if she writes that we've threatened her, is it?"

"Would she be stupid enough to do that?"

"I don't know," said Boyle. "She might. It's a tricky call how to handle her."

"Right."

"I'll have to try and meet her when we get back."

"You think meeting in person would work better than when you phoned her?"

"Eyeball to eyeball is always better," said Boyle. "She probably needs a bit of stick and carrot simultaneously."

"I know what she needs!" said O'Donnell with a leer.

"Maybe she needs that too . . ."

"So, eh, would that count as stick – or carrot?!"

They both laughed, then Boyle looked carefully out the window. "Slow down," he said, "we're nearly there."

O'Donnell eased off the accelerator, then followed Boyle's instructions when he indicated where to turn right. The heavy truck took up most of the narrow road onto which they had turned, but there was no traffic coming from the opposite direction.

"OK, pull in over here," instructed Boyle

O'Donnell hauled on the steering wheel and steered the truck onto a large patch of waste ground.

"Kill the engine," said Boyle.

O'Donnell switched off the ignition and looked out through the windscreen. There were no other vehicles parked there and nobody was around. He heard a car approaching on the main road, but it was shielded from view by a bank of trees and it passed unseen, its engine-sound gradually fading.

"Looks like we're first here," said Boyle, then both men were startled by three quick taps from the rear of the truck. Boyle spun round to look in the vehicle's outside mirror.

A man approached from the back of the truck, his gait slow and confident. He appeared young and fit-looking, but his face was masked by a motorcycle helmet.

Majid approached the cabin of the truck slowly. No point in spooking the passengers. He had already succeeded in his objective of wrong-footing them by surprising them with his presence. Both doors opened

144

at once and two men jumped down. The nearest was heavily built but overweight. The second man came around from the passenger side. This one was leaner, faster-moving. Majid knew instinctively that the second man would be the leader.

"What's with tapping the truck?" said the first one aggressively.

"Alerting you to my presence," answered Majid, deliberately avoiding any tone of defensiveness in his voice.

"Next time alert us to your presence by stepping into plain view," said the second man.

"I'll bear that in mind – if there's ever a next time," answered Majid.

"You've brought the payment?" asked the man that Majid had mentally named the leader.

"The payment is available."

"*Available*? Have you got it here?"

"It's available here," said Majid, but without specifying where. "You have the goods?"

"Yes. And when you're talking to me, take that helmet off."

Majid made no move to obey, but locked eyes with the leader. "When we go inside the truck to examine the gear, then I remove the helmet." He paused a moment to emphasise his stance, then indicated the rear of the truck. "Shall we?"

This time it was the Irishman who made no move, but Majid said nothing further. As the one who was outnumbered two to one it was important to maintain the upper hand as much as possible, and the more that time elapsed without his removing the helmet, the weaker it made the other man seem.

As though realising this, the leader suddenly nodded to his sidekick. "Open it up, Gerry."

Sloppy, thought Majid. True professionals wouldn't use names in front of a third party. He sensed that these men were in this for the money, probably a lucrative sideline that their organisation didn't know about. It was a pity to have to use such people, particularly since security on all other aspects of the project had been watertight since the lapse at Sidon. The reality however was that these men could provide equipment that would be crucial in carrying out his mission in Harrogate.

The heavier of the men opened the back doors of the truck and Majid and the leader climbed up after him into the shady interior, stepping over the tail ramp that was stowed flat on the floor.

Having made his point, Majid now removed his crash-helmet and put it down.

"That's better. I like to look a man in the eye . . ." said the leader.

Majid didn't respond but caught a brief smile on the face of the man called Gerry. The way the sentence had been left hanging caused Majid's mind to race. Could it be that the leader liked to look a man in the eye – *when he was killing him*? Was that what they had in store for him? A quick double-cross and the substantial second payment pocketed? Perhaps he was letting caution extend into paranoia, he thought, yet he found himself wishing he was carrying his Beretta.

"I think it's time to show us the colour of your

money," said the heavier man, and Majid caught the smell of drink off his breath. Ten o'clock in the morning and already he was drinking? And while on a mission? He was getting a bad feeling from these men. He could visualise the one called Gerry drunkenly boasting about his links with Middle-Eastern terrorism. All it needed was one unguarded remark and the whole Harrogate project could be compromised.

"First I see the goods, then I pay – that is the normal way, " answered Majid.

"Show him," said the leader.

The heavy man moved forward and pulled away storage sheets. "There . . ."

Majid examined the equipment, then nodded approvingly. "Good. And the weapons?"

The leader opened a wooden packing-case and Majid was pleased to see the weaponry he had ordered as part of his contingency planning.

"Sniper's rifle," said Gerry approvingly. "Remington 700, night sight and normal sight. Two Uzis, one Beretta, one Sig, ten hand-grenades, silencers and rounds for the weapons."

"Good." Majid casually picked up the Beretta as though examining it. He gauged the weight surreptitiously. *Empty*, he thought, disappointed but not surprised. "Everything seems to be in order." He reached out, apparently absent-mindedly, for a magazine for the Beretta.

"Not so fast, pal!" said Gerry, laying a restraining hand on his arm.

Again Majid was struck by the smell of drink.

"Ye don't want to be playing with loaded weapons. Not when you haven't shown us your money."

Majid shrugged as though it made no difference whether he loaded the gun before or after payment was made. "The bank draft is exactly as agreed – there's no problem."

"That's right – there's going to be no problem," said Gerry.

Majid felt an immediate stab of alarm. His English was sufficiently fluent and colloquial to pick up on the sense of irony in the other man's comment. It was only an inflexion, only a hint of amusement at Majid's expense, but Majid's senses were finely tuned to situations of danger and he had learned to trust his instincts. And his instincts told him that these men had gone from being accomplices to being a threat to his mission. Even if they weren't planning to double-cross him, the risk of leaving a drink-sodden amateur to shoot his mouth off was a problem. He couldn't take that chance. He had worked too hard, come too far; he couldn't allow the operation to be threatened at this stage.

His trainers had always stressed that when a life or death decision arose in the field it was important to act decisively. Worrying unduly about the consequences of error could waste precious time. *Weigh things up all right, but not for too long. And when in doubt follow your instincts.*

Very well then, he would do just that – and his instincts told him that these men were a danger to the mission. There was nothing for it: they would have to die. He quickly calculated the dynamics of the situation. They outnumbered him two to one, but that wasn't necessarily a major problem. Probably they both carried guns though, and that was a problem. However he had one weapon they didn't possess – surprise. They didn't know he felt threatened; they wouldn't be expecting their victim to attack them.

In spite of himself, his mind again posed the question: what if he were wrong? What if they never had any intention of double-crossing him? *Forget it!* That would simply be too bad for them, he told himself firmly. They were players in a dangerous game and they had behaved sloppily. Normally he would have had to factor in the consequences of killing men whose friends might seek revenge, but the consequences of killing every Foreign Minister in the European Union were so enormous that two more terrorists made little difference. Majid knew that in any event he would have to go to ground permanently to evade the huge manhunt that would follow a successful operation in Harrogate.

His thoughts were broken by the leader of the two men. "So, you've seen the goods. Let's see the money now."

"It's outside."

"Come on then."

Majid calculated quickly. Killing them inside the truck would certainly be more private. But they'd be suspicious now if he dallied here. Besides, the patch of waste ground was pretty isolated anyway. But he would have to strike before they got their hands on the bank draft. Once they had that, he would be surplus to requirements.

The leader moved to the back of the truck and jumped down to the ground. Majid followed, his mind racing. Could the sight of the money be the distraction he needed? Or would they already be drawing their guns as soon as he approached the hidden money order? He reached the tail of the truck and jumped down to join the leader. Without the tail ramp lowered, it was a jump of several feet and as Majid gathered himself together he realised that Gerry wasn't going to jump. Instead, the heavier man was lowering himself to sit on the end of the lorry and get down that way. Instantly Majid knew it was his chance. He looked back at the leader and the man's shrewd, knowing eyes caused Majid to hesitate. *Expect to be frightened*, his trainers had said, *then overcome your fear. Now! Do it!* he told himself.

He glanced past the leader, a look of surprise on his face. "What on earth . . .?" It was the oldest trick in the book, but the other man fell for it. Seeing Majid's bemused expression he looked around, and in that second Majid pounced. While the leader was turned away Majid lunged forward, grasping him under the chin with his left hand. He jerked the man's head viciously upwards, and in one swift movement pulled the steak knife from his pocket and slit the exposed neck. Immediately blood spurted from the carotid artery. Majid swung his victim around so that he would act as a shield, then pushed the already dying man towards the rear of the truck. He was counting on Gerry being stunned momentarily by the sight of his comrade pumping blood. All he needed was for him to be shocked into inactivity for a couple of seconds.

He never got those couple of seconds. The heavily built man jumped to the ground and already had his gun out as he found his feet. For all the man's lack of professionalism in other ways, it was clear to Majid that his opponent had seen action before.

He quickly levelled his gun-hand but screamed out in pain before he could get a shot off. Without breaking stride Maid had thrown the steak knife into his face, catching him just below the eye. He screamed in pain and raised his hands to his face. Majid dropped the limp and bloodsodden body of the first man and closed the gap with his second opponent. He lashed out with his foot as Gerry went to swing his gun-hand around. He felt the toe of his boot connecting with the man's hand, then the pistol flew in an arc through the air. Majid expected his opponent to scramble for the gun and was surprised when he came straight for him instead. Despite being overweight and dim-witted the man had the instincts of a street-fighter and he landed a knee in Majid's stomach as they closed together. Majid doubled up in pain, but managed to get both his hands forward in a blocking move. It was just as well, for Gerry jerked violently upwards with what would have been a devastating knee in the face. Majid's hands stopped the blow and he grasped the other man's raised leg and twisted it sharply. The man screamed in agony and fell to the ground. Despite his pain however he never relinquished his grip on Majid's shirt and he pulled the lighter man to the ground with him.

Majid landed on top of him, then rolled quickly to the side, his eyes seeking the gun. No sooner had he done so than he realised it was a mistake. Moving with a speed that belied his bulk, Gerry took advantage of Majid's brief distraction to roll forward and grab him by the lapels. Majid instantly ducked, saving his face from being shattered by the ferocious head-butt launched at him. He immediately jerked Gerry's head back by the hair, then jabbed him hard in the face with his elbow. He heard his opponent's nose breaking and a cry of pain, but still the man fought on as though unaffected. A full-force blow on the broken nose would disorient him, thought Majid, and he freed his right hand and punched hard.

The blow never landed. This time it was Gerry who made the blocking movement, then caught Majid's arm. He twisted hard on the arm and Majid felt a pain like an electric shock. He struggled wildly, knowing that he mustn't let a heavier and stronger opponent pin him on the ground. With his free hand he swung a punch, connecting with Gerry's ribs, but the man simply took the pain and channelled all his strength into twisting Majid's arm. By now the pain was agonising and Majid felt a wave of panic sweep through him, knowing that if the man broke his right arm the situation would be catastrophic. Calling on every ounce of strength he had, he strained against the other man's grip, both of them all the while kneeing and head-butting each other's intertwined bodies. Majid felt himself losing the battle and he thrashed wildly, trying to shift position. Just as the pain in his right arm become unbearable his left hand brushed something solid – then he grasped it exultantly and jabbed, burying the retrieved steak knife between his opponent's ribs. He was rewarded with a cry, then an easing in pressure on his right arm. He pulled his arm free and quickly withdrew the knife from his victim's ribs. While the man's eyes were still wide in shock from the first stab-wound Majid closed both hands on the shaft of the knife and buried it in his chest, piercing the heart. The man coughed blood. Majid withdrew the knife and plunged it once more into his opponent's heart. The man shuddered once more, then his eyelids flickered and he went still.

Majid lay there a moment, his breathing ragged, then he rolled off and got to his feet. His arm was sore, his stomach ached and his cheek was scratched, but otherwise he was uninjured. He surveyed the scene, his mind quickly becoming analytical now that the immediate threat had passed. Despite it being a close-run thing, both his opponents were dead and nobody had seen what had happened. If he got the bodies into the back of the truck now and scattered rubble from the waste site over the pools of blood there would be no evidence of what had happened here. He could retrieve his money order, load the motorbike in the back of the truck and drive away. Later he could strip the bodies of any ID and dispose of the corpses. By the time they were found he would be out of the country. He would also have the equipment he had collected safely stored in Harrogate. And most important of all, the threat to his mission that these men had posed would no longer exist. Satisfied that everything was still on track, he moved quickly to dispose of the bodies.

Penny sat alone at her desk, gazing into the middle

distance. The command centre that had been set up in Harrogate police station was almost deserted now, and Penny knew that most of the other officers were either out working, gone for a Friday-night drink, or relaxing at home. Mathieson was in his hotel room, preparing a briefing for his superiors, Carrow hadn't been seen since early morning and Thompson had left to visit his grandchildren, but Penny was in no rush to return to her hotel room.

She had just spoken to Shane on the telephone, her disappointment at the lack of progress on the case diffused by his infectious good humour. He had made her laugh with a description of how Aisling had found a jar of honey and smeared it liberally over some of their old vinyl records. *Abba* and *Wham!* had had their recordings artificially sweetened, Shane had reported with relish, whereas his own *Boomtown Rats* and *Pink Floyd* albums had come through unscathed.

Penny smiled, remembering how obsessive Shane could be about the pop music of his youth. She recalled him once telling her in all seriousness how right throughout his twenties he had believed that no matter how beautiful or desirable a woman might be, he could never share his life with someone who was a Michael Jackson fan. Now she was looking forward to seeing him with Aisling tomorrow night when they were all going to stay in her parents' house in Leeds.

Thompson had told her that, barring developments, she was to take Saturday night and Sunday off, that he wanted her to be fresh for the final week leading up to the conference. Although she ultimately reported to Colin

Mathieson, the intelligence officer had agreed with Thompson that, provided nothing happened, she could have the time off. She was looking forward to seeing her family again, yet she still felt dissatisfied, frustrated that more wasn't emerging from the police investigations.

The painstaking checking of hotel and car-hire records that she had requested was being done, but it was a mammoth task, and so far nothing had arisen to help narrow the net on their prospective assassin. The security check on Conference Centre and Moat House Hotel staff had been more productive, producing eleven staff members who had been hired in the past year. Five of them had been locals, whose *bone fides* were easily checked. Two of the others were also British subjects – a kitchen maid from Glasgow and a receptionist from Bristol – and again preliminary enquiries suggested blameless lives of almost boring normality.

The four foreigners were more interesting, consisting of a Sudanese chef, a Turkish waiter, a Romanian kitchen porter and a French wine waiter. The Frenchman was the easiest of the four to check out, and apart from a predilection to over-indulge in the wines he served, his background gave no cause for concern. The other three were considerably more challenging, all coming as they did from countries outside the EU. It served to make security-based enquiries both difficult and laborious, and while Mathieson had insisted that detailed enquiries would still be pursued, so far nothing suspicious had been discovered.

Penny's thoughts were interrupted by the door to the room being opened, and she looked up to see Superintendent Carrow approaching.

"Working up your brownie points?" he said.

"Sorry?"

"Dedicated copper, still at her desk when the others are down the pub . . ."

Penny was tempted to respond to the sneering tone in Carrow's voice, but she restrained herself.

"Just tidying up a few bits and pieces," she answered.

Carrow sat on the edge of her desk and looked her challengingly in the eye. "Not producing the goods, is it?"

"What's not producing the goods, sir?"

"Your so-called lateral thinking. End of week one, and we're no nearer finding this assassin bastard, are we?"

"I'm not responsible for the whole investigation, Mr Carrow."

"You're responsible for tying up manpower looking for a six-month-old trail – if such a trail ever existed."

"Because we haven't found any evidence yet doesn't mean he hasn't left a trail."

"And because officers are spending time looking for it means resources are diverted away from real police work."

"In my view, sir, it's all real police work."

"In your view? Well, let me just tell you something, *Inspector*."

Penny again had to make an effort not to show her irritation, this time at the ironic way Carrow emphasised the word 'Inspector'.

"Your views might impress your old boss," he continued, "and your old . . . *friend* – but they don't impress me."

So he knew that she and Mathieson had been lovers years ago – and he couldn't resist letting her know. Being a Chief Superintendent, however, he was decidedly senior to her and she couldn't openly challenge him. Best to deny him the satisfaction of showing any kind of emotion.

"I'm sorry you feel that way, Mr Carrow," she answered, offering no further explanation. Looking at his face, she sensed that he was disappointed that she wasn't rising to the bait.

He nodded his head, then levered himself off the desk. "You might be a lot more sorry if all you've caused is a wild-goose chase. Wouldn't do your reputation in the Met any good when we're all back in London. Think about that." He turned and made for the door.

Penny waited until he had gone before breathing out angrily, but his words chilled her. As a senior Special Branch officer he was well connected back in London, and she knew there was a threat inherent in his reference to her reputation in the Met. Of course, he had said it to make her worry about her career being damaged by his bad-mouthing her, yet she sensed it wasn't an idle threat. She had worked so hard to progress her career that it would be unbearable if it were to be undermined because Carrow simply didn't like her style. Yet the disturbing thing was that, to some extent, Carrow had a point. Her suggestions had yielded nothing so far, and they were no nearer to apprehending their quarry than when they had started.

She gathered her car-keys from the desk, rose from her chair and tried to shake off the mood of pessimism that Carrow had caused. They had all of next week to continue their investigations, she reasoned, and this weekend she would be seeing Shane and Aisling. She went out the door and down the corridor leading to the carpark, but, in spite of her desire to be upbeat, her mood was subdued. Carrow had intimated a threat to her career, which was bad enough, but she sensed that somewhere out there was a man who posed a far greater threat. And if they didn't catch him, the matter of her career prospects would be insignificant compared to the slaughter he planned to unleash.

She stepped out the door of the station, got into the car and sat staring out the windscreen, desperately trying to think what more could be done . . .

7

Saturday September 16th 2000

Laura Kennedy stopped typing in mid-sentence. She had been sitting at the desk in her study, replying to an e-mail that Declan had sent her from the film set in Prague, when she halted abruptly. The radio was playing in the background and Laura had only half-listened to the midday news until the third item on the bulletin. Now she swallowed in shock as the newsreader gave details of a double murder. She listened intently as a Garda Superintendent from Dundalk explained that although two bodies discovered in a ditch in County Meath were devoid of any form of ID, Gardai had nonetheless identified them as the remains of Fergus Boyle and Gerry O'Donnell. Both men were known to the Gardai and were republican dissidents, thought to be linked to the outlawed Continuity IRA.

Laura sat immobile as the Superintendent admitted that the injuries to the two men pointed to foul play and that a murder investigation was being launched. Pressed by the interviewer, he revealed that both men appeared

159

to have been stabbed rather than shot although nothing conclusive could be stated regarding their injuries until a post mortem had been carried out. The newsreader gave a little more background information on the murder victims, then moved on to the next news item.

Laura switched off the radio, her head swimming. What the hell was going on? Boyle had rung her on Thursday night, unhappy with the article and demanding that it mustn't be published as written. Laura had argued with him and they had parted on poor terms. She had expected him to contact her again the next day, and all of yesterday she had been dreading a call from him, fearing that he would escalate the pressure on her to revise the article, perhaps with a threat to her safety. To her surprise no call had ever come. Now she knew why. But what had occurred to cause the deaths of Boyle and O'Donnell? Could it be linked in any way to the article? No, she decided, it wouldn't make any kind of sense for someone to kill them because of an interview. Much more likely to be an internal feud, an old score being settled, or some kind of maverick operation that went wrong. Whatever the reason though, it certainly gave the article she had just done with Boyle a hugely heightened significance. No sooner had she entertained the thought than Laura felt a stab of guilt. Two men had been killed, she chided herself, and even though he had disliked them, their brutal murder was still an outrage, still of more significance than a newspaper article.

And yet . . . despite her shock and distaste, Laura couldn't ignore the part of her that said that, as a journalist, this was an opportunity not to be missed. Boyle and O'Donnell had lived by the sword after all, and the fact that they had now died in similar fashion was unfortunate – but not so tragic that she felt obliged to withhold her article in deference to their memory.

She picked up the phone, intending to ring Mac at the *Clarion*, then stopped herself. As an editor, Mac would undoubtedly be keen to run with the article as it was, but maybe there was an even bigger story here if she could unearth it. If she could discover what it was that Boyle and O'Donnell had been involved in that cost them their lives, it would be both a major scoop and a perfect accompanying piece for the article she had already written.

Laura put the phone down, biting her lip as her mind raced. She thought back to the previous Monday when she had met Boyle and O'Donnell in the pub. It was only four days before their deaths, so it was reasonable to assume that whatever resulted in their murder may well have been already in train at that stage. And if they were stabbed to death, it suggested a killer who knew them sufficiently well to get close to them.

She thought of the phone call Boyle had taken during their interview. Clearly the caller was organising accommodation for them and knew Boyle well enough to have his mobile number. Her pulses starting to race, Laura reached across the desk to where her notes from the interview were neatly stacked. She looked through them again and found the page on which she had surreptitiously scribbled the phone number that Boyle had arranged to call back. 4621272. It was a Dublin number, though she wasn't sure what part of the city it signified.

She had a friend in the phone company, however, who owed her a favour. It was against the rules, of course, but she could probably get an address to go with the number. If it was where Boyle and O'Donnell had been staying the police would probably be there already, but she might well be the first journalist on the scene. And then another thought struck her. Supposing the police weren't aware that Boyle and O'Donnell had been staying in Dublin? In that case she might get to the site before anyone. She thought about it for a moment, sensing that she might be entering dangerous territory – then she dismissed her reservations, flipped open her contacts book at the appropriate page and rang her friend in the telephone company.

Majid drove north, keeping the truck at a steady sixty miles an hour as he followed the A61 towards Harrogate. It was a warm autumn morning and the sun had shone all the way from the ferry terminal in Liverpool, but Majid couldn't relax until he had safely off-loaded the stolen lorry.

The papers Boyle and O'Donnell had provided for the vehicle had been in order, and there had been no problem boarding the night ferry from Dublin to Liverpool the previous evening. Majid had kept a low profile during the crossing and had stayed in his cabin for the entire journey, anxious to ensure that no-one would remember him if questions were asked later on. Earlier that day he had disposed of the bodies in a ditch that ran parallel to a lay-by on the road between Dundalk and Dublin. With the bulk of the truck shielding him from view, he had dragged the bodies across a field before dumping them in the ditch, well out of view from either the main road or the lay-by.

He had reckoned that it would be some time before they were likely to be discovered and it had been a shock to hear on the truck's radio that morning that they had already been found. He had been driving on the motorway, skirting Manchester, when it had featured on the eleven o'clock news. Despite knowing that he had done nothing to leave a trail linking him to the dead men, he had still found it unnerving.

Now, as he reached the approach to Harrogate, he felt that he was almost home and dry. He would still have to unload the truck and then abandon it somewhere far removed from Harrogate, but he had all of that figured out. Suddenly he felt a racing of his pulses on seeing a police patrol car on the verge of the road. Surely they couldn't already have made a connection between the dead men, the vehicle, and its presence in another jurisdiction? Yet there was always the possibility that O'Donnell had shot his mouth off at some point. Maybe the truck that they had acquired could be linked to them – and by extension to their killer, now that their bodies had been found.

Majid slowed down, hoping that the police presence was nothing more sinister than a speed trap. He was wearing a baseball cap and lightly tinted sunglasses to alter his appearance a little, but, as he drew nearer to where the police vehicle was parked, he had to consciously force himself to breathe deeply and appear calm at the wheel. In his peripheral vision he could see that there were two police officers seated in the car, but he took care not to look over at them as he drew level. He found his grip on the steering wheel tightening, then he went past, immediately glancing in the rear-view mirror. They hadn't turned to follow his progress, but were instead still looking back in the direction of the approaching traffic.

Majid sighed, relieved that they hadn't been seeking him, yet annoyed at having allowed himself to be spooked, even temporarily. He drove on into Harrogate, swinging to the right at the roundabout on the Otley Road. He turned onto York Place, then drove out along the Knaresborough Road until he reached the working-class quarter of Starbeck. He knew every twist and turn of the route, having practised on numerous dummy runs during his exploratory visit to Harrogate earlier in the year.

Nearly there now, he thought, driving along Starbeck's main street. About twenty minutes before, he had rung Jemail Zubi on the mobile so that he and the Turkish waiter, Tamaz Akmedov, would be ready when he arrived at the warehouse he had leased. He turned off the main street and drove on until he reached an industrial area of small factories and warehouses. A glance at the clock on the dashboard told him that it was twelve o'clock. Good timing, he thought. At twelve on a Saturday morning there shouldn't be too many people around. Handling the truck confidently, he pulled into a small industrial estate and made straight for the warehouse. He passed several workers surrounding a car outside a panel-beater's, but none of them paid much heed to the truck and Majid drove on without making eye contact with any of them.

At the end of the road a pillared entrance led into a long narrow compound, and even as Majid steered the truck in between the pillars he saw the gates of the warehouse sliding open to receive him. Slowing a little, he drove into the warehouse, pleased to see Jemail and Tamaz following his instructions by sliding closed the gates immediately the full length of the truck was inside the building. He drove forward as far as he could, wanting to allow space behind the truck so that they could position the ramp and off-load the precious cargo. He reached the end wall, braked smoothly and applied the handbrake.

Jemail and Tamaz came forward to greet him, Jemail smiling broadly, Tamaz a little more diffidently, and Majid allowed himself a wide smile in return. He had, after all, single-handedly acquired the equipment and transported it without a hitch all the way from the Cooley Peninsula. Pleased with himself, he switched off the engine, jumped down from the cabin of the truck and went forward to embrace his comrades.

Laura put the phone down excitedly, grabbed her car-keys from the desk and made for the door of her flat. Almost an hour and a half had elapsed since the news bulletin on the radio, but her friend in the telephone company had been out at lunch when she rang. Laura had left a message requesting her to call on an urgent matter, then had waited restlessly until finally the call had been returned. She had had to do a little persuading to get her friend to break the rules, but eventually she had acquired the address to match the phone number.

Laura left her apartment block now, quickly unlocked her car, then drove in the direction of the M50 motorway. The address she had been given was for an apartment out in Tallaght, in the western suburbs, and Laura was anxious to get over there as quickly as possible.

She drove at a faster pace than usual along the motorway, constantly having to balance her desire to get there speedily against the risk of being stopped for speeding – the very last thing she wanted today. The Saturday traffic wasn't too heavy however, and she reached the main street of Tallaght within thirty minutes of getting the address.

She pulled in off the road and swiftly scanned a map of the city, seeking the particular part of Tallaght in which the apartment block was located. It took her a minute or two to find it, then she cast the map onto the front passenger seat, slipped the car into gear and sped off down the road again. She was conscious of the fact that time could be of the essence, but as she approached the entrance to the apartment complex she forced herself to slow to a leisurely pace. No point drawing attention to herself if the police were already here, she reasoned.

She pulled into the carpark, taking in her surroundings. It was a medium-sized complex, reasonably well maintained. She drove towards a vacant parking space. Leaving the engine ticking over, she looked carefully about her, checking the area to her rear in the driving mirrors. There was no sign of the police, either in marked or unmarked cars. In fact, there was no activity of any kind in the carpark and she switched off the engine and applied the handbrake. She looked again at the address she had been given, and identified the apartment block to her left as the one she sought, but she didn't get out of the car. She knew that to take this any further might be

166

dangerous, and she paused, undecided what to do. Perhaps she ought simply to wait until the police arrived. She would still be the first reporter on the scene, probably still get some kind of scoop. But her journalistic instincts told her that she had the initiative here and that she should act while she still had it. On the other hand, anyone involved with Boyle and O'Donnell was likely to be dangerous, and going to the home of such a person in the aftermath of the murder could be foolish. Then again, sometimes chances had to be grasped. Her heroes Woodford and Bernstein wouldn't have cracked the Watergate case had they opted to leave well enough alone. She hesitated another moment, then suddenly made her mind up. She reached for her car-keys, got out of the vehicle and made for the apartment complex.

Majid sped southwards along the motorway. The lunchtime traffic was a little heavier than when he had travelled in the opposite direction earlier in the morning, but he was happy enough to be simply one more truck in a stream of cars and trucks heading towards Manchester. He had considered keeping the vehicle hidden in the warehouse until the mission was over, but had decided against it. Apart from taking up too much space, there was his desire not to retain so tangible a link with the two men he had killed. Better to be rid of the empty truck and, if the link were made between it and Boyle and O'Donnell, let the police try to trace it to republican contacts the men might have had in the Greater Manchester region. With a population of about seven million people, that would keep them busily engaged and on the wrong track.

Majid had carefully scrubbed the truck interior clean of all bloodstains the previous day in the hours between arriving in Dublin and awaiting the night sailing of the car ferry. He was satisfied that little would remain by way of forensic evidence and he would make certain that all of his own fingerprints were removed before disposing of the vehicle.

Despite being a little stiff after driving from Liverpool to Harrogate, he had resisted the temptation to dally with Jemail and Tamaz. After unloading the truck he had chatted with them over a quick cup of coffee, then freshened up in the toilet of the warehouse and had been back on the road thirty minutes after his arrival.

He had been pleased to note that the morale of the two men seemed to be good, and that they had operated smoothly on the truck's arrival and departure, opening the gates efficiently from inside the warehouse without showing themselves, lest anyone outside should glance in their direction.

He had known that Jemail could be counted on, the three years they had spent together in an Israeli jail having provided lots of examples of his tenacity and willingness to take on the system. He knew that Jemail had been a guerrilla fighter since the Israeli invasion of his native Lebanon, in 1982, when as a sixteen-year-old he had thrown rocks against the advancing Israeli tanks. Both his weaponry and his tactics had advanced a lot since then, but his reservoir of raw courage had remained unchanged. Taken in conjunction with his zealous hatred for Israel and its Western allies, it had made him Majid's first choice when seeking an accomplice for the mission.

Jemail was now thirty-four years of age, an experienced operator capable of ruthless efficiency, yet a pleasant companion when not in action. He was well-versed in bomb-making and unarmed combat, was a good marksman, and as a consequence of his almost child-like passion for playing amateur soccer, was also highly fit.

Majid had noted that Tamaz Akemov, although sixteen years older than Jemail, had deferred to the younger man as they all sipped coffees back in the warehouse. He had been pleased that the waiter hadn't demurred when asked to assist today. Tamaz was a slightly wistful-looking man of about fifty, diffident in manner but with an engaging, if infrequent, smile. His primary function of obtaining employment at the Conference Centre had long since been achieved, and Majid was pleased at how well he appeared to have settled into a quiet, strictly self-contained life in the six months that he had lived in Harrogate. Probably kept going in the expectation of riches beyond his dreams, Majid surmised. The important thing now would be to ensure that he kept his nerve. Majid had already decided to keep the operational details from him so that Tamaz could concentrate simply on being a waiter. Only coming up to the day of the assault would Majid brief him on what precisely he needed to do.

Majid drove on south now, his eyes scanning the roadside as he reached the outskirts of Manchester. After a few minutes, he saw what he wanted and he flicked on his indicator and turned off the inside lane onto an exit from the motorway. He followed the slip road bringing him to a busy motorway café and service station. As he cruised slowly forward into a large carpark, he noted that it was filled with vans and cars in the area nearest the restaurant, and trucks and articulated vehicles further back from the road.

He drove into the truck area, seeking a parking place that would enable him to point the truck so that its rear doors were facing away from the motorway and the restaurant. Because the parking lot was large there were ample spaces at its extremity, but Majid wanted to ensure that the truck didn't stand out by being parked on its own. Instead he manoeuvred it through a fuller area, eventually guiding it into a vacant space in a line of other trucks. He came to a halt, switched off the engine and applied the handbrake. He glanced out the windscreen with apparent casualness, then, happy that no one was watching, took the keys from the ignition and wiped all of the controls with a linen handkerchief. Still using the handkerchief, he unlocked the door, wiped the lock and handle thoroughly, then swung the door open and jumped down to the ground.

He stretched his limbs as though having finished a long drive, all the while checking surreptitiously that nobody was watching him. Satisfied that he was unobserved, he went to the rear of the truck, opened the back doors and quickly lowered the ramp as silently as possible. Moving swiftly, he rolled the Honda down the ramp, then pulled it up onto its stand, taking care to keep it shielded from view behind the body of the truck. He climbed back into the vehicle, pulled up the ramp, then used the handkerchief again to remove his fingerprints from anything he had touched. A quick glance about satisfied him that nothing had been missed. He stooped down, picked up his crash-helmet and donned it. He pulled the visor down to cover his face, then jumped down from the truck and closed the rear doors. A final look around assured him that no-one was about; then he wiped the handles of the truck's rear door before slipping the handkerchief into his pocket. He took a last look at the truck, one among many now, and reasoned that there was every chance it would stay parked here for quite a while without anyone paying attention to it.

Pleased with himself, he slipped the key into the Honda's ignition, then kick-started the bike. The engine didn't start, and Majid felt a quick flutter of anxiety. He tried again, kicking harder, and this time also it failed to catch. Suddenly his pulses were racing and with murder in his heart he thought of the idiot from whom he had bought it. *Engine sings like a bird. Service it meself!*

Majid breathed deeply, forcing himself to be calm. Perhaps he had just given it too much choke, flooded the engine. After all, it had started all right the day he had driven to the Cooley Peninsula. He closed the choke and kick-started again. This time it sounded healthier, but still it didn't catch. He swallowed hard, forcing from his mind the problems that would arise if he didn't have transport to take him away from here. He waited a moment, then put it on half-choke. Holding his breath, he kicked again. This time the engine caught. Majid released his breath and swung the bike down from the stand. He drove down to the end of the parking aisle, not wanting to appear suddenly on the Honda from beside the truck that he had abandoned. He turned left, then made his way at

171

moderate speed towards the exit point. He waited until there was a break in the traffic, then made for the motorway without a backward glance.

Laura walked towards the door to the apartment complex, her mind racing. She wasn't sure how she ought to play this, but she had found before that in nerve-wracking situations it was sometimes better to act on the spur of the moment rather than have a plan worked out. Plans tended to suggest dire consequence in the event of their failing and Laura sensed it would be better not to paralyse herself into inaction by too much thought. At the same time she couldn't but feel uneasy at the possible reception she might get if an associate of the murdered men was in the flat right now. She knew she was involving herself with dangerous people, and it would be difficult to argue that coming here at this time was legitimately connected with the article she had written. Then so be it. There was no going back now, she decided, as she reached the entrance door and glanced about her. No close-circuit television, she noted, relieved that at least her visit wasn't being recorded.

Laura paused, gathering her nerve to press the bell for the apartment number her friend had given her. From the conversation she had overheard when Boyle had been on the phone to the apartment owner, she had got the impression that O'Donnell and Boyle would be staying there alone, in which case there might be nobody here now. Then again, she had only heard one side of the conversation – perhaps the owner was going to stay with them. Or had been going away and had returned in the

172

past couple of days. Or had heard of the killings on the news and was making back for the apartment right now . . .

Before she could ponder any further she bit her lip, took a deep breath and pressed the bell. She waited, part of her hoping for a response, part of her fearing it. A moment passed and no answer came. In spite of her nervousness, Laura felt a sense of anti-climax. Maybe a radio was playing loudly, she thought, or they were in the bathroom when the bell had sounded. She reached up and rang the bell a second time. Again she waited, and this time the silence felt more conclusive. She was about to lower her hand from the communications panel when she was startled. A middle-aged woman had turned the corner of the lobby inside the apartment block and was making straight for the door.

Catching Laura's eye, the woman smiled. Laura realised immediately that feeling conspicuous was something that was in her own mind – to the woman she was merely a visitor using the intercom. Before she had time to weigh up what she was doing, Laura decided to seize the moment. She pretended to be pressing the speaker button with her thumb and leaned forward as though continuing a conversation.

"OK, Mary, thanks . . ." she said, then turned round towards the door as though awaiting her friend to press the buzzer from within her apartment.

It worked perfectly. She had timed it just so that the middle-aged woman would reach the entrance door at that point, and as the woman opened the door Laura smiled in greeting. The woman smiled again and Laura

173

held the door open with one hand and stepped aside, allowing the woman to exit. The woman stepped out, then Laura entered the hall.

It was a three-storey building and, going by the apartment number, Laura realised that the unit she sought was on the second floor. *The unit she sought?* The very idea of what she was about to do was outrageous. Yet even as she ascended the stairs two steps at a time she knew that at the back of her mind all along had been the notion she was now entertaining. She exited from the stairwell and entered a short, carpeted corridor. She found the door marked 217 and stopped beside it. Knock on the door, she thought, maybe the intercom is broken. She did so, but no-one replied to her knock, just as she had expected.

There was only one thing for it, she knew, but she hesitated. It would be breaking the law, it would be putting herself at risk with dangerous people, it would be crossing a Rubicon in every sense. And yet she couldn't come this far and turn back. She had to break in. She looked at the door, assessing it with the eye of a professional. She thought of the many times she had gone out on jobs with her father and she decided that the two locks on this door shouldn't present any great difficulty to a locksmith's daughter. One was a simple Yale lock, the kind she could open with a plastic card; the other was a door-mounted two-lever lock.

She opened her handbag and took out a hair-clip. She stood close to the door so that if anyone were to enter the corridor it would appear as though she were inserting a key into the lock. Instead she slipped the hair-clip into the keyhole and began to move it about as her father had taught her. Her heart was pounding in her chest, but she forced herself to concentrate on the task in hand. Chubby Kennedy had been able to open any such lock in less than twenty seconds and, while less expert than her father, Laura had mastered the intricacies of lock-making back in her early teens.

She jiggled the hair-clip around gently and after what seemed like an age she heard the lock click open. She felt a surge of relief and quickly withdrew the hair-clip, then slipped a credit card into the crevice alongside the Yale lock. Three seconds later she pushed the door open and stepped into the hall. This was the critical moment, she knew. If the apartment had an alarm, the opening of the hall door would be sure to trigger it. Laura waited for the wail, ready to step back into the corridor and walk briskly away. It never came. She breathed out deeply, pushed the hall door closed with her foot and moved down the hallway into the apartment proper.

An open door on her right led into a bathroom and straight ahead she could see what looked like the living-room. Two closed doors on the left were presumably bedrooms, and she realised that despite having rung the apartment's bell and knocked on the front door, it was possible that someone could be in either of the rooms, asleep, or too drunk to have bothered answering her. Gathering her courage, she quickly opened the first door. *Empty*. The second room was also unoccupied, and a relieved Laura closed its door over and made for the living-room.

This was a good-sized room, with a dining-area and galley kitchen off to one side. Immediately Laura walked into it, she was struck by a stale smell of food. She looked about in distaste, noting the discarded convenience-food cartons propped all over the kitchen and the empty beer cans that stood on the coffee table, mantelpiece and floor of the living-room.

She wasn't sure exactly what she was looking for, but seeing a desk and computer screen set up in one corner, she drew nearer. Computer games were scattered across the desk, on which a telephone-cum-answering-machine also stood. She checked the answering machine, but there was no flashing light, nor was there the illuminated display that indicated previously played messages were stored. A scribbling pad lay open on the desk, but to her disappointment the top sheet was blank. *What did you expect? Details of the time and place of the rendezvous with the murderer?* Her eye was caught by a large clock on the wall. 2.20 p.m. She would give herself ten minutes in the apartment. And that was an absolute maximum – for all she knew either the owner or the police could be about to pull up outside.

Thinking of the police, it struck her that she was at the equivalent of a crime scene, even if the murders had taken place somewhere else. It would be essential not to leave any fingerprints. She reached into her pocket and withdrew a handkerchief which she wrapped around her right hand, then she again turned her interest to the desk. What she needed was a diary, or an appointments book. Using her handkerchief-enshrouded hand, she opened each of the drawers of the desk in turn. She found envelopes, stamps, a pornographic magazine, coloured markers, typing paper, spare tippex and a box of floppy discs. She quickly went through the labels on the floppy discs, but all of them seemed to relate either to computer games or a local Gaelic football team.

Where else might someone like Boyle keep a diary? In his bedroom. She crossed the living-room to the hall and entered the first bedroom. A faint, sour smell of sweat hung in the air, and again were empty beer cans littering the floor. The bed was unmade and discarded clothes hung on the backs of chairs. *O'Donnell's room, no question,* she decided. She opened and closed the drawer of his bedside locker, checked the wardrobe, then quickly scanned the rest of the room. Nothing. But then O'Donnell wasn't the decision-maker anyway.

She moved quickly to the second bedroom and went in. Again the bed was unmade, but this room was neater and smelt of aftershave. *Definitely Boyle's room.* As if to confirm it, Laura found a copy of her article on top of his bedside locker. It was heavily edited with a red biro, but she resisted the temptation of checking the scribbled changes that Boyle had inserted in the margins. Taking care not to leave any fingerprints, she checked the drawers of his bedside locker, but all she discovered was a thumb-eared paperback novel about the Vietnam war and a bottle of sleeping pills. Disappointed, she moved to the wardrobe and quickly checked the shelves. Socks, underwear, shirts and sweaters were all she found. She turned on her heel, returned to the living-room and looked about again.

She made for the tiny kitchen, stepping over the spilt cartons as she checked for a possible wall-chart on which a name or an appointment might have been scribbled.

There was no wall-chart or calendar and, despite looking around carefully, Laura could see no scrap of paper that might contain a name or address. She looked across the room to check the clock: 2.25. Five minutes left. She was just about to cross to the computer when she heard the sound of a car pulling to a halt outside. Her already racing heartbeat suddenly accelerated and she felt a trembling in her knees. She ran to the window that looked out over the carpark and saw a stocky man with a shaven head getting out of a car. He seemed to Laura exactly the kind of person to be involved with Boyle and O'Donnell and she immediately regretted her impetuous action in breaking into the apartment. Standing well back from the window, she watched him through the net curtains as he went to the boot of his car. He opened the boot and took out several plastic bags full of groceries, then locked the boot and made for the entrance to the apartment block across the way.

Laura gave a huge sigh of relief, but the incident brought home to her how vulnerable her position was. She had been thinking about turning on the computer in the hope that it might contain a file with names, addresses and phone numbers, but even if the machine didn't have a password that would block her access, she felt now that she couldn't afford the time. She had a niggling thought that she was overlooking something and she stood in the middle of the room trying to think what it was. She glanced again at the clock and saw that it was now 2.27. And then it struck her. *The telephone.* It was a machine similar to her own one at home, which meant that by pressing the recall button it would list the last five numbers dialled. And if Boyle and O'Donnell had arranged to meet the person who killed them, it was possible that they had rung the killer to set it up. Pulling a pen and notepad from her pocket, Laura made for the phone, then pressed the button with her handkerchief. She jotted down the number, then pressed again, continuing until she had all five numbers and the first one had reappeared. She looked at the clock again: 2.28. Time to go.

She slipped the pen and notebook back into her pocket, then looked around to make sure that everything was exactly as she had found it. Satisfied that she had disturbed nothing, she walked down the hall, wiped both bedroom door handles with the handkerchief, closed the apartment door gently after her, and made for the stairs. She descended two steps at a time and reached the lobby without meeting anyone, then stepped cautiously outside. There was still no police presence and the carpark was deserted. Moving at a moderate pace, she went to her car, started the engine and drove towards the exit.

Majid queued at the ticket window in Leeds railway station, pleased at how smoothly things had gone. He had found his way from the motorway service station to the centre of Manchester without difficulty, and once in the city centre it had been a simple matter to locate the train station. He had stayed on the Honda however, driving about until he had found a back street in a slightly run-down area. Satisfied that he was unobserved, he had parked the motorbike at the kerb, left the keys in the ignition and walked away. He had originally toyed with the idea of keeping the motorbike, then dismissed it on the grounds that driving around Harrogate on a bike with Irish registration plates might attract attention. Instead he had walked away along the back street, keeping the helmet on just in case anyone was watching unbeknownst to him.

He reckoned that within an hour or two the bike would very likely be stolen, after which its Irish registration plates would no doubt be replaced with false ones. He had disposed of the helmet on the way back towards the station, casually slipping it into the bushes of a small park that he passed. Then he had continued on foot to the train station. Once in Manchester's busy Piccadilly station he had felt better, satisfied that the motorcyclist who had left the truck on the city outskirts had now vanished, his place taken by one more anonymous traveller amongst the thousands using the rail network.

He had taken the first available train from Manchester to Leeds, buying a ticket for that leg of his journey only. It meant purchasing another ticket now for the trip from Leeds to Harrogate, but Majid regarded it as basic fieldcraft never to leave any more of a trail than necessary when on a mission.

He reached the top of the queue and the man behind the ticket window looked at him.

"Sir?"

"Harrogate, please, day return." No need to advertise Harrogate as his final destination by buying a single, he thought.

"Four-eighty, please, sir."

Majid proffered a twenty-pound note.

"You wouldn't have anything smaller, sir? Bit low on change at the moment."

Majid suppressed a flicker of irritation. He should have had smaller change, shouldn't have done anything to bring attention, however fleeting, to himself. "Sorry," he said, smiling warmly, "I've nothing smaller."

"Not to worry," said the ticket-seller, taking the twenty and handing back the ticket and the change. "There you are, sir."

"Thank you." Majid moved away from the counter and started across the concourse towards the platforms. There was a train leaving for Harrogate in ten minutes, he noted, which meant that in another hour he should be safely back with Jemail and Tamaz.

No, he suddenly thought, chastened a little by the incident with the change. *Make no assumptions on safety. You're on a mission, so anticipate the worst, expect the unexpected, and stay alert.*

Satisfied with how things had gone, but on his guard against complacency, he made his way towards the ticket barrier.

Laura still couldn't believe what she had done. The drive home from Tallaght was a haze, and it was only now, as she sat at the desk in her study, that the full realisation of the risks she had taken hit her. She found her hand trembling when she recalled the moment she had heard the car stopping outside the apartment – it could so easily have been the owner of the unit. Yet despite the delayed reaction of shock, part of her was still on a high. She knew she had taken a big risk, knew she had broken the law too, but there was no denying the buzz that came with having been daring enough to seize the initiative.

There was only one problem, and though she had put it to the back of her mind all the way home from Tallaght, it couldn't be avoided any longer. She had to ring the numbers she had copied from the phone in the apartment. Otherwise the risks involved in the break-in would be for nothing. Yet if she rang the numbers and one of them *was* the person who had killed Boyle and O'Donnell she would be drawing herself to the attention of a murderer. No scoop, however sensational, was worth having your throat slashed. On the other hand, it wouldn't be necessary to identify herself to the person she called. And the telephone line in the apartment was unlisted – she mostly used her mobile for business communication – so even if she rang someone who had caller identification her number wouldn't show up.

Before she could be swayed by any further objections, she reached for the phone, activated the automatic taping mechanism and dialled the first number on her list. The phone rang at the other end, and Laura swallowed hard as she waited for it to be answered.

"Hello, *Pronto Pizza!*"

"Oh . . . I'm very sorry . . . wrong number," said Laura.

"You're all right. Sure you don't fancy a pizza while you have me?"

In spite of her tension Laura smiled briefly. "No, thanks. Bye."

"See ye."

She hung up, then dialled the second number listed. She waited a moment, then went through her wrong-number routine again on getting a local video-rental shop. The third number was a porn line, and when the fourth turned out to be a bookie's shop Laura had to smile wryly. *Some life these guys led* . . . The smile died on her lips however as she realised that that she was using the past tense, and that the men who had called these numbers had been brutally murdered.

She hesitated before calling the last number. It was for a mobile, and she knew that if the killer had given Boyle and O'Donnell a phone number it was more likely to be a mobile than a landline. Part of her wanted the number to be innocuous while another part knew that she would be disappointed if that were the case.

Her heart pounding, she dialled the number. It rang three times, then a man answered.

"Hello?"

He sounded surprised, Laura thought fleetingly, as though he weren't expecting to be called. She took a breath to steady herself and was pleased at how cool she sounded when she spoke. "Hi. I was asked to give you a call . . ."

"Who is this?"

"It's Allison," Laura answered, using the first name of the dentist she had visited the previous week.

"I think you have the wrong number," said the man.

He sounded foreign, Laura thought. She could hear announcements going on in the background and she thought he must be speaking from some kind of public place, perhaps an airport or a bus station.

"No," she answered slowly, "I think I have the right number: 085 7359005."

"Boarding, sir, platform seven," she heard another voice say at the end of the telephone line, followed by her man answering "all right" in a distracted fashion.

A train station, she decided, then the man was speaking directly to her again.

"Who asked you to call?"

"A concerned friend."

"There's been some mistake."

He was about to go, Laura could hear it in his voice. *Get his attention!* "Obviously there's been a mistake – and Boyle and O'Donnell made it!"

There was a silence, and Laura was struck by his lack of response. *If he'd never heard of Boyle and O'Donnell why didn't he say so, or ask who they were?*

"Will you just tell me one thing?" she asked, wanting to keep him talking.

"What?"

"Why were they killed?"

There was no response, then Laura heard the second voice, presumably that of the porter saying, "You'll have to board, sir."

"All right!" she heard the man answering before he spoke directly to her one final time. "You've got the wrong number," he said, then the line went dead.

Laura sat unmoving at her desk, then she breathed out and put the phone down. Her mouth was dry and her pulses were racing and she knew one thing for sure. She had rung the *right* number. This man was lying. He knew Boyle and O'Donnell – he had spoken to them the day before they died. In fact he could have been the last person ever to speak to either of them on the phone. And there was no getting away from it, he could well have been the person who murdered them.

Laura felt a shiver go up her spine at the thought and she wondered again at the wisdom of what she had done. Too late for that, she thought, frightened by the world she had just entered, yet thrillingly aware that there would be no turning back now.

"Serves the bastards right," said Carrow. "Couldn't happen to two nicer blokes."

The afternoon sunlight had made the command room in Harrogate police station warm and stuffy, and Carrow's animated pleasure at the news of the killing of the two IRA men contrasted with the subdued demeanour of Mathieson and Thompson. Penny knew that both the other men were aware that Carrow's brother had been killed in the early seventies while serving with the army in Northern Ireland, and she realised that they were making allowances for his attitude.

"Still a murder, Len," said Thompson gently.

"Yeah – of two murderous bastards! Nothing to lose sleep over in my book . . ."

Penny saw that Thompson was about to reply, but instead he stopped himself.

"Anyway, it happened outside our jurisdiction," said Mathieson. "Nothing to do with us."

"All terrorists are the enemy," said Carrow. "Anything to do with them has to do with us."

"I think just now we've enough on our plate," said Mathieson.

"Loads on our plate all right," agreed Carrow, "but bugger-all progress in dealing with it."

"I don't think that's quite accurate," said Mathieson. "We've done a painstaking analysis of the hotel and Conference Centre, and any conceivable source of threat."

"We haven't found our man. Haven't arrested anyone, haven't even questioned anyone . . ."

Penny felt like reminding Carrow that he too was part of the investigation. As a junior officer she couldn't make such a point, but she sensed that Carrow was waiting for either Thompson or Mathieson to tackle him. Whereupon she knew he would return to his hobby-horse regarding how much time was being wasted poring over hotel registration records. A computer file was being created of Middle-Eastern males between the ages of twenty-five and fifty who had registered in any of Harrogate's over one hundred hotels, and although Penny wasn't sure that the effort to pinpoint a previous visit to Harrogate by their target would reveal anything, she still felt it was worth pursuing in the absence of anything else.

"Any further developments on the personnel security checks?" asked Carrow.

"Yes," answered Mathieson. "Our Romanian kitchen porter seems to be clean."

"Yeah?"

"Still looking into it, but he seems OK."

"What about the Sudanese chef and the Turkish waiter?"

"Having trouble getting reliable information from the Sudan," replied Mathieson, "but it's being pursued."

"And the Turk?"

"So far so good. No criminal record, never came to the attention of the authorities on a political level."

"Where's he from?" asked Carrow.

"Urfa. It's in the south, over towards Syria."

"Yeah?" The Special Branch officer looked at Mathieson with interest. "Could he be a Kurd?"

Mathieson shook his head. "We don't think so – he's never been known to have links to the PPK."

"Could have relations or in-laws that do."

"Possibly," agreed Mathieson. "We're making more detailed enquiries. For the moment though he seems to be kosher."

"Right. Still nothing from your chums in Mossad, I presume?"

Penny knew that Carrow was asking only to needle Mathieson and to underline the fact the MI5 man's Israeli contacts hadn't yet drawn up a photographic file of Iraqis who had come to their attention or been held prisoner by them in recent years.

"Obviously, if there's any development there you'll be apprised immediately," answered Mathieson curtly.

"Good," said Carrow. "Because someone, somewhere, needs to come up trumps."

Penny saw Mathieson's jaw tighten in irritation. "Quite," he said, and she realised that he was more rattled than she had thought. Presumably he had come under pressure when reporting to his superiors in London earlier in the day.

She looked at his tired expression and found herself feeling a little sorry for him. This evening she would be meeting Shane and Aisling, when they got to Leeds. She had tonight and all of tomorrow to enjoy with her husband and daughter. Thompson too would be spending more time with his grandchildren over the weekend if nothing broke with the case. But Mathieson had no family to visit, no-one to be unequivocally on his side and to bolster him for the challenging week that lay ahead. Still, that was Mathieson's own choice, she knew. His devotion – obsession, some would say – regarding his career had cost him his first marriage, and had come between him and his one-time relationship with Penny. And yet she couldn't help but feel sympathetic now, knowing as she did that he was feeling the heat and that he would be the one to carry the brunt of the blame if a terrorist outrage occurred.

Her own career would hardly prosper on the back of such an event either, she reflected, although such matters would pale into insignificance if they failed in their task and their quarry visited carnage on Harrogate.

Her thoughts were interrupted by Mathieson bringing the briefing to a close, and she quickly gathered her notes and rose from the table with the others.

"I'll call you if there's anything, Penny," said Thompson as they followed Carrow and Mathieson out of the command centre and towards the locker rooms "Otherwise, relax and enjoy your weekend."

"Thanks, Chief."

"Come back refreshed for Monday morning," he said. "Something tells me it's going to be a tough week!"

"OK, see you Monday."

She turned and entered the locker room, Thompson's words playing in her mind. This time next week the first of the dignitaries would be arriving in Harrogate, and if progress wasn't made by then it wouldn't just be a tough week – it might well be a disaster. Chastened by the thought, she began to change, knowing that sooner rather than later they needed to get the break they so desperately wanted.

Majid sat staring out the window as the train sped through the Yorkshire countryside. The route to Harrogate went through pleasant, rolling farmland, but despite appearing to gaze with interest out the window, Majid only half-noticed it. Instead he listened to the conversation of his fellow passengers, training his ear to become in tune with the way English was spoken in this part of Britain. It was quite different to the English that he was familiar with from the south of England and from the BBC World Service. His own English was fluent, and he thought with gratitude of his father, who had sent him to English classes in a private school in Baghdad. That had been in the early eighties when Iraq had been open to Western influences, and his father, with the pragmatism of a successful trader, had recognised that English was an important tool in the world of commerce. As it happened Majid had later declined to go into the family business, opting instead to study medicine, but the good grounding in English that his father had paid for hadn't been in vain, he thought wryly.

What would his father think now, he wondered, if he knew that the fluency in English he had prescribed for his son was to be used as a weapon against the very people whose language it was? Hard to know, thought Majid. His father had died of a heart attack in 1989, when Majid was still only nineteen and before they had really established an adult-to-adult relationship.

Politically his father had been a moderate, bending whichever way the wind blew and at heart more interested in trade than in politics. They had never discussed religion, but, looking back on it, Majid suspected that his father was probably similar to himself in harbouring a distaste for religious zealotry. Although the family would have been seen as practising Muslims, Majid knew that in his own case, and quite likely in his father's also, being a Muslim was a social and cultural identity as distinct from a genuinely religious one. Certainly, when his father had died prematurely, Majid had angrily refused to accept his mother's tearful acceptance of their loss as the will of Allah.

So, what would the older man have thought of his son leading a terrorist attack on a European town? Probably that it was too extreme a response and much too personally dangerous. But his father hadn't lived to see all of the family die unnecessarily at the hands of the West. Nor had he languished for five years in an Israeli jail while the Zionists' American allies underpinned Israeli arrogance and belligerence.

Just then Majid's train of thought was disturbed by a fellow passenger ringing someone on a mobile phone to arrange a lift at Harrogate station. There in about ten minutes, the woman said on the phone, and Majid realised that he had better cease his musings and make his own arrangements now.

He slipped his mobile from his pocket, turned it on and rang a number. He had instructed Jemail to await his call in the rented warehouse and he was pleased to hear the Lebanese answering on the first ring.

"Hello?"

"I'll be in Harrogate in ten minutes," Majid said softly, speaking in English. The chances of a nearby passenger recognising Arabic, had he spoken it, were slim, but Majid was determined to do nothing to draw attention to his status as a foreigner.

"I'll be at the station," answered Jemail. "Everything go well?"

"Yes. See you then."

He hung up, then immediately switched off the mobile. Apart from the brief call to Jemail he had kept it turned off all the time since the unexpected telephone call that he had received in Leeds. He had been thrown at first by the woman calling him and asking about the deaths of Boyle and O'Donnell, but on reflection it hadn't seemed so strange. The two dissident republicans hadn't deported themselves in a professional manner, and it would hardly be surprising if they had recorded his phone number without subsequently erasing it. He just hoped that they hadn't left any evidence regarding the equipment that they had acquired for him. Although even if they had, the truck was now disposed of and everything else was safely locked up in the warehouse. Still, he didn't like loose threads and the woman being able to ring him had been disturbing.

He thought of it again now, running the telephone conversation in his head. *Why were they killed?* she had

191

asked. But no matter how you looked at it, in reality she couldn't have known that he had killed them. Probably just someone taking a chance, seeing what she might get by way of response. But who was the woman? And had she uncovered anything by way of his response? Hardly – he had given no hint of recognising the names of Boyle and O'Donnell. Though perhaps he should have actually said he didn't know who she was talking about. Still, he had stuck with his story of a wrong number and even if the woman had been a police officer she had no way of knowing where he was now. Provided he kept the mobile switched off until he met Jemail, and then disposed of the sim card, that should be the last link broken. He sat back in his seat, trying to see a flaw in his reasoning but unable to find any. Then the train slowed on approaching Harrogate and Majid rose with other passengers, eager to be on his way.

"This better be good, Kid!"

"I'm sorry to disturb your fishing, Mac," said Laura into the phone, "but I really have to talk to you."

"So talk."

"Not when we're on mobiles. I need to meet you, Mac, it's urgent."

She heard the sigh in the Deputy Editor's voice. "All right. Do you know the Leinster Aqueduct?"

"Eh, no, I don't think so . . ."

"It's where the Grand Canal crosses the Liffey. Drive to Sallins, take the track along the right-hand side of the canal for about half a mile and you'll see my car parked at a bend off the track. Park there and walk on for about five minutes. I'll be the guy with the fishing rod and the exasperated expression."

"Thanks, Mac. And look, I'm sorry again for having to disturb you."

"What the hell, it's only the first Saturday night I've taken off in a month. When will you be here?"

"I'll leave straight away. Say about an hour."

"All right, Kid. See you then."

"OK. Bye."

Forty-five minutes after the telephone call, Laura was negotiating the bumpy track alongside the canal, rehearsing yet again how she would put her proposal to her editor. It wouldn't be easy, she knew. Like any editor with good instincts Mac would want to make the most of the exclusive interview she had done with Boyle and O'Donnell, an interview that was now hugely topical in the aftermath of their brutal murder. To get him to hold off on that, she would have to hook him with the possibility of something even more sensational – a difficult task, bearing in mind the nebulous nature of what she had to offer. Still she had to try. All her instincts told her that the man she had rung on the mobile number simply had to be pursued.

Laura slowed her car, recognising Mac's vehicle parked up ahead. She swung right, leaving the track and bumping across a grass verge to park alongside Mac's station wagon. It was the only other vehicle there, and Laura quickly locked the doors of her own car, then started along the towpath.

It was a humid evening and a hazy September sun was starting to set, bathing the trees and bushes along the canal bank with a warm glow. She rounded a bend in the canal, smacking away the midges and other insects whose presence, she presumed, accounted for the lack of evening strollers. She knew that Mac was a fanatical fisherman however and it came as no surprise to see him in the distance casting his line, oblivious to the insects.

He looked up as she drew closer, gave a quick wave, then reeled in his line.

"Catch anything?" asked Laura.

"Couple of trout."

"Big ones?"

"Anorexic. Threw them back."

"Ah . . ."

Mac cast again, then placed his rod in a holder and turned to Laura. "Have a seat," he said, indicating the stone wall of the aqueduct that carried the narrow course of the canal over the waters of the Liffey far below.

"Interesting place," said Laura. "Is this a favourite spot?"

"Yes," answered Mac, sitting beside her on the wall. "Odd river, the Liffey," he said, indicating its turbulent waters below them. "It rises only fifteen miles from Dublin but takes ninety-two miles to reach the sea." He turned back. "I'm sure you'll be more direct."

Laura recognised her cue for ending the small talk and faced her editor. "OK, I'll give you the part you won't like first."

"Let's have it."

"I'd like you to hold off on printing my interview with Boyle."

"You're kidding me?"

"No," said Laura.

"The murder is a big story – it makes your piece really hot."

"Granted. But an exclusive interview with a murder victim will stay hot for quite a while."

"And what's to be gained by not publishing now?"

"I think there may be an even bigger story here."

Mac raised an eyebrow. "Is this the part I'm supposed to like?"

"Could be. I got hold of a phone number dialled by Boyle and O'Donnell the day before they were killed."

"Whose number?"

"I don't know as yet."

"Laura –"

"But I think it could be the person who killed them."

She had Mac's interest now – she had to try to press her advantage. "That's why if we wait with the interview –"

"Forget the interview, let's stay with this. How did you get the phone number?"

"You don't want to know," said Laura.

"I do."

"Mac – you don't. Please . . . don't ask me."

Laura saw the editor hesitate and she decided to forge ahead. "Look, the funerals of Boyle and O'Donnell will be next week. If we hold the article we can still run it to major effect after that. If we run it now, the police will probably want to interview me as one of the last people to have dealings with them."

"What's wrong with that?"

"It won't advance the investigation, but it will hamper me."

"How will it hamper you?" asked Mac.

"It would mean I'd have to stay in Ireland."

"Were you planning to go somewhere else?"

"Hoping to," answered Laura. "With your backing."

"Really?"

"This number I got, it's definitely one of the last ones Boyle or O'Donnell called before they were killed. It's a mobile number, and I rang it."

"And?"

"I had a strange conversation with the man who answered. He sounded surprised to be called, and I thought – maybe the only ones he gave the number to were Boyle and O'Donnell."

"What did he say?" asked Mac with interest.

"That I had a wrong number. I hadn't though. And when I asked him why Boyle and O'Donnell had been killed there was this stunned silence."

"I'll say – especially if it *was* a wrong number."

"It wasn't, Mac. I even called the number out to him and he didn't deny it. He also never asked who Boyle and O'Donnell were, or said he'd never heard of them."

"Right . . ."

"This guy knew them, Mac, I'm sure of it. He was one of the last people to speak to them – maybe the very last."

"You're saying you think he killed them?"

"I think it's quite possible."

"What did he sound like?"

"Foreign, reasonably young . . . he had good English."

"Probably not an internal IRA thing then."

"No, I'd say they were into some kind of maverick activity. But there could be a terrorist link."

"How so?"

Laura hesitated, knowing that if she presented this the wrong way it could sound flimsy and half-baked. "I taped the conversation. It sounded like he was in a train station when I rang him – I heard a porter urging him to board and there were announcements going on in the background."

"Where's the terrorist link in that?"

"I'm not absolutely certain there is one. But here's the thing. Afterwards I got the tape into a filtering programme – to try and separate out some of the different sounds."

"I thought Declan was off doing sound for a film in Prague?"

"He is, but he has lots of sound gear in the apartment. I've picked up a fair bit watching him work at home. Anyway, I isolated some of the announcements to try and find out what train was leaving from platform seven."

"Your mystery man's platform?"

"Yes. It was going to Harrogate."

Mac brushed a buzzing insect away, then looked at Laura questioningly. "You say that as though it should explain everything to me."

"At the end of next week all the Foreign Ministers in the European Union will be attending a two-day conference there. As will the American Secretary of State."

"So?"

"Boyle and O'Donnell were terrorists. If this guy was linked to them, he may well be a terrorist too. So here's a gathering in Harrogate that would make the vast majority of the world's terrorists drool at the mouth. And our man is going to Harrogate . . ."

"Lot of imponderables there, Kid . . ."

"Some, but if our man is a terrorist, going to Harrogate just now is a hell of a coincidence."

"But can you really see the Continuity IRA wanting to hit EU Foreign Ministers?"

"Who knows? Maybe Boyle and O'Donnell were freelancing."

"Then why would your guy kill them?"

"Could be they fell out over something, maybe he wanted to silence them, who can say?"

Mac looked thoughtfully out across the darkening countryside, then turned back to Laura. "So what is it exactly you're proposing?"

"Let me try to trace this guy. I presume the *Clarion* would consider sending someone to cover the conference anyway. Let me do it. If my hunch is right, there could be an explosive story here, no pun intended." Laura smiled briefly, but Mac didn't smile back.

"I was in Harrogate once," he said. "There must be fifty – sixty thousand people there. You're proposing to find a man you just heard on the end of a phone line, in a population that size?"

"He's foreign, he's male, he's aged between twenty and forty, I'd say. It can be narrowed down quite a bit."

"Not that easily. You can't just earmark every foreigner you see and start checking them out."

"I'd start with the delegates. Being a *Clarion* representative gives me access. I could legitimately request the list of diplomats from each country. Then start checking the delegates of countries that have unrest –

Spain with the Basques, that sort of thing . . . try to find some terrorist angle, some link."

Mac breathed out. "It's really iffy . . ."

"But absolute dynamite if I'm right. Think of the scoop we could have, Mac!"

"I still feel the likelihood of finding this guy is really slim. Chances are he'll have nothing to do with the diplomats who'll be attending."

"Field agents often work under diplomatic cover, Mac. And who knows what intelligence people will be there? There could be bent agents, guys on the take from terrorists."

"Even if there were, Laura, even if you did find your man – then what?"

"Then we've got a brilliant story."

"Then you could end up dead – if he's the ruthless killer you're depicting."

"I'll be careful, Mac, really careful. I wouldn't tackle him personally. I'd notify the authorities."

"I still think it's a needle in a haystack."

"Even if it is a bit, what have we got to lose?"

"Other than time, money and effort?"

"OK, OK, three scenarios, Mac," said Laura. "A) I go there and I find him: scoop of the year. Agreed?"

Mac nodded. "Agreed."

"B) I go but don't find him, and he attacks the conference. You have a reporter on the spot who's already on the story. So you're hardly losing there."

"And C)," interjected Mac, "and the most likely one. The *Clarion* underwrites the cost of a complete wild-goose-chase."

"Then I do you some colour pieces on Harrogate – I'd do them anyway while I was there. But when I come back, we still have the Boyle interview – it'll still be hot. And if we hold off printing it now I won't have to stay here making statements to the Guards – and we might just get a sensational story. What do you say?"

Mac bit his lip and looked down at the swirling waters of the Liffey. Laura held her breath, resisting the temptation to argue her case further, then Mac turned back to her.

"All right then," he said. "Nothing ventured . . ."

"Thanks, Mac, I appreciate it."

"When did you want to go?"

"Pretty quickly. There's a flight to Leeds tomorrow evening I could catch."

"OK. But I want you to keep me posted regularly."

"Will do."

"And, Laura. This is really important . . ."

"What?"

"Be careful. If your hunch is right, you'd be dealing with very dangerous people. I don't want a dead hero on my hands."

"I promise I'll be careful, Mac."

"See that you are. There's also the matter of the police. If they find the interview in Boyle's house they may want to question you."

"Tell them I'll be back in Ireland when the Harrogate conference is over."

"If you uncover anything in England that's pertinent to the Boyle and O'Donnell investigation, you should pass it on to the Guards. Especially if there's any chance it might be linked to an assassination bid."

"Right . . ."

Mac smiled briefly. "After you've written up the story, of course."

Laura smiled in return. "Of course."

"OK. Keep all your bills and receipts – and don't stay in the penthouse suite."

"Sure. Look, I'll leave you to your fishing. And thanks again, Mac!

"Yeah . . ."

Laura got down from the aqueduct wall and Mac followed suit.

"Oh and Laura?"

"Yes."

"Your father was a locksmith, right?"

"Right." *He knew she'd broken in somewhere to get the telephone number.*

"I hadn't forgotten."

"No."

"So let me say it again. Tread very carefully on this one."

"I will."

"Do. Because the *Clarion* can only shield you to a degree. After that . . ."

"I understand . . ."

"Good hunting," said Mac, then he picked up his fishing-rod.

"Thanks, Mac," answered Laura. Then she nodded farewell and set off briskly towards her car.

8

Sunday September 17th 2000

"So, ten whole days till you see me again – how will you bear it?" asked Shane.

"Stoically," answered Penny with a grin.

They were strolling across the sunlit lawns of a public park near her parents' house in Leeds, their gentle pace dictated by Aisling who was stepping out happily in a baby-walker. It was the most relaxed that Penny had felt since her arrival in Harrogate the previous week and she was savouring the time with her husband and child. She had made love with Shane the night before, and again this morning, and she felt close to him now as they enjoyed the autumnal splendour of the park.

She wondered if Shane still harboured the unease that she had sensed previously about her having to spend so much time with her old lover. Certainly he hadn't revealed any hint of jealousy since their reunion last night, but Penny had been careful nonetheless to play down her involvement with the security chief over the previous days. Shane had always been supportive of her career, notwithstanding the difficult hours and all the other pressures that went with her rank, and she felt that the least she owed him in return was the reassurance that he had nothing to fear from her old flame. At the same time were she explicitly to make that point, it might seem like protesting too much, and Shane might think she still found Mathieson attractive.

And if she were honest, she would have to admit that despite the age difference and all that had happened in the past, she did still find herself attracted to Mathieson. It was never going to go anywhere, and she wouldn't voice it to a soul, but she knew deep down that part of the reason she felt sympathy for Mathieson as he tried to cope with the pressure back in Harrogate was because she still found him appealing.

Still, soon she would be back in Windsor with Shane and all of this would be a memory. Perhaps it would be better simply to love Shane – as she wholeheartedly did – and make no reference to Mathieson other than in his role in the current operation.

"I was thinking a bit about your problem," said Shane, breaking her reverie.

"Oh . . . which problem?"

Shane smiled. "How many do you have?"

Penny felt a twinge of guilt at the warmth of her husband's smile, then she dismissed it. She loved her husband more than she had ever loved Colin Mathieson, and she would never betray him – it was time to dismiss the kind of thoughts she had been entertaining.

"I've lots of problems on this operation," she answered easily. "Which one do you mean?"

"Getting some kind of an ID for your target."

"Ah, that problem." She looked at Shane. "This probably isn't really fair though, is it?"

"What?"

"Our precious time off, and you're getting sucked into police matters."

"I think I've been sucked into police matters since . . . well, since you first threw yourself at me," he answered with a grin.

"*Threw* myself at you?"

"Well, practically. Anyway, I don't mind talking about the case if you don't."

"Fine," said Penny, changing direction to follow Aisling's erratic strides in her baby-walker, then turning back to Shane. "So, what are your thoughts then?"

"It's nothing mind-blowing, but one thing did strike me."

"Yeah?"

"The computer searches are stymied by the lack of a name or a face for this character, right?"

"Right."

"But the Israelis haven't come up with either, despite MI5 asking for their help."

"Not so far, no," answered Penny.

"Then maybe MI5 aren't the ones to do the asking."

"How do you mean?

Shane shrugged. "Maybe this is simplistic. But if I wanted a favour from the Israelis, something that might take a great deal of time and effort, I'd forget MI5 and have the favour requested by someone they'd find it harder to say no to."

"What, like the Prime Minister?"

"No, like the Americans. Israel probably wouldn't exist today if it wasn't for the support they've always had from the US. So if Uncle Sam says 'This is top priority, please drop everything and deal with it', maybe they would."

Penny looked thoughtful. "I hadn't thought of it like that."

"If the American Secretary of State is addressing the conference, it's a legitimate American concern. In fact I'm surprised the Yanks haven't already turned up the heat on Tel Aviv."

"I'm not sure our Secret Service would have shared all our intelligence with the Americans."

Shane looked surprised. "Why wouldn't they?"

"I get the impression that intelligence people guard their patches pretty jealously. They may not want the CIA muscling in on an operation that they're handling."

"You reckon?"

"I'm only guessing, Shane. But there's another week before the delegates arrive – maybe our people thought there'd be time enough to crack it with our own resources."

"But so far they haven't, and getting an ID for this guy could be the key. So why not suggest asking the Americans to twist a few arms?"

"You're right," said Penny reflectively. "With so much at stake, national pride's a luxury we can't afford."

"So what will you do?"

"Try and find a diplomatic way of phrasing it. Then

put your suggestion to my boss – first thing in the morning . . ."

Majid stared at the map, then pointed with his forefinger. "According to my calculations, it should be about here."

Majid and Jemail Zubi were seated in the front room of the house in Starbeck, an atlas spread out on the table before them.

"Cape Finisterre?" said Jemail.

"Maybe moving into the Bay of Biscay if the ship is making good time, still off the Portuguese coast if they're behind schedule."

Tamaz Akmedov was in the kitchen preparing Sunday lunch, and Majid had turned on the kitchen radio and closed the doors of both the parlour and the kitchen to ensure that the Turkish waiter would hear nothing of what was now being said. Since his arrival in Harrogate yesterday Majid had come to like the softly spoken older man, but he was determined that the mission's operational details would remain on a need-to-know basis.

"So, what – two or three more days to reach England?" asked Jemail.

"Probably a little over two. You have your mobile phone there?"

"Yes."

Majid held out his hand for it, making a mental note to get himself a new sim card for his own mobile when the shops opened on Monday morning. He had destroyed the old sim card because of the disturbing call he had received in Leeds railway station, and he hadn't had time to seek a telephone outlet in which to buy a replacement. "I've arranged to contact the ship this weekend – it may as well be now," he said. He took a slip of paper from his pocket and dialled the number written on it.

"Cellphone in their radio shack?"

"No," replied Majid. "Private link to the captain. His own mobile."

The phone rang several times, then was answered, and Majid turned his back on Jemail the better to concentrate.

"Hello?"

The captain's voice sounded distant but clear, and Majid could hear a rumbling noise in the background which he presumed to be the noise of the freighter's engines. "I'm calling about the consignment," he said.

It was understood that no names or places were to be referred to and Majid was pleased to hear the other man respond in equally non-specific terms. "All is going according to schedule."

"Estimated to arrive when?"

"ETA approximately three o'clock Tuesday afternoon."

"Excellent," said Majid. "I'll contact you that morning."

"Fine."

"Till then." Majid hung up and turned to face Jemail, who smiled.

"On schedule then?"

"Yes, due in Hull on Tuesday afternoon."

"Great. Once we get this we'll have everything we need."

Majid nodded in satisfaction. "And then we'll show them. Then we'll make them pay . . ."

With a jolt and a protesting screech from the tyres,

Laura's plane hit the tarmac and hurtled down the runway at Leeds/Bradford airport. It was the last flight from Dublin on Sunday evening and the aircraft was only half full, so that between the modest size of the airport and the flight not being fully subscribed she found herself collecting her baggage within fifteen minutes of touchdown.

Now that she was actually in Yorkshire however she wondered if her visit might not turn out to be a humiliating mistake. She had been fired up with enthusiasm yesterday, still on an adrenaline rush when she had spoken to Mac in the aftermath of breaking into the flat in Tallaght. This morning, in the cold light of day, she had weighed matters up more objectively and she had to admit that there was a distinct possibility that her journey might turn out to be a wild-goose chase. In retrospect, she was surprised that Mac had actually sanctioned it. She realised now that in order to sway him her enthusiasm must have been really strong and infectious. She still felt that there was a spectacular story to be had regarding the mystery man that she had telephoned – it was just that, now the initial excitement had abated, she could see how daunting her task was likely to be.

She hoisted her bags and made for the car-hire desk where she completed the formalities, then collected the keys to a Ford Orion. Normally she would have used taxis or hired a more luxurious car, but this time the cost would be going onto her own credit card and she decided to economise. It was a small gesture, but she felt that Mac had been generous in acceding to her request.

In return she had decided that her investment in the project, apart from her time and energy, would be to provide her own car. In terms of flexibility and access to locations around Harrogate it would be important to give herself every possible advantage – the leads she had to follow were slender enough.

She collected the car from the parking lot, placed her luggage in the boot and her laptop on the passenger seat, then drove off. Dusk had fallen, but the airport surrounds were well illuminated, and she followed the road signs without difficulty. After a few moments she reached the A61 and turned onto it, heading north towards Harrogate.

She had gone onto the Internet earlier, seeking a single hotel room, and had finally booked one in the Old Swan Hotel, which was a five-minute walk from the Conference Centre. It was also the hotel in which the novelist Agatha Christie had ensconced herself when she had gone missing back in the twenties and that, for Laura, had tipped the balance in favour of staying there. If nothing else she should be able to provide the *Clarion* with a colour article out of that. It would also entertain Declan, she knew, when she rang him in Prague later that night – particularly since the Dustin Hoffman/Vanessa Redgrave film *Agatha* had been shot on location in the Old Swan Hotel.

She knew Declan would not be so entertained if he heard that she was on the trail of a possible murderer, but she decided she would play down any element of danger, make it sound more like a case of tracking down an elusive witness. And elusive he might very well be. Despite her upbeat approach when selling Mac the idea

209

of checking out the various European delegations, Laura felt now that it was going to be a major challenge.

She had tried to approach it logically, listing all the countries that she knew would be attending the conference and checking each one off against the voice on the tape she had made. She knew at once that the man's accent wasn't Nordic and so she had removed Denmark and Norway from her list. He didn't sound Germanic either and so she had crossed off Germany, Austria, Luxembourg and Holland. Ireland and the United Kingdom were English-speaking and so they too had gone. Which left Spain, Portugal, Italy, and Greece, as the front runners in terms of accent, with France and Belgium less likely, but still possibilities. Of those, Spain had seemed like her best option, as it had a well-publicised terrorist problem with the ETA Basque separatist movement.

Very well, she decided now, as she cruised along the A61 through the gathering dusk – Spain it would be. She had to start somewhere, and first thing tomorrow morning she would begin checking the Spanish delegation. Satisfied at having some plan of action to follow, she drove on northwards for Harrogate.

The darkening September sky was still touched with streaks of blue as Penny set out from her parents' house in Leeds. She knew that within half an hour she would be back in her hotel room in Harrogate, but for the moment she still felt relaxed. The break with Shane and Aisling had done her good, and it was only now that she had unwound that she realised how much she had needed it.

The Sunday evening traffic was light, and she drove along comfortably, her mind elsewhere as she followed the contours of the road. She found herself thinking about the Israeli proposal that she planned to put to Mathieson, then she consciously stopped herself. Time enough to go into police mode tomorrow morning; for now she ought to savour her precious time off. She reached across to the passenger seat and, without taking her eyes off the road, took a cassette from the pouch of her travel bag. It was a new compilation tape that Shane had made for her, and she slipped it into the cassette player, then smiled as the sound of Bob Geldof singing the 'Great Song of Indifference' filled the car. Shane had been a fanatical Boom Town Rats fan in his youth, and this was one of his favourite tunes from Geldof's solo career. She found herself humming along to the lilting melody, then she smiled again as the next track began to play. Shane had refused to give her the list of songs, insisting that each one should come as a surprise, and now the car interior reverberated to the quirky but catchy strains of 'Bang Bang', BA Robertson's late seventies hit. Show me a person's record collection, she thought wryly, and I'll tell you all about them. Just as she was singing along about Samson and Delilah, her favourite line in the song, the car's engine spluttered, then picked up again.

Penny frowned, knowing that the unmarked cars in the police pool were normally well serviced. She had borrowed this one on Saturday afternoon and driven it without a problem all weekend. She glanced at the dashboard, but the oil-pressure warning light hadn't come on and the water temperature was normal. No sooner had the engine seemed to settle, however, than it began spluttering again. Penny immediately dropped a gear and tried gunning the engine, but as soon as she eased her foot from the accelerator she could feel the engine starting to cut out again. She pressed the accelerator once more, simultaneously flicking on her hazard lights and manoeuvring into the left-hand lane. Just then the engine cut out completely. Fortunately the traffic had remained light during the journey, and Penny managed to bring the car safely to a halt on the verge.

With the hazard lights still flashing she got out of the car, took a torch from the glove compartment and opened the bonnet. Despite coming from a family of engineers she had never been mechanically minded, but she knew enough to check the fan belt and the leads to the spark plugs. The belt seemed to be in prefect condition, and Penny pushed each of the leads in tightly and checked that nothing was loose at the distributor cap. Finally she checked that the battery leads weren't loose and that there was water in the battery. She returned to the driver's seat and slipped behind the wheel again. She turned the key in the ignition, but all she got was a coughing sound. She tried again to no avail, waited a couple of moments, then tried twice more. It was no use, the car wouldn't start and she knew she would simply run down the battery by constantly trying to start it. She breathed out in frustration, feeling that she could really have done without this. The car was safely in off the road, but she reckoned that she must be about fifteen miles away from Harrogate. She had her mobile phone with her, but she had no idea if the police mechanics operated a call-out service on a Sunday night.

She cursed her luck, then looked into her rear-view mirror as a car pulled in behind her onto the verge. *A good Samaritan, or someone wanting to take advantage of a woman stranded in the countryside?* Hopefully the former, she thought, getting out of her car and turning to face the newcomer.

"Hi," said the other driver, switching off the headlights and approaching. "Having trouble?"

In the light-spill from the flashing hazard lights she saw that the driver was a woman of about her own age and she sensed immediately that this was a good Samaritan with no ulterior motive for stopping.

"Don't know what the problem is," answered Penny. "Know anything about engines?"

"Zilch, I'm afraid. But I've got a mobile phone, or I can give you a lift."

Penny considered a moment. If she had to go through the routine of trying to get a police mechanic out tonight she would certainly be back in police mode, and she could also be waiting by the side of the road for quite a while. If, indeed, the fleet mechanics were on call on a Sunday night in the first instance. Whereas if she locked the car and took a lift, the car could be collected first thing in the morning and she could stay in off-duty mode for the rest of the evening. "Where are you headed?" she asked the woman.

"Harrogate."

"I think I'll take your offer of a lift, if that's OK. Getting a mechanic on a Sunday night could be really tricky."

"Right."

"And eh . . . thanks very much for stopping, I appreciate it."

"No problem. If I hadn't, you'd probably be inundated with offers from randy truck-drivers." The woman smiled. "Then again, maybe I'm spoiling your fun."

Penny smiled back. "That sort of fun I can live without. If you just hang on, I'll lock the car and get my stuff."

"Sure."

Penny replaced the torch and collected her gear, then locked the car and approached the passenger door of the other vehicle. The woman was moving a small case from the passenger seat onto the rear seat

"You can put your stuff in the back if you like," she said.

"Fine," answered Penny. She placed her travelling bag on the rear seat, then moved around to the front and got into the car, strapping herself in.

"All right then," said the woman. "Home, James!"

Penny smiled, then glanced over at the other woman, who indicated, then pulled back out onto the road. She confirmed Penny's first impression of being about thirty, and up close Penny could see that she was good-looking and well-dressed, albeit in casual clothes. "It was really good of you to stop," said Penny.

"No bother."

"You're not from around here?"

"The aul accent's a dead give-away."

"Irish?"

"Guilty as charged. Top o' the Mornin' . . ."

Penny grinned, already liking this woman and her slightly quirky humour. "Are you living here or over on holidays?"

"Neither actually. Just over on business."

"Ah."

"How about you?" the woman asked. "Are you a local?"

"Almost. Originally from Leeds, now I live outside London. I should introduce myself – Penny Harte."

"Pleased to meet you, Penny. Laura Kennedy – I won't shake hands . . ."

"Please don't!"

They drove on, easy in each other's company, then Laura glanced over at Penny. "So, where are you staying in Harrogate?"

"The Moat House Hotel. It's right beside the Conference Centre."

"Oh, that's handy . . ."

"Yes, it's very central."

"No, I meant it's handy for me. I'm staying in the Old Swan – it's meant to be very close to the Conference Centre."

"Yes, just up the road."

"Great. I've never been to Harrogate before, so when I drop you off I'll find out where the Conference Centre is."

"Right. So, are you attending a conference?" asked Penny.

"Covering rather than attending. I'm a journalist."

"Oh, really? Which conference are you here for?"

"The EU Ministers next week. I'm doing some articles for a Dublin newspaper."

215

"Before the conference starts?"

"Yes, colour pieces. Yorkshire Dales, the Spa town of Harrogate, the delegates arriving – that sort of thing . . ."

"Right . . . actually there's a quote on the wall in our hotel that would be really good for a colour piece. It's what Dickens said about Harrogate – maybe you've heard it?"

"No," answered Laura. "What did he say?"

"Harrogate is the queerest place, with the strangest people in it, leading lives of dancing, newspaper-reading and dining!"

"Excellent!" said Laura with a laugh. "I'll definitely work that into one of the articles."

"Good. I'll feel I've given something in exchange for the lift."

"Fair enough, we'll call it quits. So, are you attending a conference too?"

"Same one as you," answered Penny.

"Yeah? Are you with the UK delegation?"

"Not exactly."

"Let me guess. An interpreter?"

"'Fraid not."

"IT specialist?"

"I can just about use the spell-checker on my computer."

"Eh . . . the madam of an international ring of call-girls?"

Penny grinned as she shook her head. "I'm a police officer." She waited, curious to see the other woman's response. Most people seemed taken aback, then tended to respond with anything from awe to ill-disguised disapproval.

"OK, Guv, it's a fair cop!" said Laura. "I hid the diamonds under the floorboards!"

Penny laughed. "At least you didn't say 'Evening all'."

"So it's PC Harte then . . ."

"Chief Inspector Harte, actually . . ."

"Wow, I'm impressed! And good for you! You must be pretty hot at your job to get that rank so young."

"Things have gone well for me."

"Here, no false modesty! Great to see women breaking through the glass ceiling."

"Yes," answered Penny, touched by the genuine enthusiasm of the other woman. "Thanks . . ."

"I mean it. So what have you to do? Look after the security of these high-flying politicians?"

"All that sort of stuff . . ."

"Fascinating job."

"Sometimes," conceded Penny. "I'm sure your own is pretty interesting, working for a newspaper, travelling abroad."

"It has its moments . . ."

They chatted on, exchanging details on their jobs, their respective partners, their families and their lives in general. Their rapport was easy and natural and the time passed quickly, then Penny realised that they were entering the outskirts of Harrogate and she directed Laura along the route that took them towards the Moat House Hotel.

"This is the Conference Centre coming up. If you'd like to drop me at the traffic-lights, you can turn up left, and then left again for the Old Swan."

"Not at all," said Laura. "I'll run you up."

"Are you sure?"

"Absolutely."

"Thanks then, you've been very kind."

"I've enjoyed the chat."

"This is all the Conference Centre here," said Penny pointing.

"Gosh, it's big."

"Huge. Now, just in to the left here – this is the hotel."

"OK." Laura turned in off the road, then pulled to a halt before the hotel lobby.

"Great," said Penny.

"Listen, I don't know how you're fixed," said Laura, "but I don't have my boyfriend, and you don't have your husband. Maybe we could meet up for a drink?"

"Yeah, I'd really like that."

"How about the bar here – after work tomorrow night?"

"Sounds good," answered Penny, "but I probably wouldn't be free till about nine, half-nine."

"Say about half-nine then."

"I look forward to it," said Penny. "And thanks again for the lift."

"My pleasure."

Penny got out of the car, gathered her things from the back seat, then closed the door and gave her new-found friend a wave. She watched the Irishwoman turn the car and drive off, then she stepped purposefully towards the hotel lobby.

9

Monday September 18th 2000

"Think he'll keep his nerve when the time comes?" asked Jemail Zubi, putting aside his breakfast plate and looking quizzically at his partner.

It was a good question, Majid knew, but he didn't reply immediately. Instead he gazed out the kitchen window of the house in Starbeck, considering his answer. The behaviour of Tamaz Akmedov would undoubtedly be critical for the success of the mission, and should the Turkish waiter lose his nerve at the last minute it could certainly scupper their plans. It was something that had greatly worried Majid when he was originally doing his planning, but he had decided that the uncertainty associated with using an untested colleague couldn't be avoided. Every mission involved risks of some form, every plan contained elements of chance. The trick was to minimise the imponderables as rigorously as possible, and this he felt he had done.

In choosing from the list of candidates supplied by

Rahmani, Majid had deliberated at length before opting for Tamaz Akmedov. The basic requirements of being Turkish, a professional waiter, capable of speaking English and without a police record had been met by all of the candidates, but Tamaz's personal history had clinched it for Majid. He remembered being swayed by the fact that the man had had a difficult life, with years of hard work for modest wages, then a divorce, and finally the tragedy of his estranged wife and their child being killed in a car crash while visiting relatives in Amman.

The file had made for sad reading, but Majid had recognised immediately that the events outlined within it made Tamaz a real possibility for their mission. Firstly, a man without family ties could easily leave one job, move to another country and, keeping himself to himself, work unobtrusively for six months. More importantly, as a lone individual he could vanish easily in the aftermath of a successful mission. But perhaps most importantly of all, Majid had felt that Tamaz would be likely to feel that after all the knocks he had received, life now owed him something.

Majid's perception had turned out to be an accurate one, and when faced with the prospect of earning a million dollars in cash Tamaz had taken little persuading. Majid had made clear to him that he wouldn't have to act directly against the then unnamed but high-profile targets, that his role would simply be to facilitate others in striking a spectacular blow. If Tamaz had harboured any moral qualms they hadn't been evident to Majid and, having explained in graphic detail what would happen to the Turk should he be tempted to double-cross them, Majid had gone with his instincts and chosen the soft-spoken waiter from Urfa.

Having reflected on it all again, Majid now turned to Jemail Zubi. " I think he'll do what we tell him. I reckon he'll keep his nerve."

"Yeah?"

"Yes, I think so." Majid knew that Jemail respected his judgement, and he was glad to see the other man nodding as though reassured

"I'm glad," said Jemail, "I've grown to like him."

"You've grown to like his cooking."

Jemail smiled. "That too. You have to admit the *Iskender Kebaps* were good."

For Sunday lunch the previous day Tamaz had served the traditional Turkish dish of grilled sliced lamb in tomato sauce, hot butter and yoghurt. "Pretty good," Majid conceded with a smile. He knew Jemail liked his food, and in spite of working out and playing soccer regularly the Lebanese was slightly rotund at the waist. It was something Majid had kidded him about when they had last met, but now Majid knew that there was a serious side to having a good cook resident in the house in Starbeck. Although there were plenty of restaurants in Harrogate and thousands of conference delegates in the town at any given time, nevertheless he had urged Jemail to eat in as much as possible. No point in raising any kind of a profile in Harrogate, with the authorities aware of an operation being afoot.

For the same reason he had told Tamaz to lease the house for a whole year, and he had made certain that the rent went into the landlord's account on the thirtieth of every month. In consequence Tamaz had never had any contact with his landlord in the six months in which he had stayed in the house, and any minor household problems he had dealt with himself, at Majid's instruction. There had been no trouble with neighbours, no disputes about parking or noise, which meant that Jemail and Majid could now discreetly stay in the rented house without attracting any comment.

"So, what's the plan for today?" asked Jemail.

"Tamaz goes to work as usual, I get a sim card for my mobile, you fuel up the van." Knowing that they would need transport, Majid had bought a second-hand van the previous March. He had purchased it long in advance, not wanting to engage in any commercial transactions during the run up to the operation. "Other than that we lie low."

Jemail groaned theatrically. "How many times can I play soccer on the N-64?"

"As many as are necessary for good security."

"Relax, Abdullah, I'm only kidding."

"No kidding, Jemail. Patient waiting is a part of any mission."

Jemail raised his hand in appeasement. "OK. Not a problem . . ."

"Besides, you'll be out tomorrow."

"Yeah?"

"When I collect the shipment from Hull, I want you to come with me."

"Great."

"Great, it'll get you out of the house – or great, then we'll have everything we need?" asked Majid wryly, though he already knew the answer.

222

"Both, I suppose," answered Jemail. "But mostly we'll have what we need. And you know what, Abdullah?"

"What?"

"I'm dying to use it. I'm dying to show these Western bastards."

"Me too," said Majid. He looked the other man in the eye. "And just think. This time next week – you and I will make history . . ."

"I don't know, Penny," said Mathieson thoughtfully, his fingers distractedly tapping a soft beat on the top of the command-room table. "Not as simple perhaps as you think . . ."

Penny had managed to get him alone in the station before a scheduled review meeting with Thompson and Carrow, and she had presented her case for American pressure on the Israelis as persuasively as she could. His response had been noncommittal but, despite being disappointed at his lack of enthusiasm, she could understand his reservations. She realised that if he used the Americans he would be under a compliment to them, and no doubt they would then be very much in his face during the rest of the operation.

"The thing is, were we to approach the US intelligence at this stage, it would cause considerable ill-feeling," said Mathieson.

"How so?"

"They'd be annoyed at not being consulted before now."

"Surely you can argue that as the host nation, British Intelligence wished to handle it themselves initially. If the boot were on the other foot they'd probably want to do the same."

"Probably, but there'd still be resentment, believe me. There'd also be a problem with the Israelis."

"Yeah?"

"It would blatantly be going over Samuel Lubetkin's head. The equivalent of saying that he's not co-operating enough and that he needs to be reprimanded."

"But in reality he's *not* co-operating enough, not from our perspective," said Penny.

"Maybe, but he has his own, extremely difficult, agenda to deal with. And we may need his good will in the future. Which we certainly won't have if we do what you suggest."

"That's as may be, Colin, but is anything needing his future co-operation likely to be more important than an attempt to kill every EU Foreign Minister?"

Mathieson raised an eyebrow in acknowledgement. "Fair point," he conceded.

"Talking of the Israelis – something's just occurred to me," said Penny.

"Yes?"

"As close allies of the Americans, might Mr Lubetkin *already* have informed the CIA – when he was informing you?"

Mathieson shook his head. "No, the Americans would definitely have raised it with us."

"I wonder why he didn't tell them," said Penny.

"I'd say A) because we're the ones hosting the conference, so security is our responsibility, and B) while it sounded like a serious threat, Lubetkin may have figured it could still turn out to be another harebrained Arab scheme that would come to nothing. He'd covered himself by informing us – no need to have the CIA obsessively breathing down his neck when he has so many other problems to contend with."

"Except now it might really suit us to have the CIA breathing down his neck. If the Israelis could come up with a name and a face for our man, it would transform our operation here."

"*If* they could . . ."

"But supposing they could, Colin. Supposing they made a huge effort to go through all their files, all their records – and they hit paydirt? Our chances of catching our quarry would improve enormously."

Mathieson looked thoughtful, and Penny could see that she had swayed him to some extent. *Time to go for broke.* "Look, what's the worst that can happen if we do what I suggest? We antagonise Lubetkin and the Americans, and the Israelis still come up with nothing. Not a great scenario admittedly, but not a disaster. And think of the alternative. Supposing this guy carries out his attack somehow, and kills the people we're supposed to be protecting because we can't locate him. And then it turns out that Lubetkin had a dossier somewhere. Had a file, and background information, and a photograph of our man. And we never saw it – because we didn't push hard enough?"

Mathieson said nothing for a moment, and Penny consciously resisted the temptation to oversell her proposal.

"I take your point," said Mathieson eventually.

"Does that mean you'll do it?"

Again Mathieson didn't respond immediately, gazing instead into the middle distance. Penny continued to look at him quizzically until finally he turned and faced her. "I'll talk to my superiors," he said.

"Great."

"There's no guarantee they'll share your view," he warned.

"I understand. But supposing for argument's sake they do, how quickly might they move?"

"Quickly, I would think. One phone call to Washington, one call from there to Tel Aviv. If it's going to happen, it'll happen fast."

"OK. So . . . when will you talk to your superiors?" asked Penny, hoping she wasn't pushing too far.

Mathieson looked at her, then smiled. "I'd forgotten quite how tenacious you could be."

"Isn't that part of why you seconded me to this in the first place?" she replied, smiling in return.

"I'll contact them as soon as the meeting here ends. Talking of which . . ."

Penny looked round to see the door of the command room opening. She saw Thompson holding the door and indicating for Carrow to enter the room ahead of him. The Special Branch officer approached the table, curtly returning the greetings of Penny and Mathieson.

"Morning, Chief," said Penny as Thompson drew near.

"Morning, Penny, morning, Colin! Good weekend, Penny?"

No point boring everyone with the car-breakdown story, she decided. "Yes, great, thanks. And you?"

"Trounced in a bowls tournament, vomited on by a grandchild – the usual weekend pleasures."

Penny and Mathieson laughed, then Thompson turned around to Carrow. "How about you, Len? Tally-hoing after the fox this weekend?"

Penny smiled inwardly, knowing that her old boss was sending up Carrow's treasured status as a member of his local hunt. Carrow had always been keen to leave behind his working-class roots in Barnsley, and she knew Thompson enjoyed subtly baiting him regarding his penchant for social climbing.

"No hunting," answered Carrow.

"Oh?"

"Some of us were busy working on the operation here. Talking of which, can we get down to business?"

"Certainly," said Mathieson, and Penny caught a quick wink from Thompson as they all took their chairs around the table.

"OK, quick update from each of us on our respective areas," said Mathieson. "Starting with security checks on hotel and Conference Centre staff. Been some progress, both with our Sudanese chef and our Turkish waiter . . ."

"So what's the story?" asked Thompson.

"We've finally got someone reliable in the Sudan working on it. So far nothing untoward on the chef, but our chap is delving deeper as we speak."

"Presumably you've made him aware that time is of the essence?"

"Absolutely," answered Mathieson "He's conscious of the time-scale and he'll report immediately there's further data."

"And the Turk?" asked Thompson.

"We've been making enquiries in Urfa and so far everything is kosher. No police record, no known political affiliations, no family trouble. Since his late teens he's worked as a waiter in various countries. We're still checking out his work record in each location, but so far he seems above board. How about you, Len, what's the status on the UK residents?"

"We spoke to the barman who's a CND member. Total prat, but no more than that. Also the former Commie –"

"The kitchen porter?" queried Mathieson.

"Yes. In his sixties now, hasn't been an active member in yonks. Started giving us a load of blather about becoming disenchanted with the Soviet departure from pure communist ideals – whatever they might be." Mathieson's face showed a hint of a smile. "Harmless then, you reckon?"

"Definitely. Complete waste of space, but no threat."

"OK," said Mathieson. "Jack?"

"I've just spoken to the Chief Constable," answered Thompson. "We'll have an additional hundred and fifty uniformed officers arriving over the next twenty-four hours plus another sixty plainclothes officers."

"'Bout bloody time," said Carrow.

"I know it's a long time, Len, since you were a regular officer," said Thompson, not concealing the sarcasm in his tone, "but you will recall that the local commander has to balance special event requirements like ours with the need to maintain other police duties."

"Sure," replied Carrow. "We wouldn't want people

cycling with no lamps on their bikes because the local coppers were protecting the lives of VIPs."

"Yes, well, I'm sure we'll be glad of the extra manpower," interjected Mathieson, "and as we've only six days before the conference begins, can I suggest we channel our energy productively?"

"Meaning what?" asked Carrow.

"Meaning we don't waste time sniping, we get through the agenda of this meeting, and then we get on with the many tasks we all have for today." He looked round the table.

"Agreed?"

"Agreed," answered the others.

Laura pushed aside her cup and saucer and looked down at the journalist's pad on the table before her. She had had lunch in one of Harrogate's Victorian tea-rooms, but the attractive old-world atmosphere of the premises was lost on her just now. Oblivious to the clatter of crockery and the aroma of freshly brewed coffee, she scanned through the notes where she had outlined her tasks for the day and tried to remain enthusiastic. From past experience she knew how important it was to keep a positive attitude. She realised it would be vital to remain determined and creative, particularly when following a lead as slim as the one she was currently pursuing.

She had gone to the Conference Centre that morning seeking information on the various delegations attending the Foreign Ministers' Summit. As an accredited journalist she had been facilitated politely and efficiently, and in keeping with her plan she had first checked out the Spanish delegation. To her disappointment, she had discovered that the main delegation wasn't coming to Harrogate until Saturday and the advance party consisted of only three people. Under the guise of writing an article on the development of democracy in Spain, she had met the Spaniards – two females in their twenties and a male diplomat in his sixties who spoke in a high-pitched effeminate tone – and it was clear that none of them remotely matched the profile of the person she had spoken to on the phone. The Greek delegation, which was next on her list, was also arriving on Saturday but its advance party hadn't yet arrived. Having drawn a blank with her first two choices, she then made enquiries regarding the Italian delegation. There were four people listed in the advance group, two of them males, but they weren't due back in Harrogate until that afternoon, having left for a lunch-time function with the Italian consul in Leeds.

She had left the Conference Centre and strolled through the town to get her bearings, all the while analysing her reasoning to date. It had struck her that while some countries had no advance parties of civil servants or diplomats in attendance yet, the one group of people that all countries would already have in place would be their security services. Although the British would have overall responsibility for security – and already it seemed both painstaking and high-profile – each country would still have its own security personnel.

Could her man be from one such group, she had wondered? Certainly such a person would have the necessary military skills to have killed Boyle and O'Donnell. Equally certainly the names of such staff wouldn't appear on any readily available list, unlike the diplomats. In reality it didn't seem to make much sense for someone from a foreign security service to want to kill two rogue IRA operatives. Even if their deaths had been as a result of some kind of covert, counter-terrorist strike, the logical perpetrators would surely be British, whereas the man on the tape, though a fluent English speaker, clearly wasn't speaking in his native language.

Eventually Laura had put on hold the notion of pursuing the security-personnel angle. Now, having finished reviewing her handwritten notes, she left a tip on the table, slipped her notebook into her bag and rose to leave the tea-rooms. She stepped out into warm September sunshine and made her way towards the pedestrianised shopping area that occupied the interconnecting streets behind St Peter's church. She passed the imposing bulk of the church and made her way towards a telephone shop that she had seen earlier in the day. Over the course of the weekend she had tried innumerable times to get through on the mobile-phone number that she had obtained in the flat in Tallaght, but the phone had clearly been switched off, and Laura reasoned that if she were in the shoes of the man whom she had called she would simply dump the sim card from the mobile and buy a new one to acquire a different number. And if he had spent the weekend in Harrogate then getting a new sim card locally when the shops opened again on Monday seemed a plausible enough action.

She had seen no other telephone shops anywhere in Harrogate and so, on reaching the shop now, she took a deep breath, opened the door and stepped in. To her relief there were no other customers in the shop and the assistant looked up eagerly as she approached. *Probably bored*, she thought, *might make him eager to talk*. He was young too, only in his early twenties. *Susceptible to a bit of female charm*, she reckoned, hating herself for being so calculating, but knowing that she would need every break going.

"Good afternoon," said the assistant brightly. "Can I help you?"

"Yes, please," she answered equally brightly. "Want to get fifty pounds' worth of credit for the mobile, please."

"No problem."

Laura smiled and gave him her credit card, and they chatted easily as he carried out the transaction. The credit-card clearance went through quickly, but he seemed disposed to continue chatting when Laura had signed the docket and retrieved her card. *Now*, she thought – the worst he can do is refuse to help.

"Eh . . . I was wondering . . . I was wondering if you might be able to do me a favour?" she said.

The assistant smiled and raised an eyebrow playfully. "If it's humanly possible."

"It's just . . . my cousin has been having a bit of a problem . . . with crank calls . . ."

"Yeah?"

"Nothing too bad, but still a bit upsetting."

"Sure," the assistant said sympathetically.

"She teaches in a language school here in Harrogate – so the pupils have foreign accents. And this guy keeps ringing her. There are three or four pupils it might be, but she doesn't know which one it is."

"She could get call recognition – then the number of the person calling her would show up."

"That's exactly what she did. Then the last time he called her she got a bit upset and told the guy she had his number. It obviously put the fear of God in him, because he hung up immediately and kept the phone switched off."

"Once she has the number she can go to the police and they'll be able to trace it."

Laura grimaced. "She doesn't really want to go to the police."

"She should, you know. The police take that kind of harassment seriously."

"That's just it though. The calls were never really obscene or abusive, just silly . . . irritating, you know? She doesn't want to get the guy arrested, deported maybe, if he's here on a student visa."

"If you ask me she's being way too understanding," said the assistant.

"She's a really nice person," said Laura. "But *I'd* like to find out who the guy is – and give him a good piece of my mind."

"Absolutely."

"So I was hoping you might be able to help me," said Laura appealingly.

"How?"

"Well, I reckon he'll have gotten rid of his sim card after my cousin scared him with the call-recognition thing. That was late on Saturday afternoon, so I was wondering if you'd sold many sim cards since then?"

The assistant looked at her a moment, the playfulness gone from his demeanour now, and Laura wondered if she had offended him with her request.

"I've sold three since then," he said.

"Any of them to a foreign-sounding male?"

Again the assistant looked at her for a moment, then nodded. "Yes, one of them."

Laura felt a sudden racing in her pulses. "Yeah?"

"Just before lunch today. Foreign guy came in and bought one."

"Would you have his name?" Laura asked, trying to keep the excitement from her voice.

"No, it was only a sim card."

"I thought maybe he'd have paid by credit card," said Laura hopefully.

The assistant looked at her and shook his head. "Paid in cash. Sorry."

"Can you remember what he looked like?"

"About thirty, maybe. Thick black hair, brown eyes."

"Anything else you can remember?"

The assistant considered. "Reasonably tall, maybe five eleven, six feet. Fit-looking."

"Great," said Laura with a smile. "You'd be a good detective – you're really observant."

As she had hoped, the assistant was spurred a little by the flattery. "He, eh . . . he had a confident air about

234

him. Like a guy who was used to doing business, used to getting his own way maybe . . ."

"Right. And when you say he was foreign-looking – are we talking dark skin?"

"Not black, but darker than you or me."

"As dark say as an Indian or a Pakistani?"

"No, he wasn't Indian or Pakistani – not that dark, more sallow. Also I'd know an Indian accent."

"So what did the accent sound like to you?"

"Hard to pin it down . . . maybe . . . maybe an Arab?" He paused a moment then nodded. "Yeah, could have been Middle-Eastern, between the accent and the skin tone. Though of course I'm only guessing."

"No, that's fine. Anything else strike you?"

"Not really. He just came in, bought the sim card and left."

"Right. Can you recall how he was dressed?"

"Eh . . . nothing that would stand out. Wore a dark suit, looked like a businessman."

"Excellent. Anything else, anything at all?"

The shop assistant considered, then shook his head. "Sorry, but that's about it."

"OK. Listen, you've been really helpful, thanks a million."

"Not at all. Do you reckon it's the guy who's been bothering your cousin?"

Laura nodded. "Yes. Yes, I think we've found our man . . ."

Samuel Lubetkin watched the early afternoon traffic converging onto Dizingoff Circle, an area of Tel Aviv that the guidebooks sometimes fancifully compared to the Place d'Etoile in Paris. A squat, heavily built man, he sat alone at an outdoor café table reflecting on how much Tel Aviv had changed. Only a hundred years ago there had been no city here, just sand-dunes and wasteland; now there were traffic-jams at two in the morning. It was frantic and frustrating and hardly the world's prettiest city and yet Tel Aviv enthralled him. Its vibrancy symbolised for Lubetkin the triumph of the state of Israel itself. It was brash, it was confident, it had flourished in spite of a hostile environment.

Despite the noise and pollution from the traffic, Lubetkin liked occasionally to sip Turkish coffee near Dizingoff Circle. For a man whose work with Israeli intelligence called for ruthless pragmatism he had a romantic streak, and he liked the continuity of patronising the place where some of the pioneering founders of Israel had hatched their plans for wresting for themselves an independent nation.

The son of penniless immigrants who had fled in the late thirties to what was then British-occupied Palestine, Lubetkin had grown up without any of the insecurity and sense of inferiority that had marked his parents. A child of the fledgling state of Israel, Lubetkin had later served with pride and considerable distinction in the army. As a young cavalry officer he had led a squadron of jeeps that had roared into East Jerusalem during the Six Day War, driving the Jordanians back and capturing territory of huge emotional significance to many Israelis.

How straightforward it had all been back then, he thought, as he sipped his coffee. The enemy had been visible, the objectives defined and the very survival of the state had provided an unassailable motivation. Now his work with Mossad was murkier, morally dubious at times, less satisfying. And yet he believed that it couldn't be shirked, but rather was a messy job that simply had to be done.

He had gone straight from the army into intelligence work, and looking back he could see why his superiors had persuaded him to do so. He spoke fluent Arabic, he had a chess-player's instinct for long-term, tactical thinking, he was ruthless when necessary and he had a capacity for daring, unexpected field tactics that sometimes worried his superiors but more often yielded impressive results. As he grew older however the list of moral compromises grew, and now at fifty-eight years of age he found himself increasingly looking back affectionately to his youthful army days and the simplicity of the battles required of him then. Then again, maybe everyone looked back nostalgically as they got older, he thought. Maybe everyone's lives grew more complex and envying the simplicity of earlier times wasn't the preserve of ageing intelligence operatives.

He sipped his Turkish coffee again, savouring its bitter taste, then his philosophising was cut short. Approaching his table was his assistant, Avi Blumenthal.

Blumenthal was a tall, slender man in his early forties whose tailor-made clothes and slightly patrician air suggested a wealthy family background. Despite the contrast with Lubetkin's more streetwise manner the two men got on well, and Lubetkin nodded in greeting now. "Avi," he said, indicating for the other man to take a seat.

"Thank you."

"What's up?"

"We've had an interesting call," answered Blumenthal.

"Something we can discuss here?" asked Lubetkin, conscious as ever of security, despite the roar of the nearby traffic making it difficult for them to be overheard.

"Yes, it's more politics than normal business."

"Politics?"

"The Prime Minister's office were on to us. They want to know why something that could affect the security of the American Secretary of State isn't getting top priority."

"What?"

"The Harrogate conference. They're concerned about the threat."

"Damn it, Avi!" said Lubetkin. "I'm concerned too. But I'm more concerned about *intifadas*, suicide bombers, people who plan terrorist attacks on us. I've tried to help the British, but I've other stuff on my plate. Can't they see it's a matter of priorities?"

Blumenthal shrugged. "I think, Sam, the priorities have just changed."

"Yeah . . ."

"So the PM's office want some answers."

"Fucking politicians," said Lubetkin.

Blumenthal gave him a wry grin. "My feelings entirely."

Lubetkin smiled wryly in return, then nodded.

"Right," he said philosophically. "Let's get back to the office, and do our masters' bidding . . ."

Laura glanced discreetly around as she entered the crowded bar of the Moat House Hotel, quickly scanning the sea of faces before her. Since getting the description in the telephone shop she had trawled through the streets and hotels of Harrogate seeking her man, but to no avail. She had also checked out the two Italian diplomats on their return from Leeds, but one had been bald, and the other had been small and with greying fair hair.

Although she couldn't be absolutely certain that the man who had visited the phone shop was the same person to whom she had spoken on the mobile, her gut instinct and the circumstantial evidence had convinced her that he was. The initial excitement she had felt in the phone shop had energised her, but that had abated with the realisation that she still had to seek a man for whom she had no name, in a town of over sixty thousand inhabitants.

She had spoken to receptionists in each of the hotels that she had visited, giving what she hoped was a plausible story about wanting to contact a man whom she had met on the train to Harrogate. She had described his physical appearance and explained how she was anxious to meet him again. None of the receptionists had recalled a guest who met exactly the description, but in each case Laura had left her mobile phone number. She had explained that she didn't want her number given out, but had smilingly said that it would be a big favour if they let her know if such a man should show up in their respective hotels. Without having actually said so, she had given the impression that it was an affair of the heart. She knew that when asked directly most people's inclination was to oblige, particularly if the request appealed to their sense of romance.

She planned to try the same approach at more of the hotels tomorrow. Meanwhile the Moat House was a good hotel in which to hang out. It was attached to the Conference Centre and therefore a likely magnet for her quarry – assuming her theory was true and that he had some illegal agenda relating to the forthcoming conference.

She made her way through the bar, looking about carefully while keeping her body language casual.

"Laura! Over here."

She turned in surprise and saw Penny Harte waving at her. The policewoman was seated in a corner of the bar.

Laura smiled and approached. "Hi," she said.

"Hi."

"I didn't expect to see you. I'm a little early."

"I knew the place was busy so I came a bit ahead of schedule to try and get us a spot."

"*Be prepared!* I bet you were a Girl Guide," said Laura with a grin as she sat down.

"Guilty as charged. Enthusiastic member of the Primrose Patrol. So . . . what would you like to drink?"

"Think I've earned a gin and tonic," said Laura, "but please, let me get them." She saw that Penny was about to object and raised her hand to stop her. "Please. It goes on my expenses. Let the press barons pay – for the first one at least."

"Well, when you put it like that . . ."

"I do. So, what will you have?"

"I'll join you in gin and tonic then," said Penny.

"Another Girl Guide lost to the Demon Drink," said Laura with a smile.

"What would my old Patrol Leader say?"

"*Cheers*, probably. Right – two G and T's coming up!" said Laura, then she rose and made for the bar, casually taking the money from her purse while surreptitiously scanning the faces all around her.

The noise level in the hotel bar rose perceptibly as the night went on and as Penny and Laura sat in the corner sipping their third drink they no longer had to speak quietly to avoid being heard. They had chatted easily, comfortably regaining the rapport they had established the previous night on the drive into Harrogate. Penny found herself revealing her hopes and aspirations as well as the frustrations she felt in her career as a police officer, and Laura in turn spoke freely of her own job and how she loved the freedom, but also felt the insecurity of being a freelance. The gin and tonics had added to the relaxed atmosphere between them and Penny smiled when Laura put her glass aside and said, "I've a confession to make."

"Don't tell me – you know the whereabouts of Lord Lucan?"

"No . . ."

"You've evidence that Elvis was murdered?"

"I suppose you get stuff like that all the time?"

"You wouldn't believe it. We'd a guy in the station last year who swore he saw Hitler in Battersea Park."

Laura smiled briefly, then looked Penny in the eye. "Actually, I was serious . . ."

"Yeah?"

"It's not that I've committed any crime, but . . . well, I have misled you."

"In what way?" asked Penny.

"I told you I was here to do colour pieces on the conference, and I am in part . . ."

Penny looked at the other woman, her curiosity aroused. "But you've some other agenda?"

"Yes. And it's possible . . . it's possible we might be able to help one another."

"In what way?"

Laura hesitated.

Penny looked at her quizzically. "How might we help each other?"

"What I'm about to tell you is strictly off the record. For now it's just between you and me, OK?"

Penny nodded, intrigued at the turn events had taken. "OK."

"All right, " said Laura, "here it is. I am a *bone fide* journalist, and I am here on behalf of a genuine newspaper. But I'm also on someone's trail. In fact, that's the real reason I came to Harrogate."

"Can I ask who this person is?"

"I don't know his name," answered Laura, "but there was a killing in Ireland last week – you may have heard of it. Two members of the Continuity IRA were murdered."

"Yes, I read about it."

"I happened to acquire a phone number that one of the dead men had called the day before the killing. It was a mobile number, and when I rang it I got this guy."

"Whom you're now trying to locate?"

"Yes. I think . . . well, I think it's possible he may have been the one who killed them."

"What makes you think that?"

"I don't have any proof, if that's what you're going to ask for," said Laura, "but the two murder victims were terrorists, and I think this man may be a terrorist also . . ."

"I see . . ."

"And if I'm right, and he is a terrorist, then I reckon that his coming to Harrogate just when all the Foreign Ministers in the EU are due here may not be a coincidence."

Penny felt the hairs on the back of her neck rising suddenly.

"I hope you don't think I'm mad . . ." said Laura.

"No. No, I don't," answered Penny slowly.

Laura looked at her – an appraising, shrewd look that culminated with her nodding. "So . . . there's been some kind of a threat, has there?"

After a slight hesitation, Penny answered, "I'm sorry, Laura, I can't discuss that."

"I understand."

Penny's mind was racing, but she knew she had to curtail her excitement and follow a logical line. "What's the connection to Harrogate?"

"When I rang this guy he was making his way here."

"How do you know?"

"I taped the conversion," said Laura. "It's audible in the background – he was definitely boarding a train to Harrogate."

"You still have the tape?"

"Of course."

"How long did he talk to you?"

"Maybe thirty seconds. I think the call took him by surprise, and I tried to keep him talking as long as possible."

"What did he sound like?"

"Foreign," answered Laura. "Good English, but accented."

Penny felt another shiver run up her spine. *A foreigner bound for Harrogate who could be a terrorist.* "Have you notified the police in Ireland?"

"No. He was in Britain when I rang him, the conference is in Britain, I'm in Britain. Were I to notify the police officially, I think it should be here in Britain."

"Right . . ." said Penny. She felt that the other woman should still have notified the Irish police, but she wasn't going to push it right now. "You said *were you* to notify the police. Why wouldn't you?"

"I'm a journalist," said Laura, "and I feel this could be a major story. I don't want to lose this guy's trail. I don't want the police shutting me out."

"I see. But how can you follow his trail if all you have is his voice?"

"I've a description of him now. At least I think I have."

"A description?"

"I figured that after I rang him on the mobile he'd ditch the sim card – if he is who I think he is. And I'd rung the number all weekend and it wasn't functioning. So today I went to the phone shop here in town and asked how many sim cards they'd sold since Saturday afternoon. Only one was sold to a foreigner who sounded like my guy. Right age, right kind of accent and now I've got a description."

Penny nodded approvingly. "That was rather good detective work."

"Thank you," said Laura.

Penny paused, sensing that the first break in the case could be at hand here, yet knowing that she had to proceed curiously. "You said at the outset that perhaps we could help each other . . ."

"Yes," agreed Laura.

"What exactly had you got in mind?"

"A quid pro quo. Though I want to say, Penny, that I didn't befriend you with this in mind. I met you and liked you first. It was only tonight that it struck me we might be able to help each other."

"Right."

"I mean it," said Laura. "I'd hate you to think I'd been cultivating you. I mean, I didn't even know you were a police officer when I stopped at the breakdown."

"It's OK, Laura, I believe you. But now that a quid pro quo's been mentioned – what exactly are we talking about?"

"I can share with you my physical description of the guy. More importantly, I can give you a copy of the tape. Presumably your linguistics people could come

245

up with all sorts of data by analysing the voice." Penny recognised a heaven-sent opportunity, but she kept the excitement from her voice. "And in return?"

"I'd have your word that I'd be kept in the loop. I'd be allowed see how a police investigation like this is handled. I really want to see the inside track here. Of course, I wouldn't publish a word until after the event, and even then nothing that was classified. But if I'm right, and this guy is up to something, it's a huge story – and I absolutely want the scoop. And if I'm wrong and nothing happens, I get to write a fly-on-the wall article. *What life's really like for police officers at the coalface. A view from the inside.* So, what do you say?"

Penny knew that having a civilian involved to the extent that Laura was suggesting might be a little messy. On the other hand, she felt that Laura wasn't the type to create unnecessary problems. And the tape represented the first real opportunity for a break in the case.

"I'd have to sell it to my bosses," said Penny. "It's pretty irregular."

"Not as irregular as a terrorist targeting every Foreign Minister in the EU."

"Granted. But I know how they'll view your premise."

"How?" asked Laura.

"Heavily circumstantial, lot of conjecture."

"Circumstantial evidence can convict. And besides, there's no conjecture about the tape. It exists and it's there to be analysed. Provided we have a deal. So . . . are you interested?"

Penny nodded. "Yes. I'm interested."

10

Majid punched in the numbers, then pressed the dial button on his mobile phone. The early morning sunlight streamed in through the parlour window, warming the house in Starbeck with strong autumnal sunshine. Jemail Zubi looked up from the map that was spread on the table before them, and Majid nodded to him. "Ringing . . ."

The phone was answered on the third ring, and Majid recognised the voice of the ship's captain whom he had called the previous Sunday.

"I said I'd ring this morning," said Majid. "Everything on schedule?"

"Yes, slightly ahead of schedule actually."

As had been the case during his last call, Majid could hear the rumbling of the ship's engines in the background, but the man's voice was perfectly clear.

"We made good time," continued the captain. "Should be docking about one-thirty this afternoon."

"Good."

"Once we've cleared customs you can arrange collection as soon as you like."

"No, I don't think so," answered Majid. Although he was glad that the ship was ahead of schedule he had no intention of making his collection in broad daylight. At the same time he decided not to give the captain a specific time for collection that night. Considering that the man was acting under orders from Omar Rahmani, it would have been tantamount to suicide for him to have engaged in any kind of a double-cross, yet Majid was aware that this was one of the few key moments of the mission that wasn't under his own control. If anything were to go wrong, if somehow the authorities were onto them, the attempt to capture or kill them was likely to be when they showed themselves to collect the consignment from the ship. The less the captain knew about the hand-over arrangements, until the last minute, the happier Majid would be. "This evening suits me better," he said. "I'll ring you with instructions nearer the time."

There was a pause, and Majid sensed that the captain probably wasn't used to taking orders like this. *Fine*, he thought, *no harm to keep him slightly off balance*. Besides which, in this situation Majid was acting as Rahmani's representative and he knew that the captain was unlikely to want to fall foul of the powerful Iraqi.

"Stay by the phone please and I'll call you with the details," said Majid.

"As you wish."

"Until later then," said Majid, then he hung up and turned to face Jemail.

"Everything OK?"

"Arriving at one-thirty today, but we won't collect it till after dark."

"So what time do we leave for Hull?"

"Long before that," answered Majid. "I want to be sure everything is right before we make contact."

"Sure," agreed Jemail.

"If we leave Harrogate about four we'll be there with several hours to spare."

"Fine. There is one thing, Abdullah . . ."

"What?"

"Police checkpoints. I told you I saw one on the Knaresborough road – and Tamaz saw another on the A61. It sounds like they're covering the different approaches to Harrogate."

"But they're random," said Majid. "I looked where you said on the Knaresborough road, and it wasn't there this morning. Also they're checking people *making* for Harrogate. When we're in the van this afternoon we'll be *leaving*."

"But when we're coming back tonight?"

"Then we've no option but to take our chances. But remember that the checkpoints are random. And they'll be less likely to man them late at night when most of the police are off duty. Which is when we'll travel back."

"Supposing we still get stopped?"

"It's a mission in enemy territory, Jemail – it can't be done without some risk."

"Don't misunderstand, my friend. I'm not afraid to take risks." The Lebanese looked at Majid and smiled wryly. "I just like to keep them to the minimum."

"Believe me, we will. And if we do get stopped our first strategy will be to talk our way out of it."

"That may not be so easy."

"So long as you appear confident and cool, talking usually works very well."

"OK. But . . . worst-case scenario," said Jemail. "Supposing talking doesn't work?"

"What would our trainers have recommended?" asked Majid.

"Sudden overwhelming force."

"Exactly. What's the status of our weapons?"

"I stripped, oiled and loaded all of them yesterday."

"Do it again today," said Majid. "Let's be doubly certain."

"All right. What are we bringing?"

"An Uzi each."

Jemail nodded. Both men hated most things Israeli, but there was no denying the effectiveness of the Israeli-made Uzi submachine-gun.

"Let's have handguns as well," added Majid. "The Beretta for me, the Sig for you. Silencers for them all."

"OK. Anything else?"

"No. Just lie low this morning and have the weapons ready for this afternoon."

Jemail nodded, an excited glint in his eye. "Consider it done."

Chief Superintendent Jack Thompson looked thoughtful as he sat behind his temporary desk in the command room. Penny sat silently opposite him, glad that she had been able to get him alone for a few minutes at the start of their working day. She remembered from the old days how it was better not to pester Thompson when he was evaluating something and so now she waited patiently. After a moment Thompson's gaze came back from the middle distance, and he swivelled slightly in his chair, then looked Penny in the eye.

"Leaving aside all the ifs, buts and maybes, what's your gut feeling on this one?" he asked.

Penny hesitated a moment. She had told Thompson of Laura's offer regarding the tape, but she knew that when repeated in the cold light of day to a third party the whole thing could sound like wishful thinking by a journalist on the make. Except that she didn't think this was the case. "My gut instinct is that she's onto something."

"You really think the person on the tape could be our man?"

"Certainly a possibility. In the absence of any other leads, I really think it's worth pursuing."

Thompson nodded. "Maybe . . ."

"Even if it's not our man, Chief, a terrorist is still a terrorist."

"How do you mean?"

"Well, if this guy had dealings with two terrorists – who are murdered the day after he speaks to them – there's a fair chance he's not collecting for the Red Cross. Odds are he's some kind of terrorist himself."

"Could be," conceded Thompson. "And this Laura Kennedy, you're sure she's legit? I mean she could have made the tape with a friend."

"I don't think so –"

"Can't be just dismissed, Penny," said Thompson,

"however nice she seems. Journalists have been known to pull all sorts of stunts. If it's even certain she is a journalist."

"She is. I saw her press card. I also went online and checked that she's registered with the NUJ."

"OK, let's take it she's an accredited journalist. How did she get the phone number for this guy in the first place?"

"She won't say. But that's not in itself suspicious. You know yourself how journalists are about protecting their sources."

"Yeah, especially when it suits them," said Thompson. "I'm being Devil's Advocate, Penny, because if I agree to this deal I know I may end up justifying it to the Chief Constable."

"I understand."

"So, what do you know about this woman's background?"

"She's from Dublin, she's been a journalist since leaving college, her family are middle-class – brother a doctor, sister a schoolteacher. She lives in an apartment with her boyfriend."

"What does he do?"

"Works as a sound engineer on films. He's on location in Prague at the moment."

"A sound engineer?"

"I know what you're going to say, Chief – he could have made the tape for her. But you asked me for my gut-instinct, and my instinct is that whether or not the guy on the tape is our man, the tape itself is legitimate. I'd bank on that."

"Fair enough. What else do you know about her?"

"She's smart, she has a slightly quirky sense of humour," Penny hesitated fractionally, feeling a tiny stab of guilt at having to analyse so cold-bloodedly character traits that had been revealed when the women had relaxed together. "She's good-natured too – she'd no idea who I was when she stopped for me by the side of the road."

"Any inkling of her political leanings?"

"No, but . . . I doubt if they'd be anything extreme."

"And yet she got an interview with the Continuity IRA."

"She's a journalist, Chief."

"Sometimes journalists have political agendas. Maybe the Continuity IRA gave her the phone number. It's not beyond the bounds of possibility that they could even have set her up to infiltrate us."

"Theoretically, it's possible," said Penny. "But then so is just about anything. And I'd bet my bottom dollar that she's exactly what she says she is."

"You're that sure?"

"Yes, I reckon she's legit."

"All right," said Thompson. "We'll check her against our data banks. She doesn't sound like a candidate for an IRA background, but obviously we'll have to check."

"OK."

"Incidentally, there's no need to say anything about this to Mr Carrow . . . for the moment . . . "

"Whatever you say, Chief."

"I don't know whether you remember, but he's got a bit of a thing about the Irish."

"He's got a bit of a thing about a lot of people!"

Thompson smiled. "He has. But when it comes to the Irish he thinks they're either rampaging terrorists at worst, or sympathetic fellow-travellers at best."

"That's ridiculous," said Penny.

"I know. But his brother was killed serving in Northern Ireland so his prejudices are magnified a hundredfold."

"Yes, I remember hearing that."

"Anyway, let's just assure ourselves that she's kosher before Mr Carrow tries to stymie things."

"Sure. Does that mean, Chief, that you're going for Laura's offer?"

"We'd have to agree exactly what it is she gets in return, and I'll have to clear a few things at my end, but yes, I think it's worth having the tape analysed."

"Great," said Penny.

"I'll need to talk to Colin Mathieson too, but I'm sure there won't be a problem there."

"No."

"Probably be a break for him. He's had the American Secret Service like a monkey on his back since yesterday."

"From what I hear they want to be on all our backs."

"Not mine, thank you. Co-ordination between the Secret Service and MI5 is Colin's baby; co-ordination between the Secret Service and the police falls to Special Branch – Len Carrow's baby."

"No better man to keep them in their place," said Penny with a smile.

"He does have his uses," agreed Thompson.

"Talking of the Americans, any word yet on the Israeli angle?"

Thompson nodded. "Colin rang me last night."

"Yeah?"

"All couched in very diplomatic terms. But to put it bluntly, both the CIA and Mossad are seriously cheesed off with MI5. Arses have been kicked in Tel Aviv though, so we're assured top priority is now being given to trawling their files like we'd originally requested."

"I hope they come up with something soon," said Penny.

"You and me both. Meanwhile let's get our hands on this tape."

"Right. And assuming there are no hitches, Chief, how quickly can we get the voice analysed?"

"Rapidly is what I'll be demanding. It's done with computers – no reason why we shouldn't have answers fast."

"Good."

"What arrangement have you made with the journalist?"

"I'm to ring her to say if we're interested. As soon as a deal's done, she'll hand over the tape."

"Right, let me make a few enquiries first."

"Fine. I can wait here if you like," offered Penny.

"Yes," answered Thompson, "do that. Then the minute it's sorted out, let's get our hands on this tape . . ."

Laura answered her mobile on the second ring. In her eagerness to hear back from Penny Harte she would have answered on the first ring had she not been eating the breakfast brought to her bedroom by room service. As it was she quickly swallowed the muesli in her mouth and put the phone to her ear. "Hello?"

"Morning, Kid."

"Oh, Mac . . ."

"Is that disappointment, surprise or early-morning grumpiness I detect?"

"Eh, none of the above," Laura answered, trying for a tone of levity, but aware that she had been disappointed to hear the Deputy Editor's voice when she had been hoping the call was from Penny.

"Nine fifteen, Laura. Thought you'd be bright-eyed, bushy-tailed and up and at 'em."

"All of the above, Mac."

"I believe you, Kid," said McEvoy sardonically, "but thousands wouldn't."

"A million flies can't be wrong, yeah?"

She was rewarded with a brief chuckle, then her boss spoke again, his voice serious. "I've had a call from the Guards. They want to interview you."

"Yeah?"

"They found that Boyle and O'Donnell had been staying in an apartment in Tallaght, but then that's probably not news to you . . ."

Laura didn't rise to Mac's bait regarding Tallaght. "I presume they found a copy of my article in this apartment?" she said instead.

"You presume correctly. So they want to interview you, as we expected."

"What did you say to them?"

"That you were out of the country on assignment for

the *Clarion*. I emphasised that your link to the dead men was strictly limited to interviewing them for the article, and that I'd commissioned you to do it."

"Were they happy enough with that?"

"They're prepared to wait till you come back from Harrogate to take a formal statement."

"Good. And thanks, Mac."

"You'd want to tread very carefully, Laura."

"I will."

"Do. Which brings us to Harrogate. How have you been doing?"

"I've been pretty busy. You got my colour piece?"

"Yeah, it's good. Liked the Dickens quote."

"Thought you might," said Laura.

"Any progress on the main story?"

"Yes, there's been some . . ." Laura hesitated, unsure how much to tell her editor. Part of her wanted to tell him about the proposed deal with Penny Harte but, if she built it up and then Penny couldn't sell the idea to her superiors, she feared that she would lose face with Mac. Better to wait until there was something more tangible, she decided.

"Were you going to tell me what the progress was?" Mac asked, a slight edge of impatience in his voice.

"Yes, of course. I think – I think I may have a good description of my target."

"Yeah?"

"Obviously he had to dump the sim card after I called him, so yesterday I tried the phone shops in Harrogate. One of them sold a sim card to someone who sounded very like our man. I got a good description."

"Nice work. Any joy with the delegations?"

"Not so far, but I'm still working on that."

"Right . . ."

"I've also struck up a friendship with a policewoman I met by chance," said Laura, choosing her words carefully. She wanted to prepare Mac in case Penny did get approval from her bosses.

"Oh yeah?"

"Yeah, she could be a pretty useful contact."

"Have you told her the real reason you're in Harrogate?"

Trust Mac to get to the heart of the matter, thought Laura. "I've told her some of it."

"So she knows you're trying to find this guy?"

"Yes."

"And that you think he may be planning a hit on the conference?"

"Yes."

There was a pause. "Do you think I shouldn't have told her?" asked Laura.

"No, it was probably right to warn her. But I think if the British police know of this guy's existence, but the Guards here don't, there could be a problem."

"I haven't formally gone to the British police and reported it."

"Even so," said Mac, "might be wise to cover all options."

"If I rang the Guards to tell them, they might want me to come back to Ireland. And I can't leave Harrogate now, Mac, I'm making progress here."

"Yeah . . ."

"They'd also want to know where I got the mobile number," said Laura.

"I think our best bet's the ol' anonymous phone call."

"How would that work?"

"Newspapers get tip-offs all the time. I'll ring the Guards and say we've had a call from someone. Tell them about this mystery foreigner who may have been involved with the murdered men."

"You think they'll buy that?" asked Laura.

"No reason why they shouldn't. If it turns out that you're right and the murderer is in Harrogate the British police can deal with it. But it means the Guards don't look clueless. Means they can even look good if they notify the Brits and the guy is subsequently arrested."

"Right . . ."

"Lot of ifs and buts, Kid, but *if* all of this were to happen, and you got your scoop, the Guards here might well suspect that your involvement went beyond just writing an article on Boyle and O'Donnell. If they looked stupid in front of their British counterparts they could be pretty disgruntled with you. If, on the other hand, they get to tip off the Brits, they look good – and they'd be unlikely to hound the journalist who broke the story."

Laura quickly considered Mac's arguments, then smiled. "The word *Machiavellian* comes to mind . . ."

"I love it when you talk dirty."

Laura laughed.

"But seriously, Kid, be very careful here."

"I will."

"And let me know as soon as anything develops. *If* anything develops."

"I'm working all the angles, Mac. If it's humanly possible to find this guy, I'll do it, believe me."

"OK. And, Laura . . ."

"Yeah?"

"A scoop is terrific, but it's not worth dying for. If this guy is what you think he is, then he's very dangerous. So I'll say it again. Be careful – be very careful."

"Thanks, Mac, I will."

"Talk to you soon."

"Yeah, bye, Mac."

Laura breathed out slowly, then hung up, chastened slightly by the conversation with her editor, but eager to leave the line open for the call she expected from Penny Harte.

The morning rush-hour traffic had eased now, improving the traffic flow through Harrogate, and Penny drove swiftly, consciously keeping her excitement in check as she made her way through the town. Normally she would have walked from Police Headquarters to the Old Swan Hotel, but today she was anxious to get there as quickly as possible. She had rung Laura the moment Thompson had given her the go-ahead and now she wanted to finalise the deal on the tape.

She turned right into Parliament Street, noting a strong police presence as she drove down the hill and traversed the part of town close to the Conference Centre. Mixed among the uniformed police, she knew, was a sizeable contingent of plainclothes officers, carefully watching for any suspicious behaviour, anything even remotely threatening or irregular.

So far nothing of any significance had been uncovered, but Penny knew the importance of exploring every possible source of threat. It was an approach that Thompson had had to pursue in checking out Laura Kennedy, and although Penny had felt slightly guilty about yielding up every detail that Laura had revealed to her, nonetheless she had kept sight of her priorities and done so.

To her relief, none of the security checks had turned up anything untoward on the journalist. In reality, it was no more that Penny had expected. The idea that Laura might be involved in some sort of convoluted Irish republican plot that involved befriending a policewoman had always seemed farfetched to her and, unlike Carrow, she didn't feel that anyone Irish should automatically be treated as potentially hostile.

She had debated in her own mind whether or not to tell Laura that they had had to have her checked out, then had decided against it. She reasoned that as a journalist Laura was probably practical enough to know that such things needed to be done, and if the other woman hadn't realised it then there was no point in either alienating her or inhibiting her for the future.

Penny turned left into Swan Road, then swung right into the carpark of the Old Swan Hotel. She crossed the tarmacadamed parking lot and entered the lobby. The Old Swan interior was redolent of the era when Harrogate had flourished as a spa town, but Penny wasn't in the frame of mind to appreciate its old-world atmosphere this morning. Instead she quickly made her way to the residents' lounge, spotting Laura who rose from an armchair and came forward to greet her.

"Penny, how are you?"

"Pleased I got the go-ahead," answered Penny with a smile. "I got here as fast as I could."

"A quick responder – the Journalist's Dream Come True. Would you like a coffee or anything?"

"No thanks, Laura. If you don't mind, we'll get straight to business."

"Great," answered the Irishwoman. "Let's grab a couple of armchairs in the corner here."

"Fine." Penny followed Laura to a corner of the lounge where they were out of earshot of those residents and visitors who were reading newspapers and having morning tea.

"So, we have a deal then?" said Laura.

"Provided you agree to my boss's terms."

"Which are?"

"More or less as we discussed," answered Penny. "You give us a copy of the tape for analysis. In return you get exclusive access."

"Plus the results of the tape analysis."

"Yes."

"How much access is he promising?"

"Enough to write a major scoop if the tape leads somewhere dramatic."

"And if the tape turns out not to lead somewhere dramatic?" asked Laura.

"A chance to write the type of fly-on-the-wall article

you discussed. To be published after the conference has been safely hosted. OK?"

Laura looked at Penny, and Penny was conscious of a searching quality in the other woman's gaze. "I *can* trust your boss to deliver? After I've handed over the copy of the tape?"

Penny nodded. "When Jack Thompson gives his word, you can count on it."

"Fair enough."

"I did as you said too – gave him your description of the guy from the phone shop as a goodwill gesture."

"And?"

"He appreciated it. I promise you, Laura, Thompson won't let you down, and neither will I. Even if the tape comes to nothing – though I'm hoping it won't – but even if it does, you'll still get to spend time with working police officers, like you suggested."

"All right, that's good enough for me," said Laura.

"So you have the tape?"

Laura reached into her bag and produced a small cassette. "First copy of the original – it's good quality. All yours . . ."

Penny accepted the tape eagerly. "Thanks . . ."

"How soon can it be analysed?"

"Immediately. Chief Superintendent Thompson gets whatever he needs on this operation."

"How long will the analysis take?"

"Can't say exactly," answered Penny, "but it will be top priority."

"So . . . hours or days?"

"Good chance we'll know within a day, I'd think."

"And you'll let me know as soon as the results come back?"

"Absolutely. And now, I'd better get back . . ."

"Right, don't let me keep you," said Laura.

"OK."

The Irishwoman held out her hand. "Good luck, Penny."

"Thanks, talk to you soon." Penny shook the other woman's hand, then she slipped the cassette into her bag and eagerly made for the door.

Samuel Lubetkin tapped briefly on the office door, then pushed it open and entered the workspace of his subordinate, Avi Blumenthal. From behind a desk heaped with an array of files, Blumenthal looked up.

"Samuel," he said, laying aside a dossier and giving Lubetkin his attention.

"Hard at it?"

"When the PM's office says jump . . ."

"Mossad staff officers say 'How high?'," answered Lubetkin with a smile.

"Something like that. Even our friends in Shin Beth are actively co-operating."

"Wonders will never cease," said Lubetkin wryly, aware as he was of the inevitable competition between Mossad and Israel's interior security service, the Shin Beth. "Get all the extra bodies you requested?"

"Yes, most of them anyway . . ."

"*Most* of them?"

"Even with the PM's backing there's still the question of physically acquiring suitable people," answered

Blumenthal. "However, I'm promised I'll have a full complement within a matter of hours."

"Good. How's progress in the meantime?"

"Pretty good. We're still trawling through every record we can find on Iraqi terrorists and suspected Iraqi terrorists, plus the Shin Beth records on Iraqi prisoners and former Iraqi prisoners . . ."

"Going back the suggested ten years?"

"Yes. Should be a fair chance of the target being in that time-frame."

Lubetkin nodded. "We can always go back further if need be."

"Let's hope not," said Blumenthal. "There's a hell of a lot of collating to be done as it is."

"OK. So, what sort of a timescale are we talking about to plough through everything?"

"Depends on how much more shows up from the archives," answered Blumenthal.

"The PM's office hasn't been back to me yet," said Lubetkin, "but they will be. So, are we talking a day, two days . . . more?"

"I'd tell them two days, and we'll try to improve on that."

Lubetkin nodded. "All right. And, Avi. Kick some asses here if need be. Let everyone know this is top priority."

"I have – they're working flat out."

"Yeah?"

"Yeah.

"Maybe you should still emphasise the Iraqi angle," said Lubetkin.

"How do you mean?"

"Underline that for Israelis Iraq is a really hostile nation. That compiling the dossiers is a vital job and that doing it speedily and accurately is a way to strike back at the bastards who showered us with Scud missiles during the Gulf War."

"OK," said Blumenthal.

"I remember Israeli children going to school with gas masks, Avi. I remember Scud missiles whistling down from the sky and terrified civilians not knowing if Sadam had armed them with chemical weapons or not. I remember my eight-year-old niece asking me if the Iraqis could hit Tel Aviv with anthrax."

"Right . . ."

"All that kind of stuff makes this personal, Avi, for me and for lots of the people collating the data. It's good for motivating them."

Blumenthal looked at his senior colleague but said nothing.

"So use the Scuds, and use the frightened children – but only up to a point. Not to the extent that they're so driven it clouds their judgement, yes?"

Blumenthal looked searchingly at Lubetkin. "*Use the frightened children?*" he repeated.

"You know what I mean."

"Sometimes – sometimes you're a hard man, Sam . . ."

"It's a hard business. Normally I don't have to remind you of that."

"I stand corrected," said Blumenthal.

"Just come up with the goods, Avi – however you see fit."

"Right . . ."

"OK," said Lubetkin. "Keep me posted . . ."

Majid and Jemail sat in the front of the van with the
lights off. Their handguns were in their pockets and the
Uzis were at the side of the seats within easy reach.
Although they were safely ensconced in the far corner
of the carpark of a hotel on the outskirts of Hull, Majid
knew that the moment of maximum danger was
approaching. If the operation had been compromised
somehow, tonight was surely when the authorities
would try to apprehend them, but there was no way of
collecting the shipment from the freighter that had
docked that afternoon without exposing themselves to
some degree.

He had tried to cover as many eventualities as
possible when planning for tonight, but he knew from
experience that sometimes things developed unexpectedly
on a mission like this. Still, Jemail was a good man to
have along – he had seen action lots of times, and Majid
knew that his partner wouldn't be found wanting if
they had to fight themselves out of a corner. All the
same, Majid thought, no harm to run through things
one last time. "Jemail . . ."

"Yes?"

"If there are any complications at the hand-over . . .
you know the drill . . ."

"We kill whoever caused the complication and make
certain to get the shipment."

Majid nodded. "And if we have to kill anyone
present . . ."

267

"We kill everyone present – the mission can't be compromised."

"Exactly," said Majid, then his mobile rang, and he turned away from Jemail and answered the phone.

"Hello?"

"You said to call you back," said a man's voice, and Majid could hear a hint of strain in the tone of the ship's captain's voice. "The taxi is here now."

There was animosity in the tone too, but Majid didn't care. He had rung the captain earlier and, while still speaking obliquely, had made clear that any problems concerning a safe delivery would be deemed traceable to the captain personally. The man had taken offence when Majid had intimated that such difficulties would mean the captain paying a very high price, but Majid wasn't concerned for the man's feelings. There had been further friction when Majid had explained that he wouldn't be collecting the shipment from the freighter, but that the captain was to take a taxi and deliver the material personally, to a destination that would be provided later. It had become necessary for Majid to invoke the all-powerful Rahmani – without actually mentioning their mutual employer by name – before the captain had reluctantly agreed to follow Majid's instructions.

"You have the goods with you?" asked Majid

"Yes," answered the captain.

"And you're travelling alone – we want no misunderstandings . . ."

"Yes, you've already made all this clear."

"Good. Take the taxi to the St George Hotel. It's on the western outskirts of Hull."

"And where exactly do we meet?"

"Don't worry about that. Just go to the St George, and make certain that you keep your mobile switched on."

"Look, you're –"

"Keep it switched on all the time, I'll talk to you again." Majid hung up before the man could argue, then put down his own phone, pleased with how things were progressing. In the event of a double-cross or the mission being compromised, the opposition would now try to stake out the hotel. Satisfied that he had created a plausible false trail, Majid turned back to Jemail.

"OK?"

Majid nodded. "Yes. Let's go."

Both men put on their seat belts, then Majid started up the engine, turned on the lights, and drove towards the exit.

Jemail slipped the Uzi into the large inside front pocket of his jacket, waited until there was a break in the traffic on the busy main road, then opened the door of the van and got out. Majid immediately pulled away. He watched in the rear-view mirror as his partner walked with an apparently casual stride towards a petrol station-cum-roadside-café thirty metres back down the road. Majid had chosen it carefully, wanting a premises that fronted a busy road and that had a café with windows that overlooked the approach. As a bonus this particular premises occupied a V junction, with another busy road on the far side of its forecourt from which entrance could be made by drivers wishing to use the café. Majid

knew however that it wasn't possible to turn left at the
V, and so he continued on, dialling a number on his
mobile as he headed for a set of traffic-lights at which
he knew there was a left filter.

The phone was answered immediately, and once
again Majid detected the irritation in the captain's voice
"Hello?"

"Change of plans," said Majid. "Forget the St
George and tell your driver to go to the Cross Keys
service station and café."

"This is ridiculous –" began the captain.

"Don't argue, just tell him now!" ordered Majid. He
heard the captain breathing out harshly, then giving the
taxi-driver the altered instructions.

"Very well, I've told him," the man said grumpily.

"Good," said Majid. "From now until we finish, stay
on the line – I'll be giving you instructions from time to
time.

"Not another destination?!"

"No, just go to the service station. But keep the
phone to your ear and leave the line open, all the time."
Majid lay his own mobile down on the seat as he
negotiated the filter light, then he turned back toward
the service station from the opposite direction, satisfied
with the precautions he had just taken. He had timed
matters so that the taxi would not have yet reached the
St George Hotel, and lest the captain might have been
involved in a double-cross – either voluntary, or under
duress from the authorities – anyone staking out the St
George wouldn't know that the action had switched to
the service station. With the mobile switched on and

kept to his ear the captain wouldn't be able to report back on the changes. Of course if the authorities had simply been following his taxi there would still be a problem, but Majid knew that every option couldn't be covered, and he felt that he had done well to introduce the safeguards he had implemented.

He pulled into a lay-by about twenty-five metres from the garage, switched off the van's engine and killed the lights. He picked up his mobile and spoke into it while scanning the garage forecourt and noting the lighted windows of the café. "Just checking in – still there?"

"Yes, I'm still here," answered the captain.

"Shouldn't be much longer now – you were heading in the same direction anyway. Keep the phone to your ear, I'll talk to you again soon."

Majid put the mobile down, then looked again at the garage. He could see the neon lights in the windows of the café and he knew that Jemail would by now have taken a seat with a view of the forecourt and the entrance door. He settled down to wait as patiently as his excitement would allow, then after a couple of minutes a taxi came from the road on the opposite side of the V and pulled onto the forecourt. Majid immediately lifted the mobile. "Hello?" he said.

"Yes . . ."

"OK, step out here and pay off the taxi."

"Can't I take the taxi back again?" asked the captain.

"No, that's not how we do it. Pay off the taxi, please."

Majid heard the other man breathing out in

exasperation, but a moment later he saw him stepping out of the taxi carrying a Gladstone bag. The captain was a short, heavy-set man. Majid watched him paying off the taxi-driver, waited until the taxi began to pull away, then spoke again.

"All right, carry the bag casually and enter the café. Go to the men's toilets and enter the first cubicle from the door. If that's not free, take the first cubicle that is free. Lock the door, place the bag on the top of the cistern, then wait a moment before flushing the toilet. Leave the cubicle, closing the door after you. Got all that?"

"Yes."

"Go back out through the café, cross the forecourt and head back up the road by which you arrived. When you've gone a hundred metres you can stop and hail a taxi. Understood?"

"Yes."

"One last thing. You're under observation now and you'll be under observation in the café also. So do exactly as I've said, and when I finish talking now, turn off the mobile and don't use it again until you're travelling back in the taxi. All right?"

"Right," the captain answered tightly.

"And thank you for all your co-operation."

"My pleasure," said the other man, his voice dripping sarcasm.

"OK, switch off the phone and let's do it." Majid turned off his own mobile and from the distance he could see the captain pocketing his. He watched him making for the door of the café and entering. He breathed out deeply, his pulses starting to race. He had seen no sign of any vehicle following the taxi and he felt that in reality the captain was probably completely above board, but he knew also that if anything *were* to go wrong it would be within the next minute or two. He slipped his hand down onto the Uzi, its presence a reassurance as he continued to scan the approaches to the garage, but still nothing appeared to be untoward. The seconds passed with agonising slowness until eventually he saw the door of the café opening with a spill of light. He strained his eyes and recognised the figure of the captain crossing the forecourt without the Gladstone bag. Majid immediately laid the Uzi across his knees and turned the key in the ignition. He flicked on the lights, put the van into gear and indicated. He saw a gap in the approaching traffic and swiftly pulled out onto the road, then indicated left and pulled in smoothly onto the forecourt of the garage.

He glanced across the forecourt to confirm that the captain was still following his instructions, and to his relief he could make out the figure of the man heading towards the road by which he had originally approached. Even if he were now to signal someone on that road, his support would be on the wrong side of the V, and if any hostiles tried to storm the cafe on foot Majid was well placed to mow them down with the Uzi.

Majid watched the captain disappear from view, then he turned round to face the door of the café. *Come on*, he thought, *what the hell could be keeping Jemail?* Could the captain conceivably have attacked him, then left the Gladstone bag behind to put Majid off while he called in support? Suddenly the door of the café opened and his speculations were ended. Jemail was standing in the doorway, the Gladstone bag in his left hand. He closed the door and walked across the forecourt, his stride brisk yet seemingly casual. Majid continued to scan all the approaches to the forecourt while resisting the urge to shout to Jemail to hurry up. Then he was at the van, and Majid leaned across and swung the passenger door open for him. Jemail placed the Gladstone bag on the floor before quickly climbing into his seat and shutting the door behind him.

Majid immediately pulled away, turning back out onto the main road as Jemail fastened his seatbelt. They drove for a while without speaking, both of them checking the van's mirrors in case of pursuit, then when it seemed that no-one was following, Majid kept the vehicle at a steady forty miles an hour and relaxed enough to glance over at Jemail.

"No hitches in the toilets?"

"Followed him in, pretended to be washing my hands – he'd never even have seen my face. The minute he went out I got the stuff."

"Anyone see you taking it?"

"No, the toilets were empty."

"Excellent," said Majid. "Well done, Jemail."

"Thank you. I thought . . . I don't know, but somehow I thought the package would be bigger."

"Don't worry," said Majid, "there's enough there to kill hundreds, believe me."

Jemail nodded in satisfaction. " I can hardly wait."

274

Majid glanced across at him and smiled. "Me too, Jemail, me too . . ."

Penny pored over the hotel records spread out on her desk in the command room. She knew that locating her quarry from the hotel computer print-outs was a needle-in-a-haystack operation, but nonetheless she ploughed through the paperwork, hoping for something that would catch her eye. It was almost half nine at night and the command room was quiet now with most of the staff off duty, but Thompson and Carrow were still working at their respective desks. Colin Mathieson, she knew, was holding a briefing with the security representatives of all the countries attending the conference and wasn't expected back for at least another hour.

Penny looked up from her paperwork to rest her eyes for a moment and glanced across at Thompson. He sat straight-backed at his desk but with his sleeves rolled up, and she was struck by a feeling of déjà vu. During the years when she had served with him they had often worked late like this in trying to crack tough cases, and it had become a routine that Penny used to go out to a takeaway in Leeds for late-night coffee and doughnuts for herself and Thompson, whom she knew to have a sweet tooth. For a moment she considered doing it now, just for old time's sake, then decided not to. She knew from experience that for a woman to be taken seriously as a Detective Inspector she had to behave carefully, and getting refreshments might send out the wrong signal to junior police officers who saw her doing it. In addition to which there was Carrow, whose disposition was hardly conducive to the camaraderie of late-night coffee and cakes.

Penny had tried to figure out the nature of Carrow's obvious dislike for her, a dislike that seemed even more evident now than when she had been a rookie at the time of their first meeting seven years previously. She had concluded that Carrow didn't like women officers in general, and – for whatever reason – her in particular. Perhaps he had resented her original role as Thompson's protégé, perhaps he had resented her brief relationship with Mathieson, or perhaps he simply disliked her as a person. Whatever the cause, it was a dislike she certainly reciprocated, except that in her case she made the effort to be civil.

Penny's reflections were cut short by the ringing of a phone in the command room and Carrow crossed from the filing cabinet at which he had been standing to take the call at his desk.

"Carrow," he said briskly as he snapped up the phone, and Penny and Thompson both looked up, hoping there might be some development.

"Baines, what's happening?" said Carrow.

Penny glanced across at Thompson and caught his eye. They both knew that Baines was the agent in London who was co-ordinating the security checks on the hotel and catering staff. Earlier in the evening he had rung to say that nothing untoward had been discovered regarding the Sudanese chef, and that the man could be regarded as having security clearance. Which meant he must be calling about the Turkish waiter, Penny reckoned. She listened to Carrow's end of the conversation, her curiosity piqued.

"Really," said Carrow into the phone. "Yes? . . . Damn! . . . Right . . . All right, Baines, thank you for calling." Carrow hung up, then turned to face Thompson and Penny.

"Well?" prompted Thompson.

"Drawn another blank."

"The Turkish waiter is clean?"

"Seems so," answered Carrow. "God damn it, when are we going to get some good news?!"

"Well, isn't it good news – in one way – that he doesn't appear to be a threat?" said Penny.

"Not from our bloody perspective, it's not," retorted Carrow.

"What did they discover about the deaths of his wife and child?" asked Thompson.

"An accident," answered Carrow with disgust. "Their car crashed with a bus in Amman."

Thompson shrugged. "Right . . ."

"If it had been Israeli shelling or something we might at least have had a motive. As it is, whatever his name is –"

"Tamaz Akmedov," offered Penny.

"Whatever. He's got security clearance as of now. So, nothing in the line of suspects, no decent leads – we're not an inch nearer to finding this bastard!"

"There is the tape, Mr Carrow," said Penny, unwilling to have her lead so summarily dismissed.

"Oh, yes, the tape," repeated Carrow in a voice oozing sarcasm. "Let's just hope it turns out to be more fruitful than your other suggestions."

Thompson caught Penny's eye and gave an

infinitesimal shake of the head. With difficulty she managed to obey the message being sent her and refrained from rising to Carrow's bait.

"We'll know soon enough about the tape, sir," she said evenly, then she turned her back on Carrow, picked up a hotel print-out and went back to work.

Majid swore aloud then immediately slowed the van on seeing the checkpoint ahead. They had timed their return from Hull so that it would be around midnight on getting back to Harrogate, but the police were still manning the road-block, through which another car was now being waved.

"Bastards!" said Jemail, "Another half-mile and we were home."

"Relax, Jemail. We're law-abiding citizens who have nothing to fear from the police. OK?"

"Yeah . . . unless they want to check the van. . ."

"We talk them out of the need for that. Only if they insist, do we kill them."

"Right. Looks like there's just two of them."

"Could be back-up we don't see," said Majid. "Keep the Uzi to hand. If we have to shoot, I'll take these two with the Beretta, you handle anything else."

"Right."

"Act friendly and stay relaxed," said Majid as he decelerated and began to wind down the driver's window. He came to a smooth stop at the checkpoint and smiled at the nearer of the two policemen who approached the car.

"'Evening," said Majid.

"Good evening, sir," said the police officer.

Majid could see the other policeman shining his torch onto the windscreen to check the tax and insurance discs. Nothing to worry about on that score, Majid knew. Instead he kept his gaze on the policeman who now stooped to talk in through the opened van window. He had noted that both officers were uniformed and although they didn't appear to have any weapons on show, Majid knew that they could still be carrying handguns.

"May I ask where you're coming from, sir?" said the policeman.

"York," answered Majid.

"And your destination?"

"Harrogate."

"And your name, sir?"

Majid sensed an air of superiority in the man's manner, despite the use of the word "sir", but he made sure not to respond to it and kept his own tone pleasant and relaxed. "Gregori. Nicholai Gregori."

"Where would you be from, Mr Gregori?"

"Athens, in Greece."

"Yes, sir, I know where Athens is. And you, sir?" asked the policeman, looking in across the cab at Jemail.

"Mikos Karamanlos. From Cyprus."

"May I see some identification, please?"

Majid opened the glove compartment and produced a driving licence. He had deliberately moved his hand fairly quickly to see how the policeman would respond, but there was no reaction from the police officer to suggest that he felt any element of threat. Instead he accepted the driver's licence, and a blood-donor's card in the name of Karamanlos from Jemail. While the first policeman studied the identification, the second one was talking quietly into the mouthpiece of a walkie-talkie. Majid felt his pulse beginning to pound but forced himself to continue breathing normally. While the police officer could be calling in back-up, equally he could simply be calling someone in the station to have a pizza delivered.

The first officer handed back the donor car and wallet, then looked Majid in the eye. "What are you carrying in the van, sir?"

"Just ourselves," answered Majid, holding the other man's gaze yet not making a challenge of it.

"Really?"

Majid forced himself not to answer too quickly, but his mind was racing. The silenced Beretta was in his jacket pocket, and he reckoned he could kill the nearest policeman and probably his companion before any alarm could be raised. On the other hand, there could be support personnel in the shadows at the side of the road.

"Yes," Majid answered. "Just using it to get us back from York."

"Don't you have a car?"

"Hoping to get one next year. Meanwhile the van doubles for work and pleasure."

"And which were you pursuing in York, sir?"

Again Majid picked up on a needling tone behind the policeman's ostensibly polite phraseology. The second policeman had now drawn nearer to the open car window, but Majid looked instead at the first officer. He was a beefy man in his late thirties with a closely-cropped moustache and pock-marked skin, and Majid sensed that there was going to be a problem. No matter how agreeably he behaved, he suspected that in the end the policeman would still want to show who was in charge by searching the van.

"Neither business nor pleasure exactly," Majid answered. "We were at the race relations conference in York."

"Oh yes?"

"Dr Jusaif Safel from the Commission for Racial Equality gave a talk. Mikos and I do some work for the commission here in Harrogate so we went to hear it."

For several seconds the policeman looked at him impassively, and Majid feared that he wasn't buying the existence of the imaginary conference.

"Well . . . I'm sure that was very interesting, sir," said the police officer, and Majid tried to give no indication of his relief.

"Yes, he's an inspiring speaker," added Jemail with a smile.

"I dare say he is, sir," said the policeman, giving Jemail a humourless smile. The man turned back to Majid. "Nevertheless, sir, I'm going to have to ask you to open the back of your van."

Majid felt a sudden tightening in his stomach, but he forced himself to keep his voice steady. "Is this really necessary, Officer? It's late, we're tired, and we're simply returning from a race relations conference." Majid kept his left hand on the steering wheel, but

281

casually lowered his right hand towards his lap, ready to pull the Beretta out. He knew that Jemail would be doing the same with the Uzi, ready to spray any back-up officers who might suddenly emerge.

"I'm afraid it is necessary, sir. Step out of the vehicle, please, and open the rear doors."

Majid breathed out heavily as though irritated by the man's intransigence. In reality his mind was racing about how to make the kill. *Step out slowly, turn your back as though closing the van door, then draw the gun, spin round and shoot. Two shots for each target, then back into the van and speed off.* That was the theory. In practice though there could be fire from heavily armed support personnel in the background. Even with two Uzis and the element of surprise, he knew they could end up out-numbered in a fire-fight.

Majid reached for the door handle, then the second police officer stepped forward, raising a hand to stop him. "Just a second, please, sir. Frank, a quick word."

The second policeman drew his beefier colleague aside and began talking quickly and quietly to him. Majid glanced over at Jemail who raised an eyebrow and indicated the two policemen. Majid nodded no to Jemail's unspoken suggestion of striking now. While there was a risk that the second officer could be cautioning his colleague to wait until reinforcements arrived before proceeding any further, Majid hoped that instead his racist ploy might be working. If he and Jemail really were two foreign nationals who did work for the Commission for Racial Equality it would surely be a foolish white policeman who would leave himself open to a charge of harassment. Particularly with the plaintiffs returning from a conference on racial equality.

He saw the two policemen appearing to argue, then the second one raised his finger at his colleague, as though making a telling point. Majid kept his right hand resting casually on his lap, ready to pull out the Beretta. Eventually the beefier man nodded to his partner and the other officer turned away from him and strode over to the van.

Majid had decided that if he felt this man were engaging him in conversation to keep him occupied until reinforcements arrived then he would kill the two police officers and take his chances. He looked up at the second policeman, hoping this wouldn't be necessary.

The man bent down to talk in the window to Majid. "That'll be all right, sir, you can be on your way now." he said. "Sorry for having to detain you, and thank you for your co-operation."

Thank God for the Commission for Racial Equality, thought Majid, but to the policeman he simply nodded curtly. *A sober citizen whose patience has been tried a bit, but who isn't going to make too much of it . . .*

"Safe home, sir."

"Thank you." Majid let off the handbrake, put the van into gear and drove off.

He watched in the rear-view mirror to see if either of the policemen was speaking into his walkie-talkie, but neither was, and he breathed out a sigh of relief.

"That was close," said Jemail.

"They'll never know just how close."

"They may have noted the registration number."

"Doesn't matter," said Majid. "We'll have the van inside the warehouse in less than two minutes."

Suddenly Jemail laughed. "If only they knew what we have!"

Majid looked across at this colleague and smiled. "Their faces would be worth seeing . . ."

"I have a good feeling about this mission, Abdullah. It's like – it's like the Gods are smiling on us."

"Perhaps. But in the end you make your own luck by being prepared."

"We've covered everything that could possibly be covered," said Jemail.

"That's why we're going to succeed," said Majid.

"You really believe we're going to pull it all off, don't you?"

Majid glanced across at his partner, his face deadly serious. "This time next week our enemies will be devastated. Count on it, Jemail. *Count* on it."

11

Wednesday 20th September 2000

"I know Len Carrow's been giving you a hard time, Penny, and I'm sorry," said Mathieson.

They were alone in a vacant office off the command room in Harrogate police station and Penny had wondered why Mathieson had called her in for a private word.

"It's OK," she said, touched that Mathieson was concerned for her personal welfare despite the pressure he was under.

"It's not really," said Mathieson. "A senior officer shouldn't pick on a subordinate."

"It's just how he is," said Penny. "I try not to let it get to me."

"Please don't. Can't have you feeling inhibited because of his attitude – defeats the whole purpose of having you here. At the same time, if I tackle him it'll make a tricky relationship even more difficult."

"Don't, Colin, I can live with it."

"There's also the fact that . . . well, he knows that we were once . . . together . . ."

It was the first time that Mathieson had referred directly to their affair, and Penny felt a flicker of irritation that it should now be a source of embarrassment to him. She looked directly at Mathieson and spoke calmly. "A) that's history now – it was seven years ago, another lifetime, and B) it's none of his business, it hasn't affected the work we've been doing here."

"Please, Penny, don't misunderstand. I've never regretted our having what we had, and I don't regret it now. Truly."

Mathieson looked at her appealingly, and despite herself Penny couldn't help but be gratified by the obvious truth of what he was saying.

"I'm just trying to explain," said Mathieson, "probably rather badly, why I haven't taken Carrow on."

"It's all right, Colin. I'm a big girl now. I can take a bit of stick."

"It's just . . . well, I know what it's like . . ."

"Really?"

Mathieson paused, then nodded. "I never told you before, but when I left Sandhurst as a young officer my first CO really disliked me. I know what it's like to be picked on despite the fact that you're working hard."

"Why did he dislike you?" asked Penny, her curiosity aroused.

"Think he felt I was a bit too privileged. Born-with-a-silver-spoon kind of thing. That was part of it, anyway."

"And the other part?"

"Took me a while to figure that out," said Mathieson. "Quite similar to you and Carrow, actually . . ."

"How's that?"

"Envy."

"Envy?"

Mathieson nodded. "When I was posted to my unit we were serving in Aden. It was coming up to the end of British rule and there was lots of trouble. Not to hide behind false modesty, I did rather well. I'd studied Arabic, so I was useful, got mentioned in dispatches. It was only later that I twigged my CO resented my standing out."

"Really?"

"'Fraid so. Same thing with Carrow and you. He's probably not aware of it on a conscious level, but it's clear he resents working with someone who's female, who's younger, and who's really bright."

Penny smiled. "If nothing else, you're doing my ego good."

"I'm serious, Penny, don't let Carrow undermine you. You're twice as smart as he is."

"If he's so dim, how come he's a Chief Superintendent?"

"Not so much dim as prejudiced. But he's crudely effective. He's streetwise, he works like a Trojan, and he's been around a long time, so he moved up the ladder."

"Right."

"When you're his age though, you'll be more than a Chief Superintendent."

Penny smiled again and was about to reply when

there was a sudden peremptory knock, then the door was opened. Mathieson and Penny looked round in surprise to see Thompson standing in the doorway.

"Jack, what's up?" said Mathieson.

Thompson smiled broadly. "I think we've just hit paydirt." He pushed the door behind him closed, then drew nearer. "I've had a call from the language labs. They've analysed our tape and they're e-mailing the results as we speak."

"Don't keep us in suspense!" said Mathieson.

"The guy on the recording is our man, I'm sure of it."

Penny felt a thrill at Thompson's words, but she tried to curtail her excitement. "What emerged, Chief?"

"The voice is that of a – wait for it, *Iraqi* male, aged between twenty-five and thirty-five, thought to be from the Baghdad region."

"Oh my God!" said Penny.

"The lab people say he was taught English by British rather than American tutors. And as the call developed, and Laura Kennedy questioned him, the stress levels in his voice rose steadily."

"Excellent!" said Mathieson. "I think you're right, Jack – sounds like our man."

"Too bloody true!" said Thompson. "An Iraqi, with terrorist connections, coming here just at this time? Way too much of a coincidence."

"Well done, Penny," said Mathieson. "If it wasn't for your contact with the journalist . . ."

"Yes, nice one, Penny," agreed Thompson.

"Thank you. So, what's our next move?"

"Getting a name, and then a face for our Iraqi friend," said Mathieson.

"We can get onto the Irish police and see if they have anything on him entering or leaving Ireland," said Thompson.

"I'll leave that one to you, Jack," said Mathieson.

Penny looked at the intelligence officer. "Obviously you've a plan of your own."

"Electronic voice recognition. Not quite as accurate as finger-printing, but pretty damn good all the same."

"What will you compare the tape with?" asked Penny.

"Any recordings we have of terrorists or suspected terrorists who fit the age profile."

"What about the Israelis?" asked Thompson.

Mathieson smiled. "You're way ahead of me, Jack. I'll be onto Tel Aviv as soon as we leave this room."

"Would they retain tapes of every interview or interrogation they do?" asked Penny.

"Probably not," answered Mathieson, "but they'd have a hell of a lot more than we would." The intelligence officer looked at his watch. "Nine thirty. That would make it eleven thirty in Israel. If we send the recording from our computer to theirs they'll have the rest of the day to work on it."

"What about sending it to the CIA and the FBI?" asked Thompson.

"More than my life would be worth to keep them out of it," said Mathieson with a wry smile, "but I think the Israelis are by far our best bet."

"Will they be co-operative, do you reckon?" asked

Penny, "I mean after all the work we've already requested from them?"

"I hope so," said Mathieson. "We're expecting a response from them in the next day or two. That must mean they'd be starting to form a short list of dossiers to send us. Shouldn't be a huge job to begin the voice-recognition programme with recordings from those on that list."

"Assuming they have them all recorded and on file," said Thompson.

"Quite. No guarantees, Jack, but damn it all, this is the best break we've had – by a mile. Well done again, Penny."

"Thank you."

"Right, enough chat," said Mathieson.

"Aye," agreed Thompson, "let's track this bastard down . . ."

Laura sat in her hotel room wondering how to handle her phone call to the *Clarion*. So far she had always found Mac to be honest and decent, but now she was going to have to tell him something any editor would want to print, yet it had to remain off the record. Her instincts told her that she could trust the *Clarion*'s Deputy Editor, but still she felt a little uneasy. She had given her word to Penny Harte that nothing would be published, when Penny had rung her minutes earlier with the news regarding the tape analysis. Supposing that in spite of that Mac went ahead with the story, behind her back? It would be a terrible betrayal and deeply dishonourable, yet she knew that newspapers sometimes were tempted into unethical behaviour by their desire to scoop their rivals. Ultimately it came down to a matter of trust. Mac had trusted her sufficiently to send her to Harrogate on the *Clarion*'s behalf even though the trail she had planned to follow was undoubtedly tenuous. Now she needed to show considerable faith in return. She pondered the matter, then suddenly decided to go with her instincts.

She picked up the phone and dialled Mac's number, which was answered on the second ring.

"McEvoy."

"Hi, Mac, it's Laura."

"Laura, what gives?"

"Quite a bit, actually."

"Yeah? Tell Uncle Mac."

"That's just it, Mac. There's something important to tell you, but it's more off the record than anything I've ever told anyone."

"If you wanted my full attention, Kid, you have it now . . ."

"I'm dead serious, Mac."

"OK."

"You remember the policewoman I told you about?"

"Yes."

"I've done a deal with her. In return for giving her my recording for the police to analyse, I'm getting the inside track on this case. They're allowing me access that no other journalist will have."

"Nice one, Laura!"

"There's more. But before I tell you, I need your word that all this is strictly off the record."

291

"If it's all strictly off the record, where's the gain for us as a newspaper?" asked Mac.

"After the conference is safely over, we can run some brilliant exclusives," answered Laura.

"After the conference is safely over the story may not have legs. A threat that doesn't materialise isn't very gripping."

"This will be gripping, Mac, I promise you. It's *already* gripping."

"But you can't tell me how gripping unless I give my word not to print it?"

"Not to print it just for the moment."

"How long am I meant to sit on this information?"

"Until I get clearance from Penny –"

"Penny's your policewoman friend?"

"Yes, Detective Inspector Penny Harte. I'd expect to get clearance pretty soon after the conference ends."

"And you really think this is worth waiting for?"

"Absolutely, Mac."

"OK . . . it's off the record then. You have my word."

"Thanks, Mac." Laura knew that from his perspective, Mac had gone out on a limb for her again, and she felt slightly ashamed of her earlier musing on whether or not she could trust him in return.

"So, what's the big news I can hear now?"

"The police got the tape results from the language lab this morning. The man I spoke to on the phone is an Iraqi."

"And that's significant?"

"Absolutely. One of the things I learnt as part of the quid pro quo for the tape is that a terrorist attack on the conference is being actively investigated. And although the threat's not government sponsored, it's thought to stem from – you guessed it – Iraq."

"Wow! Interesting all right . . ." said Mac. "And is there some sort of IRA/Iraqi link?"

"None that's emerged so far – apart from the strong likelihood that this guy killed Boyle and O'Donnell."

"Right. Good work, Kid, you've done really well."

"Thanks, Mac."

"Stay tight on this one."

"I will. Like I said though, there won't be anything we can print till next week, so you'll have to settle for a few more colour pieces."

"Forget the colour pieces, forget the conference," said Mac. "We can get that kind of stuff from the wire services. Concentrate purely on the Iraqi thing."

"OK. So . . . you get it too then?"

"What?"

"The scent of a major story."

"Yes. Possibly an explosive story. Be careful."

"Be careful – but get the story . . ."

"Yes."

"I'm on it, Mac. And thanks for the support."

"No sweat."

"I'll keep you posted."

"OK, Kid. Mind yourself.

"Yeah. See you, Mac."

Laura put the phone down, relieved to have cleared her lines with the *Clarion,* then she rose, suddenly eager to go out and pursue her story.

Majid had sensed a problem brewing, and it came as

little surprise when Tamaz Akmedov asked to speak to him in private. It was the waiter's half-day and Majid had noticed his agitation when he had returned from work after lunch-time. Now they were seated in the parlour of the house in Starbeck and when Majid spoke he consciously kept his manner casual yet sympathetic.

"You have some concerns, Tamaz . . ."

"Yes."

Majid knew that the Turkish waiter was somewhat in awe of him and so he smiled encouragingly, wanting to relax the other man and draw him out. The worst possible situation, he knew, would be if Tamaz was becoming spooked by the operation, yet was too scared of him to discuss his problems openly.

"Tell me what's bothering you."

"I'm – I'm getting nervous, Abdullah. The security at work . . . it's everywhere. More and more police, more spot checks, people checking our passes, sniffer dogs . . . everything . . ."

"I can understand your feeling nervous," said Majid gently. "It's normal – you wouldn't be human if you didn't."

"It's not just *feeling* nervous. It's affecting me – my concentration. This morning I dropped a tray of dishes."

Majid felt a twinge of anxiety. Tamaz was scheduled to work at the Foreign Ministers' dinner next Monday evening, and the last thing Majid wanted in the lead up to that was behaviour that would attract attention. He was going to have to reassure his accomplice effectively in order to nip this in the bud.

"It's usual coming up to an operation to feel nervous," he explained. "The thing is not to dwell on it. You put your mind on what you have to do – block out all the rest."

"It's not so much what I have to do – although that scares me too –"

"No need. Your part will be straightforward, I promise you."

"It's more afterwards I'm worried about. How – how we can possibly get away . . ."

"Ah . . ."

"You've never told me how we'll escape, Abdullah."

"It's all been taken care of."

"Even if we get out of the Conference Centre undetected –"

"No, Tamaz. *When* we get out."

"When we get out then. Every policeman in England will be looking for us. How do we get out of the country?"

Majid looked at Tamaz, the older man's usual sheepish demeanour for once replaced by nervous animation, and he realised that he would have to reveal some of the operational details that he had been withholding. He had known from the start that Tamaz wasn't a seasoned subversive like Jemail, whose calm he had admired when they had been questioned at the roadblock the previous night, and so he had kept Tamaz in the dark as much as possible, not wanting to provide him with the details of what lay ahead. Now, though, he would have to be more forthcoming.

"After we've struck at the Conference Centre we'll

leave Harrogate immediately," he explained. "We'll transfer into the van and make for the motorway. We'll be gone from the town before they begin organising roadblocks."

"And where do we go on the motorway?"

"Newcastle," lied Majid, feeling that there was no need to compromise security by revealing the actual destination of Liverpool.

"Why Newcastle?" asked Tamaz.

"It places us seventy miles from the scene of our operation, but it's less than a two-hour drive. By early the next morning we'll be on a ship sailing down the Tyne. By this time next month you'll be a millionaire, you can be in Rio –"

"I didn't choose Rio –"

"I don't want to know where you chose," said Majid, holding back his exasperation. "We go to ground, we adopt new identities, then we each vanish. My point is that this time next month your waitering days will be over. Other waiters will dance attendance on you. You'll be comfortable for the rest of your life."

Tamaz looked thoughtful, and Majid placed his hand on the other man's shoulder. "Six more days and it will all be over. You've come this far, now there's less than a week to go. Just keep your nerve and everything will be fine." He looked Tamaz directly in the eye. "I promise you, it's going to be all right."

The older man nodded. "OK."

Majid continued looking at him, trying to gauge Tamaz's conviction, and to his relief the Turk nodded again and looked a little more composed.

"OK, Abdullah. And thank you."

"No problem, my friend. Any time you need to talk, I'm here."

"Thank you."

"Anything else bothering you?"

"No. No, everything else is OK."

"Sure?" asked Majid.

"I'm sure."

"Good. And, Tamaz, two things to remember any time you start to feel nervous."

"Yes?"

"Other people don't know how you feel. So long as you look normal and behave normally there's no reason for them to realise your heart's thumping."

"All right. And the other thing?"

"Hold onto a thought."

"What thought?"

"The same thought I hold onto," said Majid, wanting to engender a sense of camaraderie.

"Yes?"

"The thought that this time next week you'll be a hero. You'll be a millionaire too. And we'll have carried out our mission . . ."

12

Thursday 21st September 2000

Samuel Lubetkin came down the stairs two steps at a time, moving gracefully for a heavy man. He made his way quickly down the corridor, distractedly returning the greeting of a fellow Mossad agent, then turned into Blumenthal's office and closed the door behind him.

The morning sunshine flooded in through the windows of the office, bathing Blumenthal in warm shafts of sunlight, and Lubetkin could see from his subordinate's pallor and bloodshot eyes that he had been up all night. It was unusual to see Blumenthal looking other than suavely turned out. Despite his slightly dishevelled air however, he smiled now.

"Well?" said Lubetkin.

"We've finally hit the jackpot."

Lubetkin had rushed down from his office on the floor above, following a call from Blumenthal saying there had been a break in the case. Lubetkin kept his patience now, feeling that Blumenthal was entitled to bask a little after all the effort he and his team had put in. "So what's happened?"

"We've found a match for the voice."

"Yeah?"

"I'd drawn up a short list of about twenty dossiers on Iraqis that I was going to present to you. We tried to get recordings on as many of them as we could, and Ruth Shagam tracked this one down."

"It's a definite match?"

"Yes," answered Blumenthal, "over ninety per cent certain, so we can forget the other dossiers."

"Who is he?"

"Guy by the name of Abdullah Majid. Aged thirty, well-educated, comes from a middle-class Baghdad family. Originally captured during a raid on a training camp in the Sudan in '93"

"How long did we hold him?" asked Lubetkin.

"He served five years for terrorist offences. The tape we got was of his interrogation, when he was questioned before his trail."

"So there'd be fingerprints, photographs?"

Blumenthal nodded. "The lot."

"Great work, Avi." Lubetkin punched the other man on the arm. "Well done!"

Blumenthal smiled. "It was a team effort."

"Pass on my congratulations, especially to Ruth Shagam."

"Will do."

"In fact, tell the whole team to gather here in half an hour . . ."

"Yeah?"

"I know people have worked their butts off on this one," said Lubetkin. "I'd like to thank them all."

"They'll appreciate that," said Blumenthal.

"First though I need to get onto the Brits."

"Ah . . ."

"I know," said Lubetkin smiling wryly, "they went over my head to begin with. But in fairness they also came up with this tape."

"True."

"Doesn't make it quite right, but still . . ." Lubetkin smiled.

"Right . . ."

"Have you got this guy's file to hand?"

"Sure." Blumenthal passed a buff-coloured file across the desk.

"Thanks, Avi. I want to read through it quickly, then contact the PM's office."

"OK. What happens then?"

"We transfer all the data electronically, so the Brits can have it immediately."

"That should please them," said Blumenthal.

"They owe us big-time for this."

"Will you point that out to them?"

"Damn right I will," said Lubetkin with a grin. "Anyway, I'd better get moving. Well done again, Avi."

"Thanks. Let's just hope it helps them catch the bastard."

"Amen to that," said Lubetkin, then he turned and started briskly for his office.

Laura stepped out of the Old Swan Hotel into hazy

September sunshine. The morning air was warm and sweet-smelling and in other circumstances she would have given herself over to the mood of autumnal mellowness, but she knew that today would not be relaxed. At lunch-time she had an appointment to meet Penny and the rest of the police team, and her mind was full of the case as she walked down Swan Road towards the Valley Gardens. Now that the man to whom she had spoken on the phone had turned out to be Iraqi, Laura had given up her enquiries regarding the delegations that she had been checking out previously. Although she wasn't due to meet Penny for several hours, she had decided nonetheless to wander about, reasoning that Harrogate wasn't all that big and that it was possible she might still strike it lucky and encounter her man. She knew too that she often did her best thinking while out walking and she wanted to get her thoughts in order for her meeting with the police.

She had been briefed by Penny on each of the three senior officers working on the case, and had been eager to compare Penny's descriptions with her own impressions on encountering them for the first time yesterday. Thompson, as expected, had been likeable, a big, slightly bluff Yorkshireman with a wry sense of humour. He actually looked like the kind of police Inspectors who featured in the old Scotland Yard black and white movies that Declan sometimes inveigled her into watching. Thompson had made her welcome even though Laura knew that in reality her presence was probably regarded as a nuisance to be borne in exchange for the access to the tape.

Mathieson, the spook with whom Penny had once been involved, had been courteous but slightly distant. He had a languid, public-school-type manner which Laura knew must be something of a façade. Penny had admitted that he was a senior intelligence figure and as such was under considerable pressure regarding the security for the conference. Although now in his late fifties, he was still a very handsome man, and Laura couldn't help but wonder if Penny had been tempted to resume their liaison. Probably not, she thought – there seemed to be no hint of any erotic spark between them, and Laura recalled the night she and Penny had traded confidences and Penny had said how much happier she was now with Shane and her daughter Aisling. Still, it made for an interesting dynamic, Laura thought, to have to work cheek by jowl with a former lover.

The third officer she had met had been Carrow, the Special Branch representative, and Laura could see at once why he and Penny didn't get on. There was a combativeness about him that was off-putting, and unlike Thompson and Mathieson he had clearly felt under no obligation to make Laura feel welcome. She had tried to be fair to him and had rationalised that perhaps society needed tough, combative people in the kind of frontline, coalface work that he had do in Special Branch. Even so she had been put off by his arrogance and the obvious resentment he felt regarding her presence in the command room. Still, she knew that she was lucky to have gained the inside track to the degree that she had, and the differing personalities would actually provide a good range of perspectives when she got down to writing her articles.

Thinking of her work, she passed the Crown Hotel, where Byron had once stayed, and she smiled wryly, knowing that she no longer had to worry about working such details into colour features for the *Clarion*. She continued along Montpelier Parade, unobtrusively checking the faces of those she passed. Since getting the details on the sim-card purchaser in the telephone shop she had seen a reasonable number of dark-complexioned men around Harrogate, but so far none of them had properly matched the detailed description that the shop assistant had given her.

She crossed Parliament Street now and made for the busy pedestrian district. She felt the warm September sunshine on her shoulders and was struck by a sense of wellbeing. Yet it was more than simple wellbeing, she knew. It was the prospect too of being on the verge of a major story, the hint of danger that went with the thrill of the chase.

She recalled telling Declan an edited and bowdlerised version of what was happening, greatly playing down any element of danger, when he had rung her from the film set in Prague. No point in having him worrying unnecessarily, she had decided, just as there was no point in unnerving her parents who had also rung her. She had simply told her father that she was in Harrogate covering the forthcoming conference for the *Clarion*. She had then listened to a detailed account he gave her of a recent bridge match, all the while wondering what he would think if he knew that the locksmith skills she had learned from him had initiated the chain of events that had brought her here. They wouldn't understand, she thought. Not her parents, not even Declan, none of them would fully understand how the risk of involving yourself with someone lethal could be justified in pursuit of a story. Yet Laura felt there could be no shying away. This was the story of a lifetime – she knew it instinctively, and her instincts also told her that there would be developments sooner rather than later.

Buoyed by the thought, she headed on through Harrogate.

Mathieson crossed the command room excitedly, and Penny stopped in mid-sentence when she saw his expression. She had been talking to Thompson and both of them turned to look at a large colour photograph that Mathieson was brandishing.

"We've ID'd him!" said Mathieson triumphantly, and Carrow and several other police officers who were in the room drew nearer. "The Israelis got a voice match for the tape! His name is Abdullah Majid, and this is what he looks like."

"Oh my God . . ." said Penny. The photograph was of a handsome, dark-haired man in his mid-twenties. He had a look in his eyes that suggested danger, and Penny felt a shiver go up her spine now that she was finally confronted with her quarry.

"Bloody marvellous!" said Thompson. "This changes everything."

"Not before time," said Len Carrow.

"He looks quite like the description Laura Kennedy got in the phone shop," said Penny.

"Yes," agreed Mathieson, "seems like that was him all right."

"What else do the Israelis know about him?" asked Carrow.

"He's a hardened terrorist, served five years in one of their jails. Smart, well-educated, mentally tough. He'd been trained by the Mujahadeen in the Sudan."

"Jesus . . ." said Penny.

"Yes, sounds like a dangerous customer," said Mathieson. "He was released from prison two years ago. Since then the Israelis haven't linked him to anything specific, though of course that doesn't mean he hasn't been active."

"This is the break we needed," said Thompson. "Having a face will make a world of difference for the officers on the ground."

"Plus we have fingerprints and all the background detail on him that the Israelis had," said Mathieson.

"Getting that tape was a godsend," said Thompson. "Well done, Penny!"

"Thanks, Chief."

"Yes, damn good work, Penny," added Mathieson.

"Thank you," answered Penny, trying not to let her pleasure show too much.

"If we've finished patting ourselves on the back," said Carrow, "maybe the lads here can get back to work, and we can draw up a plan of action?"

Penny knew that the police officers to whom Carrow had referred were under Thompson's command, and she saw the flicker of irritation that crossed his face before he nodded to them and they returned to their tasks.

"OK, first thing is to run off large quantities of the photograph," said Mathieson.

Thompson nodded in agreement. "Right. And the minute that's done I want every copper on the beat to have one."

"Likewise my people," said Carrow. "To what extent do we share our information with the foreign security services?"

Mathieson considered a moment. "We'll have to let them know what we've found out. Some of them may have data on file on this guy – maybe we can find out something more about him."

"Do we provide the foreigners with the photograph?" asked Carrow.

"Yes, but with clear instruction not to attempt any interception."

"Good," said Carrow. "This is our show – anyone spots this bloke, they call us. We're the ones who take him – that must be crystal clear."

"We'll spell it out to them," agreed Mathieson.

"Talking of taking him," said Thompson, "we need a policy concerning arrest."

Mathieson looked at him. "Yes?"

"I'd suggest that if unarmed officers encounter the suspect they shouldn't try to detain him. I think we must assume him to be armed and dangerous at all times."

Carrow breathed out impatiently. "I'd have thought that's blatantly obvious!"

Thompson turned to Carrow and looked him in the eye. "Maybe not if you're a gung-ho young constable – as you once were yourself. Maybe the temptation

PAYBACK

would be rather strong to make a name for yourself and go to arrest him."

Before Carrow could respond, Mathieson answered Thompson. "Fair point, Jack. I presume then that we're all agreed. Any unarmed officer encountering the suspect calls in for support?"

"Definitely," said Carrow, and Thompson nodded agreement.

"May I ask a devil's advocate question?" said Penny.

Mathieson turned to her and smiled. "Seeing as you provided the lead, I should think so . . ."

"It's just if the situation arose where an unarmed officer encountered – what was his name again?"

"Majid. Abdullah Majid."

"Supposing a constable encounters Majid, calls in for back-up, but meanwhile Majid is about to leave? He's about to get into a taxi, or a car or whatever. If there's a real risk of losing him before back-up arrives, what does the constable do?"

Mathieson looked thoughtful and turned to Thompson. "Jack?"

"It's a judgement call. If Majid is with an accomplice the presumption must be that they'd both be armed. In that case an unarmed officer shouldn't try for an arrest, even at the cost of losing contact."

"And if he's not with an accomplice, Chief?"

Thompson shrugged. "Down to the individual officer to judge the circumstances."

"Though I think in reality we'll have so many armed officers and agents about that it's an unlikely scenario," said Mathieson.

307

"Let's hope so," agreed Thompson. "Meanwhile, I want to brief all my commanding officers on this development. The sooner we flood the streets with constables looking for this bloke, the better I'll feel."

"Absolutely," said Mathieson.

"Just to go back to Laura Kennedy for a second," said Penny. "We did promise her that she could be in on some of this."

"The Israeli data has to be treated as classified," objected Carrow.

"But for her we wouldn't have the Israeli data," countered Penny, being careful not to make her tone too confrontational.

"Nevertheless, she's a civilian and this is a classified development," said Carrow.

"But, Mr Carrow, the whole operation could be said to be classified. We knew that when we made the deal with her. The understanding was that we'd trust her to stay off the record with anything we don't want published."

"She's a journalist. You don't trust journalists."

"She trusted us. She gave us the tape."

"Then for once we've come out the better in dealing with the press," said Carrow.

Penny turned to Thompson, but before she could appeal he was already speaking.

"I gave my word we'd give her access in exchange for the tape. I don't break my word."

"What is this, the Boy Scouts? Get real, Thompson! We're dealing with a serious terrorist here. We don't need some snooping journalist tagging along and getting in the way. We certainly don't need to open the Sunday papers and find our efforts splashed across the centre pages."

Thompson looked the Special Branch officer in the eye. "We're talking about controlled access and nothing being printed until after the conference. And even then only material that's agreed as being on the record. That was the deal I made, that's the deal I intend to keep."

Carrow turned to Mathieson. "For Christ's sake, Colin! Let's have a reality check here."

For a moment Mathieson said nothing and Penny couldn't tell from his face what he was thinking. She desperately wanted him not to renege on the deal – it would be dreadful to have to go back to Laura Kennedy with such a blatant betrayal of her trust.

"I think we can rely on Chief Superintendent Thompson's judgement and experience in dealing with the press over many years," said Mathieson.

Penny felt exultant, but was careful not to show it in front of a clearly irked Carrow.

"Fine," said Thompson.

"So, I'll give Laura Kennedy a call then?" said Penny.

"Yes," answered Mathieson. He turned to the others. "Right," he said, "we've all got plenty to do – let's go to it!"

Majid pulled off his mask, then stepped back to survey his handiwork. He had spray-painted the van dark blue with Jemail's assistance and he was pleased to see how well the vehicle had come up in its new colour. The air in the warehouse smelt heavily of paint, but he saw Jemail pulling off his mask also now that the spraying was finished.

"It looks well, Abdullah."

Majid nodded. "Yes. More important, it looks different."

Majid had decided on the purchase of the paint and spraying equipment the previous March when he had organised the lease of the warehouse and bought the van. He hadn't known back then that the van would be stopped at a police roadblock, but he always strove to be thorough in his contingency planning. The capacity to change colour and replace the registration plates with false ones – obtained along with the other equipment from Boyle and O'Donnell – constituted good fieldcraft, and Majid prided himself on being meticulously professional.

"Yes, it looks different all right . . ." agreed Jemail, but Majid picked up on the lack of enthusiasm in his voice.

"You think I'm being over-cautious, don't you?"

Jemail shrugged as he peeled off the disposable gloves that he'd worn during the spray-painting. "I think the police probably never noted the white van or its registration. They believed our race relations story."

"One of them did," corrected Majid. "The other wanted to search the van."

"Only because he wanted to throw his weight around. I don't think he was genuinely suspicious."

"Either way they stopped a white Volkswagen van and they may have noted it."

"I suppose."

"There's no supposing, Jemail. The amount of security we're up against, anything we can do to camouflage ourselves, we do."

Jemail raised his hands, conceding the point. "OK, OK . . ."

"Once the paint is dry I want the van splattered in mud and covered in dust."

"Yeah?"

"The clean white van was used by two aspiring immigrants. Men who wore suits and went to a race relations conference. The dirty blue van will be used by working men wearing overalls."

"Right."

"You saw those rolls of carpet that Tamaz has stored in the loft here?"

Jemail nodded. "What about them?"

"They go in the back of the van, we throw in a toolbox, then when we make for Liverpool we're a team of carpet-fitters."

Jemail smiled. "You've thought of everything."

Majid shook his head. "The day you think that is the day you get careless."

"We won't be careless," said Jemail.

"No, we won't."

"Still though . . ."

"What?"

Jemail looked at Majid and smiled ruefully. "I wouldn't mind some time with a woman. It's been a while . . ."

Majid felt a surge of irritation, but he controlled it. He was going to have to work in harmony with Jemail to carry out the mission, so it wouldn't be wise to fight with him now that their goal was only days away. At the same time, it was really irksome that Jemail should make such a statement, even if it was half-jocular in tone. It was typical of the cheerful Lebanese, he knew, and showed a weakness Majid had been aware of when recruiting him. Jemail was first-rate once a mission was actually in operation. Then he would be cool, brave and resourceful. He was also completely loyal; and in a world where cut-throat betrayal was all around, Majid knew he could trust Jemail with his very life. The one drawback was that Jemail had a low threshold for boredom.

Majid remembered his father once proclaiming that the thing that kept many of the working-classes from advancement was an unwillingness to defer pleasure. It had seemed a little pompous to Majid at the time, the kind of remark well-heeled middle-class Iraqis could afford to make, but now he was struck by the aptness of his father's comment in Jemail's case. In fairness, he reasoned that if he himself had been forced to leave school at fourteen to work for a pittance as a van-driver's assistant, as Jemail had, then he too might be inclined to the philosophy of taking one's pleasure whenever possible. The trick, now, Majid knew, would be to ensure that Jemail did nothing that might attract attention over the next few days, yet he had to do it in such a way as not to undermine their camaraderie with the climax of the mission so close.

Majid looked the other man in the eye and smiled. "After Monday, you'll be able to afford the most beautiful women in the world."

"I know," answered Jemail with a grin.

Majid peeled off his disposable gloves, then punched Jemail playfully on the shoulder. "You'll have them screaming for mercy!"

Jemail grinned again.

"But we're really close now, Jemail. So play safe for a few more days. Then when you get your payment you can have all the women you want. OK?"

Jemail nodded. "OK."

"Right," said Majid, feeling that he had struck the right note. "Let's tidy up here."

"All right. And Abdullah?"

"Yes?"

"The carpet laying . . ."

"What about it?"

"It's good," said Jemail. "The kind of thing could get us through if we're stopped on the way to Liverpool."

"We'll probably never be stopped. By the time they're finished counting their dead we'll already be sailing out of the country."

Jemail nodded as though savouring the thought. "I can hardly wait to do it."

"Me neither, Jemail. Me neither . . ."

13

Friday 22nd September 2000

Samuel Lubetkin sat at his desk, restlessly tipping a curved paperweight back and forth as he pondered whether or not to ring British Intelligence. The paperweight was a fragment from a Jordanian artillery piece that Lubetkin's unit had knocked out during their advance on Jerusalem during the Six Day War, and the irony of its origin wasn't lost on Lubetkin. The British had trained and equipped the Jordanians, whose Arab Legion had been a considerable threat to the fledgling state of Israel. And Lubetkin had personally felt the loss of men he had served with, who fell casualty to Jordanian fire in the battle for Jerusalem. Yet here he was, debating whether or not to extend further support to British Intelligence.

On the one hand Lubetkin was pragmatic enough to know that yesterday's enemies could often be today's friends, and Colin Mathieson had once done Lubetkin a big favour when a Mossad operation in Europe had gone badly wrong. On the other hand, Mathieson had gone over Lubetkin's head in the matter of the Harrogate Conference. It was something Lubetkin could understand however, with the stakes being so high at the British end, and in fairness MI5 had done well in getting the live recording of the terrorist Abdullah Majid.

Lubetkin had spoken to Mathieson yesterday after Blumenthal's team had identified the voice on the tape, and the two intelligence officers had reached an understanding about Mathieson's having leaned on Mossad via the Americans. Lubetkin hadn't let Mathieson off the hook too lightly, and had made it clear that the British agent really owed him one. In his favour, Mathieson had accepted this and, recalling it now, Lubetkin made his mind up and lifted the telephone.

He dialled a number that Mathieson had said would reach him directly on a scrambled line at the command post in Harrogate, and seconds later Lubetkin heard the British officer's upper-class drawl.

"Mathieson . . ."

"Good morning, Colin. Samuel Lubetkin here."

"Samuel. Good to hear from you."

Lubetkin smiled. "We spoke only yesterday, Colin."

"Quite. Still good to hear from you. Know you're not one to waste time, so would I be correct in thinking Mossad have something else for us?"

"You assume I'm not ringing to call in the favour we agreed I'm owed?"

"Haven't the faintest doubt it will be called in, Samuel. But hardly a day later, old man . . ."

Again Lubetkin smiled to himself. Despite everything, he liked Colin Mathieson's sangfroid. "It may be nothing,

Colin, but I went through this Abdullah Majid's file in detail last night."

"Oh yes?"

"I read through his preliminary interrogation, when we took him from the Sudan."

"Something interesting show up?" asked Mathieson.

"No, it's not what he said – we've sent you all that anyway."

"So what was it?"

"The abduction and interrogation was led by one of our people called Moshe Avram. As you know, Majid served five years in prison as a result. Last January, two years after Majid's release, Moshe Avram was murdered in Budapest."

"Really?"

"Knee-capped, then had his throat slit, his back-up already having been shot."

"You think it may have been this Majid?"

"I haven't a shred of evidence," said Lubetkin. "At the time there were no leads, and Avram would have had lots of enemies. It's just that now we know Majid's active, the thought struck me it could be him."

"I see . . ."

"I don't have anything further on it. We hit a brick wall in following up the case."

"Right," said Mathieson.

"Two things did strike me though," continued Lubetkin.

"Yes?"

"First, Avram was very smart. He lasted a long time in the field. So whatever ruse was used to sucker him must have been good. So if it's this Majid, then he's clever."

"Quite. And the second thing?"

"Second, he must be pretty lethal. Avram was really tough, very experienced, a real street-fighter. Yet this guy managed to knee-cap him, then come close enough to slash his throat. So he's dangerous, he's ruthless and he's clever. Also he could have killed Avram with the gun presumably, but he used the knife, so maybe he's a guy who enjoys wielding a knife."

"Sounds like it," said Mathieson.

"Like I say, it may not be Majid who did it. But for what it's worth, I thought I'd mention it."

"Thanks, Samuel, I appreciate it."

"OK, then. Good hunting."

"Thank you."

"And Colin . . ."

"Yes?"

"I don't like the sound of this Majid. If I were in your shoes and I got near him, I'd shoot first and ask questions later. *Shalom*." Lubetkin hung up before Mathieson could come up with a response.

For a moment the Israeli toyed distractedly with the artillery paperweight, then he decided that he had done all he could. He pushed away the paperweight and went back to work, putting Abdullah Majid from his mind.

Laura sat in the command room of Harrogate police station, jotting down notes as she soaked up the atmosphere. The place was busy, with telephones ringing, fax machines whirring and much toing and froing of officers. At the centre of it all sat Chief Superintendent Thompson, assisted by Penny Harte, and Laura had been careful to keep her own presence as unobtrusive as possible as she absorbed everything that went on.

She had arrived at the station early after lunch, as agreed, and Thompson had made an effort to be welcoming despite all that was going on around him. Penny had found her an adjacent desk that wasn't being used just then, and had suggested that she might like to sit in on their activities. Thompson had described the chain of command, explaining that the local Chief Constable was technically the person responsible for the police element of conference security. In practice, however, Gold Command (as the senior working commander was called) was Thompson himself. Every report, every recommendation and every significant query regarding conference security was channelled to this room.

It was a massive operation, and Laura was impressed with the smoothly functioning lines of communication that Thompson had converging on the command room. All along one wall were banks of computers, their data constantly being updated. Despite giving the impression of being old-school himself, it was obvious that Thompson wasn't reluctant to embrace the advantages of new technology, and several times Laura had seen him cross to the computer screens to update himself on specific points.

Even in this busy working environment it was

obvious to Laura that Penny and Thompson had an excellent rapport, with a slightly unexpected but clearly present undercurrent of wry humour. Laura herself had taken to Thompson, and she could sense that Penny was glad that she and Thompson had hit it off.

There had been no sign of Carrow, much to Laura's relief, and Penny had explained that Colin Mathieson was in conference with the heads of the security teams from all of the countries with delegates attending the conference. Although glad to avoid Carrow's unnerving presence, Laura had felt obliged to ask after him. To her surprise, Thompson had spoken approvingly of the Special Branch officer.

"He went to the funeral of a colleague this morning," Thompson had explained.

"Someone off his team?"

"No, a constable he served with here in Yorkshire, way back when."

"Oh . . ."

Thompson lowered his voice and spoke to Laura in a confidential tone. "Whatever you might think about his – abrasive qualities, shall we say, he is strong on loyalty."

"I see."

"Always was, in fairness. I think he reckons that he owes it to the officer's family to show his solidarity."

"Right . . ."

Laura had been intrigued, the journalist in her always having found it fascinating to encounter a positive trait in someone who otherwise appeared unsympathetic. She made a mental note to observe

319

Carrow more intently during the course of the operation, then her musings were interrupted by a knocking on the command-room door. A uniformed officer in his late twenties opened the door and entered. Those who worked in the command room never knocked, and so Laura watched with interest as the constable crossed the room towards Thompson.

"Mr Thompson."

"Yes?"

"Constable Allen, sir. My sergeant suggested I see you straight away."

"Regarding?"

"The suspect Abdullah Majid, sir."

Immediately Penny and Thompson looked at the man with interest, and Laura noticed that those other officers within earshot had now stopped to listen.

"What about Majid?" asked Thompson.

"I believe I've seen him, sir."

"Really? When you say you *believe* –"

"Sorry, sir, wrong word. I *did* see him."

"Where?"

"On the outskirts of Harrogate."

"When was this?"

"Last Tuesday night."

Thompson looked at the constable quizzically "Why the hell are you only reporting it now?"

"At the time we didn't have photographic ID, sir."

"We've had it since yesterday."

"I finished night work after Wednesday night, sir. I was off yesterday, so I only saw the photograph when I came on duty again a few minutes ago."

"Fair enough," said Thompson. "Take a seat, Allen."

"Thank, you, sir," answered the young policeman, then he sat after nodding thanks to Penny who proffered him a spare chair.

"How did you encounter the suspect?" continued Thompson.

"I was manning a roadblock with another constable, sir. We stopped a van the suspect was driving and questioned him."

"Was he travelling alone?"

"No, sir, there was another man with him."

"Get a good look at him?" asked Thompson.

"Yes, pretty good. He looked Arab also."

"Right. Penny, let's have an Identikit organised immediately."

"I'm on it."

Laura was aware of Penny ringing a number and requesting immediate Identikit support, but her main attention was on the unfolding questioning of the young policeman.

"So you stopped the suspect," continued Thompson, "but didn't detain him?"

"No, sir."

"Did you note the make and registration number of the van?"

"Yes, sir," answered the constable eagerly, clearly glad to be able to offer something concrete. "White Volkswagen van . . ." He produced a small notebook and swiftly located the appropriate page. "Registration number K489 EYK."

"Excellent." Thompson turned to one of the

listening police officers. "Johnson, run that number, would you?"

"Yes, Chief," answered the officer.

Thompson turned back to Constable Allen. "So you stopped the van and questioned this Majid?"

"Yes, sir."

"Did you ask for ID?"

"Yes, sir. He had ID that showed him as a Greek, his companion as a Cypriot."

"Right. Did you search the van?"

"No, sir."

"Why not?"

The constable flushed slightly, and Laura felt a little sorry for him even as she waited impatiently for his explanation.

"I . . . eh – I suppose, sir, I bought his story. So searching the van didn't seem appropriate . . ."

"What was his story?" asked Thompson.

"He claimed that himself and his passenger were returning from a race relations conference in York."

"Interesting answer," said Thompson reflectively, then he looked around at the assembled officers. "Was there such a conference, anyone know?"

"There wasn't, sir," replied Allen. "I rang the Race Relations Board on my way over here."

Thompson nodded. "But our man knew that police officers would tread warily in their handling of anyone associated with race relations . . ."

"Quick thinking," said Penny.

"Or maybe not," said Thompson. "Maybe it was a line he had prepared. Smart thinking though, either way." He looked back at the constable. "When you questioned the suspect, how did he come across?"

"It was my colleague, Constable Green, who did most of the questioning, but he came across as – *convincing* would be the word, sir. He made the race relations thing sound pretty plausible. No sign of nerves, reasonable in his tone – he made himself sound like a law-abiding citizen."

"Interesting . . ." said Thompson. "Anything else strike you about him?"

Allen thought a moment. "Good command of English, despite the foreign accent. Able to make himself appear confident, but without being arrogant. A good actor, I'd say."

"This could be very useful, Constable," said Thompson encouragingly. "Anything else?"

Again Allen thought a moment. "I'd say – I'd say of the two men, he was the leader."

"He did all the talking, did he?"

"Not all of it, sir. The other man spoke also. He came across as plausible too. Obviously another cool customer. But the first guy, Majid . . . he'd more of an air of authority."

Thompson nodded. "Very good."

Laura longed to ask the constable even one of the many questions that ran through her brain, but she sat quietly at the desk instead. She wasn't sure whether or not the police would have reservations about her being in on developments to this extent, and so she decided to keep her head down and simply record mentally all that was said. Just then the door opened again, and Penny gesticulated to the middle-aged officer who entered carrying a laptop computer. The man drew nearer, and Penny rose to do the introductions.

"Constable Allen – Sergeant Douglas, our Identikit specialist."

"I'd appreciate it, Sergeant, if you'd go straight into action," said Thompson, "and I'd like the image the moment it's done."

"Yes, sir. Are we doing it here?"

"You can use Mr Carrow's desk – the vacant one by the window," said Thompson, then he turned back to Constable Allen. "As soon as you've finished come back to me, please. I'd like to talk some more about Mr Majid."

"Very good, sir," said Allen, then he moved to the vacant desk where Douglas began to set up his computer.

"This is bit of a break, Chief," said Penny.

Thompson nodded. "It's starting to happen. So, the minute we have a picture of Majid's accomplice, I want you to contact Colin Mathieson. Doesn't matter who he's meeting, disturb him."

"To give him the picture of the accomplice?"

"Aye. And get him to e-mail it immediately to his Israeli chums. If the second bloke's a known associate of the terrorist, there's every chance the Israelis will have him on file as well."

"Absolutely." Penny suddenly looked at Laura and smiled. "You've picked the right day to join us, Laura."

"So it seems."

Thompson looked across at Laura also and she hoped he wasn't going to ask her to excuse them. Instead, he simply held her gaze a moment then spoke.

"I won't belabour matters, Miss Kennedy. But what was said yesterday about everything being off the record . . ."

"Absolutely pertains. I understand perfectly, Mr Thompson."

"Good."

"Hard to believe, really, Chief," said Penny.

"What?"

"That we actually had our man at a roadblock on Tuesday night."

"I don't think you could say we had him," said Thompson.

"Allen seemed pretty certain of the ID."

"Oh, it was him all right. Actually taking him in though . . ." Thompson left the rest unspoken, and Penny nodded slowly in acknowledgement of what was being intimated.

"Yeah," she conceded. "He sounds like a really dangerous operator. . ."

"But now we know who he is, what he looks like, and how dangerous he is," said Thompson. "So smart and all as he may be, the net's starting to close a little."

Laura looked at Penny and her older mentor and sensed their steely determination. "You're going to get this guy, aren't you?" she said.

"I think so," answered Thompson, "and if we don't, by God, it won't be for want of trying."

"And if it wasn't all off the record," said Penny with a smile, "you could quote us on that . . ."

Majid tapped his finger carefully against the side of the van. There was no hint of stickiness, and he was pleased that yesterday's spray-job had dried out. He had come to the warehouse alone, ostensibly to check the paint-job on the Volkswagen, but also to spend some time away from Jemail. Majid had always done his best thinking alone and after they had eaten lunch together he had left Jemail watching soccer on television and made his way to the warehouse. Jemail had wanted to accompany him, but Majid had insisted on handling it himself.

Satisfied now that the dark blue paint was completely dry, he took a spare set of false number plates from a nearby shelf and began to screw the rear plate onto the back of the van. The plates looked completely convincing, but he knew there was a risk involved in using false registration numbers. Had the police at the roadblock called in his false number for checking he would have had to use the Uzi and made a break for it, but he still felt that using false number plates was the lesser of two evils. When he had bought the second-hand van the previous March he could have kept the original plates and completed all the paperwork, but that would have meant registering his address with the local authority. Better to take his chances with the phoney plates than to leave a paper trail, he had decided, and so he had ordered two sets of false plates, along with the other items supplied by the dissident Irish republicans.

Majid finished screwing on the rear plate, then went to the front of the Volkswagen and began to attach the second plate. Now that the paint was dry they would dirty up the van with mud and dust, then load the rolls of carpet and the toolbox into it, to support the carpet-laying story. They could also store the sniper's rifle and all the other back-up weaponry under the carpets in the rear of the van. That way, if a radical change of plan was forced upon them they would be ready to go at a moment's notice.

Majid finished attaching the number plate, then threw the screwdriver back into the toolbox and sat on a battered swivel-chair they had found in a corner of the warehouse. The air was still heavy with the smell of paint, but the place was quiet, and Majid closed his eyes and breathed out slowly.

He thought of all that had happened so far, looking for any flaw in what they had done. As he saw it, there had been three hiccups, an acceptable degree of deviation from plan in an operation of this magnitude. Having to kill the IRA men had been potentially risky, but in reality it had gone smoothly and created no further problems. Tamaz Akmedov's attack of nerves had also been worrying, but Majid had been pleased to note an improvement in the Turkish waiter's morale since their man-to-man chat. The encounter with the police at the roadblock however was more serious. It would only take an enquiry regarding the non-existent race relations conference to expose the fact that he had been lying. Should that happen, the police would know that two Arab-looking men had lied at a roadblock. Bearing in mind that the authorities were expecting an attack, it wouldn't be hard for them to put two and two together. So potentially there could be Identikit pictures of himself and Jemail from a description by the questioning policeman. A pity, but not a problem that couldn't be surmounted. Though of course it would be much better if the police had simply accepted the spiel at the roadblock and hadn't checked up on the race relations conference. Either way, it was done now, but it would be essential to keep a low profile over the next few days. Again not a problem, he thought. They had been extremely cautious about entering and leaving the house in Starbeck, never going out in the mornings until most of the neighbours had gone to work, and even then they had always entered and left by the rear garden gate that backed onto a small lane.

So bearing in mind that they now had everything they needed for the operation and that there were only three days to go, things were going pretty well, Majid reckoned. *And what do you do when things are going well?* his trainers used to ask. *Consider every element and try to imagine what might stop it from going well. Then devise a counter-measure for every possible problem.* Very well then, he had peace and quiet here and all the time in the world. Time to go over everything in detail so that no matter what happened he would still strike his enemies a devastating blow. He closed his eyes, breathed out slowly again, then began to review his plan.

"I've spoken to Tel Aviv," said Mathieson, rejoining the group seated around Thompson's desk in the command room. Penny noted the animation in his voice and suspected that the intelligence officer had been well received by his contact in Mossad.

"Well?" asked Thompson. "What's the story?"

"They've printed off the Identikit picture I e-mailed them. It's getting top priority – if they ID the accomplice they'll get back to us immediately."

"Excellent," said Thompson.

"Let's hope they do. Bit of a bummer not having him on file ourselves," said Carrow.

Mathieson looked at the Special Branch officer, and Penny knew that Mathieson was making an effort not to show irritation. "Quite," he answered.

Carrow had returned from the funeral early after lunch and had undone any admiration Penny had for his loyalty towards an old colleague by making another attempt to have Laura Kennedy removed from the command room. This time he had been more discreet, raising the matter with Mathieson when Laura had gone out to the toilet. Penny had been pleased when Mathieson had snapped, "We've covered this already, Len. Let's concentrate on more pressing matters, shall we?"

That had been almost three hours ago and during the course of the afternoon they had drawn a blank in trying to get a name for Majid's accomplice. The Identikit picture had been compared to police and intelligence records, but no match had been made. So far the enquiries regarding the Volkswagen van had been equally unfruitful, after it had emerged that the registration number provided by Constable Allen had been a false one. Thompson had issued immediate instructions for every second-hand car dealer within a radius of a hundred miles to be interviewed regarding sales of Volkswagen vans in the previous six months. It was worth pursuing, Penny knew, in the hope that it might turn up an address or contact phone number, yet in her heart of hearts she suspected that an opponent like Abdullah Majid would be too wily to leave a trail behind him.

"I've been giving this business a lot of thought," said Carrow now.

"Oh yes?" answered Mathieson, with just the faintest hint of sarcasm in his tone.

A barb was there nonetheless, Penny realised, when she caught Laura's eye and Laura gave a tiny smile in response to Mathieson's comment.

"Up until now we've been reacting," said Carrow. "Responding to the possibility of a bomb-threat or a sniper attack or whatever."

"We could hardly do otherwise," said Thompson.

"My point is that this bastard's made all the running, and we've had to do the reacting."

"So what are you proposing?" asked Mathieson.

"I think it's time for us to go on the offensive. Take the chase to him."

Thompson looked at the Special Branch man with ill-disguised impatience. "Surely we're doing precisely that? The moment Colin got the photograph of Majid I issued an immediate order. Every police officer in Harrogate is now actively looking out for this guy. Every single constable has a good-quality photo of him. We're checking hotels, bars, restaurants, cafés. I have dozens of officers trying to track down the source of the van. We *are* taking the chase to him."

"We need to up the ante," said Carrow.

"How so?" asked Mathieson.

"Because all the things we're doing are predictable. Necessary, I'll grant you, but predictable. Now according to your Israeli chum, this bloke is smart as well as dangerous. We know from his behaviour at the roadblock that he's cool and resourceful. So what's he going to think? He's going to think that we'll be doing exactly what we *are* doing. Looking for him in hotels and bars and cafés. So he'll avoid all those places."

Penny had been trying to avoid conflict with Carrow, but she felt that she couldn't be intimidated into not contributing. "I'm sorry to interrupt you, Mr Carrow," she said, "but he can't know we have photos of him. He has no way of realising that Laura taped the phone call and we ID'd him from his voice."

Carrow turned to Penny and looked her in the eye as he spoke. "He was stopped at a roadblock. He was questioned by police. He had false number plates. If the man has half a brain it'll occur to him that the police could still run a check on the plates."

"Though in fact we wouldn't have – if Constable Allen hadn't recognised him from the photo," said Thompson.

"But we *might* have," persisted Carrow. "There's so much high-profile security with this conference that he'll figure such checks could well be run. In which case the false plates are discovered. In which case he immediately becomes highly suspect. In which case we do an Identikit picture and issue it to our officers. Which brings me back to my starting point. If this guy is so smart, he won't be found hanging around hotels or bars waiting to be recognised."

"So how would you propose to up the ante, as you put it?" asked Mathieson.

"He has to stay someplace," said Carrow. "That's where we need to direct our effort."

"We're checking every hotel, guesthouse, and hostel in a twenty-mile radius. Plus all listed self-catering rentals," said Thompson.

"Therein lies the rub," said Carrow.

"Sorry?"

"My guess is that it won't be anywhere listed," said Carrow. "If I were in his shoes I'd be lying low in an ordinary house."

"You're not seriously suggesting we could search every house in Harrogate?" said Thompson.

"He's staying in a house in the Harrogate general area, I'll bet on it."

"For God's sake!" said Thompson, and Penny had to suppress her amusement at his complete lack of concealment of his exasperation with Carrow. "Even with all the manpower I've been given, what you're proposing's not feasible! To say nothing of the furore there'd be if we tried to have officers gaining access to every private dwelling in Harrogate."

"I wasn't thinking of every dwelling," answered Carrow. "And I wasn't thinking of actual entry – too much hassle with warrants."

"What exactly were you thinking of?" asked Mathieson.

"Targeting specific areas. If he's staying with someone, it would probably be another foreigner. Most of them live in the working-class quarters, so that's where you start."

Penny thought Carrow's suggestion smacked a bit of racism, yet there was an underlying logic to his train of thought and she found her mind racing with the possibilities.

"The photo changes everything. So we call door-to-door and produce it," said Carrow. "Ask if anyone's seen this man. We talk to shopkeepers, housewives, possible neighbours. We put the heat on, try to flush the bastard out . . ."

Thompson stroke his chin thoughtfully, then nodded. "It's not without merit. But the manpower demands . . ."

"If we say we need the manpower we'll get the manpower," answered Carrow. "Besides, we're not talking of all of Harrogate. If we start with the working-class areas, like I said, then the logistics become manageable."

Despite her dislike for Carrow, Penny had to admit to herself that his suggestion made sense, and she realised that what Mathieson had said previously about Carrow having a certain street-smartness was actually true. Now she saw the intelligence officer nodding in agreement with Carrow's proposal.

"I rather think Len's got a point here," said Mathieson. "All right, Jack?"

"All right."

"You'll organise the appropriate manpower?"

Thompson nodded. "Yes. . . somehow . . ."

"Good," said Mathieson, "let's try and move on every front."

"Absolutely," said Carrow, and Penny could see that

despite his dour expression he was pleased at having his idea adopted.

Mathieson turned to address them all. "Seems to me that our friend Majid's held most of the aces till now. Time, I think, to let him know that's changed . . ."

Laura sipped a mug of cocoa and gazed out her window at the rear of the Old Swan Hotel. It was a clear night, and faint yellow moonlight reflected off the roof-tiles that stretched away in all directions below her. It was a romantic image, and Laura was glad that she hadn't checked into one of the more modern hotels, preferring instead the ambience of the Old Swan with its labyrinthine corridors and interesting nooks and crannies. She had had a leisurely bath in her en suite bathroom, soaking in a large tub that she reckoned might well have been in place when Agatha Christie had stayed in the hotel in 1926. The bath had relaxed her, and she gathered her dressing-gown comfortably around her now and sipped the cocoa as she reflected on where she stood in pursuit of her story.

As regards the *Clarion*, all was well, she knew, and Mac had been satisfied when she had rung him earlier in the evening to bring him up to date on developments. She had also rung Declan in his hotel in Prague. He had regaled her with all the gossip from the film set and asked her how things were progressing in Harrogate. She had given him a highly sanitised version of events, and had felt guilty afterwards about misleading him. Yet she knew he would worry – and perhaps try to persuade her to drop the story – if she told him the truth about Abdullah Majid and how dangerous he appeared to be. But dangerous or not, she was absolutely committed to the story now.

She had stayed in the police station until seven that evening, but had declined an offer from Thompson to join Penny and himself for something to eat. She had sensed that Thompson had asked her out of courtesy and she decided that it would be better to let the two police officers have some time together rather than wear out her welcome. She had explained that her mother was ringing her from Dublin, back at the hotel, and instead arranged to meet Penny and Thompson at nine the next morning for the beginning of the door-to-door campaign.

In fact the call from her mother had been entirely mundane, consisting mostly of her detailing the exploits of her doted-upon grandchildren and who had said what at the bridge club, but Laura sensed nonetheless that she had done the right thing in giving Penny and Thompson some space.

Quite apart from the current case, she thought that Thompson was both likeable and fascinating, and with almost forty years' police experience behind him, he would make a great subject for an in-depth interview. She knew that he had moved out of the Moat House Hotel to sleep each night in a holiday cottage belonging to his son. The cottage was ten miles away in Blubberhouses, a twenty-minute drive from Harrogate, and she had heard him explain to Penny that he preferred the quiet of the cottage to the busy hotel. Perhaps if she continued to get on well with him she could visit him there for a relaxed interview, if the conference took place without incident.

In reality though, she knew that it would feel like an anti-climax were Abdullah Majid to be scared off by all the security that had been put in place. She felt a little guilty at the thought, knowing that it would actually be a considerable achievement by the authorities if the planned assault was prevented by the steps they had taken. But the journalist in her wanted a story, and what better story could there be than the conference going ahead safely because Majid and his accomplice were successfully apprehended? That was what she wanted, if she were honest: a high drama arrest – with Laura Kennedy the only journalist present.

She sipped her cocoa and savoured the thought, then told herself she was being over-dramatic. Still, she would know one way or the other within the next three or four days. And tomorrow she would be joining Penny and the team when they launched the door-to-door trawl. She looked out across the moonlit rooftops, finished off the mug of cocoa, then prepared to go to bed, eager for what tomorrow might bring.

14

Saturday 23rd September 2000

"Right, listen up then," said Thompson.

Penny noted the respectful attention that the assembled police officers afforded her old boss as they listened carefully to what he had to say. She had known Thompson for so long and regarded him with such an easy affection that she almost took him for granted, but it now struck her how much in awe he was held here in Yorkshire, both as the overall commander of the security operation and as a detective with an outstanding personal record.

They were all gathered around the corner from the Prince of Wales pub, prior to fanning out for the door-to-door trawl through the working-class area of Starbeck, and Penny winked over at Laura Kennedy who was standing with a notebook in her hand, no doubt trying to record the atmosphere for a future article. Laura smiled back, then Penny returned her attention to Thompson.

"I'm sure you've all been briefed already about

this," he continued, "but I'll say it again. Act carefully here. It's Saturday morning and folks are having lie-ins, relaxing, shopping, whatever. Lots of people are uneasy about the police calling to their houses – so tread lightly, and be polite. We're trying to flush out a couple of terrorists, but the vast majority of folks you'll encounter are law-abiding, so be sure you don't make them feel like *they're* being flushed out. At the same time, should our suspects be in this vicinity, we *are* anxious to actually flush them out, so don't be shy about flashing the photographs or being seen going about your business. You'll work in pairs, and if unarmed officers encounter someone who's suspicious, one of you engages the suspect in conversation while the other calls in for armed support. That support will be on hand right here, and can get to you rapidly. So no heroics. The men we seek are trained killers. Don't try and apprehend them – we don't want any dead glory-seekers. Just call it in, and you'll have armed back-up before you know it."

Penny felt that Thompson had hit just the right note, balancing a libertarian concern for the rights of the public with a nonetheless pressing need to get results. She knew that Carrow had insisted on overseeing a similar trawl that was going on in Jennyfield, a working-class area on the north-western outskirts of Harrogate, and she suspected that there would be an entirely different tone to Carrow's exhortations. She was particularly glad that Thompson had come across as balanced and professional with Laura present, and she realised that she was more concerned than she had realised that Laura, as an outsider, would get a good impression of the police.

"Penny for them!" Laura had approached and was looking at her smilingly.

Penny smiled in return. "If I told you that I'd have to kill you . . ."

Laura laughed. "I've never really understood what that means. I mean, it always sounds amusing, but I've never known exactly what it's supposed to mean!"

"Me neither," said Penny with a grin, then her attention was taken by Thompson addressing the group again.

"So," he said, looking about, "any questions?"

None of the assembled officers queried him, and after a moment he nodded. "Right, then, let's go hunt down our men . . ."

Avi Blumenthal crossed his boss's office and, with a small flourish, dropped a file on the desk of Samuel Lubetkin.

"This is getting to be a habit, Avi," said Lubetkin with a smile.

"Yeah – starting to feel like I work for MI5."

"Not quite."

"In here on the Sabbath so they can catch this guy and look good . . ."

Lubetkin raised an eyebrow. "Since when did you become religious?"

"Since never. But still, working on a Saturday, for the Brits . . ."

Strong early morning sunlight streamed through the

windows, and Lubetkin could see that his assistant looked drawn after hours of going through files. Nonetheless he sensed that Blumenthal's complaint was half-hearted, and that the team he led would be excited at having come up with the identity of the terrorist in the Identikit picture that had been e-mailed from Harrogate.

"So, who's our man?" asked Lubetkin.

"His name is Jemail Zubi. Lebanese. He's been giving us trouble since he was about sixteen."

"How old is he now?"

"Thirty-four."

"That's a lot of trouble."

"He's bad news all right," agreed Blumenthal. "And here's the thing. He was convicted on an explosives charge back in '94. Served four and a half years. And guess who was in the same prison for four of those years?"

"Our friend Majid."

"Exactly."

Lubetkin nodded approvingly. "Good work, Avi."

"Thank you. Though in fairness it was Benny Weissman who unearthed the file."

"You all put in the effort."

"There's one other thing," said Blumenthal.

"Yeah?

"The tape Kizili made last March – in the villa in Sidon?"

"What about it?"

"Majid's purpose in going there was to recruit for this mission, right?"

"Right," agreed Lubetkin.

Blumenthal looked at his boss and smiled. "Guess where Jemail Zubi has an apartment?"

"Sidon?"

"About a half-hour's drive from the villa. They're on this mission together in Harrogate, Sam – no doubt about it."

"Excellent. You and your team have put in a lot of donkey-work, Avi, I appreciate it."

"Our pleasure is to serve," said Blumenthal with a grin.

Lubetkin opened the file that Blumenthal had provided and flicked quickly through it, then removed two mug shots of Jemail Zubi, one face-on and one in profile.

"Much better than the Identikit," said Blumenthal.

"Yes," agreed Lubetkin, rising from behind his desk, "much better. Right, let's get this stuff to the Brits – and see what they can do with it . . ."

The quiet of the warehouse was disturbed by the ringing of a mobile, and Majid put down the map of greater Harrogate that he was studying and answered his phone.

"Hello?"

"We may have a problem."

Although they never used names when talking by phone, Majid recognised Jemail's voice immediately, and he felt a quickening of his pulse on hearing the anxiety in his partner's tone. "What sort of problem?"

"I went to the shops down at the main road –"

"What?"

"We needed some milk and –"

"I said stay indoors!"

"No-one saw me leave – I went out the back way."

Majid swore under his breath, then with an effort controlled his anger. "So what's the problem?"

"The police have arrived here in force."

"What are they doing?"

"Calling in to shops, going door-to-door at the houses. They, eh . . . they have pictures with them."

"Damn!" Majid knew these could well be Identikit pictures of himself and Jemail after the incident at the roadblock on Tuesday night. He had insisted that Jemail shave off his moustache, and in contrast to their dressed-up appearance on Tuesday, today Jemail was dressed casually in jeans, T-shirt and a baseball cap. Even so there was a real risk of recognition if they had a picture of him. "You don't know if the pictures are of us?"

"No, I wasn't near enough to tell."

"OK ."

"I can't walk back to the house though – the police are everywhere."

"Right . . ."

"Can you come and collect me in the van?"

"Haven't they set up roadblocks?"

"No, it's all foot patrols," answered Jemail. "They're not stopping cars."

"Are you certain?"

"Yes, I can see it all from here."

"Where exactly are you?" asked Majid.

"Opposite the Post Office. The best thing would be if I try and make my way up to the church carpark. You could pull in there without being noticed."

Majid wanted to scream, such was his anger at Jemail for jeopardising everything for a carton of milk. "This is so *stupid*. You've really screwed up."

"I'm sorry. Really. But I thought –"

"You didn't think, that's just it!"

"I'm sorry."

Majid bit his lip, knowing that now wasn't the time to vent his frustration. "Right. Make your way to the church carpark. I'll get the van out and –"

"Hang on! Hang on . . ."

"What?"

"Two of the police are approaching me."

"Stay cool."

"Yes! Of course I will!" Jemail laughed heartily, and Majid realised that the sudden bantering tone was for the benefit of the approaching police officers.

"You're some cookie!" said Jemail, laughingly. "But I suppose I'm stuck with you. All right – see you as arranged then. Bye . . ."

Before Majid could say anything the line went dead. "Damn!" he cried. "Damn you to hell, Jemail!" He switched off the phone and banged his other hand in fury against the side of the van. Jemail had acted coolly in the presence of the approaching police officers, and maybe he could talk his way out of the situation, but if he couldn't and he had to be rescued then Majid knew he would have to move really swiftly. Without wasting any more time he pulled his donkey jacket from its hook, slipped the silenced Beretta into its inside pocket, then ran towards the office and grabbed the keys to the van.

Laura sat comfortably in the police command vehicle, parked off the main street of Starbeck. Lightly holding her pencil, she added a few final strokes, then held back for evaluation the notepad on which she had made a sketch of Penny. *Not bad*, she thought. The drawing was tongue-in-cheek, but it caught the policewoman's spirit all the same. Laura had always had a flair for cartoons, and her doodlings and caricature portraits had become popular with her colleagues on the *Clarion*.

Unaware that she had been sketched, Penny sat in the front of the vehicle, issuing instructions over the phone, and Laura resisted the temptation to hold up the drawing to her. Even though Laura now felt almost as though she were one of the team herself, she didn't want to cause any problems, and knowing Penny's well-developed sense of humour she realised it might make her laugh aloud if she were suddenly shown a cartoon portrait of herself. Instead, Laura closed the flap on her notepad and settled back, waiting for Penny to finish the call.

She was happy to relax for the moment, knowing that if anything transpired with the door-to-door enquiries she would be right at the centre of things. About three-quarters of an hour had elapsed since Thompson had sent his officers to comb Starbeck, and Thompson himself had been called back to police headquarters a few minutes previously. Penny had been taking a call at the time, and Thompson had asked

Laura to tell her where he was going and that he would return as soon as possible. Laura had been glad to oblige, pleased that Thompson now obviously regarded her as part of the scene.

She had liked Thompson right from the beginning, and he had been friendly in return in his slightly bluff, no-nonsense fashion. At first Laura had thought it was a sort of 'any-friend-of-Penny's-is-a-friend-of-mine' response, but after a while she had sensed that perhaps Thompson liked her in her own right. She had taken her nerve in her hands and suggested to him that when all the drama of the conference was over she would love to have a proper chat with him, and perhaps do some articles based on his overview of forty years of police work. To her delight he had agreed without the need for any persuasion and he had even given her the address of the cottage in Blubberhouses, in which he intended to relax on a few days' leave, provided that the conference took place uneventfully. They could chat there without being interrupted, he had suggested, and if the weather stayed fine perhaps he could show her some of the Dales. Laura had readily agreed, sensing that Thompson was proud of his Yorkshire origins, and aware that he would make an excellent guide and companion.

Penny suddenly finished her call and swung around in her seat, ending Laura's musings. "Were you drawing something?" she asked.

"Guilty as charged, your honour," answered Laura, unveiling the sketch. As she had earlier surmised, Penny burst out laughing.

"Oh, my God, is that how people really see me?! I'm

like a cross between Catwoman and Cruella de Ville!"

Laura smiled. "Caricature is all about exaggeration."

"So that's what I'm like – just a bit exaggerated. Very consoling . . ."

But she was laughing, and Laura knew that she wasn't offended.

"Shane would love to see that," said Penny

"Be my guest then," said Laura and she pulled the page free along the perforation.

"I don't know," said Penny, still smiling. "He'd probably want to get it enlarged or something . . ."

Before Laura could answer, Penny's mobile rang again.

"Sorry, Laura," she said, then she took out the phone and answered it. "DI Harte."

Laura watched as Penny's expression became animated.

"Really?" said Penny. "Where?"

Laura couldn't hear the other end of the conversation but she knew something significant had happened.

"OK, I'm on my way," said Penny, then she hung up and looked back at Laura.

"Well?"

"Two of the constables have stopped a man who looks like the Identikit."

"Brilliant! Whereabouts?"

"On the High Street," said Penny, all trace of humour gone as she took her pistol from its holster and slipped it into her pocket. "OK, let's go!"

Majid pushed the door open and jumped out of the van.

He left the engine running while he quickly went to the rear of the vehicle and shut the warehouse gates behind him. He snapped the padlock closed, then moved swiftly back around the van to the driver's side. The Beretta shifted in his jacket pocket and, without pausing, he buttoned the front of the donkey jacket to keep the weapon concealed, then climbed in behind the wheel again.

There was rarely much activity in the industrial estate early on Saturday mornings, but Majid resisted the temptation to gun the engine. The worst thing now would be to panic and draw attention to himself. Conscious of the fact, he slipped the engine into gear then accelerated smoothly away from the warehouse.

Even as he quickly negotiated the turns to take him out of the industrial estate, he found himself cursing Jemail again. How could he be so stupid, putting the whole mission at risk with only two days to go? He suspected that going to buy milk was largely an excuse, and that in reality it was restlessness and claustrophobia that had prompted Jemail to leave the house. It was disappointing, and Majid was in part annoyed with himself. He had calculated that if Jemail could handle four years in an Israeli jail then he could handle the enforced inactivity in the final days leading up to their strike. Clearly he had miscalculated, but while annoyed with himself he was furious with Jemail, particularly after the conversation they had had regarding the need for security.

Still, the damage was done now, and Majid knew that he mustn't waste any more energy on anger.

Instead, he had to stay focused on dealing with Jemail's predicament. It was vital that he didn't fall into the hands of the security services, otherwise the whole mission would be fatally compromised. Whatever his other flaws, Jemail was a brave man, but Majid had been trained to operate on the principle that any prisoner could be made to talk. Of course, there was always the chance that Jemail would be able to bluff his way out – he was cool-headed and a very persuasive talker – but Majid knew he couldn't count on such a happy outcome.

Instead, he drove as quickly as was possible without drawing attention, only slowing when he reached the junction with the main road. He rued every wasted second, then the moment the traffic allowed he made a right-hand turn and drove towards the church carpark, his adrenaline pumping, and his mind frantically trying to devise a workable course of action.

Penny looked carefully at the suspect's face. He was Arab-looking and certainly bore a resemblance to the Identikit drawing. On the other hand, he had no moustache and his features didn't precisely match those in the Identikit. He was surrounded now by police officers, and Penny could see that he was being discreetly covered from behind by several armed plainclothes officers.

"Would you mind removing your sunglasses, sir?" she said.

The man sighed. "I've been through all this already, you know."

"Then I'm sorry to have to ask you to do it again, sir. But it's necessary."

The man shrugged, then took off what Penny recognised as designer sunglasses. She compared his eyes to those in the Identikit drawing and again there seemed a good similarity.

"Obviously there's some mistaken identity here," the man said.

His tone certainly didn't suggest a terrorist who had been caught by the police, she thought, and she was aware too that the Identikit was an aid, rather than a tool for foolproof identification.

"If there's a mistake then I'm sorry for any inconvenience," she said.

"I've already shown them my ID – this is ridiculous!"

"French driver's licence, ma'am," said one of the uniformed officers, handing it to Penny.

She took the licence and looked from its photograph to the face of the suspect. Unquestionably, it was the same person.

"Now, may I go?" he asked.

"We need to ask you some more questions . . ." Penny glanced down at the licence, "Mr Leclerc."

"What is there to ask? I've told you who I am, I've proven it with official ID, I'd really like to go, please."

"All in good time, sir. May I ask the purpose of your visit to Harrogate?"

"I finished some work in Leeds last night and was told Harrogate was worth visiting. So I took the train up this morning."

"What was the nature of your business in Leeds?"

349

"I was meeting a client there."

"What sort of client?"

"A client for a Japanese sports car. A special import – that's what I do."

Penny quickly produced a pen and notebook. "And the client's name?"

"John Richards."

Penny noted the name. "And where did you meet Mr Richards?

"The Queen's Hotel. Look –"

"So you stayed in the Queen's last night?"

"No. No, I stayed in Mr Richard's apartment. We've done business before, and he's just bought an apartment in the city centre. He suggested I stay there. We both did, after going for a meal together."

"And the name of Mr Richard's company?"

The man hesitated. "Something Computer Services. I don't remember exactly."

"Even though you did business with him?"

"They weren't company cars – he always bought privately."

"You've a telephone number for Mr Richards?"

"A mobile number – but he may not have it on, he's going on holiday today. Look, I've tried to co-operate here, but I really feel this has gone on long enough."

"I'm afraid I must be the judge of that, Mr Leclerc."

"If I'm held any longer I'll have to complain to my embassy."

"That would, of course, be your right, sir."

"May I have your name then?"

"Detective Inspector Harte."

The man looked Penny in the eye, then changed his tone to a more reasonable one. "Look, Inspector, I don't want trouble. Can we finish with this and both get on with our busy lives?"

Penny didn't answer immediately, knowing she had to tread carefully. Undoubtedly the man bore a close resemblance to the Identikit picture, yet if he genuinely were an innocent French citizen she didn't want the hassle and embarrassment of a wrongful arrest. It struck her too that it would require extremely cool nerves to behave as he had if he really was a terrorist.

"You have excellent English, Mr Leclerc," she said, watching his face to see his reactions.

"Thank you."

"But your accent doesn't sound French."

His face gave away nothing as he shrugged. "I'm not from mainland France."

"Oh?"

"I'm from Corsica. Different accent. And now if we're finished . . ."

"Not yet, sir."

The man was about to protest again, but Penny was distracted by the ringing of her mobile. "Excuse me, please," she said, then stepped away from the suspect and took the call. "DI Harte."

"Penny, got a report you've detained someone!"

It was Thompson, and Penny could hear the excitement in his voice. "Yes, just questioning him, Chief."

"Is he one of our men?"

"Quite possibly."

"Majid?"

351

"No, but could be the other guy. He resembles the Identikit, but insists he's a French citizen. Actually getting a bit shirty about it."

"Stay polite, but hold him for another few minutes," said Thompson. "We'll be straight up to decide it."

"Yeah?"

"Yeah, bit of good news. I was called back to meet Colin. He's after getting a positive ID from the Israelis. The bloke's name is Jemail Zubi. They've sent us good-quality photos, profile and face on. Colin's printed them off – we'll be with you in about three minutes."

"Great!"

"Yeah, the photos should decide it. Meanwhile, take no risks, Penny."

"Right, Chief. See you in a couple of minutes." Penny hung up, then returned to the suspect. "I'm sorry about that, sir," she said.

"Now can I go?"

"Shortly, sir. Your licence," she added, handing him back the French driving licence. "*Shakran*."

It was Arabic for '*thank you*', and Penny had said it almost off-handedly hoping that suspect might answer instinctively in Arabic. Her attention had appeared to be on the licence that she was handing back, but in reality she was watching the man's face carefully.

He looked at her now as though puzzled, then said, "Sorry?"

Penny held his gaze challengingly, but he continued to look puzzled and replied with another "Sorry?"

If this guy wasn't innocent, he was a real pro. "Thank you for the licence, Mr Leclerc."

"May I go now, please?"

"In a few more minutes, sir."

"I've tried to be reasonable, Inspector, I really have, but this is too much. EU citizens are supposed to be able to move freely. I *insist* you allow me to go on my way."

"My Chief Superintendent would like a word, Mr Leclerc. Then you may be released."

"Am I under arrest?"

"Not at the moment, sir."

"Good." The man made as though to move, but the armed officers instantly closed in on him.

"Please make no sudden movements," Penny said, "and stay precisely where you are, sir."

The man looked at her angrily but, seeing the cordon of officers, made no move. Penny held his gaze unblinkingly. "Two or three more minutes, then we'll sort out exactly what's what . . . "

Majid drove cautiously towards the church carpark. To his relief there had been no checkpoints anywhere along the route, and looking ahead now he could see nothing holding up the traffic ahead of him. He knew that the dirty blue van looked different from the clean white one that the police had stopped the previous Tuesday night, and he himself looked different in the donkey jacket and sporting a baseball cap, yet he knew that if he were stopped by police armed with Identikit pictures there would be a problem. Still, no point facing issues that hadn't arisen – the priority now was Jemail's situation.

He indicated left, then his heartbeat quickened

when he saw a gathering of people on the pavement in front of the Prince of Wales pub. He couldn't make Jemail out, but the location was close to the place from where his partner had rung. Majid slowed down, then turned left into the church carpark. He brought the van to a halt out of the line of vision of most people in the main street, but in a spot that still allowed him a view down the street towards the Prince of Wales. Not wanting to appear suspicious by sitting staring out of a van, Majid took a map of Harrogate from the glove compartment and spread it out on the dashboard. He pretended to study the map, but surreptitiously observed the scene unfolding outside the pub. Now he could see Jemail clearly, surrounded by about half a dozen men and two women. Two of the men were in uniform, the rest presumably being detectives or Special Branch. So the bad news was that he was decisively outnumbered. The police didn't appear to have guns drawn, but unquestionably detectives on an operation such as this would be armed. The good part was that Jemail wasn't handcuffed and appeared to be talking quite reasonably to the police officers. So he hadn't panicked, he hadn't been arrested, and there was the possibility that he might talk his way out of the situation.

Majid decided to wait and see how things unfolded, then his eye was caught by one of the two female detectives. Her face looked familiar, and Majid thought for a moment before it came to him. *The Old Swan Hotel.* When driving past the previous Monday he had seen her coming out of the hotel carrying under her arm the same type of folder in which she was now writing. She had wavy brown hair and a slim attractive figure and she had caught his eye in the brief moment it had taken for the van to pass the hotel. Obviously they had brought in police from outside the area if they were putting them up in hotels, he thought, and he wondered what her particular skill might be that would see her drafted to Harrogate. Or perhaps she had none, but, with the Western preoccupation with political correctness, women had to be represented even in the security forces. It wasn't the way in the societies in which Majid lived, but values here were different, he knew.

As if to illustrate the point, a male uniformed officer approached the group and began to report to the other female present. She too was attractive, Majid noted, with jet-black hair and sallow-looking skin, and from the general demeanour of those gathered around Jemail he realised that she was probably the senior officer present.

The woman dismissed the uniformed officer, then a squad car suddenly approached and came to a halt beside the group on the pavement. Two men got out of the back, and Majid knew immediately that these were serious players. One was a tall, heavy-set man of about sixty, the other a slimmer but athletic-looking man in his fifties. Everything about these men said 'seniority', and Majid felt his heart sink. If Jemail had been succeeding in talking his way out of trouble then top brass like this pair wouldn't have been called to the scene.

The slimmer of the two men opened a folder and withdrew photographs. He offered one to the other

older man and one to the black-haired woman, then all
of them looked from the pictures to Jemail. The heavy-
set man looked back to his colleagues and all of them
nodded. Some kind of a signal must have been given to
the other officers present, because the next thing Majid
saw was that three of the plainclothes officers had
produced weapons in support of the slimmer older man
who quickly covered Jemail with a pistol. One of the
policemen who had been behind Jemail immediately
began to frisk him, and Majid knew that if he were to
intervene it would have to be now. He weighed up the
odds then breathed out in frustration. Jemail wasn't
armed, in fact was now being handcuffed, so even if
Majid were to strike with the advantage of surprise he
would still be outnumbered by eight to one. Plus the
adjoining streets were probably full of police officers
who would be alerted by the sound of shots. He
couldn't act here, it would be suicidal. He banged the
steering wheel in temper, then tried to think clearly.
There *was* one possibility, he realised. *Always strike
where they least expect it.*

The main police station was on North Park Road.
And the authorities were only now starting to escort
Jemail way from the front of the pub on foot. If he left
immediately he could be there ahead of them. They'd
be feeling jubilant, victorious, safe on home ground –
the last thing they'd expect would be an ambush. Majid
knew that what he planned was a high-risk gambit, but
the whole operation was at stake. He started the engine,
but found himself hesitating a moment, then he realised
that he had to act before his nerve failed him. He

pushed the map from the dashboard onto the passenger's seat, put the engine in gear and pulled out onto the road.

Laura tried hard not to let her excitement show. They had bundled the prisoner into the command vehicle, a large van that could accommodate up to ten passengers, and had just begun the journey back to police headquarters. A driver and an armed officer sat in the front, then the prisoner – flanked by Thompson and Mathieson – sat in the next row, and finally Penny and another armed detective sat in the last row with Laura. Despite the significance of the capture, the police officers weren't showing the excitement that Laura knew they must feel. She tried to mirror their low-key approach, feeling that the less she drew attention to herself the more likely it was that she would get to witness whatever transpired.

Laura had managed to steal a look at the photographs that Mathieson had brought with him, and she reckoned that the prisoner was actually Jemail Zubi, the terrorist in the Israeli-supplied pictures. The man was still protesting that a mistake had been made, but Laura didn't think so, and she could tell from the demeanour of Thompson, Penny and Mathieson that they had confidence in the arrest. In spite of herself she couldn't help but take pleasure in the fact that Carrow had missed out on what was clearly a major break in the case. The Special Branch officer was still out in Jennyfield, where the other door-to-door trawl was being conducted. She knew he would be furious at having missed out on the action, and she blessed her own good fortune in having met Penny and having gained the ringside seat she had enjoyed today. She knew that what she had witnessed was the scoop of every journalist's dreams, and she recalled the risk that Mac had taken in sanctioning her trip to England on what could well have been a wild-goose chase. It would be wonderful to repay his trust with interest when she wrote what she knew would be an explosive series of articles.

Her musings were cut short by the prisoner shifting vigorously in his seat and raising his voice. "I demand you remove these handcuffs! This is outrageous!"

Laura watched as Thompson drew his face near to the man. "Don't cause any trouble, son," he said quietly, but in a voice that was decidedly unsympathetic. "You're in enough already."

"I shouldn't be handcuffed! I've done nothing wrong!"

"It's less than five minutes' drive to the station," said Penny. "We'll take them off there." Laura watched the exchange, fascinated by the dynamic that was unfolding. Were Penny and Thompson already going into good cop/bad cop mode before questioning even began in the station? She looked from one to the other and her intuition told her they were. Probably a technique that had evolved during all the years that they had worked together.

"I'm an innocent man – I want these cuffs off now!" demanded the prisoner.

This time Thompson dropped the quiet tone from his voice, but again drew his face close to the protesting man. "Cut the bullshit, son – you're as guilty as hell!"

"No!"

"Yes! And we'll prove it with fingerprints. You're up to your eyeballs in trouble here. So if you know what's good for you, drop the innocent man rubbish – and start co-operating!"

Majid drove quickly along the Knaresborough road, anxious to reach the police station as far ahead as possible of the group that had arrested Jemail. Even as he drove to set up his ambush, he knew that there were countless things that could go wrong. For all he knew Jemail might not be taken to police headquarters at all. For security reasons he could be brought to an army barracks, or he might be taken straight to some secret location where the intelligence people would want to interrogate him. Majid's hope however was that the British, with their regard for procedures, would want to charge Jemail, and that they would be sufficiently complacent to feel that they could do it without risk at the local police headquarters.

It was the scenario he had to count on – an interrogation of Jemail in any other location would mean the mission had to be aborted – and he decided not to waste time worrying over the myriad of things that were now out of his control. Instead, he knew he must concentrate on his ambush as though it were definitely going to happen. He reached the junction of North Park Road and Knaresborough Road, slowed down a little, then swung onto North Park Road. He continued on at a fast pace, then on approaching Harcourt Drive he eased off the accelerator. From his earlier reconnaissance, he knew that the police station was coming up on the right, and as he drew nearer to it he slowed right down. There was a parking area in front of the station, and he realised that if they disembarked to enter through the front door of the station there would definitely be a moment when they would be vulnerable to attack.

Pleased with what he had seen, he drove a little past the entrance, then came to a halt and pulled up onto the pavement at the far side of the road. He jumped out of the van and swiftly went to the rear doors. He pulled the doors open, climbed inside, then immediately closed the door over until just a crack enabled him to see across to the carpark of the police station. He knew that if Jemail were being brought here the arrest team would be arriving at any minute and so he immediately went to pull back the heavy rolls of carpet that ran the length of the van. The Uzis, the sniper's rifle, a selection of silencers and spare ammunition were all hidden beneath a large roll of underlay, and he was glad now of his foresight in keeping the guns so readily accessible in the van. He placed both hands under the heavy roll, swung it vigorously backwards and uncovered the weapons.

"The game is up, Mr Zubi, we know exactly who you are!" said Thompson.

Penny watched the prisoner's face, but it was hard to tell in the bumping command vehicle whether or not he'd betrayed a flicker of recognition.

"There's a mistaken identity here," said the man. "Obviously I look like someone else."

Despite herself, Penny had to admire his coolness under pressure. She was sure that he was the Lebanese terrorist in the file that Mathieson had received from Israeli intelligence, and once they got back to the station they would prove it beyond any doubt with fingerprints. Meanwhile though, the opening gambits in the psychological warfare were important, and she bided her time, knowing how the game was played. After Thompson had painted the worst possible picture for the prisoner she would present an alternative 'for-you-the-war-is-over' scenario, and suggest that he lessen his problems by co-operating with his captors. It was an approach that they had used to good effect many times in the past, though admittedly with criminals who were less impressive than the terrorists involved in this operation.

"We know all about you," continued Thompson. "We know about Abdullah Majid."

Again Penny watched the man's face. Was there a slight widening of his pupils at the mention of his partner's name? Possibly, she thought, but if there had been the tiniest hint of shock there was no sign of it now as he shook his head.

"I don't know what you're talking about."

"You know *exactly* what we're talking about," said Thompson. "We know it all, son – who you are, why you're here, what you've planned. You were walking into a trap from day one . . ."

Good move, thought Penny, *always let them think you know more than you do*. That way prisoners would often confirm things that you were only guessing about, but

361

without feeling that they were betraying their comrades. Not this guy though, she realised, as he shook his head unyieldingly.

"You're making a mistake!" he insisted.

Before Penny could go into good-cop mode, Mathieson spoke for the first time. "You're the one making the mistake," he said, leaning forward and looking the prisoner in the eye. "Thing is, your mission's had it anyway. So the question for you is simple. Are you going to persist in doing things the hard way? Or are you going to make things easier for yourself?"

"You're confusing me with someone else!"

Mathieson continued as though the prisoner hadn't spoken. "The hard way is we turn you over to the Israelis. When they finish interrogating you you'll end up in the worst jail in Israel. And believe me, you'll be an old man by the time they let you out."

The man said nothing, but Penny sensed that Mathieson's threat filled him with dread.

"Or," continued Mathieson, "you can co-operate with us and be tried here. If you play ball, you'll get a much-reduced sentence and a far less harsh regime. Either way your mission here has failed. So, what's it to be? The hard way, or the easy way?"

There was a pause, and Penny felt that Mathieson's skilful manipulation might be about to pay off.

The man swallowed, then shook his head. "It's all a mistake," he said stubbornly. "You're confusing me with someone else . . ."

Majid waited nervously in the back of the van, looking

out across North Park Road through the partly opened rear doors. He felt the van to be very visible, parked as it was on the footpath opposite the police station. It would only take the approach of one inquisitive police officer to jeopardise his hastily conceived plan, but there was nothing he could do about it. On the positive side, there was the fact that he shouldn't have to wait for long. Either they would arrive with Jemail in the next few minutes or they weren't coming here at all.

Majid could feel his heart pounding, but he knew from past experience that this was normal and that it didn't mean he couldn't still act coolly when he went into action. He also knew however that the risk assessment that was part of any operation would, in this case, dictate aborting the entire mission by now. Logically it was the sensible thing to do, but he had come too far to be sensible. The prize involved was too big. He was so close now that he was prepared to take serious risks, and he had steeled himself to pay a high price to succeed.

He glanced at his watch and realised that only two minutes had elapsed since he had uncovered the weapons. *Come on*, he thought, willing the arrest party to drive into sight. He was psyched up for action now and he wanted to get it over with, one way or the other. He looked across again at the police station, but all was still quiet there. In front of the main entrance to the building there was a parking area, and Majid was counting on the police bringing Jemail in that way rather than driving all the way round to the back of the station.

Majid realised that he had done all that he could to

prepare and so he breathed out slowly, trying to calm himself and to conserve his nervous energy. He continued his deep breathing for another couple of moments, then he heard the sound of an approaching vehicle and he stopped the breathing exercise and looked anxiously down North Park Road. A large police van came into view and Majid felt a sudden racing in his pulses. The van indicated right. As it slowed to turn into the station Majid recognised the police officers who had made the arrest and saw Jemail seated in the second row of the van between the two older men. He swallowed hard, wiped the sweat from his hands and took up his gun.

Journalism school had never prepared her for this, thought Laura, savouring the adrenaline charge of travelling with armed detectives who had made a dramatic arrest. The prisoner had continued to maintain his innocence, but it was obvious that the others were sure that he was in fact Jemail Zubi. When he had denied it for the fourth or fifth time, Mathieson had given him a smile entirely without humour and said, "Try telling that to the Israeli interrogators . . ."

He had made the implications sound chilling, and Laura knew that it was deliberate. She could see that the tactics were to unnerve the prisoner and, despite the brave front that the man kept up, she suspected that behind his continuing protestations he was actually frightened.

"Front or rear, Chief?" asked the driver now, glancing over his shoulder momentarily.

"Sorry?" said Thompson.

"Front or rear entrance, sir?"

Laura saw that they were approaching police headquarters and, now that they had reached their destination, she wondered what would happen next. With a terrorist actually apprehended there was sure to be a flurry of activity, but she had no idea to what extent she would be allowed to witness events. Would they let her watch what happened to Jemail Zubi as part of her observation of police work, or had matters now reached the point where his debriefing would be regarded as classified and done strictly in private?

"Front," answered Thompson to the driver, and Laura reckoned that she would know soon enough as the vehicle turned right and came to a halt close to the main entrance.

The driver undid the central locking, then all of the doors were opened and the passengers disembarked. Laura was first out of the rear section and she watched with interest as Thompson climbed out, then took a firm hold of the handcuffed prisoner while Mathieson climbed out after him. For a few seconds Thompson and the man stood still as they waited for Mathieson to join them, then Laura saw the most shocking sight of her whole life.

One minute the prisoner stood before her, his eyes scanning in all directions as though seeking some means of escape, the next moment his head exploded before her eyes. Spraying blood from his shattered skull, he stumbled backwards, then seemed to be spun sideways and his chest erupted, spraying Laura with more blood as he collapsed on top of her. She staggered under his weight, then felt the wetness of his bloodied remains upon her and began to scream.

Majid dropped the Remington sniper's rifle onto the roll of underlay. He knew without doubt that Jemail was now dead. The head-shot had probably killed him outright, but if it hadn't the shot to the heart had put the matter beyond doubt. The Remington 700 fired 7.62 mm cartridges, and Majid had seen before the kind of damage they did. His emotions were in turmoil, and it had taken an effort to overcome his resistance to sacrificing a comrade. He had had no choice, however; the mission had to come first, and one part of him was actually proud of having had the stomach to do what had to be done. In a detached corner of his mind, he also took pride in the coolness and good marksmanship that he had exhibited. He still felt sorrow that Jemail should have to die, but it was mixed with an anger that Jemail should have been so undisciplined as to cause the problem in the first place.

Majid's mind was racing, yet even as he coped with the flood of competing emotions he moved towards the van door. There would be a moment of shock among the group of police officers – the less experienced ones might even be traumatised – and the fact that the Remington was silenced would add to the confusion, but sooner rather than later they would seek to return fire at their assailant. Eager to be away, he grabbed a loaded Uzi, then pushed open the rear door of the van.

Mathieson screamed "Get down! Take cover!" and Penny

followed suit with the other officers and dropped to the ground. Her initial shock at seeing the prisoner shot before their eyes was giving way now to fear, and she felt her stomach tighten.

"Get behind the doors of the van!" cried Mathieson.

Although somewhat dazed, Penny obeyed and scrambled in closer to the vehicle for shelter. She glanced behind her to see what was happening with the bloodsoaked prisoner. He had staggered backwards onto Laura, but Thompson had moved quickly to lift him off the journalist, and even amidst the trauma of what had occurred Penny was impressed to see that Laura had stopped screaming and was trying to help Thompson, who had the prisoner cradled in his arms in the shelter of the far end of the vehicle.

Penny turned away, realising there was nothing she could do to help them for the moment. She pressed in tightly against the vehicle, her training kicking in as she withdrew her weapon. In the uncertainty after the firing of the two shots, the driver and the two armed detectives had ended up on the far side of the command vehicle, where Mathieson was also crouching.

"Penny! You OK?" he called out to her now.

"Yes," she answered, trying to keep her voice from croaking.

"Jack, Laura?" cried Mathieson.

"We weren't hit!" shouted back Thompson.

Penny hadn't had time to work out where the shots had come from, although all the group had gathered on the police-station side of the command vehicle, presuming that fire wouldn't be directed at them from their own headquarters. Penny's eyes darted about, seeking their assailant, then her attention was attracted by a movement out on North Park Road. She saw the rear door of a blue van swinging open and a dark-skinned man in a donkey jacket and baseball cap emerging from the vehicle.

"Colin! The blue van!" shouted Penny.

The man had swiftly rounded the rear of the van and was making for the driver's door when he heard Penny's shout. He looked over, just as Penny raised her gun and began to move out from the shelter of the command vehicle. Penny glimpsed the man's left arm, which had been down at his side, being swung up, then suddenly a hail of bullets clattered into the bonnet of the vehicle. "Jesus!" she cried as she threw herself back towards the shelter of the door. She banged against the door, hurting her hip, and her knees trembled from the knowledge of how near the silenced machine-gun fire had been. It was the first time she had ever been shot at in the line of duty, and despite all her training she found that the reality of someone trying to kill her was terrifying.

"Penny, were you hit?!" cried Mathieson.

"No, I'm OK!" Just then she heard the sound of an engine starting and realised that their assailant was preparing to drive off. She found her fear being replaced with a fury at what this man had done and she was suddenly determined not to let him away with it. She knew that Mathieson and the other officers pinned down on the far side of the command vehicle were on the wrong side for getting a clear view of the blue van, and that it was up to her to act. Almost before she knew what she was doing, she lay down on the ground, then rolled out from behind the door and rose into a crouch, raising her gun-hand. "Halt, armed police!" she cried.

The man in the van had left the door open when putting the key into the ignition, and once again wielding the Uzi with his left hand, he swung the weapon around and let off a burst. This time Penny heard the rounds whistling over her head and pinging against the tarmac behind her, then she tried to steady her gun-hand and fired. She got off two shots, both of which hit the side of the van beside the driver's door. The dark-skinned man dropped down behind the wheel and Penny realised that he might have been hit with a ricochet. No sooner had she thought it than the crouching man pulled the driver's door closed. There was a sudden roaring as the engine was revved, and Penny knew that if she didn't hit him soon he was going to escape. She swung her pistol up and got off two more shots, as from the corner of her eye she saw Colin Mathieson vaulting over the bonnet of the command vehicle. One of Penny's shots shattered the side window of the van, but the driver pulled out onto the road with a screech of tyres.

Mathieson approached at a run with his pistol drawn, but another wild burst of machine-gun fire out through the broken driver's window made Mathieson and Penny both dive for cover. The van careered across the road, and even while rolling on the ground Mathieson got off three shots that Penny heard pinging off the bodywork of the van. None of them appeared to have hit the driver however because he quickly righted the course of the vehicle and started to speed away. Penny raised her gun-hand, closed one eye and aimed at the rear tyre of the van. It was a difficult shot at a moving target, but she concentrated hard, then squeezed the trigger. She hoped to hear a blow-out, but all she heard was the sound of her shot, then the van picked up speed and disappeared down the road.

Laura crouched behind the command vehicle in a daze. There had been nothing that she and Thompson could have done to save the life of the prisoner, and she turned her gaze away, unable to bear any longer the sight of his bloody and shattered body. The volleys of gunfire that had caused her to remain under shelter had ceased now, and she saw Mathieson approaching, his pistol still in hand.

"All right, Jack?!" he called.

"Yes."

"Laura?"

"Yes, I'm . . . I'm OK. . ." she answered shakily. She didn't feel OK, but she knew that Mathieson was actually asking if she had been hit.

"He's had it, Colin," said Thompson, and Laura saw the intelligence officer looking down at the body of Jemail Zubi and shaking his head in anger.

"Damn!" he cried. "Damn, damn, damn!"

Having all travelled in the command vehicle meant that there was no car immediately available for pursuit, and Laura heard Thompson rejecting Mathieson's suggestion that they turn the cumbersome command vehicle about and use that.

"Too late, Colin, he's gone! We'll get him with roadblocks!"

"Right!"

Police officers began to spill out of the station, and Laura realised that she must look really shaky, because Thompson immediately went to her.

"All right, love?" he asked.

Laura nodded, and Thompson squeezed her arm sympathetically. She was conscious of movement behind him and saw Mathieson hurrying back to Penny, who was talking into the mouthpiece of a walkie-talkie. Laura turned around and caught sight of Jemail Zubi's shattered skull with its bloodied brain-matter spread on the ground of the parking lot, and she felt an overwhelming urge to throw up. She swallowed hard and leaned against the side of the command vehicle, but she couldn't control her trembling and was hit by a wave of nausea. Unable to hold off any longer she quickly turned away and got sick at the back of the vehicle. Her stomach heaved until eventually she was dry-retching, then Thompson touched her shoulder and handed her a handkerchief.

"Thank you. I'm sorry, but –" she began, but Thompson raised a hand to stop her.

"No need," he said. "Perfectly natural."

Laura dabbed her mouth with the handkerchief.

Then Penny approached.

"Chief?" she said.

Thompson immediately shook his head. "He's dead. Nothing we could do."

371

"I know," answered Penny solemnly. "Colin told me. Are you OK?"

"I'm fine."

"Laura?"

"I'm all right."

"I saw you on the blower," said Thompson to Penny. "Got an alert out?"

"Yes, vehicle and occupant description, got the reg. number too. All points alert, top priority."

"Good."

"We nearly had him, Chief. Two of my shots were really close."

"Pity you didn't hit him. He's some ruthless bastard – to kill his own comrade like that."

"Yeah . . ."

"He got away then?" said Laura, her voice still sounding shaky, even to herself. As soon as she'd said it she knew it was a silly question, and she realised she was probably in shock.

"For the moment," answered Penny. "But we've flushed him out now – it's just a matter of time."

"You don't look great, Laura," said Thompson, "Why don't we get you inside?"

"I'm all right . . ."

"You're not really," said Penny gently. "None of us are." She indicated the bloodied blouse. "Let's go into the station and get you cleaned up."

"OK," said Laura, then she allowed Penny to guide her by the arm. She was grateful for the solicitude of her new-found friend, yet even as she walked towards the station another part of her mind told her not to behave like a victim. The police were going to have a lot on their plate – the last thing she ought to do was to make her presence a problem by becoming a nuisance. Besides, she thought, she had craved for dramatic developments, wanted to see action and, now that she had, she mustn't complain. It was just that she hadn't ever suspected that it would feel like this. Steeling herself to be stronger, she followed Penny into the station.

Majid forced himself to slow down as the van sped towards the roundabout on East Parade. He had raced along North Park Road, anxious to put as much distance as possible between himself and the police station, but now he had to cease drawing attention and try to appear normal. He had pushed out the remnants of the broken glass from the side window with the sleeve of his donkey jacket. That still left a number of bullet holes in the bodywork, but he reckoned that most people wouldn't pay too much heed to a slightly battered passing van if it were travelling at a moderate speed.

Easing off the accelerator, he swung around into East Parade, his mind still racing. He reckoned that the authorities would already have an alert out, and with Harrogate swarming with police officers there was going to be a short time lapse between the alarm being raised and a major response on the ground. There was no question of trying to drive back to the warehouse. He had to get rid of the van, and quickly.

Even as the thought struck him, he saw a sign for a carpark up ahead. His first instinct had been to drive to a quiet suburban road, park the van and walk away.

Now though, he thought again. Every second spent driving in search of a quiet by-road increased the risk of running into a roadblock or a cruising patrol car, while parking a van with a broken window and bullet holes would have drawn attention to him had he done it on any of the main roads. The multi-storey carpark, however, meant that his vehicle would simply be one amongst many. It could take the police hours to locate his van there, compared to the likelihood of finding the van within minutes – and thus having an idea of his general location – if he parked it on the street.

His decision made, he pulled in to the left and made for the carpark entrance. As he had hoped, the entrance was unmanned, so there was no attendant to notice the missing driver's window or the bullet holes in the bodywork. He drove straight into the building without encountering any other drivers and ascended several storeys until he found a level with free parking spaces, then he drove to the end of an aisle and parked the van with the broken window and the bullet holes facing away from view. There was nobody around, and, having checked that there were no security cameras, he immediately divested himself of the baseball cap and donkey jacket, then quickly weighed up his options.

He knew that the carpark had a pedestrian bridge that crossed the railway tracks and led to the Victoria Shopping Centre and he decided that the shopping centre would be his destination. On a Saturday morning it would be full of shoppers and he could vanish into the crowds while working out his next move. Meanwhile, there was the consideration of the van and its contents.

He needed to be armed, yet he couldn't possibly take with him all the weaponry that was in the back of the van. There was also the matter of fingerprints and identity. Presumably the authorities had identified Jemail, but it wasn't certain as yet that they knew Majid's identity. And whatever Jemail's other faults, he wasn't lacking in loyalty and would never have given any information on Majid in the short time that he had been in custody. *So leave no fingerprints and just take the Uzi and the Beretta.*

There was a small hold-all on the passenger seat, and Majid shoved the compact machine-gun into it after unscrewing the silencer. He took the Beretta from the inside pocket of the donkey jacket and slipped it in also, then took a handkerchief from his pocket and wiped all of the controls and the door handle. Satisfied that he had left no prints in the cabin of the van, he took the keys from the ignition, got out and moved quickly to the rear door.

He opened the door and climbed into the back, then he swiftly wiped any prints from the Remington sniper's rifle, grabbed spare ammunition clips for the Uzi and the Beretta, and shoved the clips into the hold-all before zipping it shut. He got back out of the van and looked about. There was one family getting out of a car at the far end of the aisle, but they were intent on getting a little girl into a buggy and were paying him no attention. Majid quickly wiped the inside of the van doors with the handkerchief, then swung the doors closed and wiped the outside handle also. He paused for a second to consider if there was anything he was forgetting. *No – he had weapons, he had the keys to the warehouse, and he had plenty of cash in the wallet in his trousers pockets. Time to go.*

He picked up the hold-all, turned away from the van without a backward glance, and walked towards the shopping centre.

The command room was a hive of activity, but Penny could hear Len Carrow's voice above everything else. He had arrived back from the door-to-door trawl in Jennyfield that had now been aborted, and was giving loud instructions to his Special Branch officers over the phone. "Forget bloody armed and dangerous," he said. "It's way beyond that! This bastard's killed his own accomplice, he's fired a machine-gun at police officers. Don't pussyfoot around if you find this fucker! Understood?"

Although Carrow hadn't actually said anything condoning illegal action, Penny nonetheless had a pretty good idea of what the Special Branch officer was suggesting. She disapproved of the concept of the so-called "hard arrest" which she knew could actually translate into shooting first and asking questions later. On the other hand, she had to concede that Abdullah Majid was an exceptionally dangerous opponent who was unlikely to lay down his weapon if challenged. She watched Carrow marshalling his forces and realised that he was on the kind of high that came with going into action. In fairness though, it couldn't be denied that his suggestion to launch the door-to-door enquiries had netted them Jemail Zubi. The Special Branch man was in his element, she saw, vindicated in his tactics and now enjoying the drama and the frenetic activity that Majid's violence had caused.

In truth, Penny felt slightly guilty, recognising in herself also an undeniably thrilling adrenaline surge. The experience of being shot at had been frightening, and Jemail Zubi's murder had truly been shocking, yet she couldn't deny the sense of excitement that the events had provoked. Before she could consider it further she saw Mathieson approaching. He stopped in front of her and nodded approvingly. "You did well, Penny."

"Thank you."

"First time under fire?"

"Yes."

"Then you did *really* well."

Penny shrugged. "I got off a few shots – but I didn't hit him."

"You exchanged fire three times with an enemy who had a submachine-gun. Pretty brave in my book."

"Thanks, Colin."

"Plus you had an alert out in a matter of seconds that may well close the net. Good work."

Penny couldn't help but feel pleased with the praise, and she nodded in acknowledgement, yet knew it would be scant consolation if they didn't capture Abdullah Majid. "Do you really think we'll get him?"

Mathieson considered a moment. "Be a mistake to underestimate this chap . . . "

"Right . . ."

"Having said that, we know now who he is and what he looks like – and we've forced him out into the open. Must be a fair chance we'll nab him."

"Let's hope so," said Penny

"Quite. Look, I've calls to make, talk to you in a while."

"OK, Colin." She watched Mathieson crossing to his desk and lifting the phone, then her attention was caught by Laura Kennedy re-entering the room. Like Thompson, she had gone to the toilets to wash the bloodstains from her hands, but Thompson had returned first and now he handed her a cup of tea. Laura still looked a little shaken, with bloodstains visible on her blouse, and Penny knew that Thompson was following the established practice of offering sweetened tea to those suffering from shock.

"All right, Laura?" she asked, going over to the journalist.

"Yeah, I'm OK now, thanks."

Although Laura was sipping the sweetened tea, Penny thought that she still looked unsettled and she felt concerned for her. "Look, why don't you head back to the Old Swan for a while?" she suggested.

"I'm OK, there's no need," answered Laura.

Penny indicated the bloodied blouse. "I'm sure you'd like to change . . ."

"No . . . I . . ."

"Don't worry, we're not trying to shut you out," said Penny. "You can re-join us here – right, Chief?"

"Sure," answered Thompson.

Penny saw that Laura looked reassured, and she reckoned that her suspicions were right and that the journalist had been afraid of being frozen out were she to leave. "The prisoner died in your arms, Laura. That would be a shock for anyone. After you've washed and changed you might want to gather yourself together and take a little break."

"But there's no problem coming back here," added Thompson. "Just take a breather, then come back whenever it feels right."

"OK," said Laura. "And thanks . . ."

"No problem," answered Penny. "I'll organise a lift back to the hotel for you. And we'll get you a spare jacket to cover up your blouse."

Laura looked at the bloodied garment, then nodded. "All right. And thanks for everything."

"The least we can do," said Penny. "If it wasn't for you, we still wouldn't know who we were after . . ."

Majid knew the odds had shortened against him and yet, in spite of all that had happened, he felt charged with a sense of excitement. It was the old familiar buzz he associated with being in combat, the danger all around somehow heightening the sense of being alive. On entering the Victoria Shopping Centre he had quickly bought a necktie and jacket which he had donned on the spot in a menswear store, then he had gone to another shop and bought a Gladstone bag before making his way to a cubicle in the gents' toilets. He had locked the door behind him and transferred the weapons and ammunition from the hold-all to the Gladstone bag. He had decided that the sanctuary of the locked cubicle would give him time for some swift contingency planning before emerging into the crowded shopping centre, and had immediately set about getting his thoughts in order.

He knew that he couldn't change his physical features beyond having wetted and slicked back his hair – which he had done before entering the cubicle – but he had already discarded the persona of working man in donkey jacket and baseball cap for the conference delegate who carried his files in a Gladstone bag. The dark slacks that he had been wearing were smart enough and with the jacket and tie he looked quite respectable. Now that he had dealt with his appearance as best he could there were other, equally important decisions to be made. He couldn't go back to Starbeck now – the area would be crawling with police. Equally, he couldn't ever use the van again. He had also lost his partner, lost the sniper rifle, and blown his cover. He reckoned that if he were to abort the mission now, and if his luck held, he could probably still escape with Tamaz via Liverpool. It was the logical move, and no-one could fault him for not having tried hard enough. And yet . . . the very fact that the police had flushed him into the open and caused him to sacrifice Jemail could possibly be turned to advantage. The fact that all logic dictated cutting his losses now more than likely meant that the police too would predict such a course of action. Of course, they would still guard against attack, but they would surely expect him to be on the defensive after the setbacks he had suffered. Whereas in fact the mission could still be attempted without Jemail's assistance. It was riskier, and the odds had shortened, but he could still take them by surprise if he were to go on the offensive just when they most expected him to be on the retreat.

First though, he needed to learn more of what his

opponents knew about him. *What can you do when your enemy has you on the defensive?* he remembered his trainers asking him. *Defend bravely – or be audacious and take them by surprise.* An idea struck him and he considered it a moment, then nodded in satisfaction. Very well then, he would be audacious. No-one would expect what he was going to do next. Allowing himself a wry smile, he pushed the empty hold-all down onto the floor and took up the Gladstone bag. Then he opened the cubicle door, left the toilets and stepped out briskly into the busy shopping centre.

15

The Spanish sun bathed the landscaped gardens with golden morning sunlight, but Omar Rahmani barely registered it. He sat in the study of his villa, a state of the art communications console before him as he pondered his options. As part of the routine reporting from his source in Israeli intelligence, word had reached him that MI5 had been given detailed files and photographic records on Jemail Zubi and Abdullah Majid. It hadn't been made clear how British Intelligence had discovered the identity of the subjects, and Rahmani couldn't ask questions about it without the risk of revealing his own carefully concealed link to the two men. Unquestionably though, it put the Harrogate mission in jeopardy, and Rahmani was torn between a desire to carry on regardless and his innate sense of self-preservation which urged caution.

To have come this close – within two days of striking – yet still to have to abort the operation would be frustrating in the extreme. But to carry on, now that the authorities were on guard and knew what the assault team looked like, was a high-risk strategy. It wasn't so much the risk to Majid and Zubi that bothered him – after all they were being handsomely paid for their efforts. No, the real problem would be the danger of linkage to him should they be captured and made to talk.

In fairness, Abdullah Majid had sounded really convincing when he had proclaimed that he would take his suicide pill rather than face capture and interrogation. And knowing Majid's penchant for security, which entailed even Rahmani himself not knowing the operational details of the assault, he felt confident that he would not have revealed his identity to Jemail Zubi.

So . . . to cancel, or to let the mission go ahead – assuming that Majid still wanted to continue? It was a dilemma and, unusually, Rahmani found it hard to reach a decision. He felt that Abdullah Majid's single-mindedness was such that he might well wish to press on, notwithstanding the additional danger now that the Israelis had identified him. Either way though, he needed to be informed of developments. And if, as the man on the spot, Majid wished to carry on? Then carry on he would, Rahmani decided suddenly. A debt of honour was at stake. They must all shoulder the extra risk in order to repay so spectacularly the arrogant murderers of the West.

Rahmani lifted the phone and activated the scrambler, then dialled the number of the warehouse that Majid had rented in Harrogate. Now that he had made his decision he was anxious to contact Majid, but the phone rang unanswered, then after the eighth ring it clicked onto an answering machine. Rahmani swore under his breath, then hung up. Majid had declined to provide mobile numbers for either himself or Jemail Zubi, and the notion of Rahmani offering his own number as a contact point had never even arisen. This was the only way he could reach Majid and he would simply have to try again later. He sat immobile, his gaze taking in the manicured grounds of the villa, but his mind was firmly on Harrogate and the actions of Abdullah Majid.

Laura's taxi finally cleared the checkpoint. It was the third one she had encountered on the short journey from police headquarters to her hotel. She realised that the authorities were sparing no effort and she expected that by now every route into and out of Harrogate would be sealed off. In addition, there were plenty of uniformed constables on foot patrol, and it was obvious that Penny's alert had triggered a prompt and massive response.

Without doubt the police had moved quickly, but Laura was by no means convinced that the dragnet would yield them Abdullah Majid. The man was both lethal and quick-thinking, and Laura suspected that those police officers whom she had heard confidently predicting his early capture were underestimating their foe.

She realised that the kind of terrorist who would shoot his own partner in cold blood – presumably to prevent their plans being revealed – would stop at nothing to achieve his ends. And despite his current predicament she knew that he was capable of adapting to difficult situations speedily and with decisiveness.

384

Bearing in mind that he could have witnessed Jemail Zubi's arrest no more than ten minutes before the killing, he had acted with impressive speed to anticipate where the prisoner would be taken, to ensure that he got there before the authorities, and to set up his ambush. The combination of ruthlessness and immediate action was chilling, and Laura wasn't sure that roadblocks and cordons would be enough to catch such an opponent.

On a personal level she was still disturbed by the killing she had seen. However much a terrorist Jemail Zubi may have been, he was still a human being, and she felt that he didn't deserve to have his head suddenly blown asunder. Witnessing it at such close quarters had left her shaky, but the sweet tea and the support from Penny and Thompson had helped her to feel a little less unsettled. She was wearing a borrowed police anorak to cover her bloodstained blouse, and she decided that she would allow herself a quick shower back in the Old Swan before committing her thoughts to paper while the immediacy of events still informed her writing. She knew that she couldn't send any of it to Mac until she got the official clearance, but she wanted to keep her writing abreast of developments. Then having changed and written up her notes, she would waste no time in returning to police headquarters to watch how matters unfolded.

She glanced out the window of the taxi and saw that they were turning onto Swan Road, then she sat forward in her seat, gathered her folder, and made sure the anorak covered her bloodstained blouse.

"If we don't pick up Majid in the next half-hour, we can

take it he's slipped the net," said Mathieson, and nobody in the command room disagreed with him. Thirty minutes had passed since the lethal shots had been fired outside on North Park Road, but despite a frantic flurry of activity no sightings had yet been made. The remains of Jemail Zubi had been placed temporarily in a holding cell and the coroner's office notified. In spite of a thorough search of the victim's bloodstained clothing nothing that would provide any kind of lead had been found. Penny had hoped against hope that they might have uncovered an address via a letter or a credit-card receipt, but all that the dead man had carried on his person had been forty pounds in cash and his French driver's licence.

"I think there's a pretty good chance, Colin, that we've bottled up Majid in Harrogate," she said now, "but even if he moved before the first roadblocks were in place, he's going to find it hard to stay mobile."

"But not impossible," said Carrow. "Obviously he'll have dumped the blue Volkswagen by now, but he could have another vehicle in reserve."

"Possibly," agreed Thompson. "But if he tries to move anywhere within a twenty-mile radius of Harrogate we've a pretty good chance of picking him up. Meanwhile let's not despair too soon – we could get a call at any second saying he's spotted."

"Quite," answered Mathieson. "While we're waiting though, we need to consider the line we take on what's already happened."

Thompson looked at the intelligence officer quizzically. "How do you mean?"

"I don't think it would be advisable to go public with the shooting here," replied Mathieson.

"Do you mean with the details of it, or the fact of it occurring?" asked Penny

"Better, I think, to reveal nothing about it for now."

"Can we do that?" queried Penny.

"We can do anything we like," snapped Carrow.

"I wouldn't quite phrase it like that," said Mathieson, "but national security is an issue here – gives us considerable latitude."

"I think we'd be taking more than 'considerable latitude' if we try to deny outright that we have a fatal shooting on our hands," said Thompson.

"Indeed," replied Mathieson. "I was thinking less in terms of a denial, more in terms of a news embargo on what happened till the conference is over."

"Even though shots were fired on the public road?" asked Penny.

"Not that many," retorted Mathieson. "All of Majid's were silenced, ours amounted to only about half a dozen. We can come up with some fudge to buy time for a couple of days."

Thompson looked thoughtful. "I don't know, Colin . . ."

"What's to be gained by going public?" asked the intelligence officer. "The only ones who know for sure what happened are ourselves and Abdullah Majid. Why tell everyone else? Why allow a terrorist to put the holding of the conference at risk – which is what may happen if word gets out – why allow him to succeed in that, just when we've finally got the upper hand against him?"

"I take your point," admitted Thompson. "Impossible

though to keep all that's happened completely under wraps."

"I agree," said Mathieson. "I'll have to apprise the senior security person here of each of the participating countries and –"

"What?" interjected Carrow. "You might as well place an ad in the bloody papers if you do that."

"I didn't say I'd tell them everything. But I'll have to tell them that security will be tightened even further, and they'll want to know why. The good thing is that their vested interests and ours overlap."

"How's that?" asked Penny.

"If a country's delegates withdraw, that may well be deemed a failure by their own national security people. Not entirely logical, but professional pride is at issue. If the whole conference had to be called off, then the professional pride of every security service involved takes a dent. So my guess is that they'll go along with what we want without rocking the boat too much."

"Fair enough," said Thompson. "What about the press though?"

"To hell with the press!" said Carrow. "We've enough on our plate without worrying about them!"

"Nevertheless –"

"Nevertheless nothing!" said Carrow. "Our job isn't to keep them happy!"

Before Thompson could respond Carrow turned to Penny and pointed at her. "And you make certain that your little friend keeps her mouth firmly shut. We don't want to read about any of this in some rag of an Irish newspaper."

Penny made a conscious effort not to show her annoyance. "She's given her word, Mr Carrow," she answered quietly. "It won't be broken." And if that phraseology caused Carrow to remember that *he* had wanted the police to go back on their word to Laura, then so much the better, Penny thought.

Carrow showed no signs of discomfort however and instead looked quizzically at Penny. "Where is she now?" he asked.

"Gone back to her hotel, sir."

"Bloody typical."

"Mr Carrow, she did have Jemail Zubi's brains splattered over her," said Penny, this time not bothering to hide the annoyance in her voice. "Her blouse was soaked in blood – she needed to change."

Carrow looked slightly taken aback. "Right," he said, then he gave a quick nod as though suggesting it was time to move on to more important matters, and Penny felt a tiny stab of satisfaction at having faced him down by defending her new-found friend.

"It's still going to be tricky to handle, if the press get wind of the shooting here today," said Thompson.

"Can I suggest that you talk to the police Press Officer and explain the delicacy of the situation?" said Mathieson. "Let him earn his money by coming up with something that buys us time for a couple of days."

"OK," said Thompson, "and talking of the media, I had a thought . . ."

Mathieson looked at the policeman with interest. "Oh yes?"

"If it's a thing we don't get Majid at any of the

roadblocks, how would you feel about putting his picture out on television? Anyone who sees him to please contact the police immediately?"

"Eh . . . I don't think so . . ." said Mathieson.

Penny thought it sounded like a good idea and she decided to back her old boss. "We wouldn't necessarily have to say what it was in connection with," she argued. "We could say there had been – I don't know, some kind of incident, we could make something up – once it gave us a chance to get his face into every home in Britain. It would make it that much harder for him to evade us."

"It's a reasonable suggestion," said Mathieson, "and if this were purely a criminal matter I'd say yes, go ahead. But it's not purely criminal, it's security related, and in the context of a conference like this that makes it highly political. We can't have TV editors probing and asking questions – and they would, it's their job. My superiors are determined that this conference should go ahead. So I'm sorry, our priority is to prevent panic and ensure that the conference proceeds safely." He looked at the others. "OK?"

Thompson nodded resignedly "OK . . ."

"Len?"

"Absolutely. Keep the press vultures in the dark – handle this ourselves."

Mathieson looked at Penny, and she appreciated the courtesy involved, knowing that as her superior he didn't need her assent. "Penny?"

She nodded also. "Yes, I see your point, Colin."

"We have to find this guy ourselves," said Mathieson. "Apart from anything else, he shot to kill at our officers,

390

right here on our own turf. To my mind that makes it a matter of honour. Now we've flushed him from cover, we've a day and a half before the conference starts, and we've all the resources we need. So let's get this bastard. No half-measures, no near misses, let's just get him . . ."

Majid sat comfortably in the hotel lobby, a newspaper shielding his face from view as he surreptitiously kept watch. He knew his enemies would expect him to be running scared, and despite the risks involved he derived a thrill from the thought of striking now, just when they expected it least.

He had seen Jemail collapsing onto the pretty young policewoman, covering her in blood, and thinking about it in the toilet of the shopping centre, he had seen his opportunity. It struck him that if she had to be put up in a hotel, then obviously she had been drafted in from outside of Harrogate. Which meant that she wouldn't have a locker in the local police station and would be very likely to return to the Old Swan to change her bloodied clothes. There was a good chance too that if she came back to change she would do so alone – which would give Majid a perfect opportunity to question someone who had been at the heart of the police operation.

In order to continue with his mission Majid knew that it was important to discover how much the enemy knew about him. He also wanted to know how they had obtained the photo ID of Jemail, and, more importantly, if they had similar ID relating to him. He would find out what the woman's own role was and he would also question her about any additional but unseen security measures they might have put in place. He didn't like the idea of having to do battle with a woman, but if his adversaries chose to use female officers in the frontline then the dishonour wasn't of his making. He would do what had to be done to get the necessary information – he had a sharp knife in his pocket, and she wouldn't be long about talking when he went to work with it – and then he would have to kill her so that she couldn't reveal to the authorities how much she had disclosed to him."

First though he needed to get her alone in her room. He glanced at his watch. Ten fifty. Thirty-five minutes since the shooting outside the police station. Allow her time for being in shock immediately after the attack, for washing the blood off her hands, then driving back to the hotel. If she was coming, she ought to arrive shortly.

He turned a page of the newspaper for appearances' sake, and considered how long he ought to stay in the Old Swan were she not to arrive soon. He could probably stay another half-hour reading the paper without it seeming odd, he reckoned. After that, if she still hadn't arrived he might attract attention were he to linger further in the lobby. Just as he decided on what might be a reasonable time-limit he saw from the corner of his eye a taxi pulling up outside. The pretty young policewoman stepped out of it and paid the driver. She wore an ill-fitting anorak – presumably to cover the bloodstained top – and Majid felt his heart suddenly beginning to pound.

He held the newspaper even closer to his face to shield himself as he heard the hotel's swing-doors opening, then he listened intently as the woman approached reception.

"Good afternoon, madam," said the counter clerk, and Majid strained to hear the policewoman giving her room number. To his disappointment she was soft-spoken, and he couldn't quite catch the number for which she had asked.

Majid risked lowering the top of the newspaper slightly and he saw that the woman had her back to him. The counter clerk reached towards a row of keys, but Majid couldn't see the number of the key that he withdrew.

"Here we are," said the clerk in a deep Yorkshire accent, "238."

Majid's spirits soared and he saw the woman nodding her thanks and taking the key. He lifted the newspaper slightly so that its top again blocked his face completely, then he waited until she had crossed the lobby before glancing over to see if she was taking the stairs or the lift. The lift was already on the ground floor, and he saw her pressing the button, then stepping inside. Without appearing to hurry, he folded his newspaper once the lift door had closed, picked up his bag, rose and crossed to the stairs. He began to ascend, then once out of sight of reception he accelerated, taking the steps two at a time. Although he now knew his quarry's room number he didn't want to fall too far behind. He reasoned that once she removed the bloodsoaked blouse she would probably want to have a bath or shower. In which case she wouldn't readily answer a knock on the door. So he needed to arrive at her room pretty soon after she entered it.

He stopped on the approach to the landing below the second floor and listened for the lift arriving. Sure enough he heard the sound of the door opening, then caught a glimpse of the woman's legs as she passed by on the second floor. Majid waited a second or two, then climbed the stairs and followed in the direction in which she had gone. There were no other guests about, and so he peered carefully through the window of the fire door without showing himself, just in case the policewoman should glance backwards for any reason. He saw her reaching the end of a corridor and turning left, then he swiftly strode along the corridor she had just vacated. He slowed again on reaching the end of the corridor and heard a door closing, but in case it was another guest leaving a room he approached the corner cautiously and peered around it. To his relief, the corridor was clear and he realised that it was another fire door that he had heard closing. He rounded the corner, passed rooms 236 and 237, then came to a halt at 238. He opened his Gladstone bag, took out the silenced Beretta and tapped on the door.

The command room bustled with phones ringing and officers coming and going, but Penny Harte was lost in her own thoughts. In the eleven years that she had been a police officer she reckoned that Abdullah Majid was the most dangerous and probably the most resourceful opponent that she had encountered. At every turn so far he seemed to have covered his tracks. Thompson's enquiries to the Irish police had revealed no record of the Iraqi either entering or leaving Ireland and, apart from the Israelis, none of the other security services that Mathieson had approached had anything on record regarding an Abdullah Majid. Clearly this was a man well used to evading his pursuers. And yet such was the level of police activity now in Harrogate that it was hard to see how any fugitive could move about with ease, much less launch an attack when the conference opened on Monday. Despite which, Penny had an uneasy feeling that Majid was far from a spent force. Her reflections were cut short by a sudden animation in Thompson's voice as he took a call at the adjacent desk.

"Really?" said Thompson.

Penny saw Carrow stopping in his tracks as he too picked up on Thompson's tone.

"Brilliant!" cried Thompson, quickly scribbling onto a notepad. "Right. Thank you."

He hung up, and Penny immediately faced him.

"Chief?"

"Your computer-trawl finally paid off."

"Yeah?" Penny had been embarrassed that the massive task of checking hotel registrations, airline tickets, and car hire and sales had yielded nothing – just as Carrow had predicted – but now it appeared to have turned up something after all.

"What have we got?" asked Mathieson, who had picked up on the buzz of excitement at Thompson's desk and approached.

"The computer check showed a back-street dealer in Manchester sold a Volkswagen van last March. A constable down there showed him one of the Israeli photos this morning. Positive ID of Majid, no question."

"Buyer's address?" asked Penny.

"That's the good part," said Thompson, indicating the writing on the notepad. "It's right here in Harrogate."

"Excellent!" said Mathieson. "Fair chance he'll make for there to lie low." He quickly looked at the others. "Everybody armed?"

"Too bloody right," answered Carrow, and Penny and Thompson nodded also.

"OK," said Mathieson, "let's go then!"

Laura stopped in the act of unbuttoning her blouse. She had taken off the borrowed anorak and was divesting herself of the bloodied blouse when she heard the knocking on her bedroom door. She had ordered nothing from room service and she reckoned that any messages the hotel had for her would surely have been delivered when she picked up her key at reception. Probably something to do with housekeeping, she thought, although the room had already been cleaned and the bed made up. She crossed to the bed where she had thrown the light anorak, and slipped the garment on again to cover the blouse. Just as she did so the knocking was repeated. "Coming," she cried, then went to the door and undid the lock.

She opened the door, then froze in shock on seeing a man pointing a gun at her face.

"Don't scream!" he ordered even as he burst into the room and kicked the door shut after him.

Despite his instruction Laura felt her stomach

muscles contracting with terror and she couldn't overcome her instinct to cry out in fear. The sound never got past her throat. Moving with frightening speed, the man clasped his left hand over her mouth, swung her round, and pulled her body roughly backwards against his own. Laura felt the muzzle of the silenced gun pressing into her temple and tried desperately to keep her sense of panic from tipping her over into hysteria. Even in the brief moment of seeing her assailant's face she realised it was the man who had shot at them back at the police station, Abdullah Majid, and despite her terror she knew instinctively that if she wanted to come out of this alive she had to try to calm herself and appear co-operative.

"Don't make any sound, you hear?! No sound at all!"

Laura tried to nod in agreement, but the man was holding her so tightly that she couldn't nod properly, and so she stopped for fear that he would think she was struggling against him.

"Give me any trouble and I use the gun," he said. "It's silenced, and no-one will hear. Nod if you understand!"

Laura felt a loosening of the pressure that was forcing her head backward, although her mouth was still firmly clamped shut. Immediately she nodded, wanting to appease her captor as much as possible. Her mind was racing wildly as she tried to imagine how he had tracked her down, and why he should have chosen to come seeking her out when every police officer in Harrogate was actively looking for him.

"If you co-operate fully, I let you live," he said. "The slightest false move – the *slightest* – and your brains are all over the wall. Nod if you understand."

Again Laura felt an easing in the pressure and she nodded eagerly.

"OK, I'm going to take my hand off your mouth. Any sound and you know what happens."

The man was so close that she could smell his expensive aftershave, and somehow the intimacy made the situation even more terrifying, but she forced herself not to give in to her fear and nodded once again. Gradually she felt the pressure easing, then his hand was off her mouth and she was free again. He quickly frisked her, but she forced herself not to voice any objection.

"OK, sit on the bed. Now!"

Laura moved quickly to obey. She watched in confusion as Majid took a chair, then placed it opposite her and sat, the gun held loosely as he looked at her speculatively. His dark eyes seemed to bore into her and she looked away, frightened by his intensity and by the unexpectedness of his sitting unspeakingly before her.

"Look at me!" he said, and Laura forced herself to meet his gaze. "I'm going to ask you some questions. You'd better answer them immediately and truthfully. If you lie or if you hesitate I'll knee-cap you first, and then I'll kill you. Understood?"

Laura swallowed hard and nodded, too frightened to be able to speak clearly, yet also aware that were she to do so she could make her situation even worse. For if she spoke Majid might recognise her voice as that of the woman who had rung him on the mobile the day after the murders on the Cooley Peninsula. It had been a short call on a mobile phone, and it had occurred a week previously, but supposing he still recognised her? Supposing he made the connection and realised that all of his problems had been set in train by her snooping? If he was willing to knee-cap and kill her for not answering questions properly – and Laura had no doubt that he would, having already killed his own partner – then what might he do if he discovered that she was the catalyst for so many of his difficulties? *She had to change her voice.* And yet it was all that Laura could do not to break down, such was her fear of this man. How could she possibly tailor her answers to disguise her actions to date while simultaneously disguising her voice? *Because she simply had to.* Otherwise she was going to wind up dead. She thought of her mother's cousins in West Cork, whose lilting accents she had endlessly mimicked as a child. She would try for that accent, she decided, reckoning that it was the best she could come up with in the circumstances.

"What is your rank?" asked Majid.

"What?"

"What is your rank?!"

"I don't have a rank, I –" Laura was stopped short as Majid sprang from the chair and slapped her hard in the face. She fell backwards onto the bed, her face stinging as she reeled from the shock of being struck. Breathing heavily, she gathered herself and sat up again, by which time Majid was once more sitting impassively in the chair, watching her.

"If you were a man I'd have knee-capped you already," he said softly. "Next time I will."

"Look, I'm . . . I'm not trying to cross you," she said, seeking to find the right words while working on the Cork accent, "but when you say rank . . ."

"What sort of a policewoman are you?"

"I'm not a policewoman." Laura saw the flash of anger on the man's face and she instantly went on, eager to forestall another assault. "I'm a journalist! I'm not a policewoman, I'm a journalist!"

Majid looked hard at her, but at least he appeared to be considering her answer.

"Why are you with the police then?"

Laura knew that one wrong move here would undo her and she decided to try and slow all her answers a little in order to formulate the right kind of replies. *Always keep your lies as near as possible to the truth*, she remembered reading in some spy novel. "I'm covering the story of the conference," she answered. "I'm travelling around with the police for a sort of fly-on-the-wall approach."

"Why would they allow that when they have far more important things to do?"

"Because there's interest in women in the police force. This way the authorities can show change has taken place . . ." Laura knew that this man had already exchanged shots with Penny so he would know for sure that at least one female officer was deeply involved in the security operation. "That's the angle I'm writing from, to show how the role of women officers has changed."

"So you're a journalist, not a police officer?" Before

Laura could answer Majid raised a finger in warning. "Answer carefully, a shattered knee-cap is very painful . . ."

"I swear to you, I'm not a police officer, I'm a freelance journalist."

"Show me your journalist's card."

Laura thought for a second, then felt a sickening lurch in her stomach as she realised that she had left it in the glove-compartment of her rented car. "I – I don't have it here. It's in my car."

Majid shook his head. "Real journalists carry their cards on them."

"Normally they do, but this was different! I've been working with these officers for a couple of days so I haven't needed the card."

"You've been working with them all right. You *are* one of them." Majid swivelled the gun and pointed it at Laura's left knee.

"No! Please! It's not true!"

"Stupid woman," said Majid derisively, "trying to be brave like a man. You should have taken me seriously. You should have co-operated. Now you have to pay." He extended his left hand to steady his gun-hand, then took careful aim with the Beretta.

Armed police officers had discreetly cordoned off both ends of the street, and although Penny couldn't see all of the officers she knew that they were present in numbers. Driving at speed, it had taken only five minutes to get from police headquarters to Oakdale Drive, the address Majid had given when purchasing the van from the dealer. The houses in this part of Harrogate were modest, with small front gardens and without garages at the side in which a vehicle could be kept. Penny hadn't really expected to see the blue van parked on the street – not with a shattered side window and bullet-holes in the bodywork – but she had been confident that the blue van used by the assassin at the police station was the same one as the white vehicle stopped at the roadblock the previous Tuesday night. Which meant that if Majid had abandoned the van and proceeded on foot there surely seemed a good chance that he would make for his base.

Thompson and Mathieson had shared Penny's view, and she had been delighted that events proved Carrow's deriding of her computer searches to have been misplaced. All of which now made her disappointment all the more palpable. For yet again their target had outsmarted them. He had given as his address 21A Oakdale Drive, a plausible-sounding address on an actual road. Except that there was no 21A. There was a 21, and a 23 on one side of the road, and a 20 and 22 on the opposite side. 21A however simply didn't exist – they had already checked for rear entrances or annexes.

"Fucking wild-goose chase," said Carrow as he walked disgustedly past Penny, and this time even Thompson and Mathieson didn't argue with his sentiments.

Penny felt a surge of irritation, knowing that Carrow would have been damn glad to arrest Majid if her computer searches had uncovered a real address. It wasn't her fault, she thought, if their opponent was a thorough professional who went to elaborate lengths to cover his trail. She made no response however, knowing that any such explanation would only make her sound defensive.

"Tough cheese, Penny," said Thompson, as though reading her mind. "No blame to you though – the computer scans were well worth trying . . ."

"Thanks, Chief," said Penny, trying not to show just how disappointed she was.

"If nothing else they've shown us one thing," said Mathieson. "This operation has been actively worked on since last March."

"Yes," agreed Penny, though secretly she felt that gaining such knowledge was scant consolation.

"Should keep the computer searches going," said Mathieson. "Always the possibility that somewhere along the line he may have slipped up."

"Agreed," said Thompson. "Right then, I'm going to stand everyone down. No point hanging about here."

Mathieson nodded. "Quite. Let's get back to the station then – and hope for something else."

"Right," said Penny, then she turned on her heel and set off for the car.

Majid saw the woman's eyes widening in fear as he aimed the gun at her knee.

"No!" she cried. "I can prove it! Please – I can prove I'm a journalist!"

"So prove it," he said, still keeping the gun trained on her. He saw her looking desperately around the room, then she pointed excitedly at a folder that had been left on the top of the chest of drawers.

"That's my file. My notes are all in it," she said.

"Get it." Majid swivelled the Beretta to cover her as she rose from the bed. As she leaned forward to gain a purchase from the yielding mattress her anorak top yawned open, and he caught a glimpse of her cleavage. Despite the seriousness of the situation he couldn't help but notice how attractive she was. *Forget that she's a woman, she's the enemy,* he told himself. He knew that he mustn't think of her in any way that would influence what had to be done for the good of the mission.

"Place the folder near me on the floor, then get back to the bed," he said, deliberately making his voice harsh. He kept the gun trained on her as she approached with the folder. "That'll do," he said, before she was in range for a possible lunge at him. She did as ordered, and he waited until she was safely seated back on the side of the bed before he picked up the folder and opened it.

The folder contained written notes in a small rounded hand and Majid quickly scanned the contents. He noted a reference to Chief Superintendent Thompson, who was described as Gold Commander, and he saw a line linking him to Detective Inspector Penny Harte. There were names, addresses, telephone numbers and what looked like a sketched command structure. Interesting stuff, he thought, then he quickly flicked through the other pages of the folder before looking back to the woman on the bed. "These are notes on the police force in Harrogate," he said. "But journalists write articles. These aren't articles."

"They're my notes to write the articles from. I had to record all of that as background."

"A policewoman from another jurisdiction would write that down too."

"No!"

"Yes. It's exactly what she'd do."

"I swear to you I'm a journalist."

"Then where are your articles?"

"They're on my laptop."

"Where's your laptop?"

The woman hesitated and Majid could see the fear welling up again in her eyes.

"The laptop is in the car as well."

He stared hard at her, and she looked at him appealingly. "I swear to you on my oath – I'm not a policewoman!"

The woman sounded convincing, and Majid half-believed her, but he knew that he mustn't let her see that. In a situation like this it was always good technique to make captives think that you didn't believe them – that way they were more likely to divulge extra information. Without saying a word Majid slowly swivelled the gun and once again aimed it at the woman's knee.

"Please! Ring *The Sunday Clarion*! Laura Kennedy is my name. They'll confirm they've a Laura Kennedy on assignment here!"

"There could be a Laura Kennedy who writes for that paper. It doesn't mean that *you're* Laura Kennedy."

"You could describe me to them!"

"I don't think so . . ."

"All right, I know. Take my mobile . . . take my mobile please and ring my mother."

"Ring your mother?"

"You can say you're from the *Clarion* and you want to contact Laura urgently. If I wasn't a journalist she wouldn't know what you were talking about. But she will know because I am a journalist – and this will prove it."

Majid considered the suggestion. Perhaps the woman was telling the truth. In which case he had missed out on the chance of interrogating a police officer. But even if she were a journalist she certainly seemed to be well-connected, and he could probably still extract quite a bit of useful information from her. He kept his face a mask, wanting to keep the woman off balance as much as possible, then he looked her in the eye. "How do I know the person you'd ring is actually your mother?"

"It's programmed into my mobile. I can show you, it's just a question of scanning down till we see the entry that says *Mam*."

"And if your mother is not there?"

"She will be."

"How can you be sure?"

"She was playing cards last night. She always has a sleep-on after that."

Majid said nothing for a moment, keeping his opponent on edge, then he nodded. "Very well, you may ring."

"Thank you."

"But let me warn you. If you're lying, or if you try to trick me in any way, then I make a promise to you. Ask me what the promise is."

"What's – what's the promise?"

"I promise that if you cross me in the slightest you will not only die – you will die in great pain.

Understood?" Majid saw the woman swallowing hard, then nodding. "I said 'Understood?'" he persisted, satisfied that his threat had frightened her even further, but wanting to maximise the degree to which he had the upper hand.

"Understood," she answered quietly.

"Good," said Majid. He pointed the Beretta at her, then indicated the mobile phone. "Make the call. And remember, I'll be watching every move . . ."

Penny stared dejectedly out the car window as she travelled with Thompson back to police headquarters. Her disappointment at being tricked by the non-existent address was made worse by the fact that none of the cordons around Harrogate had yielded their man. They had been in contact with the command room, but there were still no sightings of Abdullah Majid, and Penny couldn't help but feel that with over three-quarters of an hour having passed since the shooting, their man had somehow slipped the net.

"Chin up, Penny," said Thompson. "Discovering the van purchase was good police work – not your fault that he covered his tracks so carefully."

"Thanks, Chief. It's just really frustrating the way each time we seem to get close to this guy he melts away."

"Tricky bugger and no mistake. But he's been lucky too, and no-one can stay lucky indefinitely."

"Let's hope not," said Penny.

As they spoke the traffic ahead of them slowed to a crawl, and Penny realised that the cars in front were being scrutinised at yet another checkpoint. Despite his senior rank Thompson sometimes liked to do his own driving, and he slowed now and smoothly applied the handbrake as he waited for the queue ahead of them to clear. He glanced over at the turning to his right where a side road joined the Ripon Road on which they were travelling, then he looked back at Penny. "Swan Road. Want to call down the Old Swan and offer your chum a lift back to the station?"

Penny considered the suggestion. It might be nice to make the gesture to Laura, she thought. She sensed that the journalist feared being sidelined now that the police had so much on their plate – even though she had been promised continuing access. Calling for her would certainly allay that fear, especially with the suggestion coming from someone with Thompson's clout. On the other hand Laura had had a nasty shock, and Penny wondered if it mightn't be better in the circumstances to give her a chance to gather herself together before coming back to police headquarters.

"I'm not sure, Chief," she answered. "Nice gesture, certainly. It just struck me that . . . maybe she needs time to recover a bit . . . I don't know." She looked at her boss. "What do you think?"

Thompson shrugged. "Not sure either, it was just a thought. You know her better than I do. I'll let you call it."

Penny bit her lip and pondered. It would only take them a minute to drive down to the Old Swan, and maybe Laura wouldn't want any more time on her own and would be delighted to see them.

"Need to decide, Penny – traffic's starting to move."

Penny hesitated briefly, then reached her decision.

"We'll leave it, Chief. Let her have some space after all that's happened. I'll call her later."

"Fine," said Thompson, then he let off the handbrake and they drove on down the road.

Laura felt her hands shaking as she pressed the keypads on her mobile. She watched the screen, calling up the names that were programmed. She tried to steady her nerves, aware that her fear had already caused her to let her accent slip a bit. Fortunately Majid didn't appear to have picked up on it, and she reasoned that for the most part she must have retained the lilting, West Cork tones, but she knew she would have to be very careful with an opponent like this.

She found her mother's entry on the screen, then pressed the symbol and held her breath. *Please be home,* she thought, *don't have changed your routine this week.* She heard the phone beginning to ring and she prayed that her mother would be there. The phone continued to ring and Laura found herself trembling as she silently urged her mother to pick up the receiver. *Come on, Mam! Answer the damn phone!* She swallowed hard as the phone rang out, then just as she was beginning to lose hope the receiver was lifted and she heard her mother saying hello. Immediately she held the phone out to Majid, and he took it and raised it to his face, all the time keeping the gun trained on her.

"Hello, I'm looking for Laura Kennedy, please."

Laura strained to listen and she could make out her mother's voice on the other end of the line.

"Laura's not here – who's calling please?"

"Bruno Mendez – I'm with the international desk at the *Clarion*," answered Majid smoothly.

"Oh, right . . ."

Laura noted how relaxed he was able to make his voice sound on the phone even as he kept the silenced pistol trained upon her. She was up against a real professional here, yet she knew that she was going to have to match him in sharpness if she was going to come out of this unscathed.

"I can't seem to get Laura on her mobile," Majid continued, "and I wondered if you'd have the name or the phone number of her hotel?"

"Eh, she told me the name of the hotel . . . but . . . I'm sorry . . . I can't recall it just now . . ."

"Right, well, would you have the phone number then? I'm quite anxious to contact her."

"Eh, could you hold on a second, Mr Mendez, and I'll have a look?"

"Certainly, and thank you for your help."

"You're more than welcome. One minute."

"Sure."

Laura reasoned that surely Majid should be satisfied, having rung her mother ostensibly from the *Clarion*, only to have it confirmed that Laura was in fact working on assignment for the paper. The look on his face gave nothing away however and after a moment Laura heard her mother speaking once again.

"Hello, Mr Mendez?"

"Yes?"

"I have it now. It's the Swan Hotel. The phone number is 0044 1423 500055. Room 238."

Thank God, thought Laura, then watched in fascination as Majid switched on his practised charm.

"Thank you very much for your help – I really am most grateful."

"Not at all!"

"Bye now."

"Bye."

Majid looked Laura in the eye, the mask of conviviality gone the moment he had stopped speaking on the phone. Instead he simply stared at her, and the intensity of his gaze made Laura want to drop her eyes. She didn't, however, sensing instinctively that she mustn't let him have the upper hand any more than could be avoided. "I told you I was a journalist," she said.

Majid afforded her no recognition of the fact that she had been telling the truth. Instead he put the mobile phone down and looked at her accusingly. "How did the authorities get my ID? Don't hesitate – answer immediately."

"From the Israelis," replied Laura.

"How?"

Laura knew that she had to avoid the truth about the voice recognition from her tape, but she also knew that she risked angering Majid and making him more suspicious if she slowed down her responses in order to give herself time to think. And yet she had to try and gain some breathing space between the questions and her answers. "Identikit pictures," she replied. "They made a match."

"Just my partner, or both of us?"

"Both of you."

"Since when? *Since when*?!" repeated Majid angrily when Laura didn't answer quickly enough.

"Just since this morning."

"Who is in charge of the investigation here?"

"Mr Thompson's in charge of the police, Mr Mathieson's in charge of the security services." Laura hated revealing information that had been given to her in confidence, but she knew that she had no choice. She knew too that in the present circumstances knowledge was power and that she had quite a bit of knowledge available to trade. But when she tried to formulate the best approach towards eking it out yet satisfying her captor's demands, she realised that there was one huge problem confronting her. Whatever information she gave to Majid he would be aware that immediately he released her the authorities would know that he now had that information. Unless . . . *unless he silenced her.* He had already killed his own partner, he planned to kill every Foreign Minister in the EU – why spare her? He had said he would release her unharmed if she co-operated fully, but on reflection why should he? Because she was a journalist? Hardly. Someone prepared to wipe out a group of Foreign Ministers was unlikely to be concerned with respecting the neutral status of the press. Because she was a woman? Again it seemed unlikely. Although there was the fact that he had said earlier that if she had been a man he would already have knee-capped her. So perhaps he did operate a different set of values when it came to dealing with women. Laura had always regarded the Moslem attitude to women as ranging from patronising to downright offensive, but maybe if this man was imbued with the gender values of his culture there might be scope for using it in her favour. Earlier she had noticed him looking at her cleavage when she had risen from the bed, so he was certainly conscious of being in the presence of a woman. Laura's thoughts were interrupted by another question from Majid.

"Who gave the descriptions for the Identikit pictures?"

"A constable who stopped you at a roadblock last week."

Laura saw him nodding as though irritated at having being discovered by so mundane a means, then he turned his gaze upon her again. "What brought the authorities to Starbeck this morning?"

"They'd had no progress finding you in any hotels or guesthouses. So they assumed you might be staying in a rented house."

"What brought them to Starbeck High Street?"

"They decided to start calling door-to-door in a couple of working-class areas."

Majid looked thoughtful as he digested this and Laura's own thoughts returned to the odds on his releasing her at the end of the interrogation. It was a terrifying notion, but the more she thought about it the more likely it seemed that the man before her would kill her as soon as he had extracted all the information she had to give. She swallowed hard, trying to keep her mounting sense of panic at bay. Somehow she had to get away from him before that point was reached. Her mind flitted desperately in search of inspiration, but there seemed little she could do while he kept the gun trained on her. Very well then, she had to get out of the range of the gun. She thought again about her earlier notion that he was aware of her as a woman and that perhaps he wasn't completely at ease in the presence of a female, and an idea struck her just as he continued his questioning.

"Who has overall command: Thompson or Mathieson?"

"Please, before we continue, I need to go to the bathroom." Laura watched him carefully, and, if the request embarrassed him, he didn't let it show.

"When we finish my questions," he said.

"I need to go now."

"Who has overall command?!" he demanded again, the anger evident in his voice.

"Mathieson, I think," answered Laura, wanting to defuse his anger, but immediately she returned to the subject of the bathroom, hating herself even as she put a pleading tone into her voice. "Look, it really is urgent. Please, just for a couple of minutes. I *have* to . . ."

This time she was rewarded by a flush of embarrassment on the man's cheeks, and he nodded and indicated the door of the en suite bathroom.

"Quickly then," he said, "and don't close the door."

"Can I close it over please? I won't lock it," said Laura, trying to sound as coy as possible while simultaneously trying not to let her terror show.

"Very well. Don't be long."

"Thank you." She crossed to the bathroom, her hear

pounding madly, and closed the door over while still leaving it partly ajar. Moving quickly, she ran the cold tap to cover the sound of what she really wanted to do, then she made for the end of the bathroom where a frosted window provided light and ventilation. She knew from the night when she had looked out across the moonlit roofs from her bedroom that this bathroom window would also give access to the sloping rooftops below her floor. She tried the window-frame, hoping to ease it up quietly. The frame didn't move at all, and Laura had to make a huge effort to still her sense of panic. She realised that it would require a hard pull to free it, and with Majid sitting in the adjacent bedroom he would be likely to hear it. She looked about frantically, then saw a footstool beside the bath and moved quickly to retrieve it. She lifted it soundlessly off the floor, then grabbed a large bath towel off the towel rack. She reckoned that if she wrapped the heavy bath towel around herself and shattered the glass in the window with the stool she could probably throw herself through the shattered window-frame without cutting herself too badly. After that she could slide down the sloping rooftops into the labyrinth of kitchen entrances and service areas that made up the inner courtyard of the hotel. The vital question however was whether she could slide down the rooftops before Majid burst into the bathroom and fired after her through the broken window. She knew that time was slipping away and that Majid might become suspicious and approach the bathroom door at any moment, but nevertheless she paused and evaluated the one action she could think of that might buy her precious seconds. It meant overcoming her instinctive desire not to go back in the direction of her captor, but she reasoned that if she could silently swing the bathroom door completely shut and engage the lock, then the critical moments it would buy her might be the difference between escaping and being shot while out on the rooftops. She paused a moment, terrified by what she needed to do. *Come on,* she told herself, *he's never going to let you go. It's stay here and be killed, or make a break for it and take your chances.* She knew what she had to do, but she hesitated a moment longer. Then she overcame her fear and wrapped the towel around herself. She moved to the door, silently closed it and reached for the lock.

Majid was going through the journalist's notepad when he heard the click from the bathroom door. He had been satisfied that they were two storeys up and that the woman was completely cowed by him, and so had envisaged no problems in acceding to her embarrassing request to use the toilet. Now however alarm bells went off in his head. He had specifically told her not to close the door, much less to lock it. He flung the notepad onto the ground and sprang to his feet. The Beretta had never left his hand and he held it in front of him now as he rushed towards the bathroom door. Just as he reached the door he was startled by the sound of a window being shattered and he realised that his prisoner must be escaping through the bathroom window. *Lying bitch!* he thought, then he yanked at the handle of the bathroom door.

As he feared, the door was locked. He wasted no time trying to force it, but instead stepped back and aimed at the lock. He fired three silenced shots at the lock, then immediately kicked out viciously with his right foot. The door burst inwards and he ran the length of the bathroom to the shattered window. He had expected that there would be a considerable drop from the second floor to the ground and that he might see the stunned journalist gathering herself after her fall. Instead, he saw sloping rooftops running below him in all directions and the woman sliding to the base of one of them. He swung the Beretta and got a round off, but it was a difficult shot at a moving target and he couldn't tell if he had hit her or not. The woman thudded to a halt at the base of one of the roofs, then disappeared to the right and out of view before he could fire another shot.

Majid used the sleeve of his jacket to sweep shards of glass from the window-frame, then hoisted himself up onto the window-ledge. Just then he saw a middle-aged woman looking out from a bedroom opposite him, a startled expression on her face. Almost at the same time the curtains of a nearer room were pulled back and Majid saw a heavy-set man looking at him, the man's eyes widening on seeing the Beretta. Majid ignored them both, but paused as he crouched on the window-frame. Clearly, the shattering of the window was drawing considerable attention, and he realised that his instinctive move to go after his quarry might not be the correct response. He was furious at the journalist for having duped him, and there was every chance that if he followed her down the sloping rooftops he could still catch her and finish her off – in case his earlier shot hadn't found its mark. But much as he wanted to punish her for tricking him it wasn't worth putting the whole mission at risk. And that was what the consequence could be if he were to become trapped in an inner courtyard. Even now the alarm was probably being raised, and with all of the police officers who were already scouring Harrogate for him it wouldn't take long for them to surround him. He cursed the woman silently, then swung back down from the window-ledge. He ran back through the bathroom, grabbed his bag from the bedroom floor and made for the hotel corridor. He sprinted along the corridor, turned right, then sprinted again until he came to the head of the stairs. He descended at speed, waited until he reached the landing above the reception area before slipping the Beretta into his pocket, then continued down the stairs at a moderate pace. To his relief there was so sign of any commotion in the lobby and nothing to indicate that the man on reception might have raised the alarm. He nodded casually to the receptionist, then crossed the lobby, stepped briskly into the swing-doors and exited from the hotel.

16

Omar Rahmani looked at his watch. Eleven thirty. It was almost an hour since he had first tried to contact Majid at the warehouse. In the meantime he had strolled though the grounds of his Spanish villa, the air sweet with the scent of bougainvillaea, and had tried to calculate the degree of risk in Majid and Jemail carrying on with the mission. Although he had decided earlier to be bold and to go ahead, provided Majid was prepared to, he realised on reflection the extent of the risk involved. No matter how much he rationalised, no matter how carefully he had structured things so that he wouldn't be linked directly to Majid, there was a chance that Majid would be captured alive and made to talk. In which case all of Rahmani's wealth and power might not be enough to protect him from the enraged security services of the nations whose Foreign Ministers he had plotted to kill. On the other hand, Rahmani still grieved for his murdered family, and a chance to repay his enemies so spectacularly was difficult to resist.

Immersed in his thoughts, he had wandered along a shady walk that followed the boundary wall of his meticulously maintained gardens, and by the time he had returned to the villa his mind was made up. He would stick to his original decision, despite the risk, and allow Majid to go ahead if he was prepared to see the mission through. Nonetheless, Majid had to be made aware that the authorities knew who he was, and so Rahmani entered his study now and lowered his ample frame into the leather seat before the communications console. He picked up the phone and activated the scrambler, then pressed the redial button. After a moment, he heard the phone ringing and he swallowed hard, mentally urging Majid to be present to answer the phone. The ringing continued, then Rahmani swore softly on hearing the answering machine clicking in. He hesitated, reluctant to commit such an important message to an answering machine, yet he didn't want to spend the whole day at the communications console fruitlessly ringing Harrogate. He thought a moment, then pressed a button that would distort his voice beyond recognition. Despite the cover provided by the electronic distortion he wanted to keep the message as cryptic as was consistent with making his meaning clear to Majid. "Warning – opponents know your ID," he said. "Proceed anyway, if you choose. Good luck either way."

He hung up, then breathed out heavily. He would have to ensure that the ship in Liverpool was alerted to receive its three secret passengers earlier than scheduled, in case Majid decided to abort the mission now. But in spite of the risks involved in continuing, Rahmani realised that he desperately wanted the mission to go ahead. Well, he would know soon enough. Meanwhile all he could do was hope. Hope and pray that after all the years of waiting, justice would finally be done . . .

Majid continually scanned the approaches to his hiding-place in Valley Gardens public park, but so far no-one had come near him. He had known it would be vital to remove himself from view as quickly as possible after leaving the Old Swan Hotel, and he had made for the nearby expanse of the park. Wanting to change appearance again, he had dumped the Gladstone bag containing the silenced Uzi and his jacket and tie in a dense thicket of bushes just inside the entrance gates; then, with his shirt sleeves rolled up, he had sought out a more distant section of the park in which to hole up. He had found a heavily wooded area from which he could observe any approaching searchers, then settled down among the trees and thought matters through. His biggest problem was that he couldn't risk walking back to Starbeck with every police officer in Harrogate seeking him. And with the alarm no doubt already raised by Laura Kennedy, the focus of the search was sure to shift towards the general area around the Old Swan. Which meant that he couldn't stay indefinitely in the park; even the more remote sections were likely to be combed as the search was extended. He thought with fury of the journalist who had escaped and forced him into this predicament. Lying bitch! She would pay dearly if their paths crossed again. He promised himself that much, then forced himself to remove her from his calculations. His priority now had to be to get back to the warehouse without being spotted. To attempt such a journey on foot and in broad daylight would be suicidal, yet if he were to phone up a taxi and travel by car they were likely to be stopped at a roadblock. He might have a reasonable chance of getting back to Starbeck on foot under cover of darkness, but that would mean remaining in the park for all of the rest of the day. Could he find a spot in which he could go to ground well enough to evade a search? Hardly, he thought, and if the police used tracker-dogs he could be flushed out ignominiously.

There was only one thing for it: he would have to call on Tamaz. He hated using him, but there was no alternative. He knew that Tamaz would panic if he were told about Jemail being dead, so he would have to keep that from him for the moment. He needed Tamaz to appear as normal as possible, and it was going to be hard enough for the waiter to stay cool while driving through checkpoints with Majid hidden in the boot of his car.

Majid scanned the sunlit expanses of the park once more from the copse of trees where he was sitting, but still there was no sign of any approaching searchers. He took the mobile from his pocket and dialled the number for Tamaz's cellphone. It rang out without being answered, and Majid silently cursed the Turk. *What the hell was the point of carrying a mobile on a mission if it wasn't switched on?* Just when he was angrily resigned to having to leave a message, Tamaz answered the phone.

"Hello?"

Majid forced himself to breathe out before speaking, knowing that anger wouldn't help right now. Instead, he kept his tone reasonable. "We need to meet."

It had been agreed that names would never be used and that telephone conversations would be kept cryptic.

"What's wrong?" asked Tamaz.

"Slight problem at my end," answered Majid easily, recognising the anxiety in the other man's voice and trying to allay it.

"What sort of problem?"

"Nothing too serious – I'll tell you when I see you. Can you pick me up in your car?"

"I'm working right now."

"It won't take long. Can you get out for thirty minutes?"

"My lunch-break is in less than an hour. Can it wait till then?"

Majid looked at his watch. It was eleven thirty-five, about twenty-five minutes since he had left the Old Swan. His instincts told him to get out of the park as soon as possible, yet it might seem a bit strange if Tamaz were to ask for half an hour off with his lunch-break coming so soon. "See if you can take an earlier lunch today," instructed Majid. "Say . . . say you've a toothache and the dentist has rung you with a cancellation."

"OK."

"Say you'd like to start your lunch at twelve – they'll hardly refuse you that."

"No, I suppose not."

"Good. Drive immediately then to Valley Gardens. Don't speed, but get here as soon as possible."

"Which part of Valley Gardens?"

"Go up Valley Drive, then ring me from there and I'll give you exact instructions."

"OK. And this problem . . .?"

"Will be sorted out. Don't worry about it – just make sure to get here as soon as you can, all right?"

"All right. Just supposing I can't get off early?"

"Be persuasive," answered Majid, "but if it's really not possible ring me back immediately."

"OK. It'll probably be all right – they're usually nice enough."

"Good. I'll see you in about half an hour then."

"All right. Bye."

"Bye." Majid hung up, then looked around him. It was a big park and Laura Kennedy had first to call the police and tell her story before search parties could be formed and areas to be combed decided upon. He should, he hoped, be safe here for another half an hour . . .

Penny watched admiringly as Laura sipped sweetened tea in the manager's office of the Old Swan. Sitting beside her on a large leather sofa, Penny could see that Laura sported scratches and bruises and was a bit shaken, but she was impressed by the other woman's resilience after an encounter that would have left many a person shattered.

On being rung by the hotel management, Thompson had ordered an immediate search of the hotel and the surrounding areas, then he had instructed Penny to ring Carrow and Mathieson, knowing that they would want to be present while Laura was debriefed. Penny had quickly filled Colin Mathieson in on what had happened, and the two men had arrived just now and were setting down chairs for themselves as Thompson spoke concernedly to Laura.

"You need to be properly examined by a doctor," he said.

"I'm just a bit shaken up. I'll be OK."

"I dare say. But you ought to let the doctor have a look at you when we're finished here, to be on the safe side."

"All right," agreed Laura.

Mathieson shook his head in disbelief. "This guy is unbelievable. Just when we think he's running scared, *he* attacks *us*!"

"Well, *Laura*, actually, Colin," Penny gently corrected.

The intelligence officer nodded apologetically. "Sorry, Laura. But the point stands. He thought Laura was a police officer and he went on the offensive. Ninety-nine point nine per cent of villains would have fled for cover after the killing at the police station. This guy comes after us!"

"He's an ice-cool bastard and no mistake," said Carrow.

"But how did he know I was staying here?" asked Laura.

"Well, he took off at speed from the station," said Penny, "so he could hardly have followed you. Unless maybe he tailed you some other time."

"It doesn't matter how he learnt where you were staying," said Carrow. "It's why he did it that matters. What exactly did he want with you?"

Laura didn't meet the Special Branch officer's gaze for a moment, then she looked at him. "He wanted information," she answered quietly.

"What sort of information?" asked Thompson.

"He wanted to know what the police knew about him. Had he been identified, like Jemail Zubi had?"

"And you told him?" asked Carrow.

"I said I was a journalist, not a police officer."

"And then what?" prompted Thompson gently.

"I didn't have my NUJ card on me – it was in the car. He – he threatened to knee-cap me," answered Laura, her voice becoming a little shaky.

"It's all right," said Mathieson reassuringly. "Take your time . . ."

Laura pulled herself together, then looked at Penny before continuing. "I'm sorry, Penny, but I had to show him my notebook – to prove I was a journalist."

Penny could see that the other woman was upset and she squeezed her arm sympathetically. "It's OK."

"Not really. My notes showed that I'd been associated with the security operation here. I'd jotted down details –"

"What did I tell you?" said Carrow. "I said we should never have allowed a journalist to be involved!"

"Not now, Len!" snapped Mathieson. He glared at the Special Branch man, and Carrow shook his head but said nothing further. Mathieson turned back to Laura. "Please, go on."

"He – he was going to kill me if I didn't co-operate. I had to tell him you knew who he was, that he'd been ID'd. I'm sorry."

426

"It's hardly going to make that much difference," said Thompson.

"That's not all," said Laura. "You – you have to understand that he was aiming a gun at me. And I knew he'd use it – he'd already shot his own friend."

"So what did you tell him?" asked Mathieson.

"I had to tell him that you were in charge of security and Mr Thompson was in charge of police matters. It was tell him or be shot, I'm – I'm really sorry."

"Don't be," said Thompson. "It's not worth dying to keep that much secret."

"Absolutely not," agreed Mathieson.

Seeing Laura's relief, Penny felt a flood of affection for both Thompson and Mathieson. She knew that a basic decency was prompting them to ease Laura's understandable sense of guilt.

"So what else did he discover?" asked Mathieson.

"Not much more," answered Laura. "I had to tell him it was the Israelis who ID'd him. That the constable from the roadblock had done an Identikit picture. I knew he was going to keep on pumping me for information, and I realised I had to escape, so when I went to the bathroom I jumped out the window."

"Brave move, Laura," said Thompson.

"I know what he's like. He would have killed me in the end anyway, so I had to get away."

"Still a plucky thing to do, jumping out the window," said Mathieson.

"Why don't we put her in for a Queen's Medal?" said Carrow sarcastically.

"Drop it, Len," said Mathieson. "What he's found

out isn't going to make it any easier for him to carry out his mission."

"It's still a breach of security," insisted Carrow.

"It won't make any difference if we catch him," said Thompson. "Or even if we don't catch him but we prevent him carrying out his mission." He looked at Laura as she cupped the mug of sweet tea. "You've had a bad experience, Laura, but it's done with. The important thing now is that you've come through in one piece. And I'll make certain that we get you back to Dublin safely."

Penny was watching the journalist and she half-anticipated Laura's response when she saw her putting down the mug of tea.

"I'm not going back to Dublin, Mr Thompson. I'm not running scared."

"No-one is saying you are, Laura. But this has gone beyond an article for a newspaper. Way beyond it."

Laura shook her head. "We had a deal. I gave you the tape, you promised me access."

"I think the situation has changed, Laura," replied Thompson. "I have to consider the safety and welfare of a civilian."

"Majid isn't interested in me for my own sake. I was simply a means to an end for him. His focus will be entirely on killing the delegates – he's not going to waste time and energy seeking me out again."

"Even so," said Thompson.

"He's a terrorist," continued Laura. "Terrorists thrive on disrupting the societies they oppose, you all know that. So if I go back to Ireland against my will, he's won.

He's made us change our plans. He'll have achieved what terrorists always want to achieve: he'll have set the agenda."

Penny watched the reaction of the others and she could see that even Carrow found this hard to disagree with. The anti-terrorist ethos ran deeply with these men, and Penny realised what a clever tactician Laura was in using a line of argument that resonated so strongly with them.

"If he makes us change our plans – even in something as small as a journalist having to quit a story – he wins. Let's not give him the satisfaction. Because if we deny him that, if we make him change *his* plans, then we win. So let's win here."

For a moment nobody spoke, then Thompson looked at Laura. "Why don't we go back to the Moat House first, then we can sort out what's what."

Laura glanced over at Penny, clearly unsure whether or not her pitch had worked, but Penny knew that Thompson had already more or less made his decision by not insisting here and now that Laura go back to Dublin. Penny winked surreptitiously at Laura, and the journalist obviously got the message. For the first time since they had arrived in the manager's office, Laura smiled.

"OK, Mr Thompson," she said, "let's go back to the Moat House."

Majid sat motionless in the woods awaiting the call from Tamaz Akmedov. He had done some reconnaissance since last talking to him, and was now settled down far enough into the trees not to be readily visible, yet in a spot from which he could look out across the sunlit expanse of Valley Park. The air was warm and the woods were scented with thyme, but Majid was much too focused on his own predicament to savour the early autumnal beauty of the park. It was six minutes past twelve now, yet Tamaz hadn't phoned. Majid had made it quite clear when setting up the rendezvous that should the waiter have trouble in getting an early lunch-break he was to ring back immediately. No such call had been made, which suggested that all was well, but if Tamaz had left the Conference Centre at twelve, Majid reckoned that he should have reached Valley Drive by now. On the positive side, however, was the fact that so far Majid had seen no police activity in the park. Which wasn't to say that the authorities weren't already combing the parts of the park nearer to the Old Swan.

He looked at his watch again. Seven minutes past twelve. *Come on*, he thought, *it's only a couple of minutes' drive. Unless Tamaz had been detained at a roadblock* . . . Just then his mobile went off. He had switched off the ringing tone so as not to reveal his presence in the woods, but immediately the phone began to vibrate he answered it. "Hello?"

"I'm at the location," said Tamaz.

Majid breathed out in relief, noting approvingly even as he did so that Tamaz was sufficiently cool to refer to the location rather than give details unnecessarily over the phone. It was largely academic, in that Majid would now have to give the other man specific details of where to meet, yet he still felt it was encouraging that the Tur wasn't too spooked to overlook the kind of fieldcraft that Majid had insisted on at all stages of the mission. "OK, continue up Valley Drive and follow the park boundary when the road becomes Harlow Moor Drive. Got that?"

"Yes."

"When you go up Harlow Moor Drive, you'll reach a small road on the left called Lascelles Grove. It's opposite a wooded section of the park. I'll meet you at the boundary of the park opposite Lascelles Grove. All right?

"All right."

"OK, see you there." Majid hung up, then rose and quickly made his way through the woods. After a short time he reached the edge of the woods and saw the tarmac of Harlow Moor Drive through the trees. He looked ahead, but there was no sign of Tamaz on the quiet suburban road. Majid slowed as he got to the edge of the tree-line, then he realised that his path through the woods had brought him out further up the road than he had anticipated and, on looking left, he saw Tamaz sitting in the car about fifteen yards away and opposite Lascelles Grove.

There was no passing traffic on the road and not many houses looked directly onto Harlow Moor Drive, but Majid nonetheless moved as briskly as possible to the car, then got into the front passenger seat.

"Abdullah," said Tamaz, "what's up?"

"Slight change in plans. I need to get to the warehouse as soon as possible, but I can't go on foot."

"Why not?"

Majid felt like slapping the other man for wasting precious time, yet he realised that for Tamaz – who had no inkling that there had been a shoot-out and that Jemail was dead – it wasn't an unreasonable question. He was going to have to keep Tamaz feeling as comfortable as possible, even at the cost of sitting here in a public place while providing a plausible explanation for him. "They've absolutely flooded Harrogate with foot patrols – I'd be sure to be picked up trying to get back to Starbeck."

"I can't drive you!"

"What?"

"They have roadblocks everywhere. I was stopped twice between the Conference Centre and here."

"Did they check the boot of the car?"

"No, but –"

"Did you see them checking anyone else's boot?"

"I saw one car having its boot examined."

"Just one?"

"Yes, but –"

"That's where I'll be travelling then," said Majid.

"But supposing –"

"There isn't time to argue. I have to get to Starbeck."

"If they check my boot we'll be caught!"

"Think logically, Tamaz. If they tried to check every car-boot there'd be total chaos. Traffic would back up for miles. So they'll look at every driver and only do spot-checks on the boots."

"They could still pick us though."

"They could. But the odds are greatly in our favour provided you stay calm at any checkpoints. So that's what you do. Stay calm and you'll sail through like you did on the way here." Majid looked at the older man and he could tell that the Turk was badly frightened. He reached out and laid his hand on his arm, then looked him in the eye. "I know you're a bit scared, Tamaz, but look at it this way. If I don't travel with you, I'm liable to be caught – and then we've all had it. If you just hold your nerve and I travel in the boot we shouldn't have a problem. It's *by far* the lesser of two evils. OK?"

Tamaz looked at him a moment, then nodded hesitantly. "OK."

"Good man."

"How – how will Jemail get to the warehouse?"

"He won't have to, " answered Majid. "He's already there. Now let's just get to the warehouse as soon as possible, right?"

"OK . . ."

"Good. Pull across the road here. Then park on the right-hand side of Lascelles Grove, about ten yards in."

"All right," answered Tamaz, then he put the car in gear and drove over towards Lascelles Drive.

Although there was very little traffic on Harlow Moor Road, Majid felt that it would still be risky to try climbing into the boot there, especially as there appeared to be no site that wasn't overlooked by a window or two in the houses that were strung along the road. Earlier he had done a quick reconnaissance along the boundary of the park and had decided that Lascelles Grove was about the best bet on offer. Now Tamaz pulled in to the kerb as instructed, and Majid immediately unlocked the passenger door.

"Open the boot catch," he instructed. "I'll tap when

I'm safely inside. And if you're stopped at a roadblock just stay cool. You've done fine so far, Tamaz, just keep it up." He squeezed the waiter's arm encouragingly, but saw that the older man was still frightened. "It's a question of odds, Tamaz. This way is by far our best bet, believe me. Now just stay brave like you've been, keep cool if you're stopped, and in twenty minutes it'll be over and we'll be safely in Starbeck. All right?"

Tamaz breathed out, then nodded. "All right."

"I knew I could count on you. OK, let's do it!" Majid stepped out of the car and went round to the back. The boot-catch was already undone and he immediately leaned his head forward into the boot as though rummaging for something. He pushed aside a towrope and an empty cardboard box to make space for himself, then stood up for a moment and glanced around. Where they were parked was almost a blind spot, although they could still possibly be seen from the side window of the house opposite which they were parked. Majid's apparently casual glance had scanned all likely sightlines to where he stood however, and he had seen no-one. There was also no sound of any approaching traffic on Harlow Moor Road. This was as good a chance as he was going to get, and without wasting any more time he leaned again into the boot, then quickly rolled his torso over the lip. He pulled his legs down after him, curled up into the foetal position and pulled down the lid of the boot.

He was plunged into darkness and the boot felt cramped and claustrophobic, but he told himself that none of that mattered. Getting to the warehouse safely was all that counted. He reached out his fist and tapped the inside of the wing three times. Immediately he heard Tamaz revving the engine, then the car pulled away from the pavement and they set out for Starbeck.

Laura saw the doctor to the door, shook hands and said goodbye to him, then returned to the armchair by the window of her hotel bedroom and lowered herself gingerly into the cushioned seat. As she had expected she had been given a clean bill of health, although the doctor had warned her that the bruising on her upper arm and hip would continue to hurt and would turn spectacular shades of purple and yellow over the coming days. Laura had already taken painkillers that were designed also to lower inflammation, but they hadn't kicked in yet and she still felt sore and a little shaky. She had been warned that the full effect of the shock induced by Majid's attack might take some time to manifest itself and she was glad to see Penny Harte re-entering the room, now that the doctor had left.

Penny had a large twin room in the Moat House Hotel, and when Thompson had finally agreed that Laura could stay on the case, Penny had suggested sharing her room with her, ostensibly because the hotel was full. Laura had gratefully accepted the offer, sensing that in reality it was probably a precondition of Thompson's that if she wanted to stay involved she should have the protection of sharing a room with an armed police officer.

Either way she was grateful to the other woman, and glad to have some sympathetic company, now that the adrenaline surge of her escape had given way to the inevitable reaction of thinking of how badly things could have gone. Penny had told her that Mathieson had left for a conference with the security heads of the international delegations, and Thompson and Carrow were organising groups of armed officers to search public parks, pubs, shops, libraries and anywhere else they could think of where a fugitive might seek refuge. Clearly Penny had been delegated to take charge of Laura, and she had been quick to organise the medical examination that had just concluded.

"Well?" she asked now, sitting opposite Laura on the side of the bed.

"The doctor's satisfied. No bones broken. The couple of cuts are superficial. He says the bruises will look bad for a while, but there's no real damage done."

"Good." Penny looked at Laura enquiringly. "Inside though, how are you feeling?"

Laura hesitated briefly, aware that Penny was asking out of concern rather than in an official capacity. Rather than give the kind of answers that she had felt were required to persuade Thompson to let her stay, she felt an urge now to unburden herself to the other woman.

"He frightened me, Penny. I was . . . I was really terrified . . ."

"Anyone would be."

"I suppose. And it's kind of strange. On the one hand he truly scared me, and I feel really bad about giving him information –"

"Don't feel bad about it, Laura. Your life was on the line, and what he discovered isn't that vital."

436

Laura looked at the policewoman, heartened by the obvious sincerity in her voice.

"Really you should put that from your mind," continued Penny. "I've spoken to the Chief and to Colin – they genuinely don't have a problem with what you revealed."

"Thanks, Penny, that's good to know. I don't think Mr Carrow will be so understanding though –"

"Carrow is a pain in the arse. If you were to try behaving to win his approval you'd tie yourself up in knots – and then he'd complain about the knots."

Laura smiled in spite of herself. "Right . . ."

"Sorry I interrupted you. You were saying: on the one hand . . ."

"He scared the wits out of me. But on the other hand . . ."

"What?"

"He's made me really angry. The bastard was going to kill me. I just *know* he was lying about letting me go when I'd answered his questions. So I can't let him turn me into a victim. For my own – I don't know – my own self-esteem, I suppose, I have to fight back."

"He's a professional killer, Laura. You don't need to take him on to prove anything, believe me."

"I can't walk away with my tail between my legs."

"No-one here would think any the less of you for quitting, Laura, they really wouldn't. And you'd still have a spectacular story to tell when this is all over."

"Are you saying you'd prefer me to go back?"

"I'm not saying I'd *prefer* it. I've really enjoyed having you on the case. But the more I think about what

437

you've just been through, the more I think you shouldn't feel obliged to stay on to prove some point."

Laura shook her head. "It's not really like that."

"Sure?"

Laura thought a moment, then looked Penny in the eye. "I've had a guiding principle for years now. It stems from when I was about thirteen . . ."

"Yeah?"

"Never let a bully call the shots. When I was a kid my brother Simon was bullied by a boy on the next road. He made Simon's life a misery. Eventually one day Simon couldn't take any more and he stood up to him."

"What happened?"

"They had a fight. The bully was bigger than most of the other kids – I suppose that's why he was a bully to begin with – so the odds were stacked against Simon."

"But his anger saw him through?" suggested Penny.

"No, it didn't. The bully won the fight, and Simon came home with a bloodied nose."

"Oh . . ."

"But it was a turning-point. Simon got back his self-respect. And here's the thing. Although the bully won the fight, he left Simon alone after that. Later that year the bigger brother of another kid beat the living daylights out of the bully and that was the end of that. But for me that wasn't the point."

"What was the point for you?" asked Penny.

"That as a guiding principle you mustn't let yourself be bullied. I believe the price you pay is always less in the long run than the price you pay if you *are* bullied."

"In most things, I'd agree with you, Laura. But the price with someone like Abdullah Majid could be your life."

Laura shook her head. "I don't think he's going to waste time seeking me out. And neither does Mr Thompson – otherwise he'd have insisted on my going back to Dublin."

"That's true," conceded Penny, "and I'm happy to share my room for the next few days. But in cases like this you can never be absolutely certain how things will pan out."

"There aren't many things in this life you can be absolutely certain about, Penny. So I'm not running scared. I want to be here when you get this guy. I want to see him taken away in handcuffs and I want to look him in the eye before he's taken away."

"OK," agreed Penny, "once you're sure."

"I'm sure. Let's just nail this bastard."

"Sounds good to me," said Penny, smiling at last.

"Deal then?" said Laura, extending her hand.

Penny shook hands. "Deal."

"What's going on, Abdullah?"

Majid could see the anxiety in Tamaz Akmedov's eyes, even in the gloom of the warehouse, but he knew that he could no longer shield the other man from what had happened. It was six thirty in the evening now and the Turk had arrived after finishing work, while Majid had spent the last six hours alone in the warehouse evaluating all that had happened. He had played back the cryptic warning left by Omar Rahmani on the answering machine and had thought at length about whether or not to abort the mission. The reality however was that events had overtaken the message – he already knew that the authorities were aware of his identity.

Viewed objectively, the sensible thing at this stage would be to abort the operation, yet after coming so far he was reluctant to do so. Having been ID'd and having lost Jemail made carrying out the mission more difficult, but certainly not impossible. It was a question of evaluating the odds.

Earlier Majid had discreetly entered the warehouse by a side pedestrian door and had been careful not to turn on any lights. The fact that Jemail happened to have been picked up in the High Street of Starbeck didn't necessarily mean that that was where he was staying, yet Majid had been aware that the police were likely to step up their door-to-door enquiries at houses in the general area. That in itself need not prove a problem – Tamaz was the only registered tenant in their house and presumably he had already passed a security check. No, the danger lay in the possibility of the net being cast wider and industrial premises also being searched.

As it turned out however the afternoon had passed without the police trying to gain admittance to the warehouse. A couple of police officers had driven round the industrial estate several hours earlier, and Majid had stood motionless in the darkened warehouse and watched their progress through a tiny grime-covered window. His heart pounding, he had seen them check the doors of several locked premises, then enter any units that were actually open on a Saturday afternoon. The large padlock on the main door had obviously deterred them from calling to his own location, and when several hours had passed and they obviously hadn't sought and returned with the owners of the other locked premises he had reasoned that his operational base was safe. And if that remained the case, and if he could bend Tamaz Akmedov to his will, then he could still strike a spectacular blow against his enemies.

If he could still count on Tamaz. It was going to take careful management, he knew. On the one hand, Tamaz had handled himself well on the journey back to the warehouse, keeping his nerve despite being stopped at a police checkpoint. The check had been routine, with many drivers being stopped and briefly questioned, and he had managed to come through the questioning successfully, despite the fear he must have felt. On the other hand, Tamaz was not a trained agent, and Majid knew that he was likely to be freaked by the killing of Jemail.

"What's the problem you spoke of?" Tamaz asked now.

Majid looked at the Turk, sitting on the far side of the desk in the warehouse office, then he spoke calmly but authoritatively. "It's something I couldn't tell you about earlier today. The thing is, Jemail did something really stupid this morning."

"What?"

"He disobeyed me," answered Majid, wanting to

reinforce the notion that he was in command and that obedience was expected.

"Disobeyed how?"

"He exposed himself to the authorities through carelessness – and he paid with his life."

"What?!"

"He was killed in a shoot-out."

"Oh my God . . ."

"I know it must be a shock for you."

"I – I can't believe it . . . no . . ."

"I'm sorry."

"Was it here in Harrogate?"

"Yes."

"There was . . . there was nothing on the radio – no-one said anything in work . . ."

Majid too had listened to the radio, but it had come as no surprise to him that there had been no mention of the shooting. From the authorities' point of view it made sense. If they revealed what had happened it would undermine conference security – maybe even result in the conference being postponed or cancelled. "They would have kept it quiet," he explained, "otherwise there could be pressure to call off the conference."

"How did – how did they catch Jemail?"

"It wasn't so much a case of catching him, as Jemail asking for trouble. I told him to lie low, but no – he went to a shop in the High Street. He walked straight into the police."

Tamaz looked a little puzzled "Where were you when this happened?"

"In the warehouse."

"How do you know what happened then?"

"He rang to warn me he was in trouble," answered Majid. "I went there immediately, but by then the shooting was all over."

"Oh my God . . ."

"He was a good man, but foolish . . ." said Majid.

"When did this happen?"

"About a quarter past ten."

Tamaz looked up in surprise. "Why didn't you tell me this morning in the park?"

"I knew there were roadblocks. It was nerve-wracking enough for you, driving with me concealed in the boot. If you'd just been told your comrade had been killed you'd have been agitated. That's not a criticism, Tamaz – it's just human nature. But a policeman might have picked up on it. Also you had to get through work this afternoon."

"Right . . ." the older man answered, then after a moment he looked quizzically at Majid. "If the shooting was in Starbeck, how did you end up in Valley Park?"

"I managed to escape in the van. Then I had to abandon it and proceed on foot. But I knew they were flooding the place with patrols and checkpoints. I could never have walked from there back to the warehouse."

"No. Poor Jemail . . . this is . . . it's such a shock . . ."

"I know. But you're off all day tomorrow. You have time to recover." Majid saw the look of surprise on the face of the Turk.

"You're not . . . you're not still planning to continue?"

"I am," answered Majid.

"But they'll be on full alert now. And you don't have Jemail!"

"They'd have been on full alert anyway. And yes, I wanted an accomplice, but it's not essential."

The waiter shook his head. "No, Abdullah, it's too dangerous now. I – I want out . . ."

"There is no 'out'."

"We could both be killed!"

"We won't be."

"We could be. I'm not doing this – you said it wasn't a suicide mission!"

"It's not."

"It is now. They've killed Jemail and they'll be waiting to kill us. I'm sorry, Abdullah, but I can't do this."

"You *have* to do it," said Majid, keeping his voice low, but injecting an air of menace into his tone.

"No. They'll kill us, I'm not doing it!"

Majid banged his fist down onto the desk, startling the other man. "You don't have a choice, Tamaz!" He lowered his voice, but locked eyes with the waiter and kept his tone icy. "You'll be killed if you don't do it."

"What?!"

"You heard me."

"Who'd kill me?"

"I would. And the people I'm working for would kill every living relative you have in Turkey. They have contacts in Urfa, they know the addresses, and they'd do it, believe me." Majid paused, noting the horror-struck expression on the older man's face. *Time to go for broke while Tamaz was shaken*. "And don't even *consider* agreeing and then running for it. You'd be tracked down in no time. Take it from me, your death would be a painful one. That's if you weren't picked up first by

444

the authorities here. And when they'd finished interrogating you, they'd try you for conspiracy to commit mass murder. So don't even think about making a break – *that* would be the suicidal option."

"I – I can't believe you're threatening me like this!"

"It's not personal, Tamaz," said Majid, softening his tone. "You're a good man and I like you. But there's lot at stake here and you had to be made aware of the options. Now that you realise the pointlessness of trying to quit, look at the other outcome."

"The only outcome I can see is death," Tamaz answered shakily.

"That's because you're not thinking clearly. The other outcome is that we continue as planned and succeed."

"Just like that?"

"The police were always going to be on their guard – the only thing that's really altered is Jemail's death. And I've already figured out how to continue without him."

"They're bringing in new code-words. To be issued each day for staff and vehicles going to the Conference Centre."

Majid considered this, then nodded. "That can be overcome."

"I'm scared, Abdullah . . . I'm scared."

"You're right to be scared. Because if you foul up now you'll pay dearly for it. If on the other hand you follow my instructions, all will be well – and this time next week you'll be a millionaire and safely tucked away someplace you'll never be found. " Majid looked

445

at the frightened Turk and he could see that he was weighing up the options. *Good*, he thought, *because the way he had presented things, continuing with the mission was unquestionably the least bad option*. In actual fact Majid would never have suggested to Rahmani's people that the relatives of Tamaz in Turkey should be killed or that Tamaz should be tortured if caught trying to desert the mission, but the other man wasn't to know that. Majid had briefly toyed with the idea of telling the truth about killing Jemail himself, then had decided not to. He needed to intimidate Tamaz, but admitting to assassinating his own partner might completely freak him.

The Turk breathed out wearily now, and Majid sensed that his ploy had worked. "OK, Tamaz?"

"OK . . ."

"Any time you have doubts, think of the options. Being a millionaire this time next week is the choice to go for, believe me."

"OK . . ."

Majid reached across the desk and patted the other man's shoulder. "Good man. Everything is still going to go to plan, believe me."

Tamaz nodded again, and Majid nodded back reassuringly, pleased that things had gone as well as could have been expected. Tamaz had all of tomorrow to rest and recover from his shock. Then, tomorrow evening, they would strike again. Majid had already decided what needed to be done, and he smiled to himself, doubting if the authorities would anticipate a move as audacious as the one he had planned.

17

Sunday 24th September 2000

"So how's the best girl in Britain behaving?" asked Penny.

"Missing her mother, demanding her bottle at three a.m., but sleeping next morning when everyone else is awake. Business as usual," answered Shane.

Penny smiled, warmed by her husband's wry humour at the other end of the telephone line. It was a bright autumn morning and, while Laura was showering in their en suite, Penny had taken the opportunity to ring Shane in Windsor. He had taken Aisling to visit her cousins in Bristol on Friday, and knowing that they would probably arrive home late the night before, Penny had said that she would leave ringing him until this morning. It was eight thirty now and normally she would have been on duty, but Thompson had insisted that she should have a good night's rest after her ordeal. Laura had been instructed to stay with her, and it had been agreed that the two women would meet up with the rest of the team later in the morning.

"So how have you been yourself?" asked Penny.

"Bit like Aisling."

"Yeah?"

"Missing you, feeling like hitting the bottle at three in the morning . . ."

Penny smiled again. "Only a few more days, Shane. All going well, I should be home on Wednesday."

"All going well is the worrying bit," said Shane, the bantering tone gone now from his voice.

Penny knew he was referring to the news item that the police press office in Harrogate had eventually released after media pressure. It had been stated on the television news the night before that shots had been fired outside North Park Road police station and that an arrest had been made. No reference had been made to the fact that the arrest had actually taken place in Starbeck, or that the prisoner had died as a consequence of the exchange of shots, and Penny knew that the press office would sit on the story until the conference was safely over, claiming that for operational reasons further details couldn't be disclosed as yet.

Penny felt uncomfortable. She couldn't lie to Shane and say that there was no danger involved, yet neither could she give him a detailed account of what was unquestionably a classified operation. She had heard Laura talking on the phone the previous evening to her boyfriend, Declan, and Laura had kept the entire incident with Abdullah Majid from him. Afterwards Laura had explained that with Declan stuck in Prague she didn't think it was fair to worry him about a situation about which he could do nothing. It was a reasonable, well-intentioned approach, yet Penny had always taken the line with Shane of telling him as much as she could about her job. They had agreed from the start to be honest with each other and, while Penny tended to play down the dangers inherent in her work, she didn't lie to her husband.

"Don't worry, Shane," she said reassuringly, "we're taking every precaution here, we really are."

"Good."

Penny knew that he was still concerned, but in fairness he had never asked her to give up police work. With his computer company thriving they could have managed without Penny's salary, but he had always respected the fact that she found her career deeply fulfilling. Part of why she loved him so much was knowing that in his heart of hearts he would have preferred if she held a more conventional job, yet he never put her under pressure to do so. He had once pointed out that with her leadership and management skills she would have no difficulty getting another – and probably a far more lucrative – job, but when she had said that she wasn't interested he had never raised the matter again.

"It's OK, love," she said now. "We're taking no chances here, and as soon as the conference is wrapped up I plan to get home."

"I'm glad. I've really missed you."

"I've missed you too."

"Be careful, Penny. No heroics, yeah?"

"No heroics," she answered, thinking guiltily back to the previous morning when she had left cover to exchange fire with Abdullah Majid.

"Oops – Aisling's woken – starting to cry."

"OK. Look, I'll ring you tonight, Shane, if I'm not too late finishing."

"Ring me anyway, whatever the time."

"All right."

"Listen, I have to go, Penny, she's starting to howl. Mind yourself."

"You too, love. Bye."

"Bye."

Penny put down the phone and stared into space. Some sixth sense told her they weren't finished with Abdullah Majid, yet the phone call to Shane had underlined how much her family meant to her. Very well then, she would do everything she could to catch their man, but this time without taking any unnecessary risks. She rose from the bed, crossed to the dressing-table, then picked up her Glock and slipped it into her shoulder holster.

"The bastard's out there somewhere – he should have been picked up by now," said Carrow.

Laura saw Thompson making a conscious effort to keep his patience and she watched carefully, fascinated as ever by the dynamic between Thompson and the Special Branch officer. She had had breakfast in the hotel with Penny, then joined the rest of the team in an office off the police station's command room, where they now sat around a table.

Despite the residue of shock in the hours following her encounter with Majid she had taken a pill and managed to sleep reasonably well last night, comforted by the presence of Penny in the room with her. She knew that she was still a little shaky, and she still found it unnerving to think that her assailant would probably have killed her when she had answered all his questions, but her unease was overshadowed by the sense of outrage that had steadily grown since the incident. She felt now, more than ever, that she couldn't have let him win by retreating in fear to Dublin.

"He's lying low somewhere," said Thompson calmly in response to Carrow, and Laura could see that he had decided not to rise to the bait of the other man's implied criticism. "Sooner or later though he'll show himself, and that's when we'll get him."

"You hope," said Carrow.

"I'm not in the business of hoping," snapped Thompson. "I've taken every reasonable step."

"Any joy with the discarded clothes, Chief?" asked Penny.

Laura knew that a Gladstone bag containing the silenced Uzi and a jacket and tie had been found during a trawl through the bushes just inside the entrance to Valley Park, although a thorough search of the park had failed to yield up the fugitive.

"Forensics have analysed them, but nothing new has emerged."

"No luck with the tracker dogs?"

Thompson shook his head. "The handlers are still trying, but they haven't been able to find the trail again."

"All the search parties are still out then?" said Penny.

"Absolutely," answered Thompson. "Woods, fields, parks, alleyways – anywhere a person might hole up."

"As the day goes on though we're going to have to shift more of our resources to covering the actual delegate arrivals," said Mathieson.

"What's the state of play regarding the press release on the shooting?" asked Penny.

"The press are champing at the bit, but we've managed to keep the story under wraps," answered Thompson. "And we're holding the remains of Jemail Zubi for a formal post mortem."

"It's been a hell of a job keeping the other security chiefs quiet about the shooting," added Mathieson.

"I'll bet," said Penny sympathetically.

"I emphasised to them that none of us can afford to have the conference postponed – so it's got to stay out of the press."

Carrow turned to Laura and was about to speak, but before he could Laura held up her hand. "Before you say it, Mr Carrow, I know – mum's the word."

Carrow fixed her with a searching look, but Laura could see the others smiling and she reckoned that she had accurately predicted what Carrow had been about to say to her.

"So what's the schedule now?" asked Penny.

"The VIPs start arriving over the course of the morning," said Thompson. "The hotel and Conference Centre have been swept for explosives using sniffer-dogs, we've marksmen already in position, the RAF's on alert, we've motorcycle outriders at the airport to escort each arrival non-stop to Harrogate, and we'll be issuing new code-words on a daily basis. It's basically all the safeguards we agreed on."

"At the risk of being devil's advocate," said Laura, "what happens if you still don't locate Majid?"

"Nothing – if he's given up on the conference," said Thompson.

"Somehow I don't believe he's given up," said Penny.

"Then we keep on looking for him," suggested Thompson, "and either we'll find him, or he'll come to us. Either way, this time we'll be ready for him."

Majid looked at his watch. 17.28, almost time to go into action. At 17.30 Tamaz was due to arrive at the warehouse, and Majid crossed now to the main entrance doors, ready to open them from the inside as soon as the other man's car came to a halt outside. Majid had slept on a camp bed in the warehouse the previous night, then waited all day for his rendezvous with Tamaz. Once again, his contingency planning from the previous March had paid off, so that while his stay in the warehouse was hardly comfortable, he did at least have a portable gas stove and a small supply of food and drink. There was also a dilapidated but working shower, and Majid had been able to change into fresh jeans, underwear and a T-shirt, all part of the stock of clothes he had stored in the warehouse.

The hardest part had been having to remain inactive all day long, but Majid had fallen back on his training and had adopted his philosophy of regarding patient waiting as a virtue to be embraced as part of the mission, rather than treated as an irritating waste of time.

A bigger concern by far was the mental state of Tamaz Akmedov. After having frightened the Turk with his threats the previous evening, Majid had then tried to rebuild his confidence. It was a tricky balance to strike, but Majid felt that he had done as well as was possible by the time the waiter had left. And Tamaz had had all of today to recover from the shock of Jemail's death. Of course that also gave him plenty of time to fret and work himself into a state should his nerve crack. On balance though, Majid felt that wouldn't happen. Tamaz wasn't bold by nature, but he was pragmatic, and Majid had made it very clear that going ahead with the mission would be by far the best option in terms of Tamaz's personal welfare.

Majid had resisted the temptation to ring him during the day to see how he was bearing up. Firstly, he thought that as things stood there wasn't the justification to discuss any aspect of the mission on cellphones. Secondly, he didn't want Tamaz to think that he was worried about him. Far better to take the approach that everything had been settled and that any talking could be done when Tamaz arrived at the warehouse. Having taken his decision, Majid had put his worries about Tamaz aside and concentrated instead on his own revised plans for launching his assault. He had gone over each detail from every angle, trying to anticipate difficulties, until finally he had reached the point where he believed he had thought out every move that could be anticipated. In reality he knew that his plan was risky and that vital aspects depended on how the enemy reacted on the night, but that had always been the case, and there was no risk-free way to pull off as spectacular an assassination as he was planning.

Majid's reflections were disturbed by the sound of an approaching engine and he quickly put his eye to a crack in the warehouse doors. Being a Sunday there had been no toing and froing to any of the other premises in the industrial estate, so an approaching vehicle was likely to be either Tamaz or, in the worst-case scenario, the police.

He held his breath, then a car suddenly rounded the corner of one of the factories, and Majid breathed out in relief on recognising Tamaz's car. Before the vehicle had slowed to a halt Majid was pulling on the sliding gate, then Tamaz drove forward again and entered the warehouse. Still standing unseen behind the door, Majid immediately pulled in the opposite direction until the door slid back into a closed position. Majid approached the car as Tamaz turned off the engine and got out.

"Tamaz," he said, kissing him on the cheek in greeting.

"Abdullah . . ."

Majid noted that while the Turk looked somewhat nervous he did at least try for a half-hearted smile, which suggested that he wasn't too shaken after having a day to reflect on events. And more fundamentally, he had shown up for the rendezvous, so the mission could actually go ahead.

"You brought the luggage?" asked Majid, deciding not to ask Tamaz how he was, but to go with the notion that everything was settled.

"Yes, it's in the boot."

"Let's have it out please."

"OK." Tamaz opened the boot and withdrew two suitcases. All of Jemail's stuff was in one, all of Majid's in the other. They would never be going back to the house in Starbeck, but Majid still felt it would be good fieldcraft to leave nothing to indicate their presence there, even though tomorrow would be the final day of the mission. As Tamaz removed the luggage, Majid collected the sleeping bag he had used the previous night and spread it out in the now empty boot.

"What's that for?" asked Tamaz.

"We need to take a little trip. I want to be more comfortable this time."

Majid saw the look of nervousness on the other man's face, but encouragingly Tamaz voiced no objection.

"Where are we going?" he asked.

"Blubberhouses. It's only ten miles away, and you'll be just another Sunday driver."

"What's in Blubberhouses?"

Majid smiled humourlessly. "The home of someone I want to visit. Let's go."

Laura looked out across the Stray, a fine expanse of sunlit parkland that stretched to the south of Harrogate. She was accompanying Penny, who was talking to police officers manning a checkpoint on the main road from Leeds. It was six in the evening now and the day had been incident-free, leaving Laura with mixed emotions. On the one hand, she was relieved that all of the delegates and their entourages had arrived in

Harrogate safely, yet she was disappointed that, despite continuing police searches, no trace had been found of Abdullah Majid.

Where the hell could he be, she wondered, then her thoughts were interrupted by the ringing of her mobile. She nodded in an excuse-me gesture to Penny, then stepped away as she answered the phone. "Hello?"

"Hi, Kid."

"Oh . . . Mac."

"How come you're always surprised to hear from your friendly neighbourhood editor?"

"Just – wasn't expecting to hear from you on a Sunday evening," she answered.

"Had to come in to the office to check something, thought I'd give you a buzz," explained Mac. "So, how goes it?"

"Fine."

"Anything strange?"

Yes, I escaped by the skin of my teeth from a psychopathic assassin. "No, I'm still travelling about with the local police," she answered, instinctively keeping from her editor the details of her encounter with Majid. She knew that Mac's inclinations would be in conflict if she told him the truth of what had happened. If he felt her to be in danger he was very likely to insist on her returning to Dublin, which she certainly didn't want. As a newsman however he would undoubtedly be eager to exploit such a dramatic story, yet that too would present problems because of her deal with Thompson. Either way there was nothing for it, she realised, but to keep Mac at arm's length for another little while. "The material I'm getting here is absolutely first-rate," she said. "It really is."

"Music to the ears of Uncle Mac . . ."

Laura realised that the editor was in a relaxed mode, and despite the seriousness of all that had happened she made a conscious effort to adopt an equally light tone. "We strive to please our betters . . ."

"Hey, talking of your betters, I have one for you."

Laura knew that Mac had never gone to journalism college, but that he took a childish delight in being better read than many of the graduates who worked on the *Clarion*. There was a playful rivalry between Laura and the editor, underwritten by the fact that Laura too was well-read and frequently could match Mac in recognising the quotations and maxims he came up with. "Let's have it," she said.

"Who declared 'There's much to be said in favour of modern journalism. By giving us the opinions of the uneducated, it keeps us in touch with the ignorance of the community'?"

"Eh . . . Karl Marx?"

"Wrong answer, but kind of the right neck of the woods."

"Groucho Marks?"

Mac laughed. "Nice try, Kid . . ."

Laura was glad that she had amused him, but she realised that the trauma of her encounter yesterday with Majid and the anger that had followed it were making banter feel like too much of an effort. Time to end the levity, she decided. "OK, Mac, you win, who was it?"

"Our old friend, Oscar Wilde."

"Right . . . *De Profundis*?"

"No, *The Critic as Artist*."

"Ah . . . your round so, Mac."

"Thank you," said the editor, the note of pleasure in his voice evident even over the phone. "Oh, and talking of prison –"

"Were we?" said Laura.

"Well, wasn't *De Profundis* written in jail?"

"Right."

"Just reminded me – the local boys in blue were asking more questions about you."

"Really?"

"Don't worry, Kid, I told them you were still in England on *Clarion* business. But they're still going to want to talk to you about Boyle and O'Donnell when you come back. Just so you have your story ready . . ."

"Thanks, Mac. I'll have a story for them all right. And an even better one for you. Believe me, this trip hasn't been a wild-goose chase!"

"I believe you. And Laura?"

"Yes?"

"Be careful."

The bantering tone was gone from Mac's voice, and Laura sensed his concern. "I will, I promise."

"OK, call me as soon as you've copy typed up."

"Absolutely."

"Talk to you then."

"Yeah. Bye, Mac."

"Bye."

Laura hung up, then gazed unseeingly across the

Stray. The mention of the Irish police had reminded her that she had broken numerous laws back in Dublin and that she would have to tread carefully on her return. But that was for the future. Right now all her attention had to be focused on the conference, and the possible reappearance of Abdullah Majid. Very well then, she resolved, that's what she would concentrate on. She slipped the phone into her pocket, then went to rejoin Penny at the checkpoint.

Majid found the policeman's home intriguing. It was always fascinating to explore the territory of the enemy and he had thoroughly checked out every room in Thompson's spacious four-bedroomed cottage. He had noted the address when going through Laura Kennedy's notebook in the Old Swan, and the house itself had been easy to find. Breaking in had been easy too, and he presumed that there wasn't enough crime in a small Yorkshire village like Blubberhouses to warrant the need for a serious security system. As Majid had expected there had been no car in the driveway – presumably Thompson was on duty all day in view of the conference delegates' imminent arrival – and it had been a simple matter to force a rear window open and gain entry to the secluded house.

The journey to Blubberhouses had gone smoothly, with Tamaz Akmedov's car being stopped only briefly at a checkpoint on the outskirts of Harrogate, confirming Majid's theory that while the police might speedily observe the occupants of every vehicle passing through the checkpoints, it would have caused traffic chaos were they to check the boot of every car. Of course there had still been the risk of a spot check, but Majid had long since decided that continuing with the mission inevitably entailed risk-taking, and so they had gone ahead with the journey. Once in the village of Blubberhouses, Tamaz had found a quiet pub carpark where Majid had been able to climb out of the boot unseen, then Majid had sent the Turk back to Harrogate, having first organised with him a rendezvous time for the next day.

He had gone through the house room by room, committing to memory every available detail about his adversary. He had noted that Thompson's musical taste leaned heavily towards brass bands and Frank Sinatra, then he had studied the photographs mounted on the walls, including a black and white shot of Thompson in his younger days with an attractive woman that Majid assumed to be his wife. There were also pictures of adults and younger children that Majid reckoned must be Thompson's children and grandchildren. Several of these were casually tacked onto a notice-board, and Majid had been pleased to see that the names of the children and the date of the photographs had been written on the back of the pictures. He had memorised the names, then continued exploring the house, but despite a painstaking search of every room he had failed to find the main piece of information for which he had come to Blubberhouses. He had hoped – though not really expected – that Thompson might have written down at home the crucial new code-words that were apparently to be issued each day. Majid knew that for his plan to work he simply had to be able to link up with Tamaz in the Conference Centre, and for that he needed to get Monday's vehicle-access code-word.

After searching for well over an hour, however, Majid had accepted that Thompson had probably opted to keep the codes on his person rather than leave such sensitive information in the files kept here in the cottage. By then dusk had fallen and Majid had stopped searching and instead sat quietly in the encroaching gloom, knowing that he mustn't alert the policeman by having a light shining when he returned home. He had been prepared to wait for hours if necessary, aware that Thompson might opt to work late in preparation for tomorrow's conference. His one big worry was that Thompson might not return at all that night. Even though it was obvious that he was staying in Blubberhouses rather than Harrogate and that his shaving kit and fresh clothes were all here in the cottage, there was still the chance that he might opt to stay in the hotel in Harrogate, now that the conference was imminent. If that were the case, Majid knew he would have a major difficulty, but as he sat in the dark the problem was suddenly solved for him. The drone of an approaching car became louder, then the twin beams of a car's headlights illuminated the drive outside the cottage. The headlights swung in an arc as the car approached the front door of the house, and Majid felt his excitement rising. He breathed deeply to steady himself, then reached over to the nearby kitchen worktop and picked up the silenced Beretta.

He heard the sound of a car door slamming, then the

jingling of keys in the lock of the hall door. The hallway was flooded with light, but Majid sat still knowing that he couldn't be seen sitting behind the door in the darkened kitchen. He listened carefully lest Thompson might speak to a companion, but to his relief no words were spoken, then the hall door was closed and he heard him approaching. A light switch was flicked and the kitchen was illuminated, then Thompson walked into the room. Majid remained sitting behind the door, but raised the gun and aimed it at Thompson's back. The policeman went over to the sink and picked up the kettle, and Majid smiled to himself, uncertain whether it would be more enjoyable simply to let the other man turn around and see him, or whether it would be better to startle him by speaking. He waited a moment then opted for speaking. "Lax security for a policeman," he said conversationally.

Thompson dropped the kettle in shock and spun round. Majid kept the Beretta trained on him, but smiled, enjoying the look of amazement on the other man's face. "You look surprised, Mr Thompson. Is this a bit of a shock?"

The policeman didn't answer him and Majid gesticulated with the gun. "I asked you a question. You'd be wise to answer."

"Obviously it's a shock," replied Thompson slowly.

Despite having dropped the kettle and been taken by surprise there was no sense of panic in Thompson's demeanour, and Majid suspected that given a chance this man could be a formidable adversary. Except that he wouldn't be getting any chances.

"You've done it again, haven't you?" said Majid.

"Done what?"

"Underestimated me. You keep doing it. And you know what?"

"What?"

"Even though it suits my purposes, I find it insulting. You shouldn't underestimate any foe, but particularly you shouldn't underestimate me. And you have, Mr Thompson." Majid lifted his left hand to steady the gun as he aimed it at Thompson's chest. "So now you have to pay . . ."

18

Monday 25th September 2000

"I think I'm going to marry him," said Laura.

Penny smiled, taken aback but warmed by the other woman's revelation. "That's great, Laura! I'm delighted for you."

"I haven't told Declan yet . . ."

"That'll be a nice surprise for him," said Penny with a grin.

"Yeah . . ."

The bedroom curtains were pulled back, and Penny could see the first rays of dawn light as they finished an early breakfast courtesy of room service. Today being the first day of the conference Mathieson had called a meeting for the full team at seven o'clock, and the two women had risen early, showered and dressed, then over a relaxed breakfast they had chatted and the subject of partners had come up again.

Despite the close rapport that she had developed with Laura, Penny was still a little surprised at the journalist's sudden revelation about her marriage plans. "So has this been on the cards for a while?"

"Sort of," answered Laura. "Declan was on for getting married, but . . ."

"You weren't so sure?"

"It's not that I didn't love him and want to be with him. I just felt there was no great rush, you know?"

"Right," answered Penny.

"I think marriage is important. I wanted to be certain before we took the step."

Penny nodded sympathetically. "And now you are certain?"

"Yes. The thing with Majid in my room, it was terrifying – life-threatening . . ."

"Right," said Penny.

"But . . . it also, well, it kind of clarified my thinking. Brought home to me what's important in my life. And it made me realise that Declan really is my soul mate."

Penny nodded, yet she couldn't help wondering why Laura hadn't told Declan anything about the attack if he really were her soul mate. Her uncertainty must have shown because Laura looked at her quizzically. "What?"

"Nothing . . ."

"Come on, Penny, I can see you've some kind of reservation."

"It's just . . . I'm delighted you've someone you want to be with . . ."

"But?"

"Well, if you're that close, I can't help wondering why you never confided in him about Majid."

"I wanted to, Penny, I really did. In fact, it was when we were talking on the phone that I realised for certain that Declan was who I wanted to spend the rest of my life with."

"Yeah?"

"Yeah. But I stopped myself from telling him about the attack. It seemed . . . I don't know . . . selfish almost. I mean he was in Prague and I was here. There was no way he could just leave the film without causing chaos, and I didn't want that. So all that he could have done was worry about me if I'd told him – and that's why I didn't. Can you understand that, or does it sound really clinical?"

Penny reached out and squeezed the other woman's arm. "It doesn't sound clinical at all. You're obviously a caring, loving partner."

"But you would have told Shane?"

Penny considered, then spoke carefully. "When Shane and I started we promised that we'd always be straight with each other."

"So what about situations where there's nothing he can do, but where he'll be worried sick if you tell him what's going on?"

"It's been difficult at times," admitted Penny. "I've never lied to him, but . . . well, I suppose I've tended to play things down in situations like that. It's tough, because we both believe honesty's really important – yet, like you say, it feels selfish sometimes to have another person worrying about something they've no control over."

"Exactly."

467

"It's an emotional tug-of-war I have to live with," said Penny. "I like my job, but there *are* definite drawbacks."

"Do you ever regret opting for a career in the police?"

Penny shook her head. "No, I love most of what I do. What I regret are the parts of the job that make it difficult for Shane and me."

"If those parts got out of hand, could you imagine a career outside the force?"

Penny thought a moment. "That would be kind of strange. I mean, I went straight from school into the police. Having said that, I think everyone should be flexible enough to follow more than one path through life."

"Right."

"If it ever got to the stage where I needed to change direction, I would. But in reality I don't see it happening. Shane's a pretty secure, mentally-strong sort of person. I think we can probably cope with most things my career throws at us – we've done OK so far."

"Sounds like it," agreed Laura. "Anyway, when I get home I'm going to suggest to Declan we get married." She gave Penny a wry grin. "So maybe I've something to thank Abdullah Majid for after all . . ."

Penny smiled back, but raised an eyebrow. "I still want to nail him good and proper."

"Me too," said Laura emphatically.

"OK, then," said Penny, pushing aside the breakfast tray and standing up, "let's get to work . . ."

Majid heard the alarm going off and experienced a

moment's confusion as he came to, then he realised where he was and reached out towards the bedside locker. He fumbled briefly in the dark before locating the small alarm clock and switching it off. 7.00 a.m. He threw back the sheets and swung his legs out of bed, then switched on the bedside lamp. Although the bedroom in Thompson's house was comfortably furnished, and despite having availed of clean sheets and a firm mattress, Majid had slept fitfully. There was too much adrenaline in his system, he knew, what with his confrontation with Thompson the previous evening and the prospect of what lay ahead today. There had also been the fear that someone might ring for Thompson during the night. Majid had thought it unlikely that any new crisis would arise to warrant such a call, yet the possibility of the police making contact had been at the back of his mind as he had tried to sleep. Eventually he had drifted off and although he felt a little tired now he knew that the excitement of what he was planning to do would soon have him charged up.

He had slept in his underwear, and he reached for his jeans and sweater now, postponing his shower until after he had made the first move in his game-plan for the day. He quickly donned his clothes, then reached under the pillow and withdrew the silenced Beretta. He slipped the gun into his waistband and made for the door.

Although not long awake, he walked with a spring in his step, pleased that after all the months of preparation he was finally on the brink of putting his plans into action. Last night had gone exactly as he had hoped, with Thompson having the vital code-words among the paperwork that he had brought home. He had disarmed the policeman, then tried to question him. He had already marked Thompson down as a potentially formidable opponent and it had been no surprise when the police officer had stubbornly refused to discuss the security at the Conference Centre. Majid had decided not to use up energy trying to extract information – he already knew the security set-up from Tamaz Akmedov and the plan for tonight's assault took account of the high-profile police presence. Questioning Thompson had instead been designed more to bend the policeman to his will, so that his captive would be more biddable for the role Majid had planned for him. Knowing that he must regain the upper hand after Thompson's refusal to talk, Majid had given the policeman a heavy dose of sleeping pills and ordered him to take them. Again Thompson had refused, but when Majid had calmly announced that he would handcuff Thompson to the radiator, knee-cap him in both legs, and let him slowly bleed to death while in an agony of pain, the other man had taken the threat seriously and given in.

Majid now crossed the corridor and walked through the open door into Thompson's bedroom, switching on the light. The heavy dose of sedatives had knocked the police officer out the previous night and he still snored lightly as he lay with his right hand and left foot handcuffed to the bed with two pairs of handcuffs. Majid reached out and shook him roughly until he groggily opened his eyes.

"What's . . . what's going on?" said Thompson.

Majid smiled humourlessly. "Room service. Your wake-up call." He saw recognition dawning in the older man's face and what looked like a glimpse of despairing recollection of his predicament. Majid immediately turned on his heel and made for the phone in the hall. He had deliberately arranged things so that he would force Thompson to make the call he had planned while the policeman was still groggy and half-awake. Wasting no time, he took the portable phone off its stand and brought it over to his handcuffed prisoner. "You're going to make a call," he said. "I want you to contact your office and ring in sick."

"I need to go to the toilet," said Thompson.

"After you make the call." This bastard was dangerous – Majid could sense it, and he didn't want him having time to think while he used the toilet. Far better to have him make the call while he was still not entirely awake.

"I need to go first."

Majid didn't hesitate but swung his right hand in a fast, backhand motion, smacking Thompson in the face. The older man wasn't expecting the blow, and Majid saw the shock in his eyes. Good, it was important to establish who was in control, and he would force the issue now while Thompson was thrown. "You do what I say, when I say – if you want to live. Got that?"

"I need to use the toilet," persisted Thompson, and Majid felt his anger rising at the other man's stubborn defiance. *No*, he thought, *getting angry was letting Thompson dictate how he felt. He, Majid, had to be the one establishing how the other man felt.*

"That's what your friend claimed in the Old Swan,"

471

said Majid, deliberately keeping his tone unruffled. "The toilet routine doesn't work twice."

"It's not a routine."

"When you make the call, as instructed, then I'll take you to the bathroom." Majid took the Beretta from his waistband and trained it on Thompson, then held out the telephone with his other hand, placing it on the bed beside Thompson's cuff-free hand. "Ring your office and tell them you're sick and you won't be in today."

Thompson hesitated, then looked Majid in the eye. "I don't think I can do that."

"Wrong," said Majid. "I don't think you can *not* do that."

"I don't know what your plan is, but I can't be a party to some kind of an attack on the very people I'm supposed to be defending."

"What I'm going to do, I'm going to do anyway," said Majid. "Whether or not you co-operate isn't going to protect your precious big-wigs."

"In that case you'll understand my refusal to collaborate," said Thompson.

"Wrong again. You'll ring up and say exactly what I tell you. You know why?"

"Why?"

"Because if you don't other people will die. People who matter more to you than some overfed, power-hungry politicians. I saw the pictures in the kitchen of your grandchildren. Graham, Ian and Katie. I bet Katie's your favourite – though they're all nice-looking kids. If you don't want them to be dead kids, you'll do what I say."

"You bastard!"

"Be careful what you say, Mr Thompson. I'm the one with the gun, you're the one chained to the bed."

"What kind of scum threatens children? What cause could possibly –"

"Enough! I don't have to justify myself to you. I've gone through your address book, I know where your children live, I know where to find your grandchildren. I promise you I'll kill every last one of them if you don't co-operate." Majid looked at the other man, but could see only the loathing in his eyes – he couldn't tell if the policeman was going to acquiesce to his threat. "I'll shoot Graham, Ian and Katie, and I'll slit their parents' throats. You know I killed my own comrade yesterday, so you'll understand that killing a few spoiled English brats means nothing to me. Decide, Mr Thompson, and decide right now. I won't ask you again. Do you want them to die or are you making the call?"

Majid waited, one part of him offended at the tactics he had had to adopt. In reality, he wouldn't have killed Thompson's children or grandchildren, but the policeman wasn't to know that, and Majid hoped that having had to stoop to such tactics they would at least pay off for him now. He watched Thompson closely and was relieved when the older man breathed out in defeat.

"I'll ring in," he said softly.

"Smart decision," answered Majid. "And make sure you stay smart. No warnings, no subtle hints. I have excellent English and I'll be listening to every word. Understood?"

"Yes."

"Good. Tell them you have dreadful food poisoning, you've been running to the toilet constantly, it's so bad you've had the doctor out. You're on Immodium and there's no question of you being back to work before Wednesday, at the earliest. All right?"

"Yes."

"You don't want any visitors because of your condition, you're not even encouraging phone calls you feel so wretched. OK?"

"OK."

"And Mr Thompson – be convincing. Think of your grandchildren any time you feel tempted to raise the alarm."

Majid could see the murderous hatred in Thompson's eyes, but he held the other man's stare and indicated the phone. "Make the call. And remember – one slip and this is the last day on earth for you and all your family. Now take up the phone and dial . . ."

Laura watched the changed dynamics of the command room with fascination. When Thompson had called in sick his immediate superior, Assistant Commissioner Kelch, had been notified and had assumed operational command in his place. Kelch wasn't expected on the scene for another half an hour however and with the new man not having the detailed knowledge of the operation that Thompson had, more responsibility was going to fall on the existing team. It was evident to Laura that Carrow was delighted that Thompson would miss his big day, and she suspected that th

Special Branch officer would now try to enhance his own role in the proceedings. As Thompson's assistant, Penny too would now have a more significant role, but it was obvious to Laura that she was more concerned for Thompson's welfare and disappointed that he would be missing the enormous security operation that he had helped to mastermind. Mathieson, while sympathetic to Thompson's illness, appeared nonetheless to be his usual unflappable self, yet he too would probably have to shoulder more responsibility in the absence of a key player like Thompson.

Watching Mathieson sitting at the head of the table, Laura was aware that there was a whole other dimension to conference security that she hadn't covered in the research for her articles, namely the complex issue of co-ordinating the security services of all the participating countries. A good deal of Mathieson's time had been taken up with trying to keep all the different security agencies happy – an almost impossible task on an operation of this magnitude – but Laura had decided not to try to pursue it as a newspaper topic. Apart from the fact that she knew security service procedures would be regarded as far more sensitive than normal police operations, there was also the fact that there was only so much on which she could concentrate – and her journalistic instincts told her that the battle of wits between the authorities and Majid would best be covered from the police angle.

"OK, let's quickly go through anything that needs attention, then get over to the Conference Centre," said Mathieson. "To speed things up, Assistant Commissioner

Kelch is going straight there, rather than via the station here."

"What about briefing the police commanders who are here?" asked Carrow.

"As soon as we're finished here Penny will brief the local police officers, you'll brief your Special Branch people," answered Mathieson.

Laura saw the flicker of disapproval that crossed Carrow's face and she had to suppress a smile. Carrow was smart enough however to recognise that Penny's temporary elevation was a *fait accompli*, and he made no comment.

"Right," said Mathieson. "State of play as of this morning?"

"RAF on alert to enforce the no-fly zone," replied Penny. "All roads to the Conference Centre sealed, bomb squad on standby, sniffer-dogs on hand, marksmen in position, strict exclusion from security zone of anyone without today's code-words – everything we agreed is in place right now."

"Masks and suits in case of biological attack?" asked Carrow.

Penny nodded. "Already distributed to Special Forces, ample additional supplies in the Conference Centre."

"Good," said Mathieson. "And the manhunt for Majid?"

"We've scaled it down a little to concentrate on the Conference Centre and all approach roads and pedestrian access routes," replied Penny.

"Fair enough," said Mathieson. "No hint of him leaving any kind of a trail then?"

"I'm afraid not. No residents have ID'd either Majid or Jemail Zubi so far. But we're still doing the door-to-door enquiries and unless Mr Kelch decides otherwise, we'll continue with that right through the conference."

"I know we have to prepare for an attack," said Carrow, "but I reckon this Majid bastard's thrown in the towel. His accomplice is dead and he knows now we've ID'd him. From his point of view the smart move would be to run away and live to fight another day."

"I've seen up close what this man is like," said Laura. "I wouldn't count on him running away."

Laura had spoken on the spur of the moment and she immediately regretted it when Carrow turned and looked at her balefully.

"I wasn't *counting* on it, dear. I was *commenting* – quite a different thing."

"Fine," said Laura.

"Question of probability," continued Carrow, turning back to the others. "Determined and all as he may be, I'm afraid the massive police presence round the conference location will deter him."

"You're *afraid* it will deter him?" asked Mathieson.

"Well, I'd rather catch him than deter him."

"Let's be very clear here, Len," said Mathieson. "We're not laying a bait with this conference in order to catch a terrorist."

"Don't tell me you wouldn't give your eye-teeth to get him," said Carrow.

"I want him," said Mathieson. "I'd go so far as to say I want him badly. But I want a safe, incident-free conference even more. That's the *political* priority.

Which means it's the priority for the security service, it's the priority for the police, and it had better be the priority for Special Branch too. Understood?"

Carrow didn't reply immediately, then nodded. "Understood."

"Good. What's the position with the press, Penny?" asked Mathieson.

"We're just about holding the line on the shooting story." Penny smiled wryly. "It's a mixture of stonewalling, claiming the national interest, promising favours in the future and calling in favours owed. I'd say we can just about contain it till the conference is safely over."

"We have to," said Mathieson, then he glanced at Laura.

"My lips are sealed, as per our agreement," she answered.

The intelligence officer nodded. "Good. Right, anybody got anything else?

Nobody had anything to add and Mathieson nodded again, then rose. "OK, let's hope the door-to-door flushes out our man. Meanwhile we have an operation to run, let's get to it."

Majid kept the Beretta trained on Thompson as he sa across the kitchen table from him. It was one thirty now six and a half hours since he had forced the policema to ring in sick. Time to make contact again, he reckoned Thompson's ankle was handcuffed to the leg of th chair and his right hand was secured to an adjacer chair. Majid was careful nonetheless to keep the gu aimed at his captive's chest as he reached out and handed him the portable house phone.

"Call in to check that everything is OK. When they ask how you are, say you're still feeling terrible. You're going to try and get some sleep, but first you just wanted to make sure that all was well. Assuming they tell you that everything is fine, say you won't talk to them again today, that you know they'll be busy and you don't feel well. Got that?"

"Yes."

"I'll be following every word. So no warnings, no hints – keep your grandchildren in mind if you're tempted." Majid could see again the anger in Thompson's eyes, but he ignored it and indicated the phone. "Ring now."

Thompson lifted the phone and pressed a quick-dial button. Majid rose and moved behind him, placing the silenced barrel of the Beretta against the back of the policeman's head and drawing his own head near to Thompson's so that he could hear both sides of the telephone conversation. He heard the phone ringing twice, then it was answered.

"Hello? Command room."

"Penny?" asked Thompson.

"Chief, how are you?"

"Pretty awful, I'm afraid."

"I'm sorry to hear that. No joy with the medication?"

"It takes a while to kick in. Listen, I'm going to try and get some sleep, but first I wanted to be sure that everything was all right."

"Everything is fine here, Chief – don't be worrying yourself."

479

"Right."

"All the safeguards have been implemented, Superintendent Kelch is following all your guidelines, we're still continuing the manhunt, still calling door-to-door. Everything is in hand."

"Good. Especially the door-to-door – calling to people's homes is important –"

Majid quickly cut Thompson short by jamming the gun into the back of his head.

"Chief, are you OK?" asked Penny, hearing Thompson's intake of breath.

Majid angrily swung Thompson around and brandished the gun warningly, then silently indicated for the policeman to continue.

"Eh . . . yes . . . just a cramp, sorry, Penny."

Majid mouthed the words 'You'll ring again in the morning'.

"Look, I won't ring again till tomorrow morning, Penny. Don't want to be bothering you later when you're busy."

"No problem at all, Chief. You look after yourself, everything is under control here."

"Fine. Remember corporal work number six. Talk to you then. Bye."

Thompson quickly hung up, and the moment he did Majid angrily grabbed him by the lapel. "I told you not to try any hints!"

"I didn't."

"*Calling to people's home is important*?!"

"We've been doing a door-to-door search. It was one of the main ways we hope to track you down. Not to have referred to it would have been really suspicious."

Majid stared hard at Thompson. The policeman had the look of one telling the truth, yet Majid's instinct was that the other man was trying to outmanoeuvre him. "I told you what you were supposed to say! What was the reference to 'corporal work number six'?"

"It's just a police saying."

"Meaning what?"

"A corporal is a low rank, the lowest there is above a constable. The two jobs they get landed with that everyone hates are paperwork and pounding the beat. Police paperwork entails five different filing systems – corporal works one to five. Anything involving lots of legwork – like calling door-to-door with the photos of you – is corporal work number six. It's as simple as that."

Again Majid was unsure whether or not to believe him.

"Let me ask you a question," said Thompson.

"What?"

"Why are you targeting this conference?"

"I don't have to explain myself to you."

"I know you don't," said Thompson, his tone reasonable. "Look, I'm captive here, so what you're going to do, you're going to do. But I'd really like to know what you hope to achieve, just supposing you *did* get to attack a group of Foreign Ministers. Or is it the US Secretary of State – is that the real target?"

"*Just supposing I do get to attack?*" Majid shook his head. "Your arrogance is so typical. There's no supposing. I *am* going to attack. And they're *all* targets."

"But why?"

"I wouldn't expect you to understand."

"Try me."

"Because they're the enemy."

"*All* of them?"

"Yes. When it comes to attacking us, Western countries will always band together."

Thompson looked at Majid quizzically. "*Us*, as in . . .?"

"Iraq of course! You all banded together against us. Along with your puppet Arab regimes."

"You're talking about the Gulf War?"

"What else?"

"But that was . . . nine years ago?"

"And we're to forget it because it was nine years ago? Over fifty years later the Jews still go on about the Holocaust. But our loss doesn't matter, our lives don't count," said Majid, his anger mounting. "It doesn't matter that civilians were bombed to pieces in Baghdad, and Iraqi troops slaughtered without mercy on the road to Basra! We're just to forget that, are we?!" Majid stopped himself, realising that he had allowed himself to become emotional. He saw Thompson looking at him closely, then the Englishman spoke softly.

"Obviously you lost loved ones, and I can understand –"

"You can't *begin* to understand! I lost my entire family – *my entire family*!"

Thompson nodded as though absorbing this, then he looked at Majid again. "I'm sorry you lost your family –" he began.

"*But*," said Majid disdainfully, "there's going to be a 'but', isn't there?"

"Yes," said Thompson. "On a personal level I'm sorry, but I can't be sorry we stood up for Kuwait."

"*Kuwait*? Don't make me laugh!"

"No state should be invaded like Kuwait was."

"Kuwait was never a state," snapped Majid. "It was a region of Iraq until the West turned it into a phoney little country. And don't insult my intelligence by saying the West would ever have defended it but for the oil. The whole war was about oil. Oil and commerce and power."

"It wasn't only about oil," said Thompson.

"No, it was also about resenting a Gulf nation emerging as a power. I've spent enough time in the West to know your arrogance. You couldn't bear the idea of a state like Iraq emerging as a power like France or Britain."

"That wasn't it."

"Don't deny your sense of superiority. It's in every move you people make. Well, it's time you learnt a lesson, Mr High-and-Mighty Thompson. How do you feel about begging for your life? How do you feel about begging to a *wog*, a *dago*, a *towel-head*? That's what you call us behind our backs, isn't it? So let's hear you begging a greasy wog for your life!"

Thompson said nothing and Majid levelled the Beretta at him.

"I don't think you're taking me seriously," he said.

"I've never in my life called anyone a wog, a dago or a towel-head," answered Thompson.

"How liberal you are now your life's on the line!"

"It's the simple truth."

"Beg anyway."

Thompson remained unmoving, and Majid brandished the gun. "Do it if you know what's good for you. Beg, policeman!"

Thompson shook his head, then spoke quietly. "Between the army and the police force I've been fighting wars of one kind or another for over forty years. I've shown mercy to opponents and sometimes had it shown to me. But I've never begged for it or asked any man to beg me."

"And your family. Are you too proud to beg for their lives?"

"I love them dearly, and I've already betrayed my professional calling to try and protect them. But I won't do anything further. My family are non-combatants. Either you're man enough to respect that or you're not. As for myself, I want to live –"

"But your pride won't let you beg for mercy?"

"I'm asking you not to kill anyone. It won't undo your loss or achieve any purpose."

"So you're asking me to be merciful?"

"Yes."

"But not begging?"

"I won't beg any man."

"Even if it costs you your life?"

Thompson looked Majid straight in the eye. "If you think it's honourable to murder a prisoner because he won't beg, then that's your call."

Majid held his gaze for a moment, then looked away,

impressed despite himself by the other man's demeanour. He reflected for a moment, then turned back to Thompson. "I can admire courage in an enemy. But letting you live would put me at risk. So I'm afraid, Mr Thompson, you're something of a problem . . ."

19

September sunshine lit the Yorkshire Dales in an early afternoon glow as Tamaz Akmedov drove up the curving driveway to the cottage in Blubberhouses, following the directions Majid had given by phone.

As Tamaz drove around to the back and parked out of sight of the main road, Majid made for the kitchen and the rear door of the house. He opened the kitchen door and was struck by the sweet fragrance from the rose garden, but he ignored the late flowering roses and instead looked closely at the other man's face as he emerged from the vehicle. *Anxious but not spooked*, Majid reckoned, then he smiled reassuringly and approached him. "Tamaz."

"Abdullah."

"No problems getting here?"

"Two checkpoints leaving Harrogate."

"They didn't check the boot at either, I presume," said Majid.

"No. But on the way back yesterday I saw them checking the boot of another car."

Majid considered this briefly, then nodded. "Once it's only spot checks we should be fine," he answered confidently, knowing it was vital to keep Tamaz in a positive frame of mind.

"Let's hope so . . ."

Time to change the subject, Majid decided. "Would you like something to eat before we go back?" he asked, knowing that they had plenty of time, with Tamaz not due in work until five o'clock.

"No, thanks," answered Tamaz. "But if you want to have something . . ."

"That's all right, I've already eaten." In fact after his confrontation with Thompson he had gone to the trouble of cooking himself a full meal. He hadn't really had the appetite for it, but he knew it would be his last opportunity to have a proper meal before going into action that evening and, wanting to have plenty of energy for what lay ahead, he had made himself consume it all.

"So, eh . . . you got what you needed here?" asked Tamaz tentatively.

"Yes, I did. Everything is fine. Let me just get my jacket, then we'll go."

Tamaz looked like he might be going to question Majid further, then instead he nodded. "OK."

Majid stepped back into the kitchen and retrieved the Beretta and his jacket. He looked over towards Thompson's bedroom and paused briefly, then he turned on his heel and left the house again via the kitchen door. Tamaz already had the boot open for him with the sleeping bag spread out, but instead of getting

in immediately Majid went to the other man. "I just
want to say, Tamaz, you've done really well. I'm proud
of you."

"Oh . . . well . . . thank you . . ."

"You've done the smart thing, you've been brave,
and you've stayed cool. Just keep it up, then this time
tomorrow it'll be all over and we'll be sailing home.
OK?"

"Yes, OK . . ."

"Right then. Let's get back to Harrogate and do
what we came for . . ."

At half past four the hospital's surface carpark was
about three-quarters full, and with the usual toing and
froing of ambulances, taxis and cars, no heed was paid
to the middle-aged man who parked his car, discreetly
slid the keys under the driver's seat, then walked away.

In reality though Tamaz Akmedov felt anything but
calm as he made his way across the carpark without
looking back. His heart was pounding and he couldn't
help but feel vulnerable and highly visible as he made
for the exit on foot. The logical side of his brain told him
that the sense of exposure was all in his head, that no-
one had looked twice at him, but another part of his
mind couldn't ignore the fact that he had just left in
position the getaway vehicle for tonight's operation.

Following Majid's instructions he had made sure
that the fuel tank was full, that all the tyres were at the
correct pressure, including the spare, and that there was
a working flashlight, jack and wheel brace in the boot.
The car had been serviced only a month previously and

always started first time, so there seemed little to worry about on the mechanical front. Tamaz however was far more worried about the innumerable other things that could go wrong during tonight's operation. Any single one of them could spell disaster, he knew, in which case having a getaway vehicle would be academic.

Now as he reached the hospital exit on Lancaster Park Road, he resolved to follow Majid's dictum and to think more positively. He turned left, consciously keeping his pace unhurried as he made for work. He wasn't due on duty at the Conference Centre until five o'clock so he had almost half an hour to cross town. He made for the Knaresborough Road, but despite his resolution to be positive and the therapeutic value of walking at a moderate pace, he still found it hard to dampen his nervousness.

Inside his trousers pocket he fingered a beta-blocker tablet that Majid had given him when they had arrived safely back in the warehouse premises in Harrogate. The beta-blocker was to lower the heart-rate and induce a feeling of greater calmness, and Tamaz had followed Majid's instruction to keep it until a couple of hours before they planned to make their move. Tamaz's heart had been racing however since approaching the hospital carpark, and despite having walked away from the hospital without incident Tamaz could still feel the palpitations in his heart. He was tempted to take the tablet right now, so that he would be more relaxed when he arrived at the Conference Centre. That way nobody was likely to think he was on edge, he reasoned. Then again maybe by taking it now the tablet would wear off too soon, in which case he wouldn't have the maximum benefit just when he needed it most later on.

No, better to stick to Majid's plan. He pushed the tablet down to the bottom of his pocket, forced himself to breathe out deeply as he walked along, and continued on his journey to the Conference Centre.

"I don't want to ring the Chief back when he's sick," said Penny, "especially when he said he'd ring in tomorrow."

"Sure," agreed Laura.

"But I'm curious about what he meant."

"What exactly did he say?" asked Laura.

Penny pushed her dinner plate aside as she strove to recall Thompson's exact words. She was finishing a meal in a room in the Conference Centre that had been set aside for the use of security personnel. It was six in the evening now and Penny had suggested to Laura that they should avail of the opportunity to eat before the next flurry of activity that would occur in the lead-up to the Foreign Ministers' dinner, scheduled for eight o'clock. Now she turned to the journalist, having thought again about the lunch-time telephone exchange with Thompson. "I remember telling him to look after himself, that everything was in hand here."

"Right."

"He said 'good' or 'fine', something like that. Then he said 'remember corporal work number six'. Before I could ask him what he meant he finished up quickly. Said 'Talk to you then', said goodbye and hung up. We were so busy this afternoon I didn't really have time to think about it."

"I'll vouch for that," said Laura with a smile, referring to the hectic afternoon they had all had, centred around the US Secretary of State's arrival at the Conference Centre to address the assembled Foreign Ministers.

"Now though I'm kind of curious," said Penny.

"Could it be a reference to the Corporal Works of Mercy?" asked Laura.

"What are they?"

"You're not a Catholic then?"

"No, Anglican," answered Penny, "and lukewarm at that. Why?"

"The Catholic Church used to list a series of fairly archaic good deeds that were called the Corporal Works of Mercy."

"Can you remember what they were?"

"This is really bringing me back," said Laura, then she closed her eyes as she concentrated. "Feeding the hungry, giving drinks to the thirsty, clothing the naked . . ."

"Archaic is right," said Penny with a grin.

"I know. Then there was visiting the imprisoned . . . what came next? Oh, yeah, sheltering the homeless . . . then . . . visiting the sick, and burying the dead. That's it, there were seven."

"So visiting the sick would have been number six?"

"Yes."

Penny stroked her chin distractedly as she considered her boss's comment.

"Is Mr Thompson a Catholic?" asked Laura.

"As a matter of fact he is."

"Maybe it was a roundabout way of saying he'd like you to call out to him," suggested Laura.

"But he'd insisted earlier he wanted no visitors. If he'd changed his mind why not say so? I'd have been happy to drive out to Blubberhouses when I came off duty."

"Well, you know him better than me, Penny . . ."

"He's normally very direct. Hints and allusions aren't usually his style."

"You could give him a ring."

Penny grimaced. "I'd hate to wake him if he's sleeping now . . ."

"Right."

"On the other hand maybe I should just give him a quick buzz. I don't know. I'll think about it . . ."

"Penny, Laura," said Mathieson, who now approached with a tray on which he carried his dinner. "May I join you?"

"Sure," said Laura.

"Though we're just about finished," added Penny.

"Then I'd better savour whatever moments are left to us," said Mathieson lightly as he joined them at the table.

Although the words were said jokingly, Penny felt slightly uncomfortable. She had told Laura about her one-time affair with Mathieson, and Laura had said that she felt the intelligence officer still carried something of a torch for her. Penny hadn't wanted it to be true, yet once or twice when she had been alone with Mathieson she had felt that maybe – just maybe – there was something in what Laura claimed.

"That was some afternoon," said Mathieson.

"Yes. Went pretty smoothly in the end though," said Penny, glad that the conversation had taken on a more business-like air.

"Yes, it did rather. Pity we haven't nabbed this Majid while we're at it – then it would really be a good show."

"Maybe we'll get him yet," said Penny.

"Let me guess," said Carrow who had approached unseen from behind Laura and Penny, a heavily laden tray in his hands. "You're still hoping our villain will conveniently appear for you to capture him?"

Penny felt a stab of irritation, but she made an effort to respond politely. "I'm hoping a dangerous criminal can be apprehended, yes."

"Very conscientious of you, I'm sure," said Carrow with a sarcastic smile as he laid down his tray and sat beside Mathieson.

Penny felt her irritation growing both at the snide comment and at Carrow's presumptuousness in joining them uninvited, but before she could say anything Carrow turned away from her and asked Mathieson a question about the American security contingent. Penny decided to let it go and turned to Laura.

"Fancy a desert?"

"No, thanks, I'm really full."

"Yeah, think I might skip it myself," said Penny.

"Watching our figure, are we?" said Carrow.

This time Penny's patience snapped and she looked the Special Branch man in the eye. "Actually that's no business whatsoever of yours, Mr Carrow."

"Don't be so bloody touchy!"

"I'm not touchy. But I am choosy whom I dine with. Excuse me, Colin." Penny rose and stood back from the table. She was gratified by the look of anger on Carrow's face and by the solidarity of Laura who immediately rose beside her and said 'See you later' to Mathieson, while studiously ignoring Carrow. Penny turned on her heel and the two women walked towards the door.

"Nice one," said Laura.

Penny smiled back at the journalist, though in fact her emotions were considerably mixed. Although glad that she had put Carrow in his place, she simultaneously felt annoyed that it had been necessary, and behind both those emotions was her unsatisfied curiosity about what message Thompson had been sending her earlier.

"So what do we do now?" asked Laura as they passed out the door and into the corridor.

Penny stopped, breathed out, and turned to Laura. "We put idiots like Carrow from our minds – and go back to work mode . . ."

Majid studied his altered appearance in the mirror, then nodded approvingly. It was seven thirty now and he had spent the last hour changing how he looked. He had set up a mirror in the warehouse office, spread his equipment on the table before him and gone painstakingly to work. Although it was a good many years since he had been trained in disguise technique his tutors had taught him well, and he had approached his task with quiet confidence.

The first thing he had dealt with was his thick dark hair. Using a home hair-cutting kit that he had bought in a supermarket, he shortened and thinned out his hair considerably. When satisfied that it was of a sufficient length to be visible still at the back under the cap he would be wearing, he dyed his hair and his sideboards grey. The short grey hair immediately made him look older, and when he applied gum spirit to his upper lip and gave himself a grey moustache he was rewarded by a considerable change in his overall appearance. He used a stick of white foundation make-up on his face and hands to lighten his skin-tone a little then inserted rubber padding into his mouth. The padding altered the shape of his face, making him appear older and more heavily jowled, but with suitable adjustment he was able to ensure that his speech wasn't affected. The final piece of his disguise was a pair of spectacles with wide plastic frames. Although the lens were only plain glass they were large and thickly cut and they contributed even further to making him look like a different and older person.

The final look was significantly different to the youthful-looking, dark-haired Iraqi that Majid knew would feature in the mug-shots provided by the Israelis, though he also knew that a careful study of his features could still prove a problem. In practice, though, he was hopeful that such an examination wouldn't arise and that the uniform he had changed into would be his passport into the Conference Centre. He hadn't forgotten one of his first lessons in how to avoid being conspicuous, in which he had been taught

495

that a uniform can make its wearer invisible, with people seeing a postman, or a fireman, or whatever, rather than noticing the individual.

The uniform he wore now was a good fit and Majid slipped on the cap then looked at himself again in the mirror. The transformation was good – not absolute, admittedly – but good nonetheless and he felt quietly confident that his plan was going to work. He glanced out into the warehouse and saw the vehicle that he had smuggled in from Ireland in the back of the truck. It was finally about to be used. Like the getaway car that Tamaz had parked, this vehicle also had a full fuel tank, correctly inflated tyres and an engine that started first time every time.

Majid looked at his watch. 19.32. A little over an hour to go. And then, at last, he would make his assault.

Penny watched Laura approaching with two polystyrene cups of coffee, then nodded her thanks as the journalist handed one to her. They stood together in the corridor of the Conference Centre and Laura reached out and tipped a nearby doorframe.

"Touch wood and all that, but so far so good," said Laura.

"Yeah . . ."

It was almost a quarter to nine now and the dinner for the Foreign Ministers and the US Secretary of State had begun in the nearby private dining-room at eight o'clock. Although there had been no progress throughout the day in tracking down Abdullah Majid, neither had there been any sort of assault bid on the part of the terrorist.

"I think I know what you're thinking," said Laura.

"Really?"

"It's disappointing in one way that Majid hasn't shown – kind of anti-climax, yeah?"

"Touch of that, I suppose," admitted Penny. "Though it would be premature to pat ourselves on the back just now – there's still tomorrow's conference."

"There is," conceded Laura, "but the US Secretary of State will be gone then. My gut feeling is that if Majid was going to try something, he couldn't resist such a plum target."

"You could be right."

"I really thought he'd try something today – or maybe this evening."

"Perhaps we all read him wrong," said Penny. "Maybe he threw in the towel in the face of overwhelming odds."

"So . . . '"anti-climactic, but relieved,"says senior policewoman'," intoned Laura in mock-dramatic style.

Penny smiled. "Just 'relieved', if it's going in the newspapers. And talking of relieved, I'm going to pop round to the loo."

"OK."

Penny walked down the corridor, then turned left and made for the door of the ladies'. She entered the toilets and heard a lush instrumental version of the love theme from *Titanic* coming from the wall speakers. It was a song Shane really hated, and she found herself smiling, but her moment of good humour didn't last. She paused in the empty toilets, trying to analyse the cause of her unease. For despite what she had said to Laura about being relieved, she did feel a certain unease. Perhaps it was the unresolved matter of Thompson's cryptic telephone comment – whose resolution, she had decided, didn' warrant disturbing a sick man – or perhaps it was th niggling feeling that it was out of character for Abdulla

Majid to have backed off. Or perhaps she was just tired after a hard week and was worrying over nothing. She couldn't quite make up her mind. After a moment she decided to stop fretting about it, shrugged philosophically and crossed to the nearest cubicle.

The ambulance drove over the railway bridge on the Skipton Road, then turned left and continued at a brisk pace along Grove Road. Majid sat behind the wheel in his para-medics uniform, his pulses racing but his mind focused on what lay ahead. Already his disguise had passed muster at a roadblock out on the Knaresborough road and it had given his confidence a boost. The ambulance that the two maverick IRA men had acquired for him in Northern Ireland was exactly the same type as those used here in Yorkshire, and Majid had stencilled the appropriate new lettering on the side and rear of the vehicle. The upshot had been that he was waved through the checkpoint without even being stopped.

Majid knew that it would be a different matter when he encountered the security cordon around the Conference Centre, but that too could be overcome if everything went to plan. He knew that Grove Road would bring him out onto Kings Road, north of the Conference Centre, and he had chosen the circuitous route deliberately, anxious as he was to avoid the centre of Harrogate. No point going through any more checkpoints than necessary, he had reasoned, and now as the ambulance approached the junction of Grove Road and Kings Road he turned left, then glanced at his watch. 20.44 – one minute to go.

Earlier he had synchronised his watch with that of Tamaz so that they could both go into action at precisely the same moment. The plan was that at 20.45 Tamaz would make sure to be in the private dining-room with the Foreign Ministers and the US Secretary of State. He would than collapse, simulating a heart attack. Almost certainly a seriously ill Tamaz wouldn't be moved from the room until medical assistance was forthcoming, and Majid, aware of exactly when the waiter was going to collapse, would be sure to arrive, siren blaring, within a minute or two.

Majid slowed down, then pulled in to the side of Kings Road. Just in case anyone might be observing, he pretended to go through some paperwork that he had in the cabin of the vehicle, but he couldn't stop himself from glancing at his watch. Months of careful preparation had led to this point yet within the next ten minutes a series of imponderables would determine whether he pulled off the most spectacular of assassinations or whether the mission failed. His heart was pounding and his mouth felt dry, but he knew that sort of nervousness was normal. And in spite of all the precautions the authorities had taken he still felt confident, still felt that the odds favoured his succeeding.

He glanced at his watch once again, then suddenly the alarm went off. He immediately pressed the button to switch off the alarm, then turned on his siren, gunned the engine and sped down Kings Road towards the Conference Centre.

Tamaz lay sprawled on the polished wooden floor of

the private dining-room. A shattered wine bottle was in smithereens nearby, where he had dropped it, apparently wracked by a spasm of chest pain while serving the dignitaries at the Foreign Ministers' dinner. Tamaz had then slumped to the ground, where he now lay surrounded by waiters and guests. He felt his head being raised as someone tried to make him more comfortable with a makeshift pillow and he cried aloud and grimaced as though suffering another searing spasm of pain.

He had been told the symptoms to exhibit and had rehearsed exactly how to behave with Majid, whose one-time training as a medical student had ensured a suitably realistic response. Majid had made him practise over and over until the performance was entirely convincing, and from the activity around him now Tamaz could tell that no-one had any doubts but that he was seriously ill.

"Chief Superintendent Carrow! Make way please!"

Tamaz heard the instruction, then saw the surrounding group parting for a heavy-set man in his late fifties with receding ginger hair. The man wore a dress suit despite his police rank and, having glimpsed him, Tamaz let his head fall back and closed his eyes, then felt someone feeling for his pulse.

"Pulse seems strong," said the man.

Tamaz opened his eyes again and saw it was the ginger-haired man who had introduced himself as Carrow. Tamaz looked at him and spoke haltingly. "What's . . . what's happening?"

"You'll be all right," said Carrow, then turned back

to the gathered waiters. "Has anyone called for an ambulance?"

"Doing it now, sir," answered a voice that Tamaz recognised as that of the head waiter.

"Tell them to make it snappy!"

"Am I . . . what's . . . what's going on?" said Tamaz.

"You're all right," said Carrow consolingly. "Everything's going to be fine."

Let's hope so, thought Tamaz then he closed his eyes and grimaced again.

Majid brought the ambulance screeching to a halt at the checkpoint on Kings Road, killing the siren but leaving the light flashing.

"Where's the emergency?" asked the nearest of two uniformed policemen manning the barrier, as Majid quickly rolled down the window.

"Conference Centre – cardiac arrest!" he answered, keeping his voice urgent-sounding. He noted that both officers carried Heckler and Koch machine-guns, but neither of them had raised a weapon, obviously taking the presence of the ambulance at face value.

"The Conference Centre?"

"Yes, I have clearance. Code-word *Othello*." Majid's pulses were racing, but his confidence was boosted by the fact that neither policeman had paid any attention to his altered appearance. Clearly they saw before them an ambulance driver in a hurry, which was exactly what he had been hoping for. "Can you ring ahead and tell them I'm coming? I need to get to the patient as quickly as possible."

"Right . . ." answered the first policeman.

"Thank you!"

Before the man could say anything further Majid let off the handbrake and flicked on the siren again. He put his hand on the gear-stick as though there was no doubt but that the barrier was about to be raised immediately, and was rewarded with hearing the first officer shout to his companion: "Lift the beam!"

The second policeman nodded, and Majid revved the engine as the barrier began to rise.

Laura stood alone in the Conference Centre corridor, awaiting Penny's return from the toilets. She looked about her, comforted by the level of security. In addition to armed police at checkpoints on all roads leading to the centre, there were uniformed officers carrying machine-guns here in the corridor and more discreetly armed plainclothes officers from the security services outside the doors leading to the private dining-room.

The dinner for the US Secretary of State and the EU Foreign Ministers was an intimate affair with only about fifty guests, and Mathieson had explained to Laura that armed security agents posted about the dining-room would have been deemed intrusive. Nonetheless the Americans had insisted on close protection for the Secretary of State, despite all the other security measures, and it had been agreed that an American agent would sit at the Secretary of State's table, blending in with the other male guests by dressing in a tuxedo. Unwilling to have a foreign agent as the only one seated among the guests, the British hosts had decided that they too would insert someone and it had been agreed that it should be a senior officer. Mathieson however had his hands full liaising with the heads of all the different security services, and Laura had been quietly amused by Carrow's obvious satisfaction when he had managed to appropriate the task to himself.

Now as she stood in the corridor she was struck by an unexpected sound. She cocked her ear, realising that it was the sound of an approaching siren. She frowned in puzzlement, then looked down the corridor towards the reception area and the entrance doors, wondering what was going on.

Tamaz breathed shallowly and noisily as he lay on the floor of the private dining-room. The dinner had come to a complete halt, as planned, with most of the waiting staff and a good number of the diplomats and their aides gathered solicitously around him. He had heard the man who had called himself Chief Superintendent Carrow talking by radio to what he referred to as Gold Command. From what Tamaz could hear of the conversation, it seemed that an Assistant Commissioner Kelch was discussing restoring normality to the dining-room, with the suggestion that Tamaz might be removed while awaiting the ambulance.

This was the one thing that Tamaz knew mustn't be allowed to happen. Without his presence in the dining-room the whole plan fell apart, and Majid had given him precise instructions of what do in the event of anyone trying to move him. He saw Carrow beginning to bend down towards him now and he closed his eyes and clutched his chest as though racked by another spasm of pain.

"Perhaps we could make him more comfortable outside – while we wait for the ambulance," he heard Carrow say.

Tamaz grimaced again in apparent agony, holding his chest and groaning loudly.

"I really don't think we should move him, sir," Tamaz heard the head waiter respond. "It might make things worse. The ambulance won't be long."

Tamaz groaned again, then gripped the ginger-haired policeman's arm and reverted to fast shallow breathing.

"Yes . . . yes, maybe you're right," said Carrow.

Tamaz felt a surge of relief, but he kept up his grip on the policeman's arm and lay back on the makeshift pillow, groaning softly.

Majid pulled to a halt at the barrier on the driveway of the Conference Centre's main entrance. Once again he switched off the siren, but left the lights flashing as uniformed police officers armed with machine-guns approached the driver's door. He had left the window rolled down to save time and he immediately called to the approaching officers: "Code-word *Othello*, can you lift the barrier, please?"

"Just confirming the emergency," said the policeman, indicating one of his partners who was speaking into a walkie-talkie.

"There's a heart attack victim inside, it's really urgent," said Majid.

"Hang on a tick," said the policeman who quickly crossed to the officer using the walkie-talkie. The second man spoke into the walkie-talkie, then turned to his partner and said something that Majid couldn't hear.

Majid swallowed hard, knowing that this was the crunch moment. All his hopes were pinned on the emphasis being placed on the ambulance, and its access to the centre. By immediately quoting the correct code-word he felt that he had deflected attention away from himself. Any second now he would know if it was going to work, he thought nervously.

Before he could agonise any further the first officer came back to the ambulance, his machine-gun still cradled in an apparently casual fashion. "OK, you can drive right up to the door. We'll accompany you inside to explain you've been cleared."

Majid felt a surge of exultation, but confined himself to a quick nod. "Good," he said briskly. "Let's get there as quickly as possible."

Even as he spoke the barrier was raised and he immediately drove the short distance to the entrance door, two armed police officers from the barricade following immediately behind on foot. As he waited for them to join him he swiftly reversed the ambulance so that the stretcher-trolley could be wheeled straight out the back of the vehicle, then he turned off the flashing lights and switched off the ignition. He jumped out of the cab, ran around and opened the rear door just as the two policemen arrived at the entrance. Majid began to organise the trolley and his bag of emergency medical supplies as from the corner of his eye he saw th policemen explaining the situation to the other security personnel who had emerged from the reception area of the centre.

He was going to get away with this – it was going to work. He hoisted the bag, then quickly rolled the trolley down the ramp.

"Where's your partner?"

"Rang in sick. Bloody stomach bug," answered Majid without pausing.

"Right . . ." said the policeman,

Majid moved forward, determined not the pursue this line of conversation. "Let's go," he said, then he gripped the trolley and made for the doors of the Conference Centre.

Her curiosity aroused by the siren, Laura walked down the corridor towards reception. She could see a commotion ahead, then a group of armed police officers came towards her at a trot, flanking a paramedic who ran pushing an ambulance trolley.

"Emergency! Clear the way please!" cried the leading officer, and Laura immediately stood back against the wall to let them pass.

The corridor led directly to the heavily guarded doors of the private dining-room, and Laura wondered what could have gone wrong at the Foreign Ministers' meal. Presumably someone had to have taken ill – if there had been any kind of attack she would surely have heard shots or an explosion, notwithstanding the sealed-off room and the heavy teak doors. Distracted by the thought she stood flush with the wall as the trolley rattled past, escorted by the uniformed officers. She glanced across as they ran by, only glimpsing the grey-haired ambulance man who steered the trolley while flanked by his escorts.

She watched with curiosity as they continued along the corridor. Her reporter's instinct was to follow them, but she knew that without Penny she would never be allowed into the private dining-room. As she watched the departing group she was suddenly struck with a feeling of déjà vu. For a second she couldn't place it, then it hit home and her heartbeat accelerated. She looked again at the departing group, but all that she could see of the para-medic was a diminishing rear view. He seemed to have the short grey hair of an older man under the cap of his uniform. And yet . . . a particular movement she had caught when he was going down the corridor brought her back to her room in the Old Swan hotel. The movement was exactly similar to the way Abdullah Majid had moved when he had retrieved her file from the dressing-room table.

She swallowed hard, wondering if she was imagining things in her eagerness for a dramatic end to the conference story. After all, Majid was young and had longish, thick black hair. The paramedic had come across, in the glimpse she had, as being older and had short grey hair. Then again hair could be cut and dyed. And he had moved in exactly the same manner as he attacker, whose movements she would never forget. She tried to be logical, arguing to herself that it could be a simple coincidence that someone else had moved in way that reminded her of Majid. Except that as reporter she had been taught not to believe in coincidences . . .

She hesitated a moment, reluctant to make a fool of herself. Then unable not to act, she started down the corridor.

Majid slowed down as the trolley reached the door to the dining-room. Seeing the journalist from the Old Swan had given him a bad scare, but he had shielded himself with the policemen as they ran past. For a second or two he had feared that she might call out after him, but nothing had happened and, thanks to the disguise and having shielded himself from her, he reckoned a potential catastrophe had been averted.

Now though he had to get past the final significant barrier of the security presence at the dining-room door. The policemen who had escorted him were talking animatedly with the security detail on the door and Majid proffered his ambulance driver ID card as one of the security officers approached him. "Saeed Guptar, access code-word *Othello*," he said, anxious to provide some degree of distraction as the man studied his face. The photograph had been taken the previous April when he had cut his hair short and disguised himself exactly as he was disguised now. The man looked at the ID card, then at Majid. *Don't avoid his eye, don't look nervous, but don't look at him challengingly either*, Majid told himself as he tried to maintain the air of a paramedic in a hurry, but who understood also the security needs of others.

"That's fine," said the man, handing back the card,

"but I need to frisk you." He approached Majid and began to pat him down professionally, starting at his shoulders and working downwards.

Majid had deliberated about bringing the Beretta with him. It wasn't strictly necessary, he knew, and if his main weapon worked as planned there would be no need for a gun. Yet he hated the idea of not having any firearm to hand during a mission. In the end, he had opted to bring the silenced weapon. Fortunately he had anticipated that even in the medical-emergency scenario he was still likely to be personally searched, and so he had attached the gun to the underside of the trolley with masking tape, then cellotaped a sheet of white paper over it. Only a thorough search would unearth it, and Majid had gambled that with his ID and code-word in order, and with an apparently genuine medical emergency to hand, there wasn't likely to be much checking of the ambulance equipment.

"Can you open the bag, please?" said the security man, indicating the black nylon container in which portable oxygen cylinders, a face mask, syringes and other emergency equipment were kept.

"Of course," answered Majid, trying hard to keep the anxiety out of his voice, yet seeking to project a sense of urgency, "but I do need to get to the patient urgently – it's a heart attack."

"I know that," said the officer as he looked among the contents of the bag. He went through them quickly then looked at Majid. "OK, you can go through."

"Thank you," said Majid, hoping the relief didn't show in his tone. He placed the emergency bag on to of the trolley, swung the trolley round as the security detail pulled the heavy doors outwards, then pushed it forward and entered the private dining-room.

Penny looked round in surprise as Laura rushed into the ladies' toilet. She had been applying lip-gloss in front of the mirror, but she immediately forgot the cosmetics on seeing the journalist's face. "What's up?"

"The driver of the ambulance, Penny. I think maybe –"

"What ambulance?"

Laura looked surprised. "Didn't you hear the siren?"

Penny indicated the wall speakers. "Piped music and closed doors – I heard nothing. Where's this ambulance?"

"Right outside. Someone took ill in the private dining-room."

"Yeah?"

"Penny – I think I saw Abdullah Majid."

"What?!"

"The ambulance driver ran down the corridor. He was surrounded by policemen, but –"

"You think he was Majid?!"

"I can't be certain, Penny – I only glimpsed him from behind. But I think . . . I think it may have been."

"Oh, Christ!"

"I could be wrong –"

"And he's made for the private dining-room?"

"Yes. That's if it *is* actually him . . ."

But Penny was already making for the door, the Glock in her hand. "Let's find out!"

"Careful – gently does it," said Majid as an assortment

of waiters and diplomats helped him to hoist Tamaz onto the trolley. In spite of the need to show concern for his patient, however, Majid found it hard to suppress his excitement. Exhilaration and satisfaction vied for precedence in his emotions now that he had successfully made the critical move that would mean death for so many of the overfed Western diplomats gathered here tonight.

A Trojan Horse variation had been the premise on which he had counted since beginning his planning the previous February and now he had successfully introduced his lethal Trojan horse without his victims realising it. When in prison in Israel he had once met an amateur magician, and the man had explained to him the vital importance of focussing the attention of the audience. The key moment in any trick was when you focused their attention on something that seemed important but actually wasn't, thus keeping their attention away from where you didn't want them to watch. It had formed the basis of Majid's plan, and with the confusion and trauma of Tamaz's life apparently being in danger there had been enough movement and activity for Majid's critical move not to appear significant.

He had rushed over to Tamaz on entering the room and after a quick examination had pretended to give him a thrombolytic injection. Immediately afterwards he had slipped an oxygen mask onto the fallen waiter and attached it to one of the two cylinders from his emergency bag. To his apparent chagrin the cylinder had registered empty just as Tamaz had gone into another spasm of pain, and Majid had quickly put the cylinder aside behind one of the chairs that had been pushed back to make space around the fallen waiter, then attached the mask to the reserve cylinder, which worked perfectly. It was a move whose timing they had rehearsed thoroughly, and Majid reckoned that those surrounding them would have had their attention fixed on the patient in spasm with little attention paid to the discarded cylinder.

Majid knew then that what he had to do was maintain the sense of crisis around the well-being of Tamaz, so that he could swiftly vacate the room and rush his accomplice to the waiting ambulance before anyone remembered the first cylinder. After that very little time would be required to get Tamaz into the ambulance and to speed sway towards the hospital and the getaway car left there by Tamaz, while back in the dining-room death would – literally – be in the air. For the cylinder, collected from the ship in Hull by Majid and Jemail Zubi, contained Sarin, the highly toxic nerve agent used in the Tokyo subway attack.

During that assault twelve people had been killed and over five thousand injured when a liquid form of the lethal gas was delivered via lunch boxes and punctured soft drinks containers. Majid's delivery system was more sophisticated, with a small explosive enclosed in the false bottom of the cylinder. Once past the police checkpoint on Kings Road, Majid planned to trigger the charge by remote control, thus exploding the cylinder and showering the dignitaries in the private dining-room with vaporised Sarin.

First though it was essential that the attention remained on Tamaz and away from the discarded cylinder so that a successful exit could be made. And now, right on cue, Tamaz began to groan loudly behind the oxygen mask as soon as the helpers laid him on the trolley. The cries of pain held the attention of all those gathered around. *Right,* thought Majid, as he quickly strapped the restraining belt across the waiter's chest, *time to go.*

Laura and Penny entered the dining-room unobtrusively. Penny had slipped the Glock into her pocket when Laura had emphasised again that she wasn't sure about the ambulance man being Majid, and that it could be really embarrassing to alert the security detail outside the dining-room door only to have them storm in amongst the Foreign Ministers and apprehend an innocent paramedic.

Laura had been relieved when Penny took her point, and she was impressed at how quickly the policewoman thought on her toes. They had still made their way briskly towards the dining-room, but instead of alerting the agents at the door Penny had claimed to need to speak to Carrow about the medical emergency. Laura had half-expected that the security detail might object to her accompanying Penny into the dining-room, but Penny had been so central to all security planning, and the police and MI5 contingents had become so used to seeing them together that Laura hadn't been challenged.

Now they moved swiftly towards the right-hand side of the room where a group of people was gathered around a man in a waiter's uniform lying on an ambulance trolley. Laura saw Penny slipping her hand into the pocket to have the Glock ready. They drew nearer, and Laura's eyes were fastened on the ambulance man who stood with his back to them as he leaned over the patient. She followed Penny who made her way over to the left. Many of the guests had remained seated at their tables, but there was still quite a crowd around the stricken man and Laura and Penny had to thread their way through those observing the scene. Laura could feel her heart pounding in her chest and she had to fight hard against a swelling fear brought on by the knowledge that this man could be her assailant from the Old Swan. She prayed that she had been wrong and that the ambulance man would be someone she had never seen before. Just then, the man swung the trolley round and they came face to face. He looked older with short grey hair, a fatter face and heavy glasses, and Laura thought for an instant that she had made a mistake. But the unmistakable look of surprise in the man's eyes when he saw and recognised Laura turned her blood to ice. Different as he looked, she knew that they had found Abdullah Majid.

Fucking bitch, thought Majid, *he should have killed her in the Old Swan*. He felt a sickening stab of despair at the journalist finding him now, just as he was about to exit successfully. He felt anger too – partly directed at the woman for her persistent interference but also directed at himself. She had looked him in the eye, admittedly, but his disguise was good and he knew that what had truly given him away was the expression of surprised recognition that he had shown. He knew the journalist had seen it, and now she was turning to her companion and nodding. *Time to act.*

Majid moved fast, reaching under the trolley. As he did he swung it round and backwards, taking himself out of the direct line of sight of the journalist and the accompanying policewoman, whom Majid recognised from the day of Jemail's arrest. Even as he ripped off the camouflaging paper and pulled the Beretta out from the supporting masking tape his mind was racing. The original plan was now redundant, but before he could consider any other option he knew he had to disarm the policewoman.

Now that he had gone into action mode his training kicked in and he acted swiftly and decisively. He pushed the trolley hard, forcing a path through the surprised onlookers, then he rammed it into the policewoman as she went to withdraw her weapon. The trolley caught her on the hip and she cried out in pain, and the instant during which she was distracted was enough for Majid. He leaped forward towards the nearest table of diplomats and yanked to his feet a distinguished-looking silver-haired man in his fifties. Before anyone could react Majid had the silenced Beretta to the man's head. "One wrong move and I blow his brains out! Drop your weapon! Drop your weapon now!" he said to the policewoman.

She hesitated for only a second, then dropped a standard-issue Glock pistol to the floor. Majid swung around, gripping the diplomat hard by the throat, but pointing the Beretta at a heavily built ginger-haired man whom Majid also recognised from the day of Jemail's arrest. Taken by surprise, the man had belatedly reached into his jacket, but Majid had his gun aimed straight at the policeman's chest.

"Don't try it!" he warned. "Take out your weapon. Keep the barrel pointed towards yourself and drop it on the floor. Do it, now!"

He kept his left hand wrapped tightly around the terrified diplomat's throat, knowing from the man's demeanour that there would be no resistance there.

"Do it or I blow his brains out," snapped Majid, then the ginger-haired policeman complied with his order.

Even while acting to counter the most immediate threat, Majid's mind was running ahead. He had seen that the entrance doors to the dining-room were heavy and rubber-sealed around the edges and he reckoned that the private dining-room was probably close to being soundproof. Which meant that if he could prevent shouting or shots being fired he could at least temporarily avoid confrontation with the heavily armed security detail out in the corridor. *Provided they weren't alerted by radio.* But Majid had seen no earpiece or mini-mike being sported either by the ginger-haired policeman or the female officer that he had disarmed. And if there had been another officer in the dining-room who was in radio contact then surely the corridor guards would have burst in by now.

Another officer. He quickly scanned the faces before him, his finely honed instinct for danger susceptible to any potential source of threat. He saw confusion, shock,

and outrage, but in his quick survey of those before him
he saw nobody whose behaviour looked threatening. It
wasn't altogether surprising. He knew that for private
functions at this political level it would be regarded as
intrusive to have clearly identifiable security personnel
mixing with the distinguished guests. Lots of security
outside the room was normal, and a cordon of steel
around the venue was mandatory, but in a scenario
where the guests were already deemed to be secure
then discretion was the norm. Majid reckoned that the
tuxedo-clad, ginger-haired officer was probably there
as an additional gesture of comfort to the Americans
who tended to be particularly security conscious –
especially when protecting someone as high-profile as
the Secretary of State.

"Kick the guns over to me here," ordered Majid.
"Everybody else, no raised voices, no alarms – or he dies."
Just to reinforce his point Majid rammed the gun into the
temple of the captive diplomat who whimpered and
breathed raggedly, but who offered no hint of resistance.

The two police officers kicked their weapons over to
Majid who bent, still holding the Beretta to the
diplomat's head and forcing the man to bend with him.
Majid slipped both pistols into the jacket of his
paramedic's uniform, his mind already seeking a way
out of his dilemma. There were only three possible exits
from the dining-room, he figured. A doorway to the
right led to the kitchens, but Majid knew from Tamaz
that the entrance to the kitchen from the Conference
Centre proper was heavily guarded, which ruled it out.
Opposite him and behind heavy drapes was a row of

windows, but Majid knew that the area outside the private dining-room would almost certainly be overlooked by police marksmen, thus making impossible an exit via the windows. That left the corridor by which he had entered, and which he knew to be manned by the security detail and police officers armed with Heckler and Koch submachine-guns. So the corridor wasn't on either. Unless . . . *unless he exited the same way as he had entered, in the guise of a paramedic.*

Majid considered the idea for a second or two, then quickly moved to act on it, knowing that improvised and risky as it might be, it was his best chance of escape. He pulled the gun from his captive's forehead for a second and pointed it at a woman in an expensive-looking evening gown at the nearest table "You, get that cylinder," said Majid, indicating the discarded cylinder that he had placed behind the chair. "Get the cylinder and put it on the table there. Now! Do it!"

The terrified woman moved from her seat immediately and did as she was told. As the cylinder was placed on the table, Majid placed the Beretta to the diplomat's temple again and, using the man as a shield, retreated to behind the trolley. Then he indicated the cylinder.

"It's not an empty oxygen cylinder. It's full of liquid Sarin. That's the nerve agent that killed the people on the Tokyo underground!"

He heard a gasp of horror and watched with satisfaction as those nearest the cylinder immediately pushed back their seats and scrambled away from the lethal cargo.

"And it's all for you!"

He pushed the diplomat away, swung his gun-hand round, took aim and fired three times at the cylinder valve. It wasn't a large target and the silencer lessened his accuracy, but Majid knew he was an excellent marksman and the third round hit the target. As he expected, pandemonium erupted, but Majid was already pushing the trolley towards the doors as screaming diplomats trampled each other to escape the gas emanating from the punctured valve. Suddenly there was a bang and Majid felt a burning pain in his shoulder. He spun around, realising to his shock that he had been shot. He saw a young man in a tuxedo, whom he had taken to be a junior diplomat, aiming to fire again despite the chaos of fleeing dinner guests. Majid threw himself to the side as the man fired, then he heard a cry from the trolley as Tamaz was hit. Despite the pain in his left shoulder Majid swung up the Beretta, fired two shots in quick succession and saw the man drop. Even as he saw his assailant collapsing to the ground Majid was aware of the dining-room doors opening and he pocketed the Beretta and pushed the trolley with all his might towards the door. The fact that the doors had had to be opened outwards into the corridor meant that the security detail had lost several precious seconds after they reacted to the shots, and now Majid collided into several armed agents as they rushed into the room.

"*Terrorists!*" screamed Majid in warning, but without stopping his outward flight. "They've got Sarin gas!" Majid never slowed for an instant and he knew

instinctively that the fact that he was wounded and that
Tamaz was groaning on the trolley and pumping blood
made them look like victims fleeing from an onslaught.
The warning about the Sarin had been good too, giving
the security detail something major to worry about as they
faced into the pandemonium of the dining-room. Majid
sprinted down the corridor, pushing the trolley before him
"Terrorists!" he screamed again as police officers ran
towards him, their submachine-guns at the ready.
"Terrorists in the dining-room!" Majid never slackened his
pace and almost mowed down another group of armed
officers as he careened into the reception area. "They're
killing the ministers!" he cried. "They've got Sarin gas!"

"Jesus!" cried the leading policeman, then the group
sprinted towards the dining-room and Majid crossed
the last ten yards to the entrance door, exited from the
building and pushed the trolley towards the open rear
door of the ambulance.

Chaos reigned in the dining-room with guests
stampeding away from the main entrance doors and
toward the kitchen exits in their desire to escape the
hissing cylinder of Sarin gas. Penny had grabbed the arm
of the agent who had been shot and she called to Laura
to help her to drag him to safety. The man was covered
in blood and only semi-conscious yet somehow he had
managed to hold onto his gun, a Sig automatic pistol.

"Under the shoulder, Laura, quick!" cried Penny as
she took the weapon from him, then swiftly draped his
arm around her own shoulder. Even as Laura did as
instructed and they began to haul him, Penny could see

that the confused security agents were torn between avoiding the threat from the cylinder of Sarin and taking unequivocal action to secure the room.

"It was the ambulance man!" Penny cried. "The terrorist is the ambulance man!" Panic was in the air however, and between shouting, screaming and the distraction of the agents having to assist terrified guests who had fallen in the mêlée, Penny's warning went unheard.

Damn them, thought Penny, then she concentrated again on what she was doing. The wounded man that they were dragging was more of a dead weight than Penny had expected, and frightened by the threat from the colourless gas, part of her was tempted to leave him and flee. She knew however that Sarin was heavier than air and that if she left him lying on the floor she would be condemning him to death. Instead she redoubled her efforts to get him to the kitchen door as quickly as possible, mentally noting that Laura had never hesitated when called on to delay her own escape to help the wounded man.

Penny knew that time was of the essence here and that the sooner an alert was raised the better the chance of trapping Majid within the security cordon around the Conference Centre. The seconds that would take however were seconds she simply didn't have. *No use stopping to raise the alarm and being overcome by Sarin*, she thought, and so she stumbled on, dragging the bloodsoaked agent towards the kitchen exit and safety.

Its siren wailing, the ambulance roared up Kings Road.

Majid forced the accelerator to the floor, aware that he would have very little time before the alarm was raised and that he had to get past the second barrier before that happened. The one thing working in his favour was that the barrier personnel expected him to be returning at speed with an emergency case – a fact that had been evident when the inner barrier had been raised immediately when Majid had rushed out of the Conference Centre.

His shoulder stung him now, but even as he drove at speed he tried to plan ahead. It wouldn't be long before pursuit was organised so he would have to ditch the ambulance quickly rather than drive to the hospital to collect Tamaz's parked car. If he were to steal a car immediately though it should still be possible to exit from Harrogate before additional cordons and roadblocks could be thrown around the town. Once past the Kings Road checkpoint he would be outside the inner cordon and there was a sporting chance of getting out into the countryside with its myriad of side roads. Only then could he afford to stop and tend to Tamaz and to his own wounded shoulder. And provided he didn't linger too long, there would still be a reasonable chance of getting to Liverpool under cover of darkness.

The thought of the exit point from his mission jogged his mind and he realised that what with the pain in his shoulder and all the confusion, he hadn't been thinking straight. *The detonator was in the glove compartment.* It might still be possible to kill a number of his enemies.

The checkpoint was looming up ahead, but as he sped towards the officer raising the barrier he stretched out his left arm, ignoring the pain from his shoulder, and reached for the detonator.

Laura watched in amazement as Carrow moved at speed through the chaos of the dining-room. He had tied a handkerchief around his face and held in his arms a large tablecloth. As Laura helped Penny to haul the wounded security agent toward the kitchen doors, she realised what Carrow was about to do. She had disliked the Special Branch officer from the moment they had met, but there was no disputing his bravery now as he ran forward, leaping over several people who were lying on the floor retching, and threw the tablecloth over the leaking cylinder. Then Laura saw him quickly clasp the cylinder through the heavy tablecloth, lift it and sprint towards the windows.

Police and security officers were now arriving in numbers and even as Carrow approached the windows with the wrapped cylinder Laura saw agents with gas masks going to the assistance of those guests lying on the floor. Penny had screamed again that the ambulance driver was Majid Abdullah, and the officer she had screamed at had looked amazed for a second, then nodded and immediately used his radio to pass on the message and issue an alert. Now just as Laura and Penny finally hauled the wounded agent though the doorway that led to the kitchen corridor Laura heard a loud crash. Instinctively she turned back towards the dining-room. *The cylinder of Sarin*, she thought. It mus have been the sound of the windows shattering as Carrow threw it out. No sooner had she thought it than she heard another bang that sounded like an explosion, causing a frightened surge from those dinner guests who had followed them through the doorway to the kitchen corridor. Everyone pressed forward, then suddenly they burst through a set of swing-doors and found themselves in the kitchen, its abandoned but still-steaming pots suggesting the terror with which the kitchen staff had fled. Laura felt a draught of cold fresh air, then she saw that on the far side of the kitchen were two emergency exit doors through which the fleeing guests were streaming. As they did, another team of police and security agents entered the kitchen at speed from the passageway leading to the Conference Centre, and Laura was enormously relieved to see that part of the contingent was a first-aid unit.

"Over here!" cried Penny. "Follow us!"

Without stopping, the two women carried the stricken agent out the emergency doors and into what seemed to be a rear delivery yard. Only now that they were in the open air and presumably safe from the Sarin gas did Laura realise what they had just come through, and she felt almost dizzy with relief. The first-aid team that had followed them immediately went into action on the wounded agent, and Laura felt a further relief that she and Penny would no longer be responsible for the man, whose bloodsoaked appearance didn't auger well for his chances.

As Laura and Penny stepped aside to allow the first-aid team to get on with the work, further guests spilled out from the kitchen and more gas-mask-equipped officers converged on the site. It was obvious to Laura that the situation was being brought under control and she gathered herself together, and for the first time since her sighting of Majid paused a moment to reflect. "How the hell did he do it, Penny?" she asked.

"What?"

"How did he bypass all the security checks?"

"The ambulance ruse was clever," answered Penny ruefully. "The collapsed waiter made it plausible."

"But I thought all staff were security checked?"

"They were. Obviously he inserted a sleeper months ago – somehow he got an accomplice with no track record . . ."

"But even an ambulance driver would have to state the code-word."

"Yeah . . ."

"And weren't new ones issued twice each day?"

"Someone gave them to him," said Penny. "It's the only answer."

"How many people had access to them?"

"Dozens once they were issued."

"And before that? Who held them?"

"Only Thompson and the Assistant Commissioner," answered Penny, then her face clouded. "Oh, no," she said. "Oh, Jesus, no . . ."

Laura saw the look of horror on her friend's face and she too felt a sinking feeling. "You think maybe . . .?"

"I should have fucking rung him!" said Penny in anguish. "I should have gone to see him!"

Laura felt her mouth go dry, but she forced th

words out. "Corporal Work Number Six, Penny . . . *visiting the sick* . . ."

"He was trying to warn us! Christ, why didn't I see it?"

"Maybe – maybe we're adding two and two and getting five?" said Laura, but she knew that she was speaking more in hope than in belief.

"I'll call now," said Penny, pulling out her mobile and pressing the speed-dial facility. She listened for a moment, and Laura prayed that they were wrong and that Thompson would come on the line.

"Answering machine," explained Penny. "OK," she said, her face suddenly set in determination. "Let's get to Blubberhouses – fast."

Majid drove at speed, each bump in the road sending a jolt of pain through his injured shoulder. He tried not to think too much about the pain, not to think too much about anything, other than the immediate steps needed to make his getaway.

He had abandoned the ambulance soon after roaring past the checkpoint on Kings Road. Having switched off the siren and flashing light he had pulled down a side street, parked, and checked on Tamaz. To his shock the Turkish waiter had been dead, the shot from the security agent having pierced an artery in his neck. Majid had felt a stab of guilt on seeing the bloodsoaked body of the mild-mannered waiter, then he had reminded himself that Tamaz had been in this for the money. He had also felt a little guilty at the sense of relief that he wouldn't now have to contend with a badly wounded partner and this guilt had been less easily dismissed, but he had nonetheless moved on swiftly, leaving the ambulance and hot-wiring a car from a nearby street.

His thorough knowledge of Harrogate had stood to him then as he drove at speed through the north-western outskirts of the town, avoiding the sites of previous roadblocks and aiming to get into the countryside before being spotted by pursuers or hemmed in by the additional cordons that would undoubtedly be organised.

Now as he drove through the Yorkshire countryside he allowed himself to ponder his mission. Despite all that had gone wrong, he *had* managed to infiltrate the Conference Centre, and while some of his targets had no doubt fled the private dining-room, there was still a good chance that he had detonated the cylinder soon enough to douse a number of the enemy in Sarin. If he had accomplished that, and were to escape via Liverpool, it would still count as a successful mission.

No sooner had he savoured the possibility of success than the stolen car hit a pothole, and he felt a sharp stab of pain in his shoulder. *Serves you right*, he thought, *forget the prospects of glory and concentrate on the here and now.* He could feel the blood oozing down his arm from his shoulder and he knew that he was going to have to deal with the wound. He knew too that there was a fair chance that the bullet was still lodged in his shoulder and he didn't welcome the prospect of having to remove it. Either way though he was going to have to stop – apart from tending his wound he needed to divest himself of the ambulance-driver's uniform and change his appearance again. He also needed to acquire a different car in case the police who found the ambulance should also discover that a car had been stolen nearby.

First though he was anxious to put more distance between himself and Harrogate, and so he crouched forward at the wheel, held the steering wheel tightly with his right hand and sped on through the night.

The wail of the siren echoed through the still evening air as Laura and Penny hurtled along the road to Blubberhouses. In addition to the siren Penny had slammed a flashing blue light onto the roof of her car, so that most of the motorists they encountered pulled aside to allow the speeding vehicle to pass. Laura glanced across from the passenger seat and saw the grim line of Penny's face silhouetted against the flashing blue light. They had spoken little at the start of the journey, each woman lost in her own thoughts, then Penny had checked in with Assistant Commissioner Kelch.

It transpired that a full-scale medical response was being organised and that the local hospital had invoked its emergency response plan. Numerous diplomats were already being treated with Sarin antidotes and while it was too early to be certain about the eventual outcome, the prospects were hopeful, largely due to Carrow's having disposed of the Sarin out the window before the cylinder exploded.

At first Laura had been a little surprised that Penny

hadn't rung in immediately they had set out for Blubberhouses. By the time she had rung in however they had been nearly halfway to their destination and, listening to the conversation with Kelch, Laura realised that Penny had cleverly presented as a *fait accompli* her personal role in investigating Thompson's fate. Assistant Commissioner Kelch had been shocked at the idea of the codes coming from Thompson, but he clearly had a great deal on his plate and he hadn't argued with Penny's initiative in acting to be first on the scene. Penny had requested armed back-up to follow her from Harrogate and had promised Kelch that she would proceed with caution until the reinforcements arrived.

That had been about five minutes ago and, although Penny had said little in the interim, Laura knew that her friend felt guilty about not acting on Thompson's phone call. She felt guilty herself and she had only known the man for a week. Penny, she knew, had been really close to him, and she sensed that when they got to Blubberhouses Penny wasn't going to be cautious and await the arrival of armed back-up.

Just then the car swung around a curve in the road and Laura saw a sign indicating that Blubberhouses was only two miles away. She swallowed hard, one part of her anxious to get there, yet another deeply fearful of what they might find.

Majid gritted his teeth in agony as he closed the tweezers on the bullet in his shoulder. He paused moment to gather his courage, then pulled on the bullet, gasping in pain as he worked it free from the shattered tissue. He breathed out heavily as the bullet came out, then threw the tweezers and bullet onto the kitchen worktop and immediately moved to stem the bleeding from his wound.

He had returned to Thompson's cottage and quickly boiled up a kettle of water, then transferred the water into a pot in which he had sterilised a tweezers taken from the bathroom. While waiting for the water to boil he had carefully eased off the bloodstained ambulance driver's jacket, then quickly weighed up his options. The priority was to get to Liverpool speedily, but he had decided that a small amount of time invested in covering his tracks and changing his appearance would be time well spent. He had parked the stolen car out of sight at the rear of the house and he would now use Thompson's car for the next leg of his journey. He had already divested himself of the cheek padding and false moustache and had decided that when he had the wound cleaned and bandaged he would make one final change. It would only take a few minutes to cut off his dyed grey hair, after which he would use Thompson's electric razor to shave his head, thus altering his appearance as radically as possible. He would then dress in a sweater and slacks from Thompson's wardrobe and set out for the ship in Liverpool.

First though, he had to ensure his wound didn't become infected and that he lost no further blood. Thankful as never before for his training as a medical student, he went to work on his wounded shoulder.

Penny felt her heart beginning to thump when she saw the lights on in Thompson's cottage. *Please God, please, let him be all right!* If anything had happened to him because she'd been too busy to check his welfare and too preoccupied to recognise a coded warning, she would never forgive herself.

She swung the car off the main road and into the drive, switching off the car lights as she did so. She had already turned off the siren and flashing roof lights a little while back, not wanting to advertise her arrival in Blubberhouses. Now she slowly followed the outline of the driveway, its borders just about visible in the weak moonlight.

On reaching the top of the drive she stopped and switched off the engine, parking in the shadow of a large tree about twenty-five yards away from the front entrance to the cottage. There was no other vehicle parked on the forecourt of the house, but she knew there could easily be a number of cars out of sight at the rear.

Penny slipped her hand into the jacket and withdrew the Sig pistol that she had taken from the wounded security agent. She would rather have had the Glock, with which she was so familiar, but having lost that to Majid she was glad to have a weapon as well-regarded as the Sig as a replacement. From the corner of her eye, she saw Laura preparing to get out of the car and felt a sudden jolt of guilty concern. With all the drama that had unfolded she hadn't been thinking straight, but now she realised that it had been unprofessional of her to bring Laura along. She had become so used to the other woman's companionship that it had become second nature to include her, but she knew now that she couldn't involve a civilian in what could be a highly dangerous situation. In

532

truth she knew that she herself ought to wait for the back-up personnel, but she felt that she had already let Thompson down and so there could be no question of anything but going to his assistance immediately.

"Hang on a tick, Laura," she said, keeping her voice to a whisper.

"What?"

"I want you to wait here in the car."

"Come on, Penny. We've been together through the whole thing."

"This is different. It could be dangerous – I can't knowingly put you at risk."

"It's OK, Penny. It's my choice to come with you."

"No. Sorry, but it's not. And I haven't time to argue. Just stay here till the back-up team arrives."

"But you're not waiting for the back-up?"

"I can't."

"Penny –"

"For years Thompson was my mentor – he was like a father to me. This is personal now."

"Penny, I really think –"

"There isn't time, Laura! Please, don't give me anything else to worry about. Just wait here till the team arrives. And if things go wrong, run and hide in the bushes." Penny sensed that the journalist was about to argue and she raised her hand. "Not another word!" she commanded, then she checked the magazine of the Sig, switched off the door-activated interior light of the car and slipped out of the vehicle.

Majid had finished bandaging his shoulder and was

about to put on one of Thompson's shirts when he heard the car engine. The kitchen was in the back of the cottage and all the doors were closed, so the noise was faint, but Majid still reckoned it was a vehicle approaching and he felt his blood run cold. Could the authorities have been on his trail so rapidly, he wondered, or could it perhaps be something more innocuous, a visiting neighbour or a family member perhaps? Either way he knew he had to act quickly and he threw down the shirt, snatched up the Beretta and started for the door to the hall, then stopped himself. On his arrival, he had turned on the lights in the hallway leading from the front door to the kitchen. No point now in presenting potential foes with his silhouette through the glass-panelled front door. Instead he opened the door leading from the kitchen into the dining-room, then crossed the dining-room to the connecting door that gave access to the front parlour.

He entered the darkened room and closed the dining-room door so that there was just enough light to enable him to find his way to the front window. He crouched down on the floor, then very cautiously eased back the divide of the heavy curtains and looked out. Although he had only opened the curtain a fraction he could see that there was no vehicle parked in front of the cottage and he shifted his position in order to look over towards the driveway. The moonlight was weak and he hadn't got his night sight so soon after leaving the lighted kitchen, but there could be no mistake. Just at the top of the drive was a parked car.

Majid felt his pulses racing, but he carefully closed back the curtains and tried to think straight. Certainly it wasn't a social call when the driver had parked so far from the house, and no car door had been slammed as the driver left the vehicle. Yet if the police knew his whereabouts they'd have sealed off the house with strategically deployed personnel – they'd hardly have driven a private car up the drive.

Whoever it was, though, Majid knew he had to deal with the intruder quickly. He moved as swiftly as he could back across the darkened parlour, then across the dining-room towards the kitchen. Had he been planning to make a surreptitious entry he would have done it from the rear of the house, and he reckoned his intruder would try to do the same. He toyed for a moment with the notion of exiting through the back door, then dismissed it. Leaving through the kitchen would expose him to view and would mean entering an uncertain environment out the back. Far better to tackle the intruder in a location of his choosing.

He reached the kitchen and was about to turn off the lights when he changed his mind and instead quickly unlocked the back door, then dropped to the floor and crossed below the level of the window until he reached the corner of the room. By standing here with the lights on he would remain unseen from outside yet he would have a clear view of anyone entering the room via the unlocked back door. It also meant that the intruder wouldn't have been alerted to the fact that his presence was known – as he no doubt would be were all the lights in the cottage suddenly to be switched off.

Satisfied that he had his tactics right, Majid held the Beretta in the ready position and waited.

Penny moved cautiously around the rear of the house, the Sig held out before her with both hands. A flood of light spilled out the kitchen window and she could see that Thompson's Rover and another car were parked here. She had visited the cottage one evening the previous week with Thompson and he had parked at the front, so that the presence of both vehicles parked out of sight at the rear of the house heightened her fears. She passed a darkened rear bedroom, then paused before approaching the kitchen window. She knew that with the lights on in the kitchen she would see anyone in there better than they could see someone outside in the dark. On the other hand, the only way into the room was by the back door, so that even if it weren't locked her point of entry would be obvious and well-illuminated. She didn't know if her approach up the driveway in the car had been heard from inside the cottage, and on reflection she realised that she should have parked out on the main road and approached on foot, despite her anxiety to go to Thompson's aid as quickly as possible. If she *had* been heard, however, her opponents might be lying in wait for anyone using the obvious entry point of the back door.

She hesitated a moment, weighing up the risks involved against the possibility of an easy entry in a part of the world where crime rates were low and rural householders didn't always lock their back doors. The temptation to chance it was strong, but her instinct held her back and, knowing she mustn't deliberate long, she decided suddenly to be guided by her instincts.

She turned on her heel and made her way back to the darkened bedroom that she had passed, and examined the window. In the faint moonlight she could make out that there was a hinged panel on the window that swung outwards, but when she tested it she found it to be locked. At the top of the window, however, a small window had been left open and Penny looked at it and quickly considered her options. Although she was slim and agile, it was too high up and too small to allow her to make an entry, but she reckoned that if she climbed up onto the window-sill she might be able to reach her hand in through the top window and reach down to turn the handle of the larger panel. The drawback was that while perched on the sill with one hand in the window she would be an easy target. But there was no safe easy way of proceeding, and she knew Thompson might be in real jeopardy. Before she could lose her nerve she suddenly thrust the Sig into her pocket and hoisted herself up onto the window-sill.

She knelt on the narrow sill, then carefully rose so that she could reach in through the opened window. There were heavy curtains hanging from a pelmet in the room so that she couldn't see in, but she could see the handle that she wanted to reach on the inside of the window panel. She stretched down to reach it only to find it inches from her grasp. She gritted her teeth in frustration then shuffled slightly along the sill to be closer to the small window. Once more she reached in, and this time her fingertips brushed the handle. She knew that if anyone came out the kitchen door now she was completely vulnerable, and the fear spurred her on to stretch painfully as far as she could. Her arm throbbed with the strain, then suddenly her fingers made contact with the handle and she pushed hard. To her relief the window panel was obviously well-used, for the handle moved down easily, unlocking the window. Penny breathed out, then withdrew her arm from the small window. She crouched down on her hunkers, pulled the window open and eased into the bedroom. As soon as she was in she pulled the window closed, not wanting to advertise her means of entry to anyone who might check round the back, then she took the Sig from her pocket and pushed the bedroom curtain aside.

The faint moonlight did little to illuminate the darkened room, but she could just about make out a large double bed over to her right. She could also make out where the bedroom door was, from the light that was visible under its base, and she started towards it holding the gun in her right hand while reaching out with her left to make sure she didn't bump into any unseen furniture.

She reached the bedroom door and paused, her heart pounding madly. She swallowed hard, then took a deep breath, twisted the handle of the door and eased it open a crack. She had the Sig in her right hand, and should she face an armed opponent in the corridor outside the bedroom, she was prepared to fire. Nothing however could have prepared her for the sight that awaited her.

The light from the corridor fell upon an armchair that she hadn't seen in the shadows just inside the bedroom door. Sitting in the chair was Jack Thompson. His eyes were open and their whites contrasted sharply with the rest of his face, which was red and black and covered in congealed blood. Penny stared in horror at the hole in his forehead where a single shot from close range had blown his brains out onto the bedroom wall, then she screamed loudly, an uncontrollable scream of terror and anguish.

Laura heard a loud drawn-out scream and her stomach contracted in fear. She had disobeyed Penny's instruction to stay in the car. She reckoned that if anything went wrong it would be better to be hidden already in the bushes rather than risk being caught getting out of an easily located vehicle. This way too she felt that she could save what might be precious seconds should the back-up team arrive – if they found her already out of the car and ready to brief them.

Right now, though, there was no back-up and the scream had been a woman's, Penny's presumably, which meant that something awful had happened. Laura knew that, being unarmed and untrained for this kind of work, the sensible thing would be to do what Penny had said and remain hidden in the shrubbery. Even as she thought it however she knew that she couldn't. If the situation were reversed she knew that Penny wouldn't leave her to her fate, and despite the terror that knotted her stomach she knew she couldn't abandon her friend.

Overcoming her fear, she pushed her way through the shrubbery, then started across the open ground in front of the cottage.

Majid heard the piercing scream and realised that his intruder – a woman – must have discovered Thompson's body. Even as he made for the kitchen door he heard a continuing cry of anguish, then loud footsteps as she ran towards the lighted kitchen.

Timing his move, he raised the Beretta and quickly swung the door inwards. He dived to one side, the gun firmly held and aimed, and stuck out his leg. The intruder tripped heavily, as Majid had planned, and Majid rolled out into the hallway, swinging round his gun-hand to cover anyone supporting the woman. Realising that she was alone, he swiftly swung back to her and kicked her hard in the stomach as she tried to rise from the floor.

The woman cried out and, seeing her face, Majid recognised her as the policewoman who had accompanied the journalist into the Conference Centre dining-room. All his frustration at the last-minute stymying of his mission came to the surface and he kicked her again, grabbed her by the hair and dragged her upwards, then flung her down onto the kitchen floor. The woman had been armed, but had dropped her weapon on being tripped, and Majid swiftly scooped up the pistol, a Sig automatic, and followed her into the kitchen.

He closed the door after him, breathing heavily and feeling the throbbing pain in his injured shoulder. Despite the two kicks the woman was climbing to her

540

feet, and Majid put the Sig down far out of reach on the worktop, then crossed to her, grabbed her throat with his left hand and pushed her back into a kitchen chair. Before she had time to recover fully he grabbed her face with his left hand, raised the Beretta in his right and pushed its silenced barrel into her mouth.

Laura stopped running on reaching the front of the cottage. She hesitated a moment, considering her next move. All the windows were darkened, but she could see through the glass panel of the front door that the light was on in the hallway. She moved swiftly to examine the lock. *Please God,* she thought, *let it not be a mortise, let security be a low priority at a rural cottage!* Between the weak moonlight and the spill of light from the hallway she was able to examine the lock and her heart soared. It was a simple Yale, no challenge to any burglar and certainly no challenge to a locksmith's daughter.

She looked in through the frosted glass of the front door, but nothing appeared to be stirring in the lighted hallway. Moving quickly, she stepped to one side so as not to present a silhouette should anyone emerge into the hall, then she pulled her wallet from her pocket. She slipped a credit-card out of the wallet, positioned it carefully, then inserted it into the doorframe to force back the tongue of the lock. She pressed hard and felt the lock click back, then she silently swung the door open and stepped into the hall.

Jenny's stomach ached where she had been kicked, and

the gun-barrel in her mouth made her want to gag, yet the fury and grief she felt over Thompson's murder overrode her pain and fear. On an instinctive level too she sensed that Majid wasn't going to pull the trigger. The gun was already silenced and he could easily have shot her without raising any alarm, either in the hall or when he had flung her into the kitchen. Placing the gun in her mouth smacked more of intimidation, yet although it was impossible not to feel fear in the presence of such a ruthless enemy, her fury at the cold-blooded murder of Thompson gave her an angry strength.

Before she could think any further, Majid drew his face close to hers. He stared her in the eye for a second and when he spoke his voice was low-pitched but threatening. "I'm going to ask you some questions. If you cry out, if you hesitate to answer, or if you lie, I'll blow you brains out, just like I did with your friend. Understand?"

Penny felt a wave of hatred sweep her and she stared back at him challengingly.

"I said 'Understand?'!"

Penny heard the anger in his response and realised that nothing would be gained by goading him into shooting her. In fact, the longer she could detain him here talking, the better the chances of the armed back up arriving before he could escape. She hated co operating with him in any way, but she forced herself to nod in answer to his question.

Majid pulled the gun roughly from her mouth, then drew back out of lunging range while keeping the gun trained upon her.

"Where are your colleagues?" he asked.

"Back in Harrogate."

"You came here alone?"

Penny was aware of the threat to kill her if she lied, but she couldn't endanger Laura. "Yes," she answered with conviction.

"Why?"

"I was worried about Mr Thompson."

"Then why didn't you come with others?"

"There's chaos back in the Conference Centre. Everyone's – everyone's caught up in that. I just made for here."

Penny could see that he wanted to believe it, and she knew she should elaborate to convince him, but her fury and disgust at what had been done to her former mentor choked the words in her throat.

"You didn't guess that I would be here?" asked Majid.

"No."

Majid looked at her intently and again Penny sensed that what she had answered was what he had hoped to hear.

"What alerted you to worry about Thompson?" he continued.

"It wasn't – it wasn't like him to opt out, even if he was sick . . ." said Penny, grief-stricken to find herself talking about him in the past tense.

Majid looked at her quizzically, then shook his head in anger. "That's not all – tell me everything!"

Penny hesitated.

"Tell me!"

"The codes," she answered, rationalising that in talking to such a hateful and murderous enemy she was buying time for the back-up team to arrive.

"What about the codes?"

"Only Chief Superintendent Thompson and the Assistant Commissioner knew the full list of codes. You had to have a code to get into the centre – you couldn't have got it from the Assistant Commissioner. So . . ."

"You guessed I got it from your boss?"

"Yes."

"It was easy," said Majid sneeringly. "I got it out of him in a matter of minutes."

"Then why the hell did you have to kill him?!"

"I had no choice."

"You had a choice!" cried Penny, unable to control her emotion. "You could have let him live! You could have left him here and still gone on your psychopathic mission! But no, you had to shoot an unarmed man, you cowardly bastard!"

Penny saw the flash of anger in her captor's eyes, but she couldn't suppress the feelings that swept her forward. "He was a father, a grandfather, a really good man and now he's dead because you wanted to shoot him, you evil, murderous bastard!"

Penny had barely said the words when Majid sprang forward, and her head snapped backward as he slapped her hard.

"Bitch!"

She cried out in pain, then her stomach tightened

with fear as Majid levelled the Beretta at her, his eyes ablaze with hate.

Laura stopped dead in the hallway of the cottage. She had heard Penny's raised voice from behind the closed kitchen door at the far end of the hall, and it had been heartening to know that whatever else might have happened, her friend was alive and well enough to raise her voice angrily.

Now though, Laura found herself rooted to the spot. There could be no doubt about the voice that had cried "Bitch!". It was Abdullah Majid, and all the terror that Laura recalled from the encounter in her bedroom in the Old Swan came back in a wave. She gritted her teeth and tried to steady the trembling of her knees. On either side of the hallway were two darkened rooms that she had passed, and she reasoned that it was unlikely that she would be surprised by anyone exiting from them, yet the longer she stayed here in the hallway the more she was at risk of discovery. She breathed deeply, but found herself unable to move. The voice of the Iraqi had chilled her, and all her instincts told her to run for her life from the cottage. After all, she had been told to wait outside until the police reinforcements arrived, so there was a tactical advantage to leaving. Yet abandoning Penny to the mercy of Majid would feel like a betrayal. At a minimum she surely owed it to Penny to find out what was going on in the kitchen, even if it were only to peek through the keyhole and then retreat to brief the back-up team when it arrived. Every nerve in her body still told her to get away from Majid, but she summoned

up all the courage she had, then steeling herself, she tip-
toed forward towards the kitchen.

Majid breathed deeply and forced himself to control his
anger. He still had the gun pointed at the policewoman's
face, but he made himself resist the temptation to kill her
on the spot. Her outburst of abuse had infuriated him,
not so much in that she had called him cowardly and a
murderer, but in her contention that someone who was
a good father and grandfather didn't deserve to die. It
seemed so typically Western that she should attach
such value to Thompson's life, yet when Majid's family
and others like them had been wiped out that had been
blithely written off. Iraqi deaths were unfortunate;
sanitised by being referred to as 'collateral damage' – if
indeed they impinged at all with Westerners like this
policewoman.

He felt his finger tighten again on the trigger of the
Beretta, but he forced himself to resist responding
emotionally. Instead he tried to think tactically. He
needed to get away from Blubberhouses fast, that much
was clear. But even if the woman had lied and the
police were sealing off the cottage, she might be of
considerable value as a hostage-cum-human-shield.
And if he were still one step ahead of the police and he
were to get out of the Dales unchallenged, he could
always kill her then and make for Liverpool and his
means of escape.

He stared threateningly into the woman's eyes
enjoying the fear that he could detect there. "You're
coming with me. Co-operate and you'll live, give m

the slightest – and I mean the *slightest* problem – and you're dead. Understood?"

The woman nodded, and Majid glanced over at the door leading to the hallway, intending to escort his captive through it en route to Thompson's bedroom where he could quickly acquire a jacket before they drove off. Now however Majid froze. There was a gap of a couple of inches at the bottom of the door and Majid had seen the movement of a shadow there. Without hesitating, he moved silently and speedily across the kitchen, the Beretta aimed at the midpoint of the wooden door. Even as he moved he was evaluating the relative threats to his safety, but he knew that the policewoman was traumatised, probably in pain still from his kicks, and sufficiently distant from the Sig on the far counter to be the lesser threat by a long shot. Instead he concentrated on the door, reckoning that the wood in it was thin enough for him to shoot the intruder through it. *No*, he thought, acting on the instinct that had so often served him well, *keep your options open by surprising the intruder and only shooting if necessary*. Instead of firing he approached the door, holding the silenced pistol in the ready position, then pulled the door open with his left hand.

Laura cried out in shock at the sudden opening of the kitchen door. She had been lowering her eye to the keyhole, and finding herself face to face once again with Abdullah Majid she was rooted to the spot with fear.

"You!" he cried, then before Laura could resist he

grabbed her by the throat, pulled her towards him and swung her around.

Laura gasped for breath, then realised that he was using her as a shield, quickly swivelling left and right as he checked the hallway. He was wearing no shirt, and locked in his embrace Laura could feel the warm moisture of the perspiration from his bare chest, then he jerked her backwards, pushed her into the kitchen and slammed the door closed behind them.

Despite her fear Laura felt a huge relief on seeing Penny also in the room. Although her friend looked shaken and was slumped in a chair holding her stomach, otherwise she looked to be all right physically. Their eyes met and Laura saw the look of surprise on Penny's face, but, before anything could be said, Majid swung Laura around and smacked her face.

She gasped and staggered backwards, but he came after her.

"You again, everywhere I look! You just don't know when to stop, do you?!"

"I'm sorry . . ."

"You just don't know when to back off!"

"I'm only – I'm only doing my job," said Laura, hoping desperately that it might be possible to appease him somewhat by quoting her profession.

"I should have killed you in the Old Swan!"

"I'm just reporting things! The press doesn't create the problems – we just report on them!"

No sooner had she spoken than Laura was taken again by surprise as Majid smacked her face once more. The force of the blow pushed her backwards and her cheek immediately stung, but she saw that Majid's anger hadn't been totally vented.

"Lying cow!" he cried. "You identified me at the Conference Centre!"

Laura tried to think up some response that might lessen his anger, but Majid gave her no chance. "You've crossed me once too often. Now you're going to pay!"

"Please . . ."

"Now you're going to *die*."

"No! Please, no . . ."

"Yes!" cried Majid, then he raised the Beretta and aimed it at her head.

Penny had been gauging the distance across the kitchen to the far counter, where the Sig lay. *Much too far*, she had decided. Even with Majid distracted by Laura it would take too long to reach it. On top of all her other emotions Penny felt guilty for having brought Laura along tonight, and had been touched that the other woman had disobeyed her instructions and come to her aid, presumably after hearing the scream.

She looked now at Laura, who had responded to Majid aiming the gun at her with a cry of "Not *now*!" The use of the word "now" had been unexpected, and Penny saw the confusion in Majid's face.

"Not *now*?"

"Not now you've achieved your aim," said Laura breathlessly. "There's no point shooting me for stopping you, when I didn't. You've got what you wanted," she continued urgently, "the Sarin exploded – there'll be dozens of people dead!"

Penny saw the flicker of hope in Majid's eyes and she realised that Laura was lying to buy time.

"It's a disaster zone back there," added the journalist, "a slaughter! You've done what you came for . . ."

Penny saw a flash of delight crossing the terrorist's face and she realised that he was buying Laura's story. Even so, the situation was grim. Penny knew that the odds had to be against Majid allowing herself and Laura to live just because he thought he had succeeded in the Conference Centre. It didn't fit into his behaviour pattern so far, and if he could murder Thompson in cold blood there seemed little reason to think he wouldn't be equally ruthless with them.

"Whatever political point you wanted to make, you've made," said Laura. "Please, leave it at that – there's nothing further to be gained by harming us."

"There's always something to be gained by harming the enemy. That's what the Allies thought when they destroyed my country and slaughtered my people. And that's what I think now."

Penny felt her blood running cold at the tone of icy determination in Majid's voice, but she tried to think clearly. The armed back-up could arrive any moment. If they could keep Majid talking there was the possibility of rescue. *If they could keep him talking.*

"Not everybody here wanted the Iraqi people slaughtered – you've got to believe that," said Laura.

"I don't have to do anything! I'm the one in control. And your pathetic pleas are a waste of breath."

"Please, just listen to what I have to say! Whateve:

about killing to pursue your goals, killing now, just for the sake of killing, won't help your cause."

"You don't give a damn about my cause – you just want to save your own neck!"

Penny sensed a bloodlust in Majid and she reckoned that his dialogue with Laura was going to end very soon. Her own heart was thumping and her mouth was dry with fear, but she tried desperately to think of some sort of strategy. She looked across at her antagonist, trying to identify any weak points, anything that could be exploited. She could see that blood was seeping through the dressing on Majid's bare shoulder, but it was his left shoulder and he was still comfortably holding the gun in his right hand. It was a neat dressing, she saw, and she realised that, utilising his medical training, he must have removed the bullet himself. There were bloodstained swabs on the counter, beside an aluminium pot of water in which he had presumably sterilised a tweezers that now also lay bloody and discarded. A thought entered her head, and even as it did she realised that they were entering the endgame when Laura went to speak but Majid stopped her.

"Enough!" he cried. "Die with some dignity instead of begging like a coward."

Penny knew then that she only had seconds in which to act and, before her nerve failed her, she forced herself to rise quietly from the chair. The two things working in her favour were Majid's attention being on Laura and the fact that the Sig was on the far side of the kitchen – she sensed that her adversary didn't regard her a serious threat because she would need to cross the kitchen in front of him to get to the gun. Penny caught Laura's eye as she rose from the chair and she gave a nod as if to indicate that Laura should keep Majid occupied. Laura seemed to catch on for she immediately held a hand up to Majid and spoke urgently.

"Let me just say one last thing," she began, and as she did Penny sprang backward and away from Majid and towards the counter near the sink. From the corner of her eye Penny saw Majid beginning to turn and she realised that, despite being focussed on Laura, he must have caught her movement in his peripheral vision. Without hesitation she grabbed the aluminium pot and in one swift motion flung its contents into Majid's eyes as he swung round to face her. She was rewarded with a cry of pain and she knew that her calculation had been right and that the water used to sterilise the tweezers must still have been hot enough to hurt his eyes.

Immediately she dropped the pot and lunged across the room for the Sig. Majid stumbled backwards, blinded by the water, and Penny reached the far worktop and grabbed for the weapon. Her hand closed around its handle, then a pewter jug on a shelf above her head shattered and she realised that Majid was firing with the silenced Beretta. She fell to her hunkers to present less of a target, then immediately swung around and raised the Sig. She saw that Laura had dived to the floor and that Majid was clasping his eyes with one hand and attempting to aim the Beretta at her with the other. Without hesitating she fired twice, the reports deafening in the small kitchen. Majid staggered, but despite two bloody holes in his chest he stayed on his feet and he still hadn't dropped his weapon. And when he shakily raised the Beretta once more, Penny fired again. He took the shot in his stomach and cried out in pain, but his strength and determination still appeared to sustain him and he advanced aggressively towards Penny. She rose to her feet and held his gaze unblinkingly, then shot twice more as he tried to raise the Beretta. This time he dropped the gun, but his momentum carried him forward and he fell to the floor feet from Penny. He stared at her and spoke in a gasping voice that nonetheless carried clearly.

"Bitch!" he hissed. "Western whore!"

Penny immediately shot him in the stomach again. "That's for Jack Thompson!" she cried. "That's for Jack Thompson, you murderous bastard!" she shouted, her voice cracking, then she shot him again. Majid's body jerked each time, but Penny kept the gun trained on him even as the tears began to fill her eyes. "That's for Jack Thompson!" she repeated, and shot him again. "That's for Jack Thompson!" she screamed, then she fired once more before finally lowering the gun.

She stood unmoving for a moment, then Laura crossed the room and gently touched her arm. Penny looked at the journalist through her tears.

Laura reached out to her. "It's OK, Penny. It's over now. It's over . . ."

Penny nodded, then something inside her seemed to give, and she put down the gun, allowed herself to be enveloped in Laura's arms, and sobbed uncontrollably.

Epilogue

Tuesday 26th September 2000

Samuel Lubetkin sipped Turkish Coffee at the outdoor café table and absent-mindedly watched the traffic converging on Dizingoff Circle. Although it was only half past eight in the morning Tel Aviv was already beginning to get hot, and Lubetkin was glad of the shade provided by the café's umbrellas. He looked away from the traffic and across at his assistant, Avi Blumenthal. Blumenthal was dressed in a handmade, light cotton suit which he wore with an open-neck shirt, and as ever the younger man contrived to look cool and dapper despite the heat.

"So, all's well that ends well . . ." said Lubetkin.

Blumenthal grimaced. "Not exactly how I'd see it if I were the Brits."

"No?"

"Despite our providing ID, Majid did penetrate their security."

"True," conceded Lubetkin.

"And if things had been just a little different the Sarin gas might have killed everyone in the room."

"Ifs, buts and maybes, Avi. The reality is, he's the one who's dead."

"For which much thanks," said Blumenthal with a smile.

"Amen to that," answered Lubetkin, then he sipped his coffee and looked thoughtful. "Reckon he was the Budapest killer?"

"We'll probably never know for sure," replied Blumenthal, "but yeah, I'd say it's likely. I hope so – I'd like to think Moshe Avram's killer got what he deserved."

"Yeah. Moshe was no angel – but an eye for an eye and a tooth for a tooth . . ."

Blumenthal smiled wryly. "Till everyone's blind and toothless – as someone once said . . ."

Lubetkin shrugged. "It's a dirty game we're in."

Blumenthal looked at his boss and nodded. "That's for sure."

"Still, this one's straightforward enough. Abdullah Majid was a Bad Guy, capital B, capital G."

"No question."

"So, here's to one less terrorist, one less bad guy to worry about," said Lubetkin raising his coffee cup.

"I'll drink to that," said Blumenthal as he raised his own cup. *"Mazeltoff!"*

Lubetkin nodded with satisfaction and clinked cups with him. *"Mazeltoff . . ."*

Omar Rahmani sat at the communications console in the study of his villa, listening carefully to the voice on the other end of the phone. The early-morning Spanish sunshine warmed the room and the garden outside was filled with birdsong, but Rahmani's attention was entirely focussed on the call. As usual the line was scrambled and as secure as the latest technology could make it, but nonetheless he kept the conversation cryptic.

"You're sure of what happened?" he asked the caller, who immediately reassured the Iraqi. "And he revealed nothing?" Again Rahmani heard the answer he wanted. "Very well then, thank you."

Rahmani ended the call, then sat, gazing unseeingly across his manicured lawns. He had heard on last night's news of the attack on the Conference Centre and had been disappointed to learn that none of the delegates had been killed, although a number of people had needed to be hospitalised after the Sarin attack. It was galling to have come so close, but despite his frustration at almost achieving spectacular vengeance yet ultimately failing, he had still felt admiration for Abdullah Majid. It had been a brave and daring attempt and there was no denying that Majid was a fearless warrior who had pursued his mission unflinchingly despite heavy odds against him. Which was all very admirable, yet Rahmani had needed to be pragmatic once the mission had actually failed, and he had suffered a sleepless night worrying over the possibility that Majid might have been taken alive. The younger man had sworn that he would swallow his suicide pill in the event of capture, and Rahmani's instinct had been to believe him, yet it had come as a relief to get the call from his source in Mossad confirming that Majid had been killed in a shooting very shortly after the Conference Centre attack.

Over the years it had cost Rahmani a great deal of money to fund the intelligence-gathering network he had at his disposal, and although the number on his payroll was limited, the agents themselves tended to be very well placed and therefore expensive. Several times in the past however it had turned out to be money extremely well spent, and once again today Rahmani felt that the funds secretly channelled over the years to Avi Blumenthal's numbered account had been a good investment.

Now however his thoughts went from the bought Mossad agent back to Majid. Unusually for Rahmani he felt a little guilty for his relief at the other man's death, but he told himself that Majid had known both the odds and the scale of the rewards before undertaking the mission. The younger man had known that the operation might cost him his life and he had nonetheless chosen to proceed. So be it, Rahmani thought, all part of the harsh business of life. *And thinking of business* . . .

He hesitated a moment, then decided that what was done was done and the sooner he opted for business as usual the better. No point leaving two and a half million pounds sitting in an account in Zurich, he thought – and it was still there, he had checked only last night. He turned back to the communications console, picked up the phone and began to punch out the telephone number of his Swiss banker.

Thursday 28th September 2000

The crowd in the graveyard for Thompson's buria
spilled right across the cemetery, and Penny took a
small measure of comfort from the enormous number
of colleagues, friends and neighbours who had show
up to offer their sympathy to Thompson's children
There had been a huge turnout too at the removal of th
remains to the church the previous evening, and agai
at the funeral mass this morning.

The cemetery was washed by weak autum
sunshine, but a cool breeze came in off the Yorkshir
Dales, and as the priest finished the burial praye
Penny felt a chill that she knew wasn't caused solely b
the weather. She sensed that the loss of Thompso
would stay with her for a long time, and added to th
death of her mentor was the loss of her vision of herse
as a police officer. Up until now she had never serious
questioned her career choice, despite the ups an
downs that went with the job, but she knew that h
behaviour when she had continuously shot Majid ha

been unacceptable, and that she could no longer continue as before.

Shane had driven up from London on the night of the killing and he had cautioned her not to decide anything too rashly. Next morning Assistant Commissioner Kelch had also been sympathetic and had insisted that she take a few days sick leave to recover from the trauma she had undergone in Thompson's cottage. First though, she had filed a report both for Kelch as her ultimate superior, and Mathieson as the person who had seconded her to Harrogate. She had described accurately all that had transpired and had opted not to gloss over the number of times that she had shot Majid in their final confrontation. Not entirely to her surprise, Kelch had responded that she had been dealing with an armed aggressor who had already murdered a police officer in cold blood and, without actually saying so, he had intimated that her use of excessive force against Majid was not a matter that he would feel required to explore much further.

Colin Mathieson had been equally supportive of her actions but more persuasive in his rationalisation on her behalf. Firstly, he had passed on congratulations from his superiors that due to her efforts there had been no fatalities among the conference delegates, as against all three terrorists having been eliminated. When she had admitted that she was thinking of resigning he had argued against it, emphasising that Majid had shot at her and that she had had no option but to shoot him in return.

"Nine times, Colin?" she had asked.

"Heat of battle," he answered. "He was advancing towards you, he was still a threat."

"Even so . . ."

"Look, you had to kill him to save yourself. What difference really does it make if you shot him twice, or four times, or six times, or even nine times? He'd already murdered twice and he was about to kill you and Laura, so you killed him in self-defence. Whatever way you look at it he's dead and nothing is gained by the force losing a first-class officer."

But despite Mathieson's arguments Penny knew that in continuing to shoot Majid she had sought vengeance for Jack Thompson, and that despite the justification of self-defence she had to some degree acted as judge, jury and executioner.

Curiously enough, her final decision on whether or not to resign had been influenced by a conversation the following day with Len Carrow. Although Penny had disliked the man from the moment of their first meeting, there was no denying his bravery in acting to dispose of the cylinder of Sarin. He had been detained in hospital after being treated with Atropine and Pralidoxime Chloride, the accepted antidotes to Sarin, and Penny had rung him to wish him a speedy recovery and to acknowledge the valour of his action in saving the lives of the trapped delegates. Carrow had been unusually modest about his own role, and when he had asked about Penny's welfare she had reckoned that he was being sympathetic in deference to her closeness to Thompson, whose murder had upset Carrow, despite the chequered relationship the two men had had.

Carrow had referred to the shooting of Majid with characteristic bluntness and far from having any reservations about excessive force had openly praised Penny for her actions. There was no doubting the sincerity of his congratulations and it had clinched the matter for her. Despite his bravery Carrow represented everything she disliked in policing, and the Special Branch man's gung-ho endorsement served only to confirm to Penny that her action in continuing to shoot had indeed been wrong.

Having mulled it over, she made her decision and told Shane that she was going to resign. This time he hadn't actively tried to dissuade her, asking instead if she was sure she wasn't acting too soon after the events. When Penny had told him that it was untenable to continue with a blind eye being turned to what she had done, Shane hadn't argued further. The decision made, he had been reassuringly positive and had pointed out that Penny had a highly impressive track record, a good degree, and at thirty years of age had a great deal more experience of leadership than most of her contemporaries. She would walk into a good job, he insisted.

Penny looked at him now with affection as they stood together by the side of the grave. He was standing between Laura and Penny, and as people began to drift away from the graveside he reached out and squeezed Penny's arm. Penny looked at him and nodded, then stepped forward and held out the single red rose that she had been carrying. She dropped it into the grave and stood there a moment, the tears welling in her eyes, then she turned away and walked with Shane and Laura to where Thompson's children were shaking hands with departing mourners.

The three of them offered their condolences once again, then began to thread their way through the crowd as they made for where Shane had parked his car.

"Penny!"

She turned to see Colin Mathieson approaching, his expression sombre. "Colin," she said as she stopped and faced him. Laura and Shane stopped also and Mathieson exchanged low-key greetings with them. The two men had met for the first time on Tuesday night, and despite a surface air of politeness and goodwill Penny had picked up on an underlying tension as though both men instinctively regarded each other as rivals.

"Sorry to barge in," said Mathieson to the group in general, then he turned to Penny. " I wonder could have quick word?"

"Right now?"

"Two minutes. I may have to get back to London today, and I need to talk to you first."

Penny sighed, then turned to Shane and Laura "Sorry . . ."

"No problem," said Shane. "See you at the car?"

"Yeah. Thanks, love. OK, Laura?"

"Sure."

"Thank you," said Mathieson, then Shane and Laura nodded farewell to him and set off across the cemetery towards the road.

"So, what's so urgent?" asked Penny.

"Your future," answered Mathieson.

"Oh?"

"I know this shooting business has thrown yo

Penny, but even if you're not happy with what you've done, you can't let it damage what could be a glittering career."

"Can't I?"

Mathieson looked at her enquiringly. "I hope you're not saying what I think you are . . ."

"I'm resigning, Colin," Penny interjected. "I've made up my mind."

"Oh come on, Penny!"

"What?"

"You're being way too scrupulous."

"I am what I am. If I can't be the kind of police officer I always aimed to be, then I can't be one at all. I'm sorry if you think that's being precious, but it's my call."

"Have you told the Assistant Commissioner?"

"Not yet."

"Why don't you take a sabbatical? Take a break and think things over before making such a big decision."

"There's no point, Colin. What I did won't change, my values won't change, I'm finished with the police, it's a closed chapter."

Mathieson said nothing but looked at her thoughtfully. "Supposing – supposing you were to leave the police but remain in the security field?"

"The security field? As in?"

"Intelligence work. You have a flair for it. I'd be happy to offer you a post."

Penny was taken aback, and in spite of herself felt a little flattered.

"We'd make it worth your while. And you'd be

based in London, no need to move house or anything. You're a first-class operative, Penny. I'd really like to work with you again."

Penny looked at him, his well-coiffured grey hair softly lit by the autumn sun, and Mathieson gave her a small grin and held his head to one side as if to say 'What about it?'.

Penny considered what was potentially being offered, then she met Mathieson's gaze. "Thanks, Colin – but no thanks."

"Sure? It could be exciting?"

"Positive. This is where our paths divide – this time forever."

Mathieson looked at her for a moment, then nodded slowly. "So be it. In which case – let me wish you luck."

"Thank you."

"Goodbye, Penny."

"Bye, Colin."

He held his hand out formally and she shook it, then she nodded in farewell and set out across the sunlit cemetery to join her husband.

Friday 29th September 2000

Laura gazed out the window as the train traversed the rolling Yorkshire countryside. The mid-morning train to Leeds wasn't heavily occupied and she had found a seat with a table on which to place her laptop. She waited as the machine booted up, her mind reliving the momentous events of the past few days as she gazed distractedly at the passing landscape.

She had said her goodbyes to Penny and Shane, promising to keep in touch. When Penny had first told her that she was leaving the police Laura had thought it a mistake, but after listening to the other woman's reasoning she had seen that maybe for Penny it was the right move. She had no doubt though that whatever career Penny chose she would be successful in it, and she had told her friend this, for which Penny had thanked her with touching gratitude.

Her own career, Laura knew, had shifted gear dramatically. With the attack on the Conference Centre the Majid story had suddenly come out into the open, and Mac had been thrilled at the *Clarion* getting a major scoop by having its journalist right in the thick of the action. The last few days had been frantic, with Laura writing stories and e-mailing them back to Dublin. She had negotiated successfully with Mathieson and Assistant Commissioner Kelch to use some of the material gained during her privileged access in the days leading up to the conference, and Mac had printed her material as exclusives, then syndicated the stories to a range of other newspapers. To Laura's surprise she had already been approached, via the *Clarion*, by two large London publishers with a view to writing a book based on her dramatic experiences of the previous week.

It was a dream come true for any journalist, and though excited by the prospect and impressed by the large sums offered in advances by the publishers, she couldn't help but feel slightly uncomfortable to be profiting from what had happened. She had grown genuinely fond of Jack Thompson and had been saddened and shocked by his fate. On the other hand what had happened couldn't now be undone, however much she might wish it. And in fairness to herself, she had played her part in every other respect as best she could. She had made the recording from which Majid had been ID'd, she had identified him in the Conference Centre when he had been about to plant the Sarin, and she had gone to Penny's rescue when Majid had her prisoner in the cottage.

Thinking back to her break-in at the cottage would, she knew, give her nightmares in the future, but at the time she had been acting on instinct, and the knowledge that Penny's life was at risk had given her the adrenaline charge needed to go to her rescue.

It was an aspect of the story she had played down when she had contacted Declan, who was still on location in Prague. He had been horrified to hear that she was involved in the incident in Harrogate, which he had seen on the television news, and Laura had decided not to upset him further by telling him quite how foolhardy she had been in pursuing the story. Instead she had been moved by the depth of his concern for her, and she had suggested she should take a train from Leeds straight to London, from where she could fly to Prague. The sound of his voice on the phone had affected her even more than she had expected and she had been tempted to discuss marriage there and then, but had resisted. Prague, she felt, would be a more romantic venue in which to get engaged. And if their grandchildren asked them in years to come where they decided to get married, the Czech capital would sound better than over the phone from a hotel room in Harrogate. She smiled wryly to herself, knowing that she was getting a little ahead of herself in thinking of grandchildren.

Just then the laptop played a few bars of music to indicate that the programme was loaded, and the mundane sound brought Laura back to reality. She clicked on her word-processing program and brought up the file in which she had made preliminary notes for the planned book. Once again she was struck by the thought of making a lot of money from the havoc that Majid had wreaked, but this time she dismissed the stab of guilt that she had felt earlier. She believed that the press had a role in telling the public the truth about events, and though some newspapers abused that role, she still believed firmly in the value of a free press. So no more reservations, she thought – this was the world she had chosen and she would forge ahead and be the best journalist that she could be. Buoyed by the thought, she took one farewell look out the window at the sunlit Yorkshire countryside, then she moved her fingers to the keyboard and began typing up her story.

The End